GAYLORD S

# THE
# WHEEL
## OF
# JUSTICE

**Also by William E. Holland**

Moscow Twilight

Published by POCKET BOOKS

# THE
# WHEEL
## OF
# JUSTICE

# William E. Holland

POCKET BOOKS

New York   London   Toronto   Sydney   Tokyo   Singapore

POCKET BOOKS, a division of Simon & Schuster Inc.
1230 Avenue of the Americas, New York, NY 10020

Holland, William E.
    The wheel of justice / William E. Holland.
        p.      cm.
    ISBN 0-671-79953-3
    1. Political corruption—Russia—Moscow—Fiction. 2. Businessmen—Russia—
Moscow—Fiction. 3. Moscow (Russia)—Fiction. I. Title.
PS3558.O3492W44    1995
813'.54—dc20                                                        94-22916
                                                                         CIP

First Pocket Books hardcover printing February 1995

10   9   8   7   6   5   4   3   2   1

# Author's Note

The author's previous book, *Moscow Twilight,* was based on an incident that happened in Moscow in 1989—although it did not happen to the characters the author invented to carry on from there.

This book is based on three related incidents in Moscow that did not happen—at least not in 1992, the year in which the book is set. But anyone familiar with Moscow then (or now) will recognize the possibilities.

The first event is an anticorruption campaign orchestrated by the government to combat the perceived excesses of a newly freed market economy. The campaign, at the time of this writing, is still on its way.

The second is the holding of hearings on anticorruption legislation by a subcommittee of the Russian legislature. (The legislature, in Russia, is not a part of the government, a term that refers only to the executive branch.)

Committees of the Russian legislature and their subcommittees do not hold fact-finding hearings. Even after the fall of Communism, even after President Yeltsin dissolved by force the old legislature (the Supreme Soviet, as described in this book) and replaced it with a new one under the Russian Constitution, the legislature has been content to go on making laws in the pure vacuum of political theory, just as it always had done, free from the taint of reality. But there is always reason to hope for improvement; and so this book supposes that a bold enough legislator might look around and try to understand, and cope with, the real world, and in so doing decide to take evidence on what is needed in the real world.

The third incident, and the foundation of the book, is the arrest of a Western businessman for . . . well, but why give it away? It didn't happen in 1992, but it might have; and it *will* happen.

The war between the KGB and the militia, though, was real (although unreported in the Soviet press, of course), as was General Krylov and the manner of his death. Even today, however, few facts concerning Krylov's death are public, and so I have felt free to build a fiction around it.

The rest of the book is as true to life as the author could make it, although not to actual persons. But those who know him will recognize some characteristics of my friend who in the book goes by the name of Slavin. My thanks to him for his advice on Russian criminal procedure and trial strategy. If any defects remain, they do because I ignored his counsel.

But this book is dedicated to my wife, Olga. Inna's bravery and conviction are hers.

# THE
# WHEEL
## OF
# JUSTICE

*What was the feeling of Moscow at that time? It was a feeling of deep incongruity, with evil and virtue standing side by side, and the most bitter differences of opinion as to which was which. We lived like patients on the edge of cure or madness, lost between terror and exhilaration, not knowing which way our lives would fall. It was the feeling of being a child again, or a college freshman. The whole world had been created anew: but for what?*

1

AFTER DINNER JOANNA ASKED ALEX IF HE WANTED TO HELP HER CLEAR the table while Brad read Jennifer her bedtime story.

He said he'd be glad to; but Brad protested: guests couldn't be asked to do kitchen work.

"He said he'd be glad to," Joanna pointed out. "And the only alternatives are for him to sit here alone, or for both of us to look at dirty dishes until you come down." She looked around the room, a combined living and dining room. The kitchen was reached through the narrow entry hall, which had a stairway on the other side. "It's your only night at home this week: Jennifer's overdue for a reading from her father."

"All right. Are you ready to go upstairs, Jen?"

The girl nodded. Her long hair shook like flax in a summer wind. She was a slender wisp at four years, naturally girlish, though totally unconcerned with girls' ways.

" 'Upstairs.' *There's* a novel concept for Russia," Alex said. He wanted to make up to Joanna for the lack of a separate dining room. He knew she'd grown up in a big house.

"Nothing but the best for our girls, eh, Jen?" Brad said. He took her hands and lifted her giggling, hanging at arm's length, out of her chair. "What'll we read tonight? *The Three Bears?*"

"Yeah," she breathed. It appeared that *The Three Bears* was a highly desirable narrative.

"No goddamned Russian," Joanna said, "excuse my French." She reached sideways to lay a hand on Alex's arm in apology while continuing to talk to Brad. "This girl's going to start an American school in four months, and I hope she'll at least know what the English alphabet looks like."

"What kind of teacher would object to a girl who reads Tolstoy?" Brad asked, picking the girl up under one arm like a sack of flour and poking a finger in her ribs as he did it. "C'mon, Jen. Let's do it."

Joanna and Alex watched him lug the squealing bundle up the narrow staircase by the kitchen.

"Upstairs," Joanna sighed, as if "upstairs" were a treasured memory all but forgotten, although this house had one. "God, how glad I'll be to get back to a *real* upstairs. Have I told you about my house in Minneapolis?" She smiled. She had told him a hundred times.

"I've heard rumors."

"And the lake. We'll be able to look out on the *lake*. Oh, God." For a moment it seemed that tears would come to her eyes, but none did. He put his hand over hers, still on his arm, and felt her squeeze his arm. "Come on," she said, "let's get this stuff into the kitchen."

He balanced a stack of dishes that she piled onto his hands and followed her into the kitchen. At the end of the kitchen a window looked out onto white, cool evening, still lingering at ten o'clock, as if snagged in the birch grove and unable to depart.

"Leave the stuff on the counter," Joanna said as Alex started to arrange dishes in the sink. "The automatic dishwasher comes every morning." It was a joke. She meant the maid. "Lyuba's the one thing I'll miss about this . . . country." She pointedly omitted the adjective that would have filled the gap.

"It's not a bad house," Alex said.

" 'Not bad for Russia.' Jesus, I hope I never hear *that* phrase again in my life!" She sighed and looked around the kitchen. "Yes, I know I shouldn't complain. Any Russian housewife would give both her arms for this crap." Her glance took in the Finnish stove and refrigerator, the stainless steel sink with a chromed lever faucet, the German cabinets with their precise doors of white laminate and their black lacquered handles. "But I can't tell you how happy I am that it's only three months more!"

"You've had a long tour of duty here. Two years is a long time."

"A long time to hate a place. It seems like a goddamn lifetime. This place destroys your sense of reality. A month ago I was in Vienna; now I can hardly recall what it was like. There's just so much . . . so much *Russia* everywhere here! And the worst part of it is, Bradley loves it." She laid a hand on Fall's arm. "I'm sorry. I know you love it too. I wish you could teach me how. Short of falling in love with a Russian."

Fall knew this was an invitation to talk about Inna, but he didn't take it up. After a moment she pursued it anyway. "What's it like—being in love with a Russian?"

Alex didn't know how to respond. He never knew how to respond. "What's it like being in love with anybody?"

She looked at him a long time. Her eyes had the unwavering intensity that he now always thought of as the eyes of a Minneapolis girl, although she was the only one he had ever known. "Painful," she said. "Painful, sometimes." Her eyes were steel gray with a hint of gold in them, a color he had never seen in anyone else. Did all Minneapolis girls have them? "And sometimes wonderful."

"Well, you've got a good husband to love."

3

"Yeah." She started moving dishes into the sink herself. "Lovable old Bradley."

"I've been glad for his friendship here. I count on him a lot."

"Good old reliable Bradley. A man to count on."

"And Jordan counts on him more than I do. Brad's done a hell of a job with the startup. I see a lot of companies coming into the country for the first time, and I don't know of another that's done as well as Jordan Enterprises. He's turned it into a real profit-maker in dollars in two years—that's a miracle."

"Well, the company had better recognize what it's done to our lives." She stopped suddenly, as if listening for someone listening to her, but the sound of Brad's voice rolled loud down the stairwell: *"Kto khlebal v moei chashke?"* Alex recognized the words: it was Tolstoy's retelling of *The Three Bears.* "Cut out the goddamn Russian!" Joanna yelled through the door. The story stopped, then switched smoothly into English, in a middle-sized voice: "Who's been eating from *my* dish?" A little-girl-sized voice followed, giggling: "Who's been eating from *my* dish, and ate it all up?"

What *had* Moscow done to their lives? Alex wondered. He knew Brad, saw him at least weekly, sometimes daily. Bradley Chapman was Alex's favorite client, a man who not only knew how to run a business—there were plenty of *those* in the Western business community in Moscow—but was able to get Russians to run a business. Practically nobody could do that. But what Alex liked chiefly about Brad was that he always asked what the law was, and he followed good advice. "We're gonna run this company," he said, "so that if everything we do shows up on the front page of the *Wall Street Journal,* we'll be proud instead of scared." Now he had hundreds of employees and a promotion waiting when he got back to Minneapolis.

And Joanna? What had two years in Moscow done to her? Alex had seen less of her; but he dined at their house here on the edge of Moscow at least every month, and once he had gone with Bradley and her and Jen to the Black Sea coast. The famous trip to the sea. He had a fleeting memory of her emerging from the water in a slipping bikini, tanned and laughing as she held up her top. *Nor your client's wife,* he thought hastily, pushing the memory away. What had Moscow done to her?

The story stopped. A door closed. Brad's footsteps came quietly down the stairs. "Ha! Gotcha!" He slid a hand under Joanna's bottom as he came in from the hallway. The dishes she had been stacking rattled as she swatted at his hand. "Not in front of company, Bradley!"

"If you make them clean up, they're not company. Anyway, Alex's not company, he's my lawyer. Is there any law in Russia against fondling a girl's bottom, Alex?"

"Not specifically." He thought for a few seconds. "I suppose it could come under the Criminal Code article on 'hooliganism.' That covers a wide variety of sins, including 'violation of public order, insult, and cynical action.' And that was a distinctly cynical action. Not to mention insulting. It could also possibly be covered by the article on 'insult in private circumstances.' But there wouldn't be a public prosecution for that, although she could bring a private action to prosecute you."

"Well, that's more than I want to know about the consequences of feeling my wife's butt."

"Actually, almost anything you'd want to do is prohibited by the Russian Criminal Code somewhere, if I think about it long enough. But in this case, I suppose you could use the defense, 'That was no lady, that was my wife.' "

"Good idea. Excuse me while I fondle my wife's bottom."

"You will not!" Joanna said; but she said it laughing—or pretending to. She swatted at his hand again. "Get away! Get away!"

On the drive back to Moscow, it was one of those rare, clear late-spring evenings when dry polar air had pushed out the usual humidity, and the new tall buildings on the river northwest of the city might have been painted in pearl on the silver evening, like a picture on a Fedoskino lacquer box. Their sculpted white forms rose inspired from a dark mass of forest that poured over hills bounding the river. A sliver of old moon that rose behind them was no more white and glowing than they. The buildings, Fall knew, had been empty for a year in a dispute over payment. Buyers had paid the full cost of construction to the old regime, years ago. Inna's mother had been one of them. But now costs had escalated a hundredfold, and the buildings were not done, and the new government insisted on additional payments at the new rate, ruinous to almost everyone. So now the buildings sat empty, unattainable as the moon.

Like Inna herself.

He wondered what he was going to do.

# 2

HE DID NOTHING BECAUSE THERE WAS NOTHING HE COULD DO. BUT days later when his telephone rang, days with no word from her, still he answered expecting to hear Inna on the other end; but it was a man's voice: "Mr. Fall?"

"Yes."

"This is Volkov. Chief Investigator for the Moscow City Department of Internal Affairs."

The Department of Internal Affairs—the militia. In short, the police. Fall thought about traffic citations. Had he not paid the right "fine" to an officer? He answered cautiously: "How can I help you, Chief Investigator?"

"Are you acquainted with a Mr. Bradley Chapman, an American?"

"Yes, I am. Is he all right?"

"He's quite all right, yes. He's in our custody here. He has asked to retain a lawyer."

"What is he charged with?"

"There is no charge. We wish to ask him some questions; but he has requested a lawyer, and asked us to call you."

"Where are you? Where is he?"

"At thirty-eight Petrovka Street."

"I'll be right there."

"But—"

But Fall had hung up the telephone before Volkov could go on.

A gray drizzle was falling as Fall stopped his car in front of the Central Police Station at 38 Petrovka Street. The police station was eight or nine stories of pastel yellow stucco formed to look like stone, enclosing three sides of a rectangular garden. A high-barred, black iron fence with an entry gate closed the fourth side. A militiaman lounged in the glass-enclosed sentry box inside the gate. He seemed startled when Fall appeared. He leaped to his feet. "To see whom?"

"You're holding an American. Bradley Chapman. I'm here to see him. I'm his lawyer." Fall showed his passport. "Chief Investigator Volkov called me. My name is Fall. American."

The passport apparently startled the policeman all over again. He held it as if afraid it would burn his fingers. "I'll call the Chief Investigator," he said. He went back to his desk and dialed the telephone, then talked into it surreptitiously while glancing at Fall and then again at the telephone. He came back to Fall. "Chief Investigator Major Volkov will come shortly. You can go to the front entrance." He pointed toward the building.

Fall walked from the gate to the main door at the back of the garden. The paved walk leading from the gate to the door split in the center to pass on either side of a red granite column. The column looked naked without the bust that had once topped it— a bust of Felix Dzerzhinsky, the founder of the KGB. After the August coup attempt, statues of Dzerzhinsky had disappeared almost everywhere, even the giant one that had stood in Dzerzhinsky Square itself, in front of the KGB building.

Inside the high heavy doors was an empty lobby, shabby but not as dingy as in most public buildings. At the back were three elevators, with a granite stairway on either side of the elevator bank. Footsteps echoed down the stairs. Volkov, when he came, was a slender man of forty in a gray suit, pale blue shirt, and gray tie—the civilian apparatchik's uniform. "You're Mr. Fall?"

"Yes. Where's Chapman?"

"There's a little mistake, I'm afraid. Where he is doesn't matter. He can only see a lawyer. I was going to ask you to obtain one for him."

"I'm his lawyer."

Volkov's eyebrows rose slightly. "Really? Could I see your order to represent Mr. Fall?"

"I don't have an order. But he'll tell you I'm his lawyer. He must have told you already. You called me."

"If you don't have an order, do you have a lawyer's certificate?"

"American lawyers don't carry their certificates. They hang them on their office wall."

Volkov shrugged. "Different customs are certainly interesting. But I'm afraid that's not very helpful. Only a person admitted as a lawyer in our Russian courts may represent a defendant in a criminal case."

Fall thought a moment. "He has a right to see a consular representative."

"Yes, of course. Is that you?"

"No."

Volkov shrugged. "Well, then . . ."

"You said he hadn't been charged."

"Correct. He has not. To represent a person detained for questioning, the same rule applies."

"How long do you intend to detain him?"

"I'm afraid I don't know that. There are a number of questions we want to ask him."

"Such as?"

"I can hardly tell you that. As a lawyer"—Volkov smiled quickly as he said the word—"I'm sure you understand that."

"At least let me see him. Is he here?"

"That's not possible, I'm afraid. He has a right to see only a lawyer."

Not possible. *Nyevozmozhno.* Fall had heard the word in a hundred negotiations. The important thing was to recognize it for what it was—not necessarily the close of negotiations, but the opening. He said, "Yes, I understand. But he has a right to a lawyer; and if I'm going to get him one, I'll have to talk with him about it. If I could see him for just a few minutes . . ." A Russian would of course make small accommodations for friendship when the accommodation could do him no harm. Friendship was a broad concept, with a large component of usefulness in it. Fall had never met Volkov before, but a foreign lawyer could become a useful friend to an investigator. That was the thought Fall tried to appeal to without saying it. *You don't have to do this, but maybe someday you'll be glad you did.*

Volkov looked steadily at Fall for some seconds. His eyes were ice blue and steady. Volkov was a man on his own ground. Fall looked him back in the eye, knowing that if the Investigator were to concede the point at all, he would do so only to someone he judged worthy of the concession. Favors were not to be wasted.

At length, Volkov said, "All right. A few minutes. Come with me."

They got off the elevator at the third floor and walked along a corridor floored with battered linoleum over the usual battered wood herringbone. The walls were Official Office Yellow, dingy in the light of too few lightbulbs. At one point the floor was torn up and iron pipes were lying along the hall. The building was under repair: the eternal Soviet *remont*, still under way although the Soviet Union had vanished. "You can wait here," Volkov said, indicating a doorway. "I'll bring him."

The room was an office, but not a much-used one; it contained only a paperless desk, three wooden chairs, and an oak filing cabinet built, it appeared, to last a millennium. The cabinet was secured with a steel hasp fastened by a saucerlike Soviet-standard padlock at least four inches in diameter.

At first Fall stood waiting, but after a while he sat down on one of the chairs. The room looked out over Dzerzhinsky's former garden, but on this rainy evening little light came in. The room was lit by a single fluorescent fixture in the middle of the ceiling. The fixture's ballast was old and emitted a sizzling hum that seemed—Fall supposed it only seemed—to grow more intense by the minute. He wondered if the "office" were really a subtle torture chamber.

"Alex! Jesus Christ, am I glad to see you!" Volkov, who had come in with Chapman, looked annoyed at this breach of decorum, but he said nothing. "Can you get me out of this place?"

Fall stood up and shook the hand that Chapman offered eagerly. "It appears that I can't. But I'll get someone who can."

"I've threatened to call the goddamn Ambassador, but they won't let me near a phone. Did you call him?" They both knew the Ambassador, but only slightly. But maybe Chapman mentioned the Ambassador for Volkov's benefit.

"I thought I'd better come see what the situation is first. Investigator Volkov, do you mind if I talk to Mr. Chapman alone for a moment?"

"You may. I will be in the office at the end of the hall. There is a guard outside the door to this room; tell him when you are through. But please don't be long."

"Thank you."

Volkov closed the door softly behind him.

"What's going on?" Fall asked.

"Turbin's dead."

"Turbin! What happened?"

"I wish I knew. They told me after they brought me in here. I guess they think I had something to do with it."

"What could they think you had to do with it?"

"I wish the hell I knew! Are they listening to us here?" Chapman looked around the walls and ceiling as if he would be able to see the microphones. He was shivering.

"Probably. But there's nothing we can do about that. We could talk Pig Latin."

Chapman laughed, but not a real laugh; none of the tension left his face.

"What do you know about Turbin?"

"He was found dead outside his apartment building this morning. They say it looked like he fell from the balcony."

"Jesus! What are they asking you about it?"

"It doesn't make any sense."

"What are they asking you? Exactly."

"Not about Turbin, much. When did I see him last. Was he depressed. Where was I when he died."

"When do they think he died?"

"Late last night, apparently."

"Where were you?"

"Until around two, I was at the office, working. Then I went home."

"Can you prove it?"

"I can prove I went home. I was alone at the office."

"Too bad. Have they tried to make anything of that?"

"I can't tell. Volkov, he asks questions. He doesn't say what he thinks about the answers."

"Don't you have a guard at the office? Wouldn't he have seen you leave?"

"There's a guard at the front door. I didn't see him when I left. Probably he was taking a leak. I have my own key, so I didn't have to wait to get out." Chapman seemed uneasy. Finally he added, "Mostly they aren't asking me about Turbin at all. Mostly it's about the business. What do we make. Where do we get our supplies. How much do we pay our workers. Who keeps our books. What banks do we use. I don't know what the hell they're after." He looked aside. "There was something about stolen property. It didn't seem to be much either."

"Could Turbin have stolen something? Is anything missing?"

"The cash is all kept in the bank, and it's all accounted for. Other property . . . What do we have that he could use? You know our business. We're an express-mail company. Practically everything we use, we lease from one state organization or another. We don't own anything but a few moldy buildings; and nobody could carry those away."

"Probably they're after someone else. Maybe one of your suppliers. Maybe even the bank. God knows what goes on in a Russian commercial bank."

Chapman went to the window and glanced out into the garden, then turned back into the room. He moved in a clumsy shuffle.

Chapman followed Fall's glance. "Yeah, they took my shoelaces. My belt, too. Not to mention my watch and my billfold and my pocket calendar. I'd bet I never see *them* again."

"Have you been answering their questions?"

"Yeah, sure. I don't know how many rubber hoses they keep in the back here. Anyway, none of it's secret."

"Did they tell you you have a right to a lawyer?"

"Volkov told me. Told me just before he called you. That's why you're here."

"Don't answer any more questions. If they try to ask you anything more, tell them you're not going to answer without talking to your lawyer first."

"Isn't that just going to piss them off?"

"Maybe. But that's what you pay lawyers for—to tell you when you should piss people off. And to get them pissed off at the lawyer instead of you. Don't answer any more questions. Volkov says you're not charged with anything."

"If I'm not charged with anything, then let's get out of here."

"They can detain you for questioning. They *have* detained you for questioning."

"How long?"

Fall shrugged. He wasn't sure. He didn't handle Russian criminal cases, and he knew litle about the procedure, but he didn't tell Chapman that. Chapman had enough reason to feel insecure as it was. "Let's get a Russian lawyer in here, and we'll let him handle it."

"A *Russian* lawyer! *You're* my lawyer, Alex! At the rates I'm paying, you ought to get diplomatic immunity for the devil himself! I don't want any Russian lawyer! How the hell do I know who he's working for? This is not funny, man; and I need a *real* lawyer!"

"Here, sit down," Fall said. Chapman sat in the chair Fall pointed to, and Fall sat on the desk, looking down on him. "Now. You need a lawyer. They'll only let you have a Russian lawyer. They make the rules, we don't. I know a Russian lawyer who's good and who's smart. He knows more about Russian law than I'll learn in the rest of my life. He'll only be working for you, nobody else. And besides that, I'll come with him."

"Ah." Chapman blew out a long breath. "Yeah. If I've got to have him, all right. Go get him. But then you come get me out of here."

"I'll go after him. I'll call the consulate too. Did you call Joanna?"

"They wouldn't let me call anybody. They said they'd make one call for me, to get me a lawyer, and I used it on you. Not that I don't love Joanna." He bit his lip and bowed his head for a minute—not to show tears, Fall thought. "I was afraid she'd go to pieces. All she could have done was call you, so I thought it was better to get that done first."

"I'll call her," Fall said. "I'll make it sound like she shouldn't worry."

"Sure. And get diplomatic immunity for the devil, while you're at it. Oh . . . and . . . call Alexandra and tell her where I am." He seemed to think this over before saying it.

"Your secretary?"

"Yes. She needs to know that I'm in here. People may be looking for me."

"All right. Do you want me to have her call anyone? Or send anything?"

"No. Not yet, anyway. But bring me a sweater. No, bring me three. And your long johns, if you've got any. It's colder than death back there in the jail." Fall realized for the first time that Chapman's shivering was not emotional release. He put an arm around his friend's shoulders.

The guard outside the door led them up the hall. He stopped Fall at the last office on the right, where Volkov was sitting with the door open. Fall and Chapman shook hands without speaking, and the guard led Chapman away.

The office was furnished identically to the one they had just left and looked just as unused. Volkov was reading *Izvestia*, the evening newspaper. He folded it and left it on the desk when he came to the door. Fall thanked him for his kindness.

"Not at all. Consider it a professional courtesy. I'm a lawyer too—although, like you, I'm not an advocate. I couldn't defend a client against criminal charges, for instance." He smiled as he said this.

# 3

ALTHOUGH HE WANTED TO CALL AS SOON AS POSSIBLE, FALL DIDN'T want to use the telephone at the police station. There was bound to be a pay phone not far away outside; but he wasn't carrying change small enough to make a call from a pay telephone. They had been designed for two-kopeck calls back in Stalin's time, and most of them still took only two-kopeck pieces, or two ones, although a kopeck was now worth only a hundredth of a U.S. penny. Kopecks were worth so little that it was ridiculous to carry them—unless you needed to make a telephone call.

He thought of driving to Petrovsky Boulevard to call from the Malyi Theater Club restaurant; but what he had to say he didn't want to say in a restaurant. He decided to drive back to his apartment. This late at night, in light traffic, it was only ten minutes. He was glad he didn't live in a foreigners' ghetto in the suburbs where Chapman lived.

From his apartment he tried the number of Mikhail Slavin, but there was no answer, so he telephoned the U.S. Embassy. A Marine guard answered.

"I need to speak with a consular officer."

"I'm sorry, sir, there's no one here now." The voice implied that any sensible person would have realized that already. "The Embassy is open tomorrow at nine A.M. Could you call back then, sir?"

"I'm the lawyer for an American who's in jail, and I want to get him out. I need a consular officer to go with me to the police station."

"There's nothing we can do tonight, sir." The Marine's voice had now taken on the tone of one who has heard this before. Fall wondered if he really had. How many Americans were ever detained by the Moscow police? "I'd be happy to leave a message for the Consul. Someone will call you in the morning."

"Give me his home phone number and I'll call him myself."

"I'm sorry, I can't do that, sir, but someone will definitely call you in the morning."

"Look, my client is an important American businessman. If he sits in jail overnight because the Consul wouldn't wake up, a lot of people are going to be disturbed, and one of them may be the Ambassador."

"Well, maybe you should call the Ambassador yourself, sir."

"Not a bad idea. Give me his number."

"I'm afraid I can't do that, sir." Of course not. Anybody who could really call the Ambassador at home would already have the number. Although Fall was hearing it from a U.S. Marine, that was a quintessentially Russian principle—if it was a number you had a right to know, you should already know it.

The Marine added, "But I'll take a message that you called; or if you'll call in the morning . . ."

"Never mind." Fall hung up.

If not the Ambassador, there was Cotten.

John Cotten was the commercial attaché, and he and Fall were friends, or at least close personal acquaintances. They sometimes played deck tennis on the court in the backyard of the Ambassador's residence. Close enough for this moment of need. Not close enough for Fall to remember his number, and he didn't have it in his pocket diary either. That meant a trip to the office. But first try Slavin again, and then Joanna.

Again Slavin's telephone rang for a long time with no answer. This cramped Fall's plans. He wanted to call Joanna right away; but he also wanted to be able to assure her, when he called her, that something was being done. If he called now, he'd have nothing to say except that he'd been unable to contact the Consul and hadn't found a lawyer for Brad. The hard part of deciding his course of action was knowing why Slavin didn't answer. Probably he was out; but an unanswered telephone in Moscow often meant just that the call wasn't actually going through—a condition that could go on for days. In that case, the best thing to do was to drive to Slavin's apartment, but if it turned out that he really wasn't home, that would be a wasted hour.

Fall decided to drive to his office and try Slavin again from there, and then to telephone John Cotten. He hoped he'd have some positive development to report before he had to call Joanna.

Before leaving for the office he dug four sweaters out of the armoire in his bedroom. Though winter was barely past, he couldn't find his long johns—maybe his maid still had them in the laundry; but he came across one of Inna's slips mixed in with his shirts, and at the touch of it memory of her struck him like a blow. He had bought the slip for her at a hard-currency store, when she was staying here. He pushed it aside and went out, closing the door as if that could shut the memory behind him in the bedroom.

All of the windows in the office were lit up when Fall arrived. Yellow light, diffused by the closed fabric blinds, spread the shape of the iron window grills in long woolly shadows across the walk and into the street that ran along the riverbank.

The night guard awoke with a start when Fall opened the door. Although it was still early and he was supposed to be awake all night, the guard had been stretched out asleep on the floor behind the reception counter. The blue jacket he always wore—a civilian sport coat but with a row of military medals pinned to the left breast pocket—hung neatly from the back of the reception-ist's chair. He leaped to his feet, grinning sheepishly, pretending to be wide-awake. "Oh, it's you," he said, trying to give the impression that he had been ready to fend off an attack by intruders bent on stealing the computers. The office, with facilities for six lawyers, contained computer equipment that could be sold on the black market for rubles enough to pay off the whole Moscow Militia and still leave the seller rich as a district Party boss in Central Asia. The only barriers between the Mafia and this wealth were a steel door, one sleepy guard, and—strongest of all—a certain privacy about what the office contained. As the history of warfare had long shown that most castles fall to trea-son, Fall had decided not to garrison the building to withstand a determined robbery, but to hire a guard service with a good reputation and give the guard orders to sound the alarm and not get hurt. This one, he was sure, would definitely not get hurt.

"As you were, Vasya," Fall said in English.

The guard, Vasya, didn't understand either the military reference or the irony, but the tone was friendly, and he relaxed. "It's been quiet," he said, a sort of explanation.

"Easy is the sleep of those with clean souls." The guard grinned and nodded his head, happy to agree with the proverb.

From his office Fall tried Slavin's number again, but there was still no answer. Finally he gave up, turned on his computer, and brought up Cotten's number on Hypercard.

Cotten answered the phone on the first ring. Fall identified himself. "You must have been waiting for my call."

"Nothing else to do these long spring nights," Cotten said. "What's up?"

"I need to speak with the Consul. What's his name—Murchison? I've got a client in jail, and I need a representative of the Embassy to see him. I thought you'd probably have the Consul's home number."

"I have it. And if you promise never to tell a soul that you got it from me, you can have it too. Who's in jail? Anyone I know?"

Fall didn't want to tell. This might blow over completely, and then the fewer people who had ever known about it, the better. But he could hardly ask for a favor and then turn aside a friendly question. "Brad Chapman. Jordan Enterprises."

"Brad Chapman! I know him. Jesus, what's he in for?"

"He hasn't been charged with anything. But they're holding him for questioning. It seems really to be about someone else, as far as I can tell."

"Jesus! Look, here's Murchison's number. Let me know how it comes out, will you?"

"Sure." Fall had hoped that Cotten, since he knew Brad, might offer to call the Consul himself. But Cotten was a commercial attaché, not a lawyer, and few people besides lawyers wanted to get involved with unpleasantness. He couldn't blame them. Unpleasantness tended to rub off on everyone around it.

Murchison answered his phone eventually. He listened to what

Fall had to say and then replied, in a voice as sympathetic as cold fog, "You could have called me in the morning, you know."

"Of course I know. That's what everyone keeps telling me." That was what Fall wanted to say, but he didn't. He needed Murchison's help. "I'm really sorry to disturb you," he said. "But an American citizen is being detained without charge, and the police won't let him see anyone but you."

"Or a representative of my office."

"Or a representative of your office."

"It isn't that I'm not sympathetic," Murchison said, sounding completely not sympathetic. "But my people could spend day and night on this sort of thing, and there's very little we can do anyway. At best, we could help the man find a lawyer; and it sounds as if you've got that arranged already."

"Even if nothing can be done immediately, it would help him if he could talk with an American."

"But you've already talked with him, haven't you." It was an assertion, not a question.

"I doubt I'll be able to do it another time."

Murchison sighed deeply into the telephone. "I assure you I'll send someone over in the morning."

"Thanks." Fall made himself hang up before he lost his temper and said something that might damage his client's chances of getting any help at all from the Consul for the United States of America.

He decided to try Slavin one more time before calling Joanna.

"Alloo?" Slavin, as always, sounded a little sleepy over the telephone. He wouldn't really have been sleepy. It was barely eleven o'clock now, and even on nights he was home, Slavin never went to bed before midnight. He also sounded, as always, a little quizzical, as if wondering who could possibly be calling him at this time of night—although most nights his telephone was in constant use until he went to sleep. Mikhail Slavin had an active telephone life, even by Moscow standards, where most people had a wide circle of friends and a major entertainment was telephoning them in the evening.

"Misha, it's Alex."

Slavin switched into English. "Hello, Alex. How are you?"

Slavin, when in America, had been charmed by the American custom of asking everyone how they were as a form of greeting rather than inquiry, and he used it with all his American friends at every opportunity.

"I'm well, Misha. How are you?"

"I'm well, thank you. It's very nice to hear from you."

"I'm in a little bit of a hurry, Misha. I've been trying to call you most of the evening . . ."

"I'm sorry. I was out."

"It doesn't matter now. I've got a client in jail, and I need your help to get him out."

"Ah. Well, of course I'll be very pleased to do whatever I can for you. And for your client too. Tell me the facts."

After Fall quickly described the events at the police station, Slavin asked, "Do you know the basis for the detention?"

"No. The Investigator wouldn't tell me anything, and Chapman didn't know either."

"Well, that's a little strange. He should have signed a protocol on detention; and if he did, it would state the basis for detaining him."

"It sounded like he was just a witness. He wasn't charged with anything."

"He couldn't be detained just as a witness. A witness is always free to go. He'd have to be a suspect, at least. But he wouldn't necessarily have to be charged. The police can hold a suspect for three days without charges. But something isn't quite right here. I'm surprised that they've detained a foreigner, just to ask questions of this sort. And especially an American. With our country trying so hard for American economic help, I wouldn't expect the authorities to want the police to detain any American, and especially not one whose business is an example of how foreign companies can make a profit here. Well, no matter. In the morning I'll go to the legal advice office to get an order to represent Mr. Chapman, and then I'll go to the police and see what the situation is."

"Morning! This is my most important client, Misha! We've got to get him out tonight!"

There was a long pause. Then Slavin said, "If I show my bar

membership certificate, I suppose they'll let me see him, and see the documents of the case. I can bring the order tomorrow. But you know I'm a little bit cautious: I don't like to promise something and not be able to do it. They don't have to release him for three days, and not then if the Prosecutor approves holding him. As I said, it doesn't all sound quite right, so maybe I can convince them that the detention is illegal. But frankly that doesn't happen often. And sometimes, you know, a client is more grateful for release after a night in jail."

"This is a big client, Misha. Chapman is the personification of Jordan Enterprises in Russia. You've heard of Jordan Enterprises."

"Yes, of course. The JorSov joint venture."

"And he's also a friend of mine."

"Ah! Well, you should have said he was a friend! All right, I'll be on my way shortly. I'll call this Investigator first, to assure him you've done your duty. What is his name?"

"Volkov."

"Ah." Slavin breathed the acknowledgment softly.

"Do you know him?"

"Yes. I know him."

"I hope you're old buddies."

"I've known him a long time. I wouldn't say we were friends, exactly. Neither would he, I expect."

"What kind of man is he?"

"He's a fair man. Smart. Not one to let friendship interfere with his duty. Well, I'll call him."

"I'll meet you at the police station."

"It's not necessary. If there's anything to be done, I can do it. But if you want to be there, of course . . ."

"He's my friend, Misha."

"Yes, of course. And also your most important client."

"My most important client and my friend."

"I will wait for you."

Fall called Joanna then. She sounded tired. He didn't know how to start. "I've talked to Brad," he said.

"Has he got you working this late too? He's a slave driver.

But no harder than he drives himself, damn him. I wish he could come home earlier when he's in town. He travels so much as it is."

"I don't think he'll be home tonight, Jo." He told her then what little he knew.

She said nothing for a long time. "Jo?" he asked at last, wondering if she had fainted.

"Yes, I'm here," she said. "Is there anything I can do?"

"I don't think so."

"Poor old Turbin. What about his family?"

"He didn't have one. Just a career."

Because Turbin spoke no English, she had not known him well. Now there was nothing for a woman's heart to fasten on. "What about Brad?"

"I'm going back to the station now to try to get him out. Don't worry. I've got him a great lawyer. . . ."

"This is no time for immodesty, Alex."

It startled him, that she had a joke in her at this time. But she was the offspring of Vikings. "Not me. Michael Slavin." He Englished Slavin's first name to make him—to make the whole process—seem more domesticated. "I've worked with him a lot. He really is a terrific lawyer."

"If you say he is, I'm sure he is. But tell me the truth: how much should I worry?"

"You shouldn't."

"The truth, goddamn it."

"I think it is the truth. From what Brad says, they're asking about other people."

"Then why have they got him in jail?"

"It's a vestige of the old system. They can hold on to witnesses, too, during the investigation." Not quite correct, but he didn't want to say the word *suspect* to her.

"What a country! How long does this go on?"

He avoided the question. "I'll tell you when you should start to worry. I promise."

"Bring my man home to me, Alex." Her voice was steady. "And call me as soon as you know anything."

"I will."

# 4

WHEN FALL GOT BACK TO THE POLICE STATION, SLAVIN WAS ALREADY there, a small, slender person made owl-eyed by thick glasses, writing notes on a legal pad under the nervous eyes of the duty sergeant. Bent over his work, he had the huddled, uncertain look of a Woody Allen character. But when he became aware of Fall, he looked up and smiled—a beatific smile that glowed in his eyes. "It's as I thought," he said. "I had a look at the file with Volkov, and a little talk. Our client didn't explain matters to you *quite* precisely." It seemed a relief to him to have freed himself of confusion.

"What's the situation, Misha?"

"Did you know that Mr. Chapman has been interviewed by the police twice before during the past month?"

"No! Has he?"

"He has."

"Why didn't he tell me?"

Slavin shrugged. "I haven't yet seen him myself. I thought probably you'd want to introduce us, with the Investigator's permission. It might make him feel better about being represented by a stranger."

"Will the Investigator permit it?"

"I suggested it to him. He didn't say no."

"You're a persuasive person."

"Probably he won't let us say more than a few words."

"Every little bit helps."

Slavin was right—as Fall, knowing Slavin, had expected. The Investigator sent Chapman with a policeman, who left them alone in an office with three minutes for introductions.

Chapman shook Slavin's hand unenthusiastically. Fall introduced them in English, hoping that Slavin's command of the language would give Chapman some comfort; but still he could see that Chapman was suspicious of the Russian lawyer. He looked at Slavin like a cat eyeing a tiny dog—not with real concern, but without any great hope of benefit, either.

Fall realized that, after knowing and working with Slavin for a year, he had forgotten just how unprepossessing Slavin was at first sight, in his Woodyesqueness. "Misha's one of the world's great lawyers," he said. He said it to encourage Chapman; but he meant it.

"Wonderful," Chapman said, still not sounding enthusiastic. "Well, Great Lawyer, what do we do now?"

"Now we wait to see what questions the Investigator will ask you," Slavin said. "Then we'll have a better idea what he's after."

"Do I have to go through this crap? I haven't broken any laws."

"The only way to stop it would be to convince the Procurator that you're being held unlawfully."

"The Procurator's the public prosecutor," Fall explained, but Chapman turned him away with an annoyed reponse: "I know that, Alex."

"But the Procurator's not going to come to any conclusions before the police have even presented their case," Slavin went on. "He'll give them a chance to put a case together. Still, we should have better grounds for an opinion soon. Volkov intends to question you again at once."

"In the middle of the night?" Both Fall and Chapman were shocked. "What's the hurry?"

Slavin shrugged. "Sometimes the police think suspects are more tender at night. If you're prepared, it doesn't matter."

The policeman opened the door without knocking.

"I need twenty minutes with my client," Slavin said to him.

"The Investigator said three minutes."

"He said three minutes together with my co-counsel," Slavin said, gesturing toward Fall. "I have a right to talk with my client before he is questioned."

The policeman backed out of the room. "He'll be back," Slavin predicted; but the show of strength seemed to give Chapman at least a little confidence in his Russian lawyer.

True to Slavin's prediction, the policeman was back within a minute. "The Investigator gives you your time," he said, "but *he* goes." He pointed to Fall.

"Of course he does," Slavin said. "But the Investigator doesn't give me my time: the law does." He turned to Fall, switching back into English. "You'll wait, Alexander?"

"Of course." He added to Chapman, "I called Joanna."

"Is she all right?"

"Sure. She's a tough person. I'll call her again now, to tell her you're all right."

"Oh. Thanks. And Alexandra?"

"Shoot. I forgot."

"Forgot! Jesus Christ, Alex, I only asked you for two things!"

"I was mostly worried about getting you a lawyer, and letting Joanna know how you are." Fall was embarrassed that he had forgotten, but Alexandra hadn't seemed important. No one was going to be calling her for Brad Chapman this late at night. "It's late. I'll call her in the morning."

"Since you're waiting around, call her now."

"I'll have to get her number. I guess Joanna will have it."

"It's one four eight, five seven nine four."

"All right. Sure." They stood awkwardly. Fall said, "Well, knock 'em dead."

"Is that a military exhortation, before battle?" Slavin asked.

Chapman and Fall both laughed. "No, it's what you say to an actor going onstage," Fall said. "Or else, 'Break a leg.' "

"English has some wonderful expressions," Slavin said.

Fall called Joanna from the duty sergeant's telephone at the sentry box. The sergeant seemed doubtful that this should be permitted; but he was used to taking orders from people who seemed authoritative and giving orders to everybody else, and he surrendered to Fall's polite insistence.

Joanna answered on the first ring. Fall told her parts of the truth, carefully shaped, to let her worry as little as possible. They couldn't get Brad out tonight, he said, but there was good hope for tomorrow, and she should go to bed.

Next he called Alexandra Shubina. It was a long time before she answered, sleepy-voiced, but she came alert quickly. "Alex? Bradley's in jail? Oh, it's terrible! First poor Vladilen Viktorovich, and now this!" There was a break in her voice. "Tell Bradley . . . tell him . . ." She stumbled over just what to tell him. Russians were more emotional than Vikings.

"If anyone calls for him tomorrow," Fall instructed her, "just tell them he's out of the office. Nothing else." In times of trouble, it was better to keep things simple.

"Won't they let him out tomorrow?"

"We don't know yet. Maybe they will. He isn't arrested; they're just asking him some questions. But don't talk about that with anyone. Just tell them he's out of the office."

"I'll tell them. Will you call me? I want to know how he is."

"I'll call you."

Then he went back to wait in the cold, drafty entry hall, glad he had brought Brad the sweaters, wishing he had kept one for himself. There was a bench where he might have stretched out, but he supposed there was some limit to the sergeant's sense of decorum, and he also felt he had his own side's dignity to maintain, so he sat straight on a hard chair and waited for Slavin to come.

When Slavin did come, it was three in the morning; but he seemed none the worse for it. He was wearing a raincoat and a wool cap, looking like a schoolboy that an overanxious mother had stuffed into this getup. He carried a battered litigation bag—what he would call a *portfyel*, or portfolio—that had started life as a series of pockets buckled with straps but now was more nearly a series of patches. He said nothing to Fall until they had walked beyond the pillar in the garden. Then Fall asked how it had gone.

"Our client likes to talk," Slavin said. "He is required to answer questions, of course, but not to tell his life's history."

"What did Volkov learn?"

"As little as I could let him." Slavin lifted a hand to forestall further questions until they were outside the gate. He showed his lawyer's identity card to get them outside—the policeman on duty prevented unauthorized departures as well as entries. Out-

25

side the fence, Slavin said, "Come to my apartment. We'll have a cup of tea."

"Shall I follow you?"

"Come in my car. We can talk on the way. I'll bring you back afterward."

"You won't get any sleep at all."

"I've nothing scheduled in the morning. I live the free life of a Moscow lawyer."

They climbed into Slavin's Zhiguli. When Slavin turned the key, there was a click and then a whir and finally the starter groaned, but the engine didn't start. "It's cross with me," Slavin said. "I left it standing in the rain."

"We can take my car."

"It will go. It always goes." After a second try, and then a third, it did go. Slavin smiled. "It's like Russia. It takes a lot of kicking to get it to wake up; but when it does, there's no stopping it."

"You mean the brakes don't work either?"

"Something like that. Like the Revolution. A great burst of energy, and then a long, long time coasting to a halt, in the dark by the side of the road."

The Zhiguli lurched away from the curb. As they moved, the accumulating drizzle blurred the windshield. Slavin turned on the wipers, but the wipers clearned only a narrow track on each side of the windshield. The blades had been removed, and the wiper arms, like the bandaged wrists of an amputee, rested each on a pad cut from a scrap of inner tube, designed to keep the arms from scratching the windshield.

"Maybe you should put on the blades," Fall suggested. Like all Muscovites with cars, Slavin kept his windshield wiper blades in the trunk so they wouldn't be stolen.

"It's not far." Slavin bent down to peer through the thin track cleared by the pad. "If I put them on, I'll get wet, I'll have to take them off at my apartment, I'll get wet again. . . . There's a line by one of your American poets, Emerson, I think. Do you know it? 'Things are in the saddle, and ride mankind.' "

"I didn't know you read American literature."

"It's the duty of all educated people, isn't it, to know the great poets of mankind?"

"It's not a duty many of us fulfill."

"The spirit is willing, but the flesh is weak." The car lurched from side to side as Slavin dodged potholes and ridges in the crumbling Moscow streets.

"What about our client, Misha?"

"Ah, yes, our client. I was hoping you'd forgotten." A bounce over a ridge of paving sent Fall nearly to the roof of the car. "Officially, I'm not allowed to tell you anything. The evidence in the case is secret until it is presented in court. Only his lawyer is entitled to be informed about it; and as we've already established, you're not his lawyer. Not in the eyes of the law here."

"But in the eyes of the client . . ."

"Yes, of course. But what I was about to say, there's the well-known line from another poet—I forget his name—'What they don't know will not hurt them.' "

"I think I've heard of it. So what's the situation?"

"The crime Mr. Chapman is suspected of is theft of state property."

"Brad? That's crazy! What is he supposed to have stolen?"

"Not *he*, exactly—but the business. It was done in the ordinary course of business. The Investigator's hypothesis, I believe—although he certainly didn't say so—is that Turbin killed himself when it appeared the crime would be revealed. But he isn't sure that our client didn't kill Turbin."

"How could they have stolen state property in the course of the business? Brad's checked the legality of every aspect of the business. You know that."

"But of course we still operate mostly under the laws of the Soviet Union, as the legislature hasn't got around to adopting all-new laws yet. And the laws of the Union were designed to make business a crime."

"So how did this theft of state property work?"

"The Investigator is still working that out. But I gather that the theory is that Turbin as co–General Director of the company transferred state property to the business."

"Of course he did. That's no secret. It's the whole point of the

27

business—to take this worthless postal system that the state has lying around and convert it into something that works—something that people will actually pay for using. It's *receipt* of state property; but it sure as hell isn't theft!"

"Looking at it from the Investigator's point of view, I suppose it all depends on the price, doesn't it."

"The price is perfectly legitimate. It was set by state authorities."

"One of which, incidentally, is the Ministry of Posts and Communications, whose Deputy Minister at the time—and ex-Deputy, until today or late yesterday—happened to be . . . V. V. Turbin, the co–General Director of the JorSov joint venture, of which the other co–General Director is Bradley Chapman."

Slavin slowed the car, swerved, crashed over the curb and up onto the sidewalk. Fall stiffened, thinking they had gone out of control at last. But then Slavin shut off the engine, and Fall realized they were at Slavin's apartment. He had been there many times, but through the steamed windows it was hard to tell where they were, and Slavin lived in a Brezhnev-era building much like every other building in that street, concrete-panel construction that had looked as dilapidated when new as it did now. Slavin did not move to get out of the car.

"So Volkov suspects that Turbin, or his minister, gave the joint venture a sweetheart price?" Fall asked.

"Police investigators are paid to be suspicious. And you know we have a saying, 'Where there's loose firewood, even the priest will steal.' "

Slavin still didn't get out of the car, and Fall remembered now that Slavin hadn't spoken until he got into it. Fall asked, "Will anyone be listening to what we say in your apartment?"

"Oh, that's very unlikely, I think. Those days are past." Still, Slavin didn't move. "But you know I like to be a little bit cautious. I wouldn't want to be heard discussing the details of the case with anyone who isn't entitled to know them."

"How do I become entitled?"

"I've been thinking. If you were appointed by your Consul as his official representative, I think the Prosecutor would be obliged to let you participate in Mr. Chapman's defense."

"I've already talked with the Consul. He'd rather have been

asleep. But I'll go to his office in the morning. Meanwhile, how do we get Brad out?"

"It's always a question, whether to use sharp struggle or diplomacy. I'm inclined to diplomacy, for now. But I gave a petition to the Investigator, asking him to release our client on the ground that he is illegally detained because no crime has been committed. I'll give a copy to the district Prosecutor tomorrow. It will show them that we're prepared to struggle. But it very seldom works."

"How did you get a petition prepared on that short notice, Misha?"

Slavin looked at him strangely, as if puzzled. "Why, I just wrote it out on the spot. When I go to the police station for a client, I always carry some small paper, and copy paper. What do you call it in English?"

"Carbon paper."

"Yes. So, I wrote a petition and kept a copy for myself and for the prosecutor. For you too." He opened his portfolio and handed Fall a flimsy carbon copy of a handwritten sheet.

Fall felt, again but for the first time in months, that jolt of dislocation that he had felt so often when he first came to Moscow. He still thought of a petition as something done on a typewriter—no, on a computer; something sweated over and corrected; something typed by a secretary and presented in multiple flawless copies. But still what he held in his hands, a handwritten carbon copy on paper that would melt in the rain, was something *done,* something accomplished, not a mere strategy but a concrete act to get Brad Chapman out of jail. Fall felt a sudden surge of gratitude, a renewal of confidence in Slavin and his easy knowledge of the system.

"Probably it will not be granted," Slavin said, glancing at his copy of the petition before he put it back into the portfolio. "But it will make them think about the consequences. Though I guess they've already thought about that." He picked up the portfolio and got out of the car. "Did you lock that door?" he asked before turning the key in the lock on his own door.

They entered the dark hallway of the apartment house, a cold, dank space that smelled more of a jail than the police station had.

29

"What consequences have they thought of?" Fall asked.

"Volkov wouldn't detain a foreigner without having done good background work. He knows it will not be a secret."

"I'll say it won't! Every foreign-company rep in Moscow will know about it within two days. All Brad's company has done is make a profit out of something worthless."

The elevator clanked to a stop within its shaft, and the door opened. They stepped inside. It was big enough for three friendly people, though not for two enemies. The door closed on them, and the elevator jerked as it started up.

"But people here grew up with the notion that profit is a moral wrong," Slavin said. "Some still think, even if it is now *lawful* to make a profit, that something crooked must have happened in the making of it, and if they look into it deeply enough, they will find out what."

"Volkov didn't strike me as that sort."

"Volkov does his job. He keeps his head down and does his job."

The elevator lurched to a stop, but the door didn't open. Slavin banged on it and then pushed the edge of the door until it grudgingly released them.

"Have you read the newspapers in the last several days?" Slavin asked.

"I skimmed them. I've been busy."

"Yes, I know your work habits." It was hard for Fall to tell if that was politeness or irony. Slavin knew about Inna, and so he knew Fall had been distracted the last weeks.

Two apartments opened off Slavin's end of the hall, but before it reached them the hall had been blocked by a steel cage door welded from girders and reinforcing bars. Its frame was cemented into the wall. A huge padlock on the inside held it shut. Slavin reached through the bars and fumbled at the padlock with a huge key. "Life is not easy in the former Soviet Union," he muttered. Getting the padlock free at last, he swung the cage door open, then locked it again behind them.

"What do you do in case of fire?" Fall wondered.

"My neighbors would forgive me for burning alive," Slavin said. "But they'd never forgive me if their worldly possessions were stolen." He confronted the next obstacle—his apartment door itself, set with four separate locks around its perimeter.

The telephone began to ring in Slavin's apartment. They could hear it through the door, but it stopped as Slavin struggled with the last lock. "No, don't go!" he called out, but the only answer was silence. "People always give up so easily!" he grumbled.

"There have been several articles in the *Russian Gazette* and other papers," Slavin went on as he continued to attack the lock. "Articles critical of corruption in official circles. They put me in mind of several periods under former regimes." He got the door open at last and swung it aside for Fall to enter. He took off his coat and cap and hung them on the pegs inside the door, removed his shoes and put on a pair of slippers, handing another pair—far too small—to Fall. As Fall wrestled the slippers, Slavin wandered through his apartment switching on lights—in the hall, in the sitting room, in the bedroom, in the third room outfitted as an office, last in the small kitchen, where he turned on one burner of the gas stove and lit it with a match. He said as Fall came into the kitchen, "When Gorbachev first came into office— perhaps you remember, it was in the middle 1980s—his first act was to attack corruption." He paused for the screech of water in the pipes as he filled a battered blue teakettle, then went on as he sought out cups, tea, spoons, and honey from a jumble of things on counters and shelves. "Anticorruption campaigns are always a pleasant diversion from difficult issues, like a drive in a large, swift machine—with the pleasure enhanced by the fact that driving is a duty. The drivers, of course, are well insulated from the cries of those the wheels are rolling over." He added, "I defended a number of persons charged with corruption at that time. A professor I knew was charged with taking a gift to help a friend's child be admitted to Moscow State University. He gave the child special tutoring. The child was a friend of the family, but of course there was a gift."

"I assume you got him off."

"Practically. He was sentenced to five years in prison. But it was only at soft labor." Slavin added, "Of course in those times no one ever was found not guilty. Success was getting a favorable sentence."

31

"You're a great source of reassurance, Misha."

"I try to be realistic."

"Are you sure you want anyone to overhear you saying this?" Fall asked, thinking of Slavin's caution in the car.

"If they're listening, they need to hear it." He added, "This doesn't involve my obligations as a lawyer. It involves the obligations of the state to its citizens. Let them prosecute me."

"Would they prosecute you?"

"Now? No. Yesterday, yes, of course. Tomorrow . . . who knows?"

"How well do you know Volkov?" Fall asked, curious about his adversary.

Slavin didn't answer at once. He filled a teapot with boiling water and threw loose tea leaves into it. "I've known him for many years. We were both on the staff of the Academy of the Ministry of Internal Affairs. Under Krylov." The Ministry of Internal Affairs controlled the militia. The Militia Academy was its highest training center. Slavin said Krylov's name as if Fall should know the significance of it; but to Fall it meant nothing. "Who is Krylov?" he asked.

Slavin motioned Fall toward the sitting room, where he kept his table. He led the way, his voice floating back over his shoulder in the narrow hall. "Krylov was the great reformer of the Moscow police. The Director of the Academy, where I worked. And so did Volkov." He pointed Fall to a chair, poured tea. "That was in Brezhnev's time. Not a good time for reformers. Krylov died in disgrace. His staff was dispersed and went this way and that. Volkov went to be a police investigator. I became an advocate, defending criminals. We talk very little since then, Volkov and I." He added, "We talked a little tonight; but only a little. He suggested that I not expect any favors." Slavin smiled, that luminous, off-centered smile that had in it something of childish innocence, but now something of loss as well. It invited no further questions.

They went on to talk, over tea and indifferent cakes on the edge of staleness, about strategy and the chances of getting Brad out, and set a time to meet in the morning. Fall, looking into his pocket diary, saw that he had a breakfast meeting with another client, set days ago—saw just in time, for it was already morning.

# 5

THE SECRETARY WHO ANSWERED THE TELEPHONE AT THE CONSUL'S OF-
fice in the morning said no one was there except her, and she had
no knowledge of anyone's having been sent to visit Chapman in
jail; so Fall decided to go to the Consul's office in person.

The Consul had by then arrived. He was a wide man with a
mustache, an impressive person but evidently not given to making decisions. "I'll send someone when I've got someone to
send," he said. "Believe me, I will, Mr. . . ."

"Fall."

"Mr. Fall."

"But the thing is, as I keep telling you, I don't want you to
send anyone. I want you to make me your respresentative."

"And the thing is, as *I* keep telling *you*, I can't make you my
representative. I already have people who are my representatives.
You don't work for this office. You don't work for the United
States. It's just not possible."

"*Nyevozmozhno*," Fall said, disgusted.

"What?" The Consul didn't speak Russian.

"I said, 'Not possible.' I hear it all the time from Russians. But
I didn't expect to hear it here, in the U.S. Embassy, when there's
an American citizen sitting in jail."

"Well, some things *aren't* possible."

"Sure. You can't sew a button on a fart, as my grandfather
used to say. But most things you can do if you've got the right
incentive."

The Consul smiled. "Your grandfather was a witty man. But
let's say I don't have the right incentive."

"Have you heard of Jordan Enterprises?"

"Of course. But you can't buffalo me with big names, Fall. I know my job, and I do it the best I can. If what I can do isn't good enough for you, I'm sorry. But I won't give you a piece of paper to go around passing yourself off as a representative of this Consulate. Big names aren't a big enough incentive."

"Then I'll have to find a better one, won't I?"

"I guess you will."

"See you later."

Fall was unhappy. His unhappiness wasn't just from his failure to get the Consul's agreement to appoint him, or even from the failure of his awkward threat. Mostly he was unhappy because he wanted to think of himself as a person who would never use political influence to get his way, and now he was going to have to try to use it. And partly he was unhappy because he wasn't sure the political influence was there. It was true that Brad Chapman *was* Jordan Enterprises in Moscow; and it was true—or at least all the television networks reported it to be true, which was close enough to truth for Fall's purposes—that Hawke Jordan could dine at the White House any night of the week, his choice. But did that convert to an order for Ira S. Murchison, Consul, to appoint Brad Chapman's lawyer as consular representative? There were a lot of missing terms in that equation.

By now it was ten o'clock in the morning. One A.M. in Texas. Not a bad time to talk to a tycoon, if you could find his telephone number. Two A.M. in Washington, D.C. Not a bad time for a tycoon to talk to the President of the United States.

Fall called Joanna. "Alex!" she said. "Have you got Brad out yet?"

"No. But I'm working on it. We're about to apply the Small World Principle."

The Small World Principle holds that no one in the world is more than three personal acquaintances away from anyone else, if you pick the shortest possible chain. But, as the number of chains between any two people is almost infinite—the number of each person's acquaintances to the fourth power—the Small World Principle is not as useful as it might be. Success may be as much a matter of luck as good planning.

The space between Alexander Fall and Hawke Jordan, though,

was a crowded one, by Small World standards. A number of chains would have fallen within the principle's parameters; but the one that actually reached from Fall to Hawke Jordan that morning ran from Joanna Chapman to the wife of Brad's boss in Minneapolis to the wife of Hawke Jordan in Odessa, Texas. It was, coincidentally, a chain of the same length that reached back to Fall on the other side an hour later: Hawke Jordan to the President of the United States, to the U.S. Ambassador to the Russian Federation (then sleeping in a hotel room in Washington, D.C.), to Ira S. Murchison, United States Consul in Moscow, to Alexander Fall, newly appointed Special Assistant Consul.

The jail was a cubic pile of cream-painted bricks standing free in the central court of the police station at 38 Petrovka Street. The structure was so rough it looked to have been stacked rather than built, and to be held together mainly by the welded grids of iron channel that were bolted over every window. The barred windows looked in every direction at the high-windowed inner walls of the police station, and at the paved yard filled with police cars that separated the jail from the station itself. The cars were mostly Russian-made Volgas, but among them were many unmarked white BMWs. The Moscow militia was increasing its status in the new world of the free market.

The wood door of the jail was opened from the inside to admit Fall, Slavin, and a militia guard.

The jail was as cold as Brad had said it was. Just walking the steel-walled corridors toward the cell, Fall could feel the warmth seeping from his bones. He understood now why Slavin had come out from the cellblock the night before dressed in his raincoat and wool cap. He was wearing them now.

The warder stopped at a door of solid steel set into the wall of solid steel.

"This place is as secure as your apartment, Misha," Fall said.

There was a steel flap at chest height on the door, closed and secured with a huge padlock, apparently the mate of the one on the file cabinet Fall had seen the day before, or of the one on the cage door outside Slavin's apartment. The warder put a key into the main lock on the door. It appeared to turn hard. The lock sounded full of gravel. Fall hoped he never heard it turn behind him. The warder pried the door open.

Chapman was alone in the cell, although there were bunks for eight. It was a cell about the size and shape of the kitchen in Chapman's apartment, but instead of appliances, four bunks were stacked two high along either wall, and the small barred window looked onto the inner windows of the Central Police Station instead of a birch grove. In one corner, crammed so close between the bunks and the wall that it could barely be reached, was a bucket that served as a latrine. Once it had been white enameled, but now it was brown with rust or worse. The place smelled as if no air had ever come in or out, but Chapman seemed no longer to notice.

Fall had expected to be welcomed with despair, but instead Chapman was angry: "It took you guys long enough to get here today! I thought you were coming this morning to get me out!"

"Christ, Brad, we've worked our tails off just to get me in here to see you!" Fall told him.

"I'd a lot rather you worked your tails off getting me out there to see you."

"That's a little harder, unfortunately."

"I thought your superlawyer here could do anything."

Slavin had let Fall enter the cell first, but now he stepped up beside him. "It's not in anyone's power to get you out yet," he said to Chapman. "I've petitioned for your release, without success. The fact is, as you know, you're a suspect in a rather serious case. The police have a right to hold you for at least three days."

These words quieted Chapman, who looked at Fall with the look of someone changing the subject. "I thought they weren't going to let you see me. Lawyers only."

"Or consular representatives. And that's me."

Chapman seemed to take some hope from this. "No kidding? How did you swing that?"

"It wasn't easy. I finally had to put the fear of God into the Consul. I invoked the name of Hawke Jordan."

Chapman's eyes narrowed. "How did you do that?"

"I got Jordan to call the President, in person."

"You did *what?*"

Fall was filled with pride, but not too much to share it. "Joanna did it, really. She got on the line, and an hour later, Hawke Jordan telephoned the President of the United States and demanded that his lawyer—that's me—be appointed as consular representative for his man in Moscow. That's you."

"Oh, God!" Chapman sat down on the nearest bunk, looking pale. "How could you do this to me, Alex?" he demanded. "Hawke Jordan is the straitest-laced Baptist this side of the Jordan River. If he gets any hint that anybody working for a company with his name on it was suspected of a crime . . ."

Fall was taken aback. "Well, Brad, do you want out, or don't you? We can sure as hell leave you in here."

"I'd rather sit in jail than have Mr. Jordan think I've got his company in trouble."

"Is that why you didn't tell me you've been questioned by the police before?"

"Who told you that?" Chapman glared at Slavin: it was clear who he thought had told him that.

But Slavin, for all his meek appearance, was not to be pushed around. "*I* told him," he answered, "not that it matters. The interrogation record in the case is available to your lawyers. If you don't want them to read it, probably you should have other lawyers. Certainly *I* wouldn't be able to help you."

Chapman said nothing for a moment. Then: "I'm sorry. I didn't mean that." He sat down wearily on one of the bunks. "This has been a little hard on me. I took a job everyone said couldn't be done, a business nobody could make work; and I did it—I made it work. And now . . ." He looked suddenly as if he hadn't slept in weeks, although the bunk he was sitting on looked as if it had been slept in for more than one night. In fact the bunks all looked as if they had been slept in for more than one night, for more than a few weeks even, although Chapman was alone in the cell.

"The business is in good shape," he said. "This is all BS! That's why it's so unfair! We didn't steal anything, we didn't pay any bribes. . . . You know that's true, Alex. Every one of their goddamn crazy rules, we asked you about, and we did what you told us."

That was true, Fall reflected. Or at least as close an approximation of truth as anyone doing business in Russia was likely to be able to claim. The rules, some of them, were still the rules of the old system; and those rules, as Slavin had said, had been designed to prevent business.

"So how come I'm sitting in jail?"

"You are a suspect to an investigation concerning theft of state property," Slavin said, "and a witness in the death of an ex–deputy minister, although the police don't know what to think about *that* case yet." Slavin, Fall had found over the years, was sometimes literal-minded to a fault. His was a wonderful lawyer's brain; and his lawyer's brain took the facts presented and pursued them through all the far corners of the law to their logical end. But what Chapman wanted, Fall saw, wasn't a statement of his case. What he wanted was comfort.

"We'll get you out," Fall said. He didn't have a basis for saying it, but it was what Chapman wanted to hear. Ordinarily Fall didn't believe in telling the client what he wanted to hear, but this wasn't ordinarily.

"When? *When* will you get me out?"

"We don't know yet. Misha has petitioned the Investigator to release you."

"And what are the chances of that?"

"Not really good," Slavin said. "The only grounds for release are that you're being held illegally; but unfortunately you're *not* being held illegally. A suspect may be held for up to three days for interrogation. At the end of three days, they must either charge you with something or release you. Usually, if they've gone to the trouble to detain someone, they want to keep him for the whole three days. And since you're a foreigner, there will be a little bit of interest in this, out in the world. I think they won't admit easily that it was done for nothing."

"So they'll charge me with something."

"Certainly they'll want to," Slavin said. "But they can only charge you with what the facts will bear."

"I didn't steal any state property."

"Of course not. And that is what we need to establish."

Chapman lay back on the bunk and covered his eyes with his

arms. "What happens if they charge me with something? Do I stay here forever? How long does this last?"

"Well, if they charge you, probably then we have a *good* chance to get you out," Slavin answered. "If it's nothing too serious, the Prosecutor may release you on your promise not to leave the city."

Chapman uncovered his eyes, looked hard at Slavin. "Is 'theft of state property' too serious?"

"It's hard to say. In a case involving a foreigner . . . ? Well, I'd be hopeful."

"I like the way this guy commits himself," Chapman said to Fall.

"I find it's better to be conservative," Slavin said, sounding a little hurt. "I've had some success, it's true, in getting my clients released before trial. But it's nothing I can promise. But now, I'm most interested in establishing that you are not guilty of the crime of which you are suspected. Perhaps we could begin to discuss that."

"Misha has told me what's in the record of your interrogations," Fall said. "Otherwise, we know nothing. We think we should point out to Volkov the facts that are in your favor. To do that, we need to know everything."

"You already know everything about the business, Alex. Who have I been asking for legal advice? If I go to jail, you ought to be in here with me." Chapman said this as a joke, but his voice had an edge of something deeper than humor.

"Then we'll both be safe," Fall said, "because nothing I know of would send anyone to jail. But we have to look at this with new eyes. Assume I know nothing at all. Now, the investigation concerns theft of state property. We know Volkov's questions all related to your company's business. Let's talk about what your company does and how it involves state property. If it seems stupid to tell me things I know already, assume you're telling them to Misha. He hasn't worked on your case."

Chapman closed his eyes, folded his hands on his stomach. Lying on the filthy bunk, he looked like a man composing himself for death. "My company is called JorSov," he began in an expressionless voice that matched his expressionless face. "The name is a combination of *Jordan* and *Soviet*."

"It was formed before the Soviet Union disappeared, then," Slavin noted.

"Yeah. It was one of the joint ventures established under the 1987 decree that first let foreigners own part of a business here. It's not *my* company, of course. It just didn't go anywhere until I got here. It's a fifty-fifty joint venture. The American half is owned by Jordan Enterprises, which is a multinational conglomerate owned entirely by one family."

"The Jordans, I suppose."

"Yes. The head of the family—the owner of the whole conglomerate, for practical purposes—is Hawke Jordan. Who Alex kindly alerted to the fact that I'm in jail."

"Who owns the Russian part of the venture?" Slavin asked. He was not changing the subject on Alex's behalf; he simply was interested only in relevant information, and right now his client's embarrassment was not relevant.

"The Russian owner is an enterprise that belongs to the Ministry of Posts and Communications. It's called the Special Deliveries Combinat. I think the Ministry formed it especially for this purpose."

"And Turbin was its head?"

"Yes."

"What does the joint venture do?"

"It's an express-delivery service," Chapman said.

"You may have been under the impression that Russia already had a postal system," Fall said to Slavin.

"It has a postal system," Chapman said. "In fact, it has at least three. One for the government, one for the military, and one for the people. The military system or the government one I might be able to use, but the military and the government won't let go of them. In fact, we lease some airplanes from the military. They're one of the few organizations you can count on here.

"The people, as usual, get what's left. The people have a post office. But we provide delivery *service*. Real delivery, every time. Something that customers will pay real money for."

"You mean hard currency?" Slavin asked.

"Yes. Real money." Hard currency meant money that could be changed into other countries' money, unlike Russian rubles. It was a criminal violation to change rubles into other countries' money, except through state-licensed banks. Hard currency also meant money that could really be exchanged for goods, unlike Russian rubles, which were sometimes described as a license to forage for goods. The state stores would sell goods only for rubles, but the state stores had few goods to sell. A person could always buy goods for hard currency. Also, the state had developed the habit of occasionally carrying out a "currency reform" in the course of which old rubles became invalid and new rubles were issued—but invariably fewer rubles were in the hands of the population after the "reform" than before. For such reasons, every Russian wanted hard currency instead of rubles. And for that reason, the state had made it illegal to sell goods or services in Russia for any money other than rubles, except with permission from the state.

"Do you have a license to sell your delivery services for hard currency?" Slavin asked.

"My lawyer insisted on it," Chapman said, indicating Fall.

"You have a good lawyer," Slavin said.

"So he tells me. So what am I doing in this place?"

"How does your service involve state property?" Slavin asked.

"The business works like this. The Russian postal system is a mess. I'm sorry to say it, but it's a mess. The equipment is a mess; the buildings are a mess. I hate to say it, but the workers are a mess too. So we said to the Ministry of Posts and Communications, 'Look, for a postal system you really need only three things. You need physical plant—buildings and equipment—you need workers, and you need customers. Your physical plant is terrible, but your workers can be trained, or some of them can; and your customers are all right, or some of them are—the ones with hard currency. There should be enough of those to pay for a real postal system, or at least for important deliveries. We can't afford to rebuild the whole system from the beginning, but let's do it a piece at a time. 'Step by step,' as the central planners used to say. So if you give us your customers and let us charge some of them hard currency, we'll show you how to run it. We'll use the income to lease your plant and upgrade it as we can. And to make you feel good, we'll use your buildings.' So that was the deal. We even offered to bring in fancy electronic data-transmission equipment, if and when CoCom will let us. We'll do it too."

"What is CoCom?"

"Damned if I know. Ask my lawyer."

"The Coordinating Committee," Fall said. "It's not really a committee; it's a group of countries, basically the Western countries plus Japan, which agreed in the old days, when the USSR still existed, to coordinate their export policies to keep the USSR from getting its hands on technology that had military value. Electronic data transfer has military value."

"So I understand that Jordan Enterprises' contribution to this business was know-how," Slavin summarized.

"That's right. We know how to run a post office. That's more than you can say for the Russian postal system."

"And the Russian partner's contribution was customers."

"The right to serve Russian customers, actually," Fall said. "Plus the buildings. Plus some information. 'Technology.'"

" 'Technology!' " Chapman said scornfully. "The only reason for that was to pretend that the Russian side had put enough value into the deal to claim a contribution equal to ours, so they could own half. The only information we ever got was where the buildings were, and where the customers were. But we could have run the system from a road map and done just as well."

"The road map would have been technology too, though," Fall said. "You'd have had to give them credit for it."

"What was the value of the property the Russian side contributed?" Slavin asked.

"You want to know the truth?" Chapman sat up on the bed, suddenly animated.

"Yes, of course." Slavin's English did not yet include a good grasp of rhetorical questions.

"Not a damn penny! That's what it was worth. We *said* it was worth eighteen million dollars. But it wasn't actually worth a damn thing."

"What about the customers?" Slavin asked.

"They weren't worth anything either. Because they weren't really customers—they were captives. If we could have come along with our service and just left the Russian postal system to compete with us, every worthwhile customer we wanted would have signed up with us, whether the Ministry of Posts and Communications liked it or not. But of course customers weren't allowed to sign up with us until the state gave us the right to serve customers. 'The right to serve customers'—*that* was worth something. What the state had, you see—the *only* thing it had that we didn't have—was the police. The state could stop people from using our service even if the people wanted to. So what the state gave us was its promise not to interfere with our business. It was kind of a protection racket. Do you understand what a protection racket is?"

"Oh, yes. It's probably another thing that was invented in Russia, like the helicopter." Slavin pondered a moment. "And the buildings? Did they have no value?"

"Oh, they were worth *something*. They sure as hell weren't worth five million, or whatever we valued them at. We didn't care. We had to have the protection. *That* was worth eighteen million. They could hide the price for it however they wanted. If they wanted it to be five million in buildings and five in equipment and eight in 'technology,' what did we care?"

"If they say now—and maybe they do—that these buildings are worth more than five million dollars," Slavin said, "maybe we *do* care. And the value of the American contribution was also eighteen million dollars? All for 'know-how'?"

"Not all for know-how. We put in a million dollars in cash. But basically it was know-how, sure. That's the difference between being able to make a business work and not being able to make it work. We could do this without them. Except for the state's protection racket, they couldn't do it without us."

There was an uneasy silence from both Chapman and Fall.

"Who approved the prices?" Slavin asked.

"Turbin." It was Fall who answered.

"Who was also the co–General Director of JorSov, the business which received the buildings."

"Worse. He was also a deputy minister then," Fall said. "He

resigned from that not long ago because there's a rumor that Yeltsin will prohibit government officials from holding outside jobs. Turbin liked being co–General Director better than being a deputy minister, he said. But when the joint venture got the buildings, he was deputy minister. He said he had authority from the Minister himself. There isn't any doubt the Minister knew the price. He knew everything about the deal."

"Is the Minister's signature on any of the documents?"

"He didn't sign the company documents. He signed a permission for the Special Deliveries Combinat to enter the transaction."

"Is there a price stated in the permission?"

"No."

They all sat for a while, digesting this. At length, Slavin asked, "Why did Turbin resign as a deputy minister instead of resigning as co–General Director? That's a big job to give up lightly. Was he paid for his services as co–General Director?"

"We tried not to," Chapman said. "But it was no deal if we didn't pay him."

"How much was he paid?"

Chapman started to answer, but Fall stopped him, holding up a hand and then pointing to his ear. *Was* no one listening? "Have you been asked about this by the Investigator?" Fall asked.

"No."

"And he shouldn't be," Slavin said. "The case is about theft of state property. Other questions are not relevant." It appeared he had changed his mind about this line of questioning.

It was only after Fall and Slavin had left the jail that Slavin came back to the question. "It was a good thing you stopped our client from talking about the co–General Director's compensation," he said. "I shouldn't have asked it. Not there."

"Well, as you said, it's not relevant."

"Not yet. They can always decide to investigate other issues. They may come back to this one yet. You were right to stop me."

"Do you think anyone was listening?" Fall asked.

"Probably not. But I remember once, I was interviewing a client who was being held in Butyrskaya Prison. We were in an interrogation room I hadn't been in before, and it looked a little strange. There were some bookshelves on the wall. I was curious

why there would be books in such a room, and I went over to
see what they were. I touched a book and it fell over, and there
behind it was an eye looking at me! I moved some more books,
and I was looking into a man's face through a hole in the wall
behind the books. We were both so surprised, we looked at each
other for a minute; and then he said, "I suppose you think we're
listening to you."

"What did you do?"

"I put the books back, and my client and I communicated in
writing the rest of the period." Slavin laughed at the memory.
Then he asked, "How much *was* Turbin paid?"

"I don't know exactly, now. It was ten thousand rubles a
month, something like that."

"Only rubles? I'm surprised he'd threaten to cancel a deal if
all he got was rubles. Ten thousand rubles is three times the
average monthly salary, but it's only twenty dollars. Jordan Enterprises can afford it."

"He got paid in dollars too," Fall admitted. "But only when he
was out of the country." Under the curious and arcane Russian
regulations on currency, a Russian citizen could be paid only in
rubles in Russia; but for work done outside the country he could
be paid outside the country in any currency as long as, on his
return, he deposited it in an authorized bank in Russia and reported it for taxes.

"And how much was his work worth?" Slavin asked. "Or perhaps I should amend that. How much was he paid?"

"Twenty thousand," Fall said. "A year."

"Not rubles, I assume."

"Dollars."

"So he could afford to be modest in his co–General Director's
ruble salary. Did he report this income to the tax inspectorate,
do you know?"

"I hope so. I told Brad he had to require Turbin to do it."

"I hope so too. If we get our client out of detention, we can
ask him about it. But until then, I think it will be better not to
discuss it with anyone else. It's not only in Petrovka jail that the
walls have ears."

# 6

WHEN HE WAS AWAY, SHE USED TO SLEEP ON HIS SIDE OF THE BED. It made her miss him less, somehow, not to wake up and reach for where he should be, and feel that he was gone. Not to look toward that side of the room, and him not in it.

Since she had moved back to her own apartment, she had given that up. She slept on her side of the bed. He had not stayed here at her place as much as she had stayed at his, just that brief period they called their honeymoon. But that wasn't the reason. He was still as much with her here as anywhere. There were times when she felt, suddenly, *here is where he used to be.* But she kept her mind from it, and now day by day it grew less. But would there ever come a time when he was gone?

She woke in the gray three-A.M. daylight, wondering, *have I done the right thing?* There was no answer.

There was never an answer. At least not until long afterward. That was her father's answer. *You'll know, too late, if it was right. Nothing to do, now, but to do.* So now, like her father, she did.

She struggled awake. Before, she always woke in a flash, like sunrise. Now something held her back. She knew what it was. That heart-deep unwanting to face the day without him. But she wouldn't name it to herself. No blaming him. Not ever.

Her feet felt for her slippers. Walking in a slow shuffle, not to lose them, she crossed the few steps to the garderobe—old, black-patinated, carved with lions and eagles and angels, an icon of her parents' youth. The knobs were missing, but she used an angel as a door-pull, worn smooth with decades of this familiarity. She took out her blue robe, belted it around her, felt closer to life in its warmth, although its warmth was only her own contained a fraction closer.

The garderobe, she supposed, was her mother's choice. Her father's taste was different: spare, simple, dawn in a birchwood. But perhaps it had not always been? Perhaps that, like so much else in him, was from the camps.

He had two university degrees; but in the camps he had been schooled longest.

Thoughts of her father kept her from thinking of Alex for a while. She wondered if her father would have objected to this use of him.

She ran water to clear the rust from the pipes and then filled the two-liter kettle and lit the gas flame on the stove. She thought of Alex snatching the match back to save his fingers. He had never learned to light it from above, as she did, from the center, where it seemed her hand would be in the flame, but where the flames shot out all around her hand and not toward it, and did not burn it. She put the kettle on to boil for tea—what she called her tea, but wasn't.

She loved strong tea, bitter, just as it came from the pot that in the old days everyone kept heating on top of the samovar. She did not even cut it with hot water as the custom was. *Zavarka* most people called it, and few people could drink it full strength; her father called it *chefir*, and he drank it uncut. He had learned that in the camps—both the name and the habit—where tea was the only drug, and prisoners drank it to forget, or to pretend to. Years ago, while he was gone, she drank it full strength in honor of him. Sometimes she added lemon, which cleared it but added its own clear bitterness. But now he was dead, and she had to save her strength for other things, and now she drank only boiled water with lemon squeezed into it.

When the kettle sang, she poured a cup, swirled it around over the sink to work the heat into the china, poured it out at once into the sink, and refilled it to the very top. She was a maximalist. She loved all things overflowing. Into the cup she squeezed half a lemon—but squeezed it only lightly. At fifty rubles, a lemon was too big a part of her salary to take half of one in her morning tea. Half a lemon lasted her a week.

She drank it too hot, not willing to wait. Her heated breath made little puffs of steam in the chill air of the unheated kitchen.

But she did not drink it fast. She made it last a long time. There was a lot of day ahead of her.

At six o'clock she stepped from a cab at Belyi Dom, the White House, the central office of the Russian parliament. She got out on Konyushkovski Street opposite the back of the United States Embassy, beside the site proposed for a memorial to the people who had erected a barricade here to defend the government during the August coup. Many had wanted to save the original barricade as the most fitting memorial. She had wanted that herself. It had been a stupid barricade, nothing but a tangle of scrap iron, old chairs, cobblestones—whatever had been at hand that night of August 18, certainly nothing that would have stopped tanks. It was a symbol, really, more than a barricade—a line drawn in the dirt: cross this, and we are enemies. It was the symbol that had stopped the tanks, not the scrap iron.

It had been a stupid barricade; but it was a powerful symbol, and it would have been a good memorial. Or so she thought. Her colleagues in the legislature had not agreed. The scrap-iron barricade, the stuff of life itself, was alien to their idea of a proper memorial. Russia was a country stuffed with memorials, nearly all of them Soviet—memorials to the Revolution, memorials to the fallen heroes of the Great Patriotic War in which the forces of socialism had defeated the Nazis, monuments to heroic Soviet workers and selfless Soviet children. They were grand and sentimental, but the life had gone out of them long before Soviet power ended. Not just out of the things themselves, the statues and the stones and the inscriptions, but out of the *making* of them. They had become a form: they were not *created*, but *manufactured*.

That was why she had tried to cling to the barricade, why she had voted to resist all attempts to remove it, to "clean up the area and make a proper memorial." It had been both symbol and reality. It was the thing itself. Nothing that could come after, no marble, no fine inscriptions, could replace it. "Proper" memorials came after the flame had gone out. The thing itself had the hearts of the living in it, in it still.

"Good morning, Inna Romanovna." The guard at the members' entrance greeted her politely, using her first name and her *otchestvo*, the middle name that was taken from the name of her father: "Inna Roman's-daughter." For a long time it had seemed that would be the only thing in the world left of her father, a name stuck to a young woman who was barred from any trusted work because of it, or because she would not betray it. He had died before the day came when it was a name trusted by the people above any other, and when because of it his daughter was elected to the Congress of People's Deputies and in turn was chosen by the Congress to be a member of the Supreme Soviet, the smaller body that acted for the Congress when the Congress was not in session. And now she was head of a subcommittee of the Supreme Soviet. That was a day he had certainly never expected to come, not in his lifetime or any other; he persisted not from any hope of being proclaimed right, but because he knew he *was* right. But when the day came, his daughter knew it had come because of him and not because of her; and this left her with a combination of sorrow and of anger—that he was gone and that on her had fallen the burden of his fame and his principles, a burden that, after his death, could never be lifted.

The elevator delivered her to the hall outside her office—a hall wider and better lit than those of most Moscow buildings, but still done in the ubiquitous governmental yellow that she had never noticed until Alex pointed it out to her.

She unlocked her office—it would be hours before her secretary arrived—switched on the lights, and went straight to her desk, where seventy years on a road to nowhere waited for her to devise a turnaround. Or so Alex had said. "After seven decades, you can't be expected to set it all right yourself," he had once said when she came home after midnight. And she knew he was right, but it hadn't been his father who died in the camps. She wondered, sometimes, seeing a new flood of papers pour daily onto her desk, whether her father during his time in the camps had cut any of the trees that had been pulped to provide this inundation.

She sorted into new stacks the papers she had left strewn across her desk the night before. In the process she uncovered the telephones. There were three of them, two beige and one white with a gold crest. In a country without multiplex switchboards, the importance of a person was shown by the number of phones on her desk. Inna was always bemused by the proliferation of her telephones; she had lived so many years without any. But finding them buried there now gave her a sudden jolt, as if she had stumbled into a different life—a subdued echo of the feeling that had swept over her when she first came into this office and sat down in the chair behind the polished desk. The feeling was gone in an instant, buried by months of familiarity as the telephones had been buried under the papers of her work.

The white telephone had amused her most when she first occupied the office. Molded into its case was the state crest of the USSR. It was her connection to the *nomenklatura*, the "list of names" of those who governed.

She could not think of the white telephone as really hers. It really belonged to whoever had occupied this office before her, when this was an executive office of the Russian Soviet Federative Socialist Republic. But after the failed coup, the executive branch had moved over to the real seat of power, the Communist Party's buildings on Old Square, where the halls were even wider and brighter, leaving the Russian White House to the legislature. The telephone had been left behind, forgotten—seadrift left on the beach when the tide of politics went out. It was still here, still working.

The white telephone was part of the separate telephone system that the Party had installed for itself, a real Party line that provided direct access to anyone who mattered in the Union. She had always known—every citizen did—that the government of the Union was a closed, separate system, barely connected to the lives of ordinary people. But it was when she first picked up that telephone on her desk and dialed a number in Vladivostok six time zones away, and it was answered, that she felt for the first time the enormous gulf that had come to separate the Party from the people, the leaders from the led. No outsiders were connected to that telephone. No one outside the few could call it. It was part of a nationwide telephone system built to serve a few thousand people, entirely separate from the system that served the rest.

For weeks she called people around the country. It was an

exploration, a voyage of discovery, just learning who was out there in this vast country. Her calls were always taken or were answered promptly. There were polite voices at the other end, not like Soviet phones that were let to ring for hours, or were picked up and set down again unanswered, or were answered in surly voices. It might have been another country she was calling, on the white telephone.

She used it for weeks, and then gradually she stopped using it at all.

The system still functioned. It was one of the few things that did function; a pity to let it go. So everyone said, those in the government now, both those long in power and those who four years ago had been dangerous dissidents, watched by the police. So few things work now. This does. Let us decide to keep it.

So they, Communists and democrats, had kept their telephones on which they could call anyone who mattered.

But she couldn't call Alex on it.

She turned to the task at hand, the stack of papers that had been closest to her for weeks now. Only the one on top was new, a summary completed late last night by her assistant. By now, copies of it would be on a few desks scattered throughout the White House, and on a few desks scattered throughout the government's offices in Old Square.

A title ran across the top of the page: "Concerning Corruption in Governmental Operations."

She picked up a telephone and dialed. After only one ring it was picked up. "You're in early, Inna," a man's voice said. It was one of those deep male voices that made Russian church choirs so powerful.

"How did you know who it was?"

"No one else is ever here at this hour."

"Except you."

"Ah. But historians are light sleepers. We have the weight of ages pressing on us."

She laughed. "That must be a very heavy blanket, in such warm weather."

"In any weather. I suppose you're calling about the report."

"Yes. Did you see it?"

"I've just begun to read it. But already I can see how convincing it is. 'Soon the malefactors will know regret.' " This comment, an ironic quotation of standard Party bombast, was a mocking in-joke among those whose lives had been shaped by opposition to that kind of rhetoric.

"Don't forget the meeting at ten."

"Innochka! Would I ever forget to be where you are?"

"Be there whether I am or not, Vasily Ivanovich. You're needed."

"By you?"

"The important thing is, by the task." She hung up the telephone. She was pleased.

# 7

---

## DECISION
### On Charging as a Defendant

City of Moscow                                      30 May 1992

Chief Investigator of the Investigation Department of the Department of Internal Affairs of the City of Moscow Major of Militia Volkov M.N. after studying the materials of Criminal Case no. 1157 concerning theft of State property,

### DETERMINED:

Under this case sufficient evidence has been gathered to provide a basis to charge that Chapman Bradley Allen carried out theft of State property on a large scale.

---

In July 1990 State property consisting of buildings, equipment, and technology was transferred from the Special Deliveries Combinat of the Ministry of Posts and Communications of the USSR to the Soviet-American joint venture "JorSov." The property was received by the joint venture "JorSov" as a contribution to the capital fund on behalf of the Soviet participant, the Special Deliveries Combinat. Receipt of the property was evidence by a Protocol dated July 20, 1990, signed by Chapman as American co–General Director and by Turbin Vladilen Viktorovich as Soviet co–General Director. The value of the property credited to the Soviet participant was thirty million rubles, whereas the actual value was at least three hundred million rubles.

The joint venture "JorSov" has continued to own and use the above-referred-to property as its own.

Also in July 1990 property consisting of cash, technology, and know-how was contributed to the joint venture "JorSov" by the American participant, Jordan Enterprises. The property was received by the joint venture "JorSov" as a contribution to the capital fund. Receipt of the property was evidenced by Protocols dated July 20, 1990, and July 23, 1990, signed by Chapman as American co–General Director and by Turbin as Soviet co–General Director. The value of the property credited to the American participant was thirty million rubles, consisting of six hundred twenty-five thousand rubles in the form of one million dollars in cash and twenty-nine million three hundred seventy-five thousand rubles in the form of technology and know-how. The actual value of the property contributed by the American participant was no more than five million rubles.

Thus Chapman committed a crime as provided in Article 93 Prime of the Criminal Code of the Russian Federation.

On the basis of the above, being guided by Art. 143 and 144 of the Code of Criminal Procedure of the RF

**DECIDED:**

To charge <u>CHAPMAN, BRADLEY ALLEN</u> as a defendant in this case, by presenting to him an accusation of having committed the crime set forth in <u>Article 93'</u> of the Criminal Code of the RF, about which he/she is being informed. A copy of the Decision is being sent to the Prosecutor of the City of Moscow.

Investigator: *Volkov*
(signature)

This Decision has been made known to me on <u>30 May</u> 199<u>2</u>, and its text read personally by me and the substance of the charge explained to me.

**Defendant:** *B. Chapman*        **Investigator:** *Volkov*
(signature)                 (signature)

It has been explained to me that according to Art. 48 of the Code of Criminal Procedure of the RF I have the right: to know what I am accused of; to give explanations concerning the accusation with which I am presented; to present evidence; at the end of the preliminary investigation to be acquainted with all materials in the case; to have a lawyer from the moment provided in Art. 47 of the Code of Criminal Procedure of the RF; to participate in court proceedings in the court of first level; to object; to protest actions and decisions of the Investigator, Prosecutor, and court; and to have the last word in court.

Defendant: *B. Chapman*
(signature)
30 May 1992

I presented the Decision and explained the rights.

Investigator: *Volkov*
(signature)

**Taking Under Arrest**
**Chapman Bradley Allen**

# Sanctioned

**Procurator of the City of Moscow**
**Chief Investigator**
**Major of Militia**
*Volkov*

## Decree

**Concerning Measure of Prevention**
**In the Form of Taking the Accused Under Arrest**

City of Moscow                                    30 May 1992

Chief Investigator of the Investigation Department of the Department of Internal Affairs of the City of Moscow <u>Major of Militia Volkov M.N.</u> after studying the materials of Criminal Case No. <u>1157 concerning Chapman Bradley Allen,</u> accused of committing the crime provided in Article 93' of the Criminal Code of the RF,

DETERMINED

In July 1990 Chapman B.A., acting as co–General Director of the joint venture "JorSov" received on behalf of the joint venture "JorSov" State property having a value of not less than three hundred million rubles, for which the State received credit for the sum of thirty million rubles. In the same time period Chapman B.A. acting as co–General Director of the joint venture "JorSov" received on behalf of the joint venture as a contribution of the American participant property having a value of no more than five million rubles, for which the American participant received credit for the sum of thirty million rubles.

At this time, clarification of circumstances needed to convict Chapman B.A. of the crime of which he is accused is not completed, but taking into consideration the gravity of the crime of which Chapman B.A. is accused and also that because of his status as a foreign citizen he could flee the jurisdiction, under Articles 89, 90, 91, 92, and 96 of the Code of Criminal Procedure of the RF,

DECREED

1. To use against Chapman Bradley Allen, born 16.9.59, U.S.A., citizen of the U.S.A., no previous convictions, resident at River Street, House 3, Moscow, place of work JorSov joint venture, Cosmonaut Street, Building 14, the measure or prevention "taking under arrest," as to which he is informed over his signature in this Decree.

2. This Decree shall be sent for execution to the Chief of Butyrskaya Prison, Chief Department of Internal Affairs of the City of Moscow.

Chief Investigator
Major of Militia <u>Volkov</u>

Decree presented to me 30 May 1992
<u>B Chapman</u>

The rain had gone. In the long, white evening Muscovites lingered on the streets of the city, celebrating their freedom from foul weather. Cold bound them so much of the year, now even a day of rain seemed unfair, in springtime.

The long, white evening was a mockery to Brad Chapman, who stared angrily out the window of the interrogation room of the Petrovka Street police station. "I thought you people were getting me *out* of this hole!" he said to Fall and Slavin. "What am I still doing here?"

"You continue to be under investigation; but also you are now

awaiting trial on the specific charge of theft of state property,"
Slavin said. He looked again at the document, as if to confirm
that the words hadn't changed since Chapman had signed it in
his presence. "Yes, there's your signature."

Slavin turned the paper toward Chapman and pointed to his
signature at the bottom. "Previously, you were detained for questioning; now you're under arrest."

"Wonderful! You guys have really done a job for me. Look at
this crap! This Investigator says the Soviet contribution was
worth ten times what we gave them credit for! I've told you
what their contribution was worth—not a plugged nickel. And
he claims ours was worth a sixth of what we got credit for. BS!
That million dollars cash alone was worth more than the whole
Soviet contribution! They say it was worth six hundred and
twenty-five thousand rubles? At their fake exchange rates,
maybe. The government set the exchange rate. They said a ruble
was worth sixty cents U.S. Well, the ruble wasn't really worth
three cents. In 1990 we could have sold the million dollars alone
for thirty million rubles on the street! Well, if this crap is what's
keeping me in jail, it's time for me to start looking for competent lawyers."

"If you don't think we're competent, Brad, you can have my
resignation right now," Fall told him. Fall was angry. The Petrovka jail was no health resort, but he didn't think that only
two days of it warranted falling apart. He was already tired of
hand-holding.

For Slavin, the emotionalism of a criminal defense practice was
nothing new. He simply waited while Chapman exhausted his
rage on the bare walls of the interrogation room. Then he said,
"On Monday we'll petition the Prosecutor again to release you.
We can say the situation has changed now that you've been
charged. Nothing *has* changed, but it's customary to say so
anyway."

"Monday! I want out of here tonight! Is this Saturday? I'm
already losing track of the goddamn days! I've been here so long
I'm starting to dream about it. At first I dreamed I was out; but
now I just dream I'm here. I dream I'm chained to a wall, and

there's a machine coming at me, a huge machine, and the last thing I see is this wheel . . . It's time to get me out of here, Alex!"

"There's no hope until Monday," Slavin said. "The Investigator made a special trip here to his office today to sign the charge protocol. He must want to keep you, or he wouldn't have come in on Saturday. And since he wants to keep you, you may as well be calm until Monday. The Prosecutor isn't going to read our petition on Sunday; and a judge isn't either—even if they would grant it over the Investigator's objection, and they won't. If you want to see your lawyers struggle, we can struggle all weekend; but nothing will be done. Sometimes calm discussion succeeds where struggle doesn't. But calm discussion can't happen until Monday."

"Screw calm discussion! You guys should be raising hell! That son of a bitch Volkov doesn't own my life!"

"Perhaps we should treat him as owning this small piece of it," Slavin advised. "The other possibility is that if we annoy the Investigator enough, he'll feel obliged to try to clear up the question of Turbin's death. It's not convenient for him to have that remain open, neither accident nor murder, not one thing or another. The easy way to clear it would be to bring a charge of murder."

"Murder!" Slavin had Chapman's full attention. "Against me? That's BS and you know it!"

"But maybe Investigator Volkov doesn't know it. Or maybe he'll just consider what's convenient for him."

"He couldn't make a jury believe that! Do you have juries in this country?"

"In criminal cases we have a professional judge and two people's assessors—lay judges, really. The lay judges do what the professional judge tells them. It's good to remember that we aren't far from the days when no defendant was found not guilty. In fact, I can't recall a recent instance either. No, I don't think we want to annoy Investigator Volkov excessively. And I can tell you that badgering him on the weekend will seem excessive to him, even if it doesn't to you."

Chapman subsided into angry but private grumbling.

"Anyway," Slavin said, "you won't be in Petrovka long, one

way or another. Now that you've been charged, they'll move you to a prison, as the decree says. 'Butyrka.' "

"If this isn't a prison, what the hell is it?"

"This is just a jail," Slavin said.

"What's the difference?"

"Prisons are organized for holding people longer."

"I imagine they're like summer camps," Chapman said. " 'Butyrka.' Where's that? Is it a fun place? Is there a lot of entertainment?"

Slavin said, "No, I wouldn't say it's a fun place." Irony is not always easy to comprehend in a foreign language, and they had been speaking English.

Once they were outside the jail, Fall asked Slavin, "Volkov wouldn't really charge Brad with murder just out of pique, would he?"

"Oh, no, I don't think so," Slavin answered. "Volkov is a very calm person. But some investigators would. That isn't the worst thing I ever heard of."

"Could he really get a conviction?"

Slavin shrugged. "Remember how recently a five-year sentence was a good result for an innocent defendant."

"But Brad's right—there's no evidence. Surely you can't convict even a guilty defendant without evidence."

Slavin repeated, "Remember how recently a five-year sentence was a good result for an *innocent* defendant. Anyway, all we can say is that there's no evidence that we've seen. We don't know what Volkov is holding back: the only evidence we have a right to see, until our client is charged, is the transcripts of his interrogations."

"Maybe he's holding nothing back. Maybe there's no evidence because Turbin really did kill himself."

"Maybe. The evidence doesn't contradict that. As I understand, his apartment door was locked from the inside; apparently nothing had been stolen; and the medical investigator concluded he died from injuries suffered in a fall from his balcony. The same evidence is consistent with an accidental fall. But why would he kill himself? Not for fear of the law, I don't think. From what we know, this charge, 'theft of state property,' would not be a strong case against Turbin. Maybe a good lawyer could even get him off, in today's conditions. Even in 1985, I'd have got him off with five years. That's nothing for a man to kill himself over. Certainly not an ex–deputy minister."

"Are deputy ministers tougher than other people?"

"Turbin was a child of the system. Under the system, only people who looked out for themselves became deputy ministers." He hunched his shoulders, as if against cold, although it was a warm evening. "No, accident seems more likely—except for one thing."

"Which is?"

"The body was found five meters outside a vertical line from the balcony railing. A person doesn't 'fall' in an arc that wide. He is propelled—by himself or someone else. It's not good to hypothesize without evidence. But it wouldn't be my first hypothesis that Turbin killed himself."

"Who would have killed him?"

"Of course we don't have any evidence on that. It *could* have been our client, as Volkov would like to suspect. It would be so convenient for Volkov to find a murderer and a thief both in one. From Volkov's point of view, our client had the motive—to keep Turbin from giving evidence about this theft of state property. And he had the possibility—he was, he says, alone at the office for many hours the night Turbin died; but no one saw him there, not even the night guard, whose duties included walking rounds of the building. Curious. I certainly wish he'd had some company." Slavin shrugged. He was owllike when thinking. His shrug was like an owl settling its wings. He closed his eyes slowly and opened them slowly, owl-eyed behind his glasses. "But if someone else killed Turbin, I wonder why whoever it was didn't try harder to make it look as if Chapman did it."

"Do you have a hypothesis?"

"No."

"This is a day remarkable for its absence of hypotheses," Fall said.

Slavin refused to be joked at. "A wrong road is worse than none. Well, I'm off." They had reached Slavin's car.

"Sorry to keep you from whoever we've kept you from on a Saturday night," Fall said. "Have I met her?"

"Oh, it's just Lidiya. I've known her since law school. She called me last week. We agreed to go to dinner. Lidiya's a very good lawyer: she can afford any restaurant in Moscow."

"I thought you had resolved to date no one over twenty-two, Misha."

"Yes, but what good are resolutions! I couldn't say no. My mother likes her. But maybe you'd like to come along. I'm sure Lidiya can find a friend."

"Thanks. I'll pass this time, Mish."

"Probably she could find a friend who would pay for herself."

"It would make me feel awkward to let a woman pay for her own dinner."

"That's a very bourgeois attitude." Then Slavin became more serious. "It's not good to think too much about one woman, Alex. Probably I'm not a very good source of advice on women, but . . ."

"It's good advice, Mish. I just don't know how to follow it."

"All right, then. Good night."

"Good night, Mish."

# 8

OVER THE YEARS PRISON OFFICIALS HAVE TRIED VARIOUS STRATEGIES TO prevent their guests from wandering. Forest, desert, and Siberian wasteland have all played their part. Islands are also a favorite: the sea is an unsleeping guard, endlessly patient.

The makers of Moscow's Butyrskaya Prison, lacking these resources, had another idea. They created an artificial island, afloat in the ocean of Soviet citizenry. Butyrskaya Prison—"Butyrka" to its acquaintances—is built within the central courtyard of an apartment building. The prison is surrounded by the windows of ordinary citizens, apparently on the theory that, day or night, someone will be watching. For Russian conditions, the theory may be correct. There are no recorded escapes from Butyrka. Or at least they have not been made public.

Inside Butyrka is another courtyard where the prisoners take their exercise by walking out the circles of their lives within the circle of buff brick within the circle of watching windows. Circles within circles.

In an interrogation room in Butyrskaya Prison, Fall and Slavin were waiting for another interrogation of their client. Chapman had been moved there from the Petrovka jail after he was charged. Nothing they had tried, so far, had got him out. The Investigator did not want his prize foreign defendant to miss his trial, and so far the Prosecutor agreed.

A fly was buzzing around the upper reaches of the interrogation room. Otherwise, the silence was tomblike.

The door opened. Brad Chapman came through it, followed by a guard, and then by Investigator Volkov. The guard looked around the room as if to be sure there was no one in it but lawyers—although no one else would have been admitted—and then without a word went out and closed the door.

"What's on my busy schedule today?" Chapman asked. There had been a series of questionings, review of the record, more questionings, even after he had been charged. The most serious game becomes routine after enough of it; and after two weeks, he had seen enough. Brick walls, empty rooms, no longer terrified him. He seemed simply tired. He slumped into a chair.

"Today, only a few little papers," Volkov said. He, too, seemed tired, the Investigator—perhaps tired of his part in a play gone stale with rehearsal. Although he was a major of militia, he was dressed as always in a civilian suit, the same gray suit, pale blue shirt, gray tie—perhaps the very same ones—the uniform of the nonuniformed apparatchik. He could have been one of the *Putshchists*, the members of the August coup, who had dressed so for their inglorious news conference before the coup faded from sight.

Fall and Slavin rearranged themselves to account for Volkov's presence. They had been sitting opposite each other; now Fall moved across to sit beside Slavin and Chapman, with all of them opposite the Investigator.

Volkov took from his briefcase a clothbound volume, which he laid on the table. He opened it, paged through it. It contained pages of different sizes, different printing, some blank pages with photocopies pasted to them. He turned to a section where a compact sheaf of uniform white pages had been wired to a cardboard backing. They were not the usual Soviet papers, thick and yellowed and typed with faded ribbons. These were white, precise, laser-printed pages, covered with columned figures. "We will talk about these."

Slavin took them first, studied the first few intently before passing the volume to Fall, and only then to Chapman.

"You know what those are, I believe?" Volkov asked Chapman.

"Do I?"

"It is my question to you. Please identify them."

"They appear to be financial records of the JorSov joint venture. At least, that's what they *say* they are." Chapman pointed to a caption on the top of the first page: "Payments, July 1991."

"And are they what they appear to be?"

"I couldn't say."

"They have the name of the company on them, do they not?"

"Yes."

"Do they show payments to people with the names of employees of your company?"

"Yes."

"Including yourself?"

Chapman took the papers, leafed through a few pages, turned them around, and tossed them back across the table to Volkov. "To someone with my name."

"Are the amounts correct for your salary?"

Chapman took back the papers, studied them again—this time slowly—and put them down on the table. "Yes."

"Was anyone outside your company familiar with your salary?"

"Sure. The home office. Probably our bank." He thought a moment. "Barton's Bank in London made a loan to the company. So it got our financial records."

"But if you are claiming that these are not genuine, they could have been faked by very few people, isn't that so?"

"I'm not saying they're not genuine. You're saying they are, and I'm saying I don't know."

"All right. Look at them again. Take your time. Do you believe that the numbers shown there are correct?"

"I couldn't tell that. It's a waste of time to look. I couldn't possibly remember all of our payments."

"Perhaps not. But do look. Is there anything you find unusual that would make you claim these are not your company's records?"

"I don't think I could tell."

"Let us not play games. Your lawyers have been diligently petitioning for your release. If you will not cooperate with a lawful investigation *here*, what reason is there to think that you would *there*?" With his head he motioned toward the window, or toward the world outside it. "Now, is this your company's record?"

"It appears to be."

Volkov put the volume aside, then took from his bag a second stack of printouts. He passed them to Chapman. "And these? Do you recognize them?" Brad flipped through them and shrugged. "They look like another copy of the same records."

"Have you looked at them carefully?"

"No."

"Please do so."

Slavin and Fall watched over Brad's shoulders as he flipped slowly through the printout. "I don't see any difference," Brad said in a bored voice.

"Look at July seventh," Volkov suggested. He was sitting back in his chair, his arms folded, watching Chapman.

Brad turned to the page dated July 7. He looked at it a moment, then closed his eyes. "Let me see the other one," he said, reaching for the first printout. Volkov slid it over to him. Slavin and Fall both reached out to turn the page toward themselves. Each deferred to the other. They settled on bending closer over Chapman's shoulder.

"Is there a difference?" Volkov asked.

Brad spoke angrily, without looking at Volkov. "You must know there is. Where do *these* come from?"

Volkov ignored his question. "What is the difference between the two sets of records, Mr. Chapman?"

Brad didn't answer.

"This one shows a payment to a certain V. V. Turbin on that date, doesn't it?" Volkov said quietly. "Is that the difference?"

Still Brad did not answer.

"A payment by wire transfer to a foreign bank, 'to be held for receipt by Mr. V. V. Turbin.' "

"That's what it says."

"A payment in the amount, I believe, of some ten thousand dollars?"

"So it says."

"It isn't illegal to make payments to employees in dollars," Slavin said, inserting a hint to Chapman. "The payment was sent outside the country, presumably to Turbin while *he* was outside the country. In that case, if it was for work done outside Russia, it was legal."

"I'm not questioning whether the payment violated restrictions on payment of Russian citizens in currencies other than rubles," Volkov said. "Not at the moment. I'm only wondering, if it *was* legal, why Mr. Chapman's computer contained records which do not show that the payment was made."

"Where do these records come from—the ones which do show the payments?" Fall asked.

"These, as it happens, were on a separate computer disk which was found in Mr. Chapman's office, which was searched while he has been enjoying our hospitality. It took some time for us to go through everything produced by that search. We only just printed these records. I surely would have told you if I'd known about them sooner. I'm quite curious, you know: why is there a difference?"

"We'd like to talk with our client," Fall said.

"I'm sure. For my part, I'd prefer that he answer my question."

"What is your question?" Slavin demanded. He leaned forward across the table, his eyes intent on the Investigator's face.

"Two questions. The first, why there are two different sets of accounts for Mr. Chapman's company."

"I don't know," Chapman said. "I told you I don't know where these come from."

"And the second, whether JorSov in fact made any payments in dollars to Vladilen Viktorovich Turbin."

"There's no law against that," Fall said.

Volkov ignored the interruption. "Mr. Chapman?" he said.

Chapman looked sidelong at Fall. Both Fall and Slavin were looking at him intently, nodding their heads. "Yes, JorSov made dollar payments to Turbin. Our lawyer advised us it was legal."

"Who was your lawyer, just out of curiosity?"

"Alexander Fall."

"Ah." Volkov made a note in his leather-bound notebook. "Then a third question: why would your computer contain records showing no such payments, if, as you say, payments were made? How could such records come to exist?"

"I don't know."

"And why would the payments, which you admit were made, be recorded only on a single disk, kept separate from any of the computers?"

"I don't know."

"When we brought your computer in, we found it to be password protected. You were kind enough to tell us your password during our first discussions; but it leads me to wonder: who else knew your password, Mr. Chapman?"

Chapman seemed to think a moment. "No one," he said.

"Then it would seem that you must have created the records that were on it."

"It would seem so."

After Volkov left the room, Fall was so furious he forgot about whether anyone might be listening. "Jesus H. Christ, Brad! How could your computer contain accounting records that didn't show payments that you knew were made to Turbin?"

"Who cares?" Chapman said. "Those payments to Turbin *were* legal, weren't they?"

"I told you they didn't violate the currency restrictions, and they didn't, if you made them the way I told you. And I'll tell you who cares: you do. Now it looks like you were trying to hide payments to Turbin, whether they were legal or whether they weren't."

"If they were legal, why would I have tried to hide them?"

"I can't imagine. But I can tell you what Volkov might consider: that although the payments weren't illegal, the purpose was. And in that case, Volkov asked a good question. Why would anyone keep records with everything in them *except* payments to Turbin? Volkov is thinking *bribes*."

Chapman said nothing for a long time. Then he said, "I was making a file of payments to Turbin. When I made the new file, I must have cut those entries out of the original file instead of just copying them."

"So you did it yourself?"

"Yeah, probably. By accident."

"But he said they found the complete record on a separate disk. How did that happen?"

"I guess I saved it to a floppy, along with other files I was saving. I don't know. I can barely remember what it's like to be outside this hellhole, let alone everything I did when I was outside."

"I hope we can convince Volkov of that! I wish you'd told him all that when he asked."

"I forgot I was working on that file. I didn't think of it until just now."

"Then there should be a file with nothing in it but payments to Turbin," Slavin said.

"If it's still there. God knows what's left, after they've been digging through my hard disk. Volkov's boys didn't exactly strike me as computer experts."

"Expert enough to find the documents he showed you," Fall said. "So why didn't they find the other, the one with nothing on it but payments to Turbin? Surely Volkov would have asked about it if they'd found it. We could ask him to look for it. At least it's some sort of explanation for the file he already has. Better late than never."

"If they can find it," Chapman said. "It's more likely they'll screw up that hard disk six ways to Sunday."

*"They're* not the ones who cut Turbin's entries instead of copying them," Fall said.

"I'll talk to Volkov," Slavin said. "I'll ask him to look for the file of payments to Turbin."

"Do that," Chapman said. "But don't be surprised if he can't find it."

"Perhaps I should offer to have you help him."

"Yes. That's a good idea."

But when Slavin turned in his petition, Volkov refused the offer of Chapman's help and the request to look for the missing file as well. He could have simply denied the petition; but Slavin had handed it over in person, and the Investigator took the opportunity to let loose his feelings. "We don't need your client's help to learn what's on his hard disk," Volkov said. "Westerners seem to think they're the only ones who know how to use computers. We have our own expert. Tell Mr. Chapman we know everything that's on his hard disk and everything that isn't. And a file of payments to Turbin isn't."

"Our client's company would also like its computers back," Slavin said. "They're needed in the business."

"They're evidence. We'll give them back when we're ready to give them back. And while you're here, we may as well deal with this." He handed over a paper.

It was another Decision charging Chapman with a crime—this time violation of Article 174 of the Criminal Code: paying bribes.

9

PREPARING TO SPEAK, INNA HAD THE FEELING SHE ALWAYS GOT AT THE podium of the Supreme Soviet, that someone was looking over her shoulder. Behind her was nothing but the red curtain that now covered the wall where, in the old days, the image of Lenin had looked down on the proceedings, as he had looked down on all proceedings everywhere in the Union. She did not know whether Lenin had been removed or merely covered over with the red curtain. One day, not long after the coup, deputies coming into the chamber had found the red curtain, and Lenin no longer watching. Although she was a member of the Supreme Soviet, duly elected, she had never pulled the curtain aside.

The proceedings of the Russian Supreme Soviet had not meant much, of course, in the days when Lenin hung over them. Not even the proceedings of the Supreme Soviet of the USSR had meant much then. What mattered was what the Party said, The Party of Lenin. In those days the country had had a President, but no one cared much what he thought, unless he happened also to be the General Secretary of the Communist Party—as sometimes he did. What mattered was what the General Secretary thought.

But although a curtain had been drawn over his image, the presence of Lenin hung over Inna still, over all of them, over all that they did here.

But behind her, too, whenever she spoke here, was the presence of her father. His face was not clear, as Lenin's was. His was a face that had been not everywhere, like Lenin's, but nowhere. She had hardly known it, as a child. It was a face she had seen only in that brief time between his terms in the camps. For, though he might be released at the end of his sentence—or might not—the camps were always waiting for a man who had not repented, and Roman Kornev had not repented.

She arranged her papers, using them as a device to arrange her emotions, looking out over the tiers of faces—faces she knew now, after four years among them. They were old faces, most of them—old not only in years, but in attitude. They were the faces of the *Nomenklatura*, the *Apparat*, the Party members who had got onto the ballot through long service at the command of the Party. They had been elected at an end and not a beginning—not long before the attempted coup, and therefore at the end of the Union rather than the beginning of Russia—and the faces reflected that. To look out on the assembled faces of the Supreme Soviet was to see a hillside of dry winter grass.

At the beginning, when she had first been elected, she thought of it as a hillside that, although dry, had on it a few flowers blooming. The flowers were the new faces, people who had here and there become known before the end of the Union in spite of the Party's efforts to bury them.

She had often wondered why Boris Nikolayevich, President Yeltsin, had not called new elections after the coup, in that brief time when all things seemed new and possible. But he had not; and the dry hillside remained and now seemed likely to prevail.

But for the moment, it seemed, those dry faces were to be on her side at last. What she was about to say would be an embarrassment to the government, to President Yeltsin and his reformers, who were her natural friends. For that reason alone she would be supported by the dry hillside whose support she was about to seek. But what she was about to say was truth, and it was right to say it, whoever supported or opposed. Still she looked for flowers on the hillside. She wanted their support too: Rusanov, the young mayor of St. Petersburg; a few delegates from Moscow—scientists and writers and even some dissidents elected on the strength of hidden admiration; a scattering of mavericks from the provinces, hardheaded romantics that Russia seemed doomed forever to produce. And one of them, whom she looked at last and for luck, was Antipov, the square, bearded face with its peasant strength, the strength to overcome anything by outliving it.

She began.

"Honorable Deputies, this is the report of the Subcommittee on Lawfulness of the Committee on Problems of Lawfulness, Law and Order, and Crime Prevention.

"You know—in this time it is impossible not to know—that corruption of officials has become an increasing problem in our society: one that in the opinion of some has come actually to threaten the ability of the people to govern themselves.

"Our subcommittee, with the support of the Chairman of the whole committee, has conducted its own preliminary investigation. We recommend today that we be authorized to hold public hearings to take testimony about the problem, with the intent to produce legislation that will radically reduce the possibilities for officials to profit personally from their powers that they hold only in the name of the people.

"We know it is not customary for a subcommittee, or even a committee, to take public evidence; but we ask for your support. In only a preliminary investigation, our subcommittee has found evidence of widespread bribery, corruption, and subversion of public office. These are not rumors: they are acts attested by persons who know of them." She laid out the list of deeds that her subcommittee had cataloged in the course of its brief investigation—some of them crimes, many of them not crimes under existing laws, although they should have been. "We believe that only the full light of day can destroy such deeds. We need to know more, before we can know how to act; and we need to know that the people know, and that they support our actions."

She caught the face of Antipov, though she avoided looking squarely at him. His eyes had not left her. He was smiling grimly.

Stepping down from the podium she was surrounded at once by a congratulating crowd. Not all of them were people whose congratulations she wanted. But a politician's business was votes, and to get theirs she would take their congratulations.

As the others dropped away, Antipov joined her. "It was done well."

# 10

THE TWO LAWYERS HAD TAKEN TO WORKING IN FALL'S OFFICE. SLAVIN was shy there, at first—confident in himself, but careful of asking anything of others. If he envied the surroundings—the clean painted walls, the carpeted floors, the doors that hung straight— he was careful never to show it; but he always let his eyes linger on the machinery—the computers, the fax, the typewriters. "I love machines that work," he said once. Then he added, "And people too. My father always used to say that machines should work so people could rest; but we seem to have got to the end without passing through the beginning. A great Socialist achievement. Lenin would be proud." But mostly he watched the activity in the office with a wary ambivalence, as if half-convinced that when his back was turned it all fell still and only jumped back to life if he turned his head suddenly to catch it. Slavin himself worked like a fiend when his mind was engaged; but in employees he was accustomed to the glacial pace of a Soviet office.

He had come in early—early for Slavin: eleven o'clock, in time for a cup of coffee before lunch. He often maintained that the human brain functioned only after the sun had crossed the meridian. He let the coffee—dark substitute for the sun—warm him before getting to business. Then: "Have you seen the *Russian Gazette* today?" he asked Fall.

"I'm too busy keeping clients out of jail to wonder what your government is up to," Fall answered. In spite of his answer, he read that newspaper daily, although he had not yet today; for the *Russian Gazette* was the official newspaper of the Supreme Soviet of the Russian Federation. It published news, but also the texts of laws and other official propaganda. Every lawyer needed to read it.

"My government is up to something that won't help," Slavin said. "Or not the government, actually; this time the legislature is up to something."

"No man's person or property is safe when the Supreme Soviet is in session." Fall had discovered, as so many travelers do, that a reputation for wit could be founded on a store of old saws in a foreign language. "What are your legislators doing to our clients?"

"Something unprecedented. They're holding hearings."

"Odd." The Russian legislature did not hold public hearings on legislation. Its tradition was that of the Party: introspection, followed by announcement of the results. "But I don't see the danger."

"The danger's in what they're holding hearings on. Corruption in government." Slavin rummaged through the sections of his old pigskin briefcase, which had once been brown but now was just old, a collection of stains. He pursued his quarry through small pockets on big pockets on bigger pockets, unbuckling and rebuckling as he went. At last he found the newspaper and slid it across to Fall. "I told you before, didn't I? When we first got into this? I thought I saw the shape of this coming, from the articles in the newspapers then. Now here it is: an anticorruption campaign, full grown. But this has a new side. It's not being run just by the executive offices of the government. They've enlisted the Supreme Soviet."

Fall read quickly the article that Slavin emphasized with his thumb. "But this can't be part of a propaganda campaign!" Fall said.

"I don't believe I specified 'propaganda.' This looks like more than just propaganda. This looks like preparation for action. But, as far as that goes, why can't it be both?"

"Look who heads the subcommittee. It's Inna!" Fall spun the paper around for Slavin to see.

Slavin looked at it once again, out of courtesy, although he had read it all before. He hesitated to say more; he knew the history of Fall and Inna Korneva, Roman's daughter. But he had a duty to his client. "If this has spawned an unprecedented procedure for the Supreme Soviet," he said, "there must be bigger forces at work than just the will of the head of a subcommittee, even if the subcommittee head is a woman of unprecedented talents. Certainly she wouldn't be associated with a *mere* propaganda campaign. But more than one pair of hands can be warmed at a fire. And you see that the other name mentioned is Antipov's. He's the head of the committee above the subcommittee, and he's no friend of foreigners. And we represent a foreigner charged with corrupt acts—theft of state property and bribery. We have to view this as a danger."

"It's a danger," Fall agreed. "But maybe we can use it as an opportunity too. It's true our client is charged with corruption; but the truth is, the corruption is on the other side. You say it's an unprecedented procedure. Let's use it to make an unprecedented statement. It's like judo—using the enemy's strength against him. Let's tell the Supreme Soviet what's going on. Let's tell the world."

"I always admire a bold approach," Slavin said. "Struggle, not diplomacy. But still . . . are we entirely sure we know what the truth is? Will our client have the world's admiration when the world has heard his story?"

"What are his chances of winning at trial?"

Slavin sighed. "Tell me who the judge will be, and I'll give you a guess."

"I don't know the judges. That's your business."

He sighed again and shook his head. "I do know the judges. That's the trouble. Some are easier to persuade than others; but they're all from the same cloth—the Party's cloth. They believe what the Prosecutor tells them. We might be lucky and get Dubinsky. He's only been on the court for three years. His brain hasn't hardened yet. Or Portnoy. I knew him at law school. Or maybe Pskova. She's hard-boiled, but she's smart. She can be convinced by facts. But most of them . . ."

"So, what are our chances of winning at trial?"

"I've had easier cases."

"Then there's not much to lose by going to the Supreme Soviet, is there?"

"All right. You've made a convincing argument. When are you going to talk to the head of the subcommittee?"

"When am *I* going to? I meant for you to."

"But you're the obvious choice. Some things in this work I have to do. You can't stand up for our client in court, not being an anointed Russian advocate. But anybody can talk to the Supreme Soviet. And besides, you know the head of the subcommittee."

"I can't ask any favors from her."

"We don't need a favor. We just need what's fair." A subtle look often came into Slavin's eyes when he smiled, as if he knew something you ought to know but didn't. It was there now. "Of course, if you're afraid to talk to her . . ."

"You're more persuasive than I am, Misha."

"Not with Inna Romanovna, I don't think."

# 11

FALL HAD NOT BEEN TO THE RUSSIAN WHITE HOUSE SINCE BEFORE HE last saw Inna. He had asked for a meeting at her office. He told himself that the purpose was to make the meeting as easy as possible for her by making it strictly business. But he didn't try to fool himself: her office was a safe meeting place for him too. He didn't want to risk having her decline to meet him socially.

Inna's secretary was a young woman whom Fall had sometimes seen well-dressed in restaurants and casinos, before he met Inna. She gave Fall what he took to be a knowledgeable look before letting him into Inna's office.

Inna had separated herself from him with her desk. She did not come out from behind it. But she stood to welcome him. "You're looking well," she said, for lack of anything better to say.

"You're looking even better." But she was pale, even though it was summer. As chairperson of a subcommittee she could have had a government dacha at her disposal, where she could weekend in the sun. He was glad to see she hadn't fallen into that.

An awkward silence held them for a moment. She pointed to a chair, across the desk from her.

"Well, I didn't come just to compliment you on how well you look," he said.

*"That's too bad. I was hoping you might have."* She wished she could have said that, but she couldn't. She said nothing.

"I really came to compliment you on the work you're doing."

"That's certainly an acceptable form of flattery. I wish I were doing something worthy of it."

"You seem to be curing corruption in government."

"Ah. You saw the article."

"May I talk with you about it, in confidence?"

75

"You know you can, Alex. But I've got only a few minutes. You know how my time is."

He knew how her time was. She had her father's reputation to live up to—a reputation that made her seem closer to the people than any of the other people's deputies; and so their love affair had been a series of interruptions, by telephone and in person, by day and by night, by people bearing every imaginable woe of the fall of Socialism, as well as some imaginary. She always listened to them. It was one thing he loved her for. *"You have to tend your sheep,"* he had said to her once when she seemed to feel a need to defend her practice; but he had had to explain the reference. "Who is it this time?"

"People needing apartments. Real need," she added, because in Moscow, everybody needed apartments. "Refugees from Nagorno-Karabakh. They've been living in the Paveletski train station for two years. Families with children. Two years in a train station!"

"What can you do for them?" he asked her.

"I don't know. Probably nothing but call a friend in the Mayor's office. But if I don't do it, who will? It's more than anyone else has done for them."

That was Inna: *if I don't do it, who will?* He said, "I'd have thought you'd be loaded down with the corrupt."

"I am. That too. But if we let the corrupt—or even the fight against them—displace the needy, what good is it having a government?"

"May I add one more to your burden?"

"Corrupt, or needy?"

"Both."

"Talk fast."

"I have a client accused of bribery and theft of state property."

"So much for the corrupt. What about the needy?"

"He's innocent. *That's* the corrupt part. Something strange is going on. I don't know what, yet; but something strange, Innochka." He used a pet name without thinking. When he realized what he had said, he blushed, but she only smiled.

"What do you want me to do?" she asked.

"I don't want to have Brad Chapman testify to your subcommittee. That just looks self-serving. But if we have other people testify for him—other foreign businessmen, who see Brad's case as an attack on all foreign investment—then it may carry some weight with the Prosecutor."

"*Is* that how they see it?" she asked. "Isn't this, as you say, apparently just an ordinary investigation of ordinary corruption? 'Ordinary' corruption," she laughed at her own phrase. "We grow so used to our chains, don't we. Well, if you can find your foreign witnesses, my committee will hear them. But I wonder what they'll say."

In the end, they said nothing.

Fall made phone calls. He went to the offices of every foreign company where he knew anyone—and that was a large fraction of the foreign companies in Moscow. For foreigners, Moscow was a small town. He had breakfast meetings and lunch meetings and dinner meetings. The first was breakfast with Ed Miller, head of the Southwest Oil Company's representative office. Alex had pinned his hopes on Ed Miller and called on him first, because the Millers lived next door to the Chapmans. The code of the Southwest, he hoped, wouldn't let a man let down his neighbor.

"Alex, you know I like Brad," Miller said. "And I'd stick up for him, whatever he's done." He didn't add "but." He didn't have to.

"Brad hasn't done anything, Ed. That's the problem."

"Okay, whatever."

"Everybody pledged support, Ed." Fall named no names, but he didn't need to. Miller knew his name was one of them. "But when we need that support, where is it?"

"Well, son, I tell you where it is. It's where it always was. We said we support Brad and it's a damn shame what's happening to him and we'll do what we can for him; and that's all true. But that's between him and us. When you want to get my company into it, things change. I don't run things out here in a vacuum, you know. I can tell you, 'Sure, I'll tell the Supreme Soviet that my company sees what's happening to Brad Chapman as an attack on all foreign investment.' But the problem is, they don't. They don't know Brad Chapman from a hole in

77

the ground. They don't know what he did or didn't do. And another thing. If I get before this subcommittee, I suspect they're going to want to know about *my* company. Do we have any problems with corruption? Well, we sure do, but we don't necessarily want to talk about them up close and personal. I can testify that some bureaucrat in the Moscow Property Committee needed a bribe to let us lease a building, even though the building has been empty for fifty years and will be for another fifty if a foreign company doesn't fix it. But if I do that, I'll be gone before the words are out of my mouth. Because back in Houston, they don't want to hear about bribes, and they don't want me talking about bribes. They don't want *bribe* and the name of our company to come up within two miles of each other, ever. And that ain't because we *paid* one: we didn't pay one, although we sure as hell got asked. No. It's because our lawyers back there have heard of the Foreign Corrupt Practices Act and they ain't about to let us folks out here do anything where the words *foreign* and *corrupt* would show up in the same sentence in a newspaper. And I'll be damn surprised if anyone else in this town feels different."

No one else did feel different. Or if they did, Fall couldn't find them. Several days of effort convinced him that in the end no foreign-company witnesses would appear before the Subcommittee on Lawfulness.

He confessed to Inna by telephone. He would rather have seen her in person; but he didn't want to see her under these conditions.

"It's all right, Alex," she said. "In some ways it's better. If we listen to foreigners, some people will always say that we're only doing this to please them."

"Do you mean Antipov?" he asked.

"It doesn't matter who. This isn't a foreigners' problem, and it isn't going to be solved by them. It's *our* problem, and we're going to solve it."

"Innochka . . ."

A pause. She was considering whether to respond to that name. "Yes?"

"Thanks for your help." What more was there to say?

"It's nothing. I'm sorry it was *really* nothing."
"Did you find homes for your lost sheep?"
"Oh. I'm working on it. Still."
"You always will be."
"I hope not. Someday everything will be solved."
"When the billy goat loses his beard."

# 12

---

## Undertaking Not to Leave

**City of Moscow**                    **June 19, 1992**

I, Chapman Bradley Allen, resident in the City of Moscow on River Street, House 3, hereby undertake the obligation that, until trial on the crimes provided for in Articles 93 Prime and 174 of the Criminal Code of the RF, I will not leave the City of Moscow, will not change my place of residence without the permission of the Investigator, the Prosecutor, or the Court, and will appear at their first demand.

I have been informed that if I violate this Undertaking Not to Leave, under Article 93 of the Code of Criminal Procedure of the RF this Undertaking may be replaced by a more severe measure of prevention.

Defendant: _____

I received this Undertaking:
Investigator: _____ *Volkov* _____

---

"Do I sign this?" Chapman asked.
"Do you want to get out of jail?" Slavin asked him in return.

" 'May be replaced by a more severe measure of prevention,' " Chapman read. "What's that? A Russian euphemism for 'shot on sight'? Remember when they shot down the Korean airliner and said 'the flight was stopped'?"

He said this looking at Volkov as he took the pen Volkov had offered him.

Volkov watched as Chapman signed.

"Are we done now?" Chapman asked. "Can I go? Have you made it official?" Slavin hushed him with a hand on his arm.

Volkov didn't look up. He was busy with the papers in his briefcase. "Yes," he said, "it's official."

As the others left the room, Volkov added Chapman's signed undertaking to the other documents in the briefcase, the City Prosecutor's resolution to free Chapman until trial. As he clipped the papers together, Volkov's eye was caught for a moment by the circular stamp on the resolution, the stamp of the Prosecutor's office, with its circles of words like the concentric walls of a fortress enclosing the crest of the Russian Federation.

The crest at the heart of the stamp was still the old crest, the crest of the Socialist Republic. The Socialist Republic had vanished with the Union it was part of, but the crest had remained behind. It still ushered people in and out of jails, whether they were the jails of Russia or of the Russian Soviet Federative Socialist Republic. Volkov did not care greatly about that, about the label for his state or about the Union that was gone. He did care greatly about justice, and about the fortress that was the law, safeguarding the state and its people. He thought of the stamp of his office sometimes as a map of that fortress, a schematic of the wall of laws that encircled the state and its people. And sometimes he thought of the stamp as a wheel, the wheel of justice, bearing down on those, like Chapman Bradley Allen, who would break into the safety of that circle.

Bradley Chapman emerged from Butyrskaya Prison like a bear from hibernation, blinking against the sudden light. Although his belt had been restored to him, his hand kept wandering to the waist of his pants as if still wary of a sudden drop.

Joanna, not permitted to enter the prison, stood on the sidewalk outside the apartment building that encased the prison. At first she clutched Fall's arm; but then as Brad came out the gate, she gathered her own forces and stepped away from Fall. She did not cry nor call out. She only went to the gate and waited a step away from it. When Brad came out, she stepped forward and put her arms around him. Neither of them spoke. Her chin rested on his shoulder. She was almost as tall as he. After a while she said over his shoulder, "Welcome back, stranger. How does it feel to be a free man?"

"I wish I knew. I'm not free: I'm just out. I can't leave Moscow."

"Alex told me. But it's a big improvement, no matter what."

"Facing trial for bribery and theft of state property? I can't call it *much* of an improvement. The only good thing is I know I'm innocent. Where's Jen?"

"I left her with Lyuba. It's not good for her to see her parents cry."

"You're not crying."

"I could be. Don't make me."

"I thought maybe you didn't bring her because you didn't want her to see her old man getting out of prison."

She pulled back. "You *will* make me cry, damn you."

"Hey, I'm sorry." But she had stepped back, she was out of his reach.

She turned to Fall and then Slavin, standing on opposite sides of her and Brad—Fall where he had been waiting with her, Slavin at the gate where he had come out with Brad: she had not even seen him until this moment. "All right, let's go, you guys," she said roughly. "We're not a show for you."

\*     \*     \*

WILLIAM E. HOLLAND

She was not a woman to hold a grudge. At home later she stroked his arm in the brief dark of Moscow summer. But it was tenderness lost on a man who seemed only part of the one she had known, as if he had left some part of himself somewhere. "What was it like?" she wanted to ask, but did not. He had never been the kind of man to tell things like that. And asking only made it worse. She determined to live without that knowledge. She was not sure she even wanted it. Prison in a strange land was the worst fate she could imagine. But that was what Moscow had been to her for two years already. "I understand," she wanted to tell him, but did not, knowing that he would not understand. She had never been the kind of woman to tell things like that.

Their daughter stirred in the dark. All the time he had been gone, Jen had waked at night calling out for her father. Joanna had learned to listen for her. Now Jen only murmured, said something indiscernible. Joanna rose, went along the hall to Jen's bedroom. She paused outside the door, which was open a crack. She did not enter. She stood listening. She heard nothing. After a time she went down the stairs and through the dining room. Although it was dark, she touched nothing; she was guided by the feel of the house, knowing where everything stood, like the panther who has paced her cage daily for a lifetime. She opened the terrace door from the dining room and stepped outside. Although it was summer, the night had turned cold as the skirts of the great polar air mass, never far away, dragged across Moscow. The birch trees beyond the small cleared yard were pale exclamation marks on the darkness. Joanna stepped across the lawn toward the grove. The icy dew felt like a series of tiny electric shocks to her bare feet.

Among the trees it was at last black dark; but she went without hesitation, and there among them, still within the fence of their small property, she found by feel the rustic bench some carpenter had hewn from birch logs. She sat down on it, and there at last she cried.

She permitted herself only one minute. Then she dried her tears on the edge of her nightgown and went silently back to the house.

82

# 13

CHAPMAN HAD BEEN IN JAIL ONLY THREE WEEKS, BUT HE FELT AS IF HE'D been gone a year. In his Sunday-quiet office, everything was the same; yet everything was strange. His in-box was full of papers— last week's cash flows, a service contract from a new customer. He ruffled through them. They were all dated after his detention. Everything before that, the police had kept. His computer was gone too. Its empty stand reproached him that he had left the computer behind, a hostage in the hands of the police.

The furniture in his office was vaguely out of place, as if the room had been stirred once by a giant spoon and left to settle again almost where it started. The picture of Joanna and Jen was still on his desk, but not where he thought it should be. Or was it right? Had he always placed it there, so far into the corner? The case of his desk chair was clearer. His own chair was gone. In its place was a typist's adjustable swivel chair, armless. Had someone sat here to type? To search his computer? Where was his own chair?

He wandered out into the outer office, by Alexandra's desk. Her computer was gone too, but the typewriter had been left. He pulled open some file drawers. The files were mostly empty. He felt lobotomized. It was going to be hard to run a business with no records.

He had insisted that JorSov hire its own guards, twenty-four hours a day, against just this danger, the theft of records. But the police had been more thorough than thieves, and guards couldn't stop them.

He went into Turbin's office, which opened off the opposite side of the reception area. The office was dark. The blinds were down, and it was a gray day outside. He turned on the light.

The office was as bare as if no one had ever worked there. The shelves were clear; the desk drawers were empty. There had been a computer there too; gone too, but Turbin had never used it anyway.

He went back into his office and sat down at his desk. The papers were there, but the will to work wasn't. He stirred through the papers. Will or no will, things had to be done. Deal with the things that had to be done first. A message from Hawke Jordan. Congratulations on being out of jail. Just the message every field manager wanted from the owner of the company. That one wouldn't wait.

It was a long time since he had written with pen and paper, but he was composing a reply when he heard the office door open. It closed. He heard the click of heels from the door to the desk. "Sasha?" he called.

She came to the door. She waited there, not coming in, resting one hand on the doorframe. "I was afraid for you," she said at length. "I was so afraid."

"Me too."

"What will happen now?"

"We'll see. The lawyers got me out. The Investigator is still investigating. He'll tell us when he's ready and not before."

"And poor Vladilen Viktorovich. How did it happen?"

"Do you think I know?"

"No. Of course not! But I thought you might have heard. Something. In jail."

"They don't tell you things. They ask questions."

"Of course." She looked around behind her, around the reception area with its missing files. "They took everything. While you were gone."

"I noticed. Well, we didn't have any files when we started. We're no worse off."

"You're so calm. I wish I could be. I haven't slept since . . . they took you." She hovered in the doorway, but he said nothing, and so she turned to go back to her desk.

"Sasha."

She turned back quickly. One hand was still on the doorframe. "Yes?" She was wearing her white knit dress that clung to her all over. He knew the dress. He knew she had worn it today for his appreciation: welcome back. But he ignored it. An end of all that.

"There was a document. The Investigator showed it to me." She waited, silent. "It was this year's accounts. Off of my computer." Still she said nothing. "Everything was on it except the payments to Turbin." Nothing. "Where did it come from?"

"I don't know . . ."

Too tentative. "No one has access to my computer but me. And you."

"Did you tell them? That I have access to your computer?"

"I should have."

"You didn't tell them."

"No."

Her voice quavered. "I was afraid for you. I thought . . . maybe I could help."

"How could that help?"

"I knew they were asking you about the business. They wanted to know how much credit was given for state property contributed to the business. If they knew how much Vladilen Viktorovich has been paid this year, in dollars . . . No Russian is paid so much just for work. They'd have to think it was for the state property. That you paid him instead of the state."

"They did think that," he admitted. "And do, probably."

"So I came in at night, that first night you were gone. And I fixed the records."

"You 'fixed' them."

"Yes. I took out the payments to Vladilen Viktorovich."

"Those were legal payments, Sasha! There was nothing to hide!"

"Oh, yes, your foreign lawyer said they were 'legal.' But it wasn't smart to make them. You said yourself—now the Investigator thinks the company paid Vladilen Viktorovich for stealing state property for you."

"How the hell did you think you could hide the payments from the police?"

"I took them off all the records."

"*All* the records?"

"Yes. I only kept one copy on a separate disc, and I put it in a special place. I didn't think they'd find it."

"Where was it?"

"I taped it inside your desk. Under the top, up inside the middle drawer. I never thought they'd look there."

"Wonderful! Christ, Sasha, what have you done?"

"I only wanted to protect you, Bradley!" Her voice trembled, and her chin too. She was holding on to the doorframe with a hand on each side, as if to keep from falling. "I'm sorry if it was the wrong thing."

"All right."

"What did you tell them?"

"I told them I was making a file of payments to Turbin, and that I must have cut them instead of copying them. That bastard Volkov told me the only copy without Turbin on it was on my computer. I knew *I* hadn't put it there; so I figured it must have been you, trying to 'help' me. I know you, don't I."

"You always did."

"It was on all the computers?"

"It didn't make sense to have it only on one."

He waved her over to him. He had intended not to. That was all over now, he had told himself. It was time to tell her. But he didn't want to tell her at a distance.

She laid a hand on his shoulder. "Will you tell them I did it?"

"One story's enough for now. It's going to be damn tough to take it back anyway. So let's see what happens."

She touched his shoulder. Her hands kneaded the back of his neck gently. "Yes, let's see what happens."

"That's not what I meant."

"Are you sure?"

"It's time for that to be over, Sasha."

"Over? Why?"

"It's . . . it isn't safe for you. You're not in this. Let's keep you out."

"I'm not afraid. Is that really the reason?"

He said nothing.

"I thought about you, while you were . . . there. I thought, maybe this will make him forget about Alexandra."

"Why would it?"

"Jail makes people think. I've known people who went to jail. People who expected it, people who didn't. People who didn't, they think about why they deserve to be there. Sometimes it has nothing to do with why they are there. I thought, 'Maybe this will be what sends him to his wife.' "

It was so exactly what he had been thinking that he had to deny it. "I just don't want you involved in it."

"But I'm already involved in it!"

"How?"

She laughed. "I'm involved in it if you are." Standing behind him, she leaned forward; and when she leaned forward, the back of his head was between her breasts. At twenty-eight she still had a classic Russian young woman's figure—full breasts, broad hips, slender waist. She was not wearing a bra, and he could feel the firmness of her breasts and the warmth. It was a dress, he knew, you could feel everything through. He put a hand around behind himself, behind her, and found her leg and slid the hand slowly up inside her dress behind her leg. She was not wearing stockings either.

"I missed you so much!" she said. "I worried so much!"

This wasn't going to happen again, he had thought—had promised himself in jail; he would do nothing ever again that deviated in the least from open truth that could be declared in court; but now he knew he had never really thought it. He turned and took one breast in his mouth through the dress. She clasped his head to her. He swiveled the chair, used his hand on her leg to pull her onto himself as he sat there, to pull one leg across his lap. When the knit dress slid up, he could see that she was wearing no underpants either; and there was nothing to keep her from getting at his zipper, and then there was nothing between them but their modesty, which had long been banished.

She took him in her hand and raised herself a little to slide onto him. Her dress, he found, could be slid above her hips, above her waist, all the way above her breasts. The nipples were like cranberries. He tasted the left cranberry with his tongue, then took it into his mouth, ran his tongue around its perimeter. She arched her back to thrust more of her breast into his mouth, and with the same motion pulled the dress off, back over her head, and tossed it onto the floor.

Looking over her shoulder, after a time, he found himself looking into the eyes of his wife in the picture, and then his daughter. Alexandra moaned when he swiveled the chair away and thrust harder against him. Then she laughed without reducing her efforts. The laughter ran through him, spreading from his loins.

"What is it?" he gasped.

"Your family. They're watching us." When he turned away from them, he had turned her to face the picture.

"Ah."

"Did you turn away from them?"

"Ah."

"Your wife. Is she good at this?"

"Mm. I don't want to think about her."

"She'll never do better for you than I can," Alexandra said. "See if she'll do this." She lifted her feet from the floor, pulled her legs up and locked them around him and around the back of the chair. Her arms were around his neck. She shifted her hands down his back and grasped the adjustment knob on the chair back, behind the middle of his back. "You're my prisoner," she said, whispering into his ear, then thrusting her tongue into it. "Now you're to be tortured." She began to move her loins in a slow, small circle, ending each time in a small thrust at him that increased slowly in strength and urgency.

"Oh, God, Sasha!"

"Confess!" she whispered. "Confess that you love me."

"I love you!"

"Confess that you love me more than your wife!"

"I love the way you do this to me!"

"Do I do this better than your wife?"

"God yes!"

"Do you love me more than your wife? Confess!"

"Anything! I'll confess anything!"

"Say it! Say it in words!"

He didn't, but she continued to thrust at him. Her breath came in quick gasps, and in some of them was a voice: "Confess!" "Confess!"

"I love you!"

"More than . . . you love her?"

"More than her!"

"Say it in English!" They had been speaking Russian. She spoke English, but not fluently. "Say it in English!"

"Why?"

"I want . . . to hear it . . . in English."

"I love you . . . more . . . than her."

He was sorry at once that he said it. In Russian it was a game. In English, it was more than that: it was a betrayal. That made no sense to him, but he felt it.

But only for an instant.

The words spoken, she released the back of the chair, moved her hands to the backs of his shoulders, where her painted nails bit deep into his flesh. She was crying out in rhythm to her—their—movements. He thought he was going to come; but every time he was on the edge, she slowed her rhythm, leaving him hanging on the edge, desperate for her, desperate to finish and desperate not to. She pulled back an instant to smile at him, a wonderful glowing smile, and then kissed him and then plunged her tongue into his mouth and withdrew it and plunged it in again and continued to withdraw and thrust and withdraw and thrust and withdraw in time to her movements on him. She was moaning into his mouth; or was it himself moaning? She began to rub her breasts back and forth across his chest in time to all of her other movements, but still not letting him come, until he felt a swift, convulsive grasp that seemed to take him everywhere at once as she came, and then he exploded into her.

## 14

MIKHAIL SLAVIN HAD GROWN UP WITH THE CLEAR, COLD AIR OF MOSCOW summer nights, and for nearly two score years he had survived it. But even knowing nothing else, he had never loved it. Not one night in a hundred was truly warm. Even when the day was hot, the night was apt to be cold, cold as an old lover's kiss. As he walked toward his car, he pulled the earflaps on his summer cap lower and dreamed determinedly of tropic heat. Costa Rica, Puerto Rico . . . what marvelous names there were in southern climates. Names freighted with warmth and riches. Venezuela. Cuba. No, not Cuba. His father had been in Cuba; that was long ago, but already then Castro was hurrying it to Socialist despair. Cuba was warm, but it wasn't *that* warm. Save his thoughts for Puerto Vallarta. The Virgin Islands. Wonderful name.

Shivering, he wished he had parked closer; but two blocks was not too far from this house, because who could know when the woman's husband might come home? Better to be safe than sorry. He pulled his cap down and hurried, wondering why it was the devil poured honey into other men's wives.

He was surprised at first to find that his key didn't work in the car door. He turned it in the lock, but even so the door didn't open. He tried it again and discovered that he had not unlocked the door, but locked it. Strange; he must have left it unlocked, then. Although he never did. But now he unlocked the door, opened it, and got in, feeling his way into the driver's seat because there was no inside light.

"Mikhail Alexandrovich, we thought you'd never come."

Slavin's head banged the roof of the car. He felt he had jumped from his skin. The voice came from the seat beside him, where he now saw that a very large man was sitting.

"Wha . . . who . . . ?" Slavin croaked.

The man laughed, and another voice echoed it from the back seat. "Now we've startled him," the backseat voice said.

"Fair enough, he's kept us waiting so long," said the one in front.

Slavin started to get out, visions flashing through his mind of an *Izvestia* headline—PROMINENT DEFENSE LAWYER SLAIN BY ENRAGED HUSBAND; how would he explain that to his mother?—but the man next to him caught him by the arm. The hand that caught him was the size of a ham of the pre-Revolutionary period. The fingers completely encircled his arm, even over his summer coat with lining. Slavin promptly postponed his departure. "What do you want?" he asked. His voice was firm. He was proud of his voice. It was well trained to argue in public or in private, and it didn't desert him, however shaky he might feel.

"Just a little conversation, Mikhail Alexandrovich. Just a little conversation."

"I am all attention."

"Why, that's kind of you, and it's only fair, Mikhail Alexandrovich, after we waited for you so long."

"I didn't ask you to." Slavin began to notice a strong odor of alcohol in the car.

"He's got you there, Joker," the voice from the back seat said.

"Well, we could have speculated about what it was that kept you so late," Front Seat said. "But we were polite and didn't. Just as in the best families of London."

"Well, we *speculated*," Back Seat said. "We just didn't ask you. We did speculate how she was. Just as in the best families of London."

"Now that you mention it," Front Seat said to Slavin, "how was she?"

"I don't believe I mentioned it," Slavin said. If this was the woman's husband and a friend, or even two thugs sent by her husband, he didn't want to make things worse than they were. He tried testing the grip on his arm and realized that he wouldn't be leaving soon.

"No, he's right," Back Seat said. "He didn't mention it. That's fair. But still, Mikhail Alexandrovich—how was she, actually?"

"I can't discuss client confidences," Slavin said.

"Client? It's 'client,' is it? I've never heard them called that," Front Seat said. "It must be this new slang young people are using. How about you, Brick?"

"No, that's true. We never called them 'clients' at all, as far as I can remember."

"Still, that's been a lot of years, in your case, Brick. You could have forgotten a thing or two, or even three, in that time."

"The memory *is* the first to go."

"Second, I think."

"Possibly in your case, Joker."

"Yours too, but maybe you've forgotten."

"Wait," Slavin said. "You didn't invade my car just to audition for a comedy act, did you? How did you get in, anyway? I never leave it unlocked."

"Ah, Mikhail Alexandrovich!" said Front Seat, the Joker, who seemed to have settled in as group spokesman. "Of course you didn't leave it unlocked! To get into a Zhiguli, a little thing like this . . . we would be insulted if you thought we couldn't!"

"No insult intended, of course."

"And none taken. You couldn't have been serious. But no, we haven't come to audition. Although it's pleasant to have one's repartee recognized and appreciated."

"It certainly is," Back Seat seconded.

"Then why are you here? I take it it's not about my client."

"Oh, there you're quite wrong. It *is* about your client."

"If her husband sent you, you're quite mistaken . . ."

"Oh, no, Mikhail Alexandrovich, not the woman! We're interested in another client altogether. No, no, what you do in your spare time is entirely up to you. It's your professional reputation we're concerned about."

"My professional reputation."

"Correct. A professional's reputation is his most important possession, after all. Don't you agree?" The hand tightened on Slavin's arm in emphasis.

"Yes, of course."

"And once that reputation has been lost, it's all but impossible to restore."

"Of course."

"It's good that you're so agreeable. But I knew you would be. So. It's been brought to our attention that you've accepted a representation that, well, might be harmful to your reputation. You wouldn't want that, would you."

"Certainly not."

"Yes. You see, Brick?" The man turned halfway toward the back seat, or turned his head: he was so large that his body wouldn't turn in the Zhiguli's cramped space. "You see? I told you he was a reasonable man." He turned back to Slavin. "Brick thought we'd have to be prepared for trouble with you. But I knew we wouldn't. Well, it's settled then."

"What is?"

"Why, you'll give it up, won't you. Representing this American."

"American?"

"Yes. Mr. Chapman. You aren't representing two, are you?"

"He'd be a lucky man if he was," came from the back seat. "All those dollars he'd be earning."

"I can't just 'give up' a client," Slavin protested. "The court won't allow it. It's against the law. Once I've accepted a case, I've got to continue, as long as I'm being paid."

"Oh, Mikhail Alexandrovich, I'm disappointed in you," Front Seat said. "There are all kinds of ways to give up a client, aren't there? There's illness . . ."

"And accident," Back Seat added. "People meet with accidents. Severe bodily injury results, sometimes. That would be a reason."

"Yes, but that's not the reason," Front Seat said. "You know what the reason is that you're going to give up this case, Mikhail Alexandrovich? I know it; and I knew this before we talked with you. Brick can tell you I did, because I told him. I said, 'Brick, Mikhail Alexandrovich is going to give up this case when we point out to him that he should; because, Brick, Mikhail Alexandrovich is our kind of people.' And, Mikhail Alexandrovich, do you know how I knew that you're our kind of people?" The hand tightened still further on his arm, which now felt to be going numb. "It's because you've proven what side you're on, Mikhail Alexandrovich. Remember once you were asked to defend a dissident, Mikhail Alexandrovich, and you didn't do it, even though the dissident was your father's childhood friend? Because you had to choose which side you were on; and you chose. 'You can't be a defender of the people if you defend an enemy of the people.' Do you remember that, Mikhail Alexandrovich? Remember Kornev?''

Slavin remembered. Roman Romanovich Kornev—his father's oldest friend. When Kornev came to him and begged him to defend him, he had agreed. What else could a man do? He had agreed at first. But then he had reconsidered. He had been persuaded to reconsider.

A man couldn't be a lawyer who defended the enemy of the people. That was true then. To defend a dissident meant the end of his career. He would never work again, except for other dissidents, and there were precious few of those. And for what? Not to save Kornev. There was no saving him. There were no not-guilty verdicts. Not in those days. "I can't help you," he had said to Kornev, had said to his father's oldest friend.

"It's not the same," Slavin said. "It isn't like that anymore."

The hand tightened yet again on his arm. "The world doesn't change, Mikhail Alexandrovich," Front Seat said. "Personnel change, but the world doesn't. It's always the same choice. 'Which side are you on?' And what does it matter anyway, this time? It's just some American who's tried to steal state property. Why should you care? He deserves to go to prison. For the good of the people, he should go to prison. Aren't you on the side of the people anymore, Mikhail Alexandrovich?''

"It's the money," Back Seat said, a new coldness in his voice. "All those American dollars. That's what matters."

"He'll get another lawyer anyway," Slavin said. "If not me, someone else."

"Maybe. But it won't be you. Not someone with your reputation and your cleverness, Mikhail Alexandrovich. Not someone the judges have to listen to."

"And maybe it won't be anyone," Back Seat said. "Lawyers are reasonable people."

"You can't scare off everyone," Slavin said. "The court wouldn't believe it; the Prosecutor wouldn't believe it. Worst of all, the newspapers wouldn't believe it. No, it isn't possible. It's stupid."

"It isn't polite to call names," Back Seat said.

"I've got a better idea," Slavin said.

There was a short silence. "What's your idea?" Front Seat asked. The hand grip did not loosen.

"I'll stay on as his lawyer," Slavin said.

"Not much of an idea."

"I haven't finished. I'll stay on as his lawyer, but I won't get him off. If I quit, it looks strange. Someone else comes along, they quit, it looks stranger. But eventually, someone will defend him. They won't be as good as I am, but they'll prepare a defense. Maybe they'll get lucky. But if I defend him, I can guarantee he won't get off."

The grip loosened slightly. "You'll throw the case."

"Let's say I'll be able to avoid mistakes that might free a guilty man."

Another short silence. "Why would you do that?"

"As you said, I haven't forgotten which side I should be on."

"That's clever," Back Seat said.

The hand released Slavin's arm. "That's why we need a Jew lawyer."

"How do we know we can trust you?" Back Seat asked.

"If you can't, I guess you'll know where to find me. You knew where to find me tonight."

Front Seat laughed. "That's right, Mikhail Alexandrovich. We'll know where to find you."

"I'll want something in exchange," Slavin said.

"Lawyers always do," Back Seat said.

"Jews always do," Front Seat said. "How much do you want, Mikhail Alexandrovich?"

"He's already being paid by the American," Back Seat objected.

"I don't want money now," Slavin said. "As he says, I'm being paid by the American. But later, the company's going to need a lawyer. The company this American won't be running anymore."

Front Seat laughed again. "And you want to be it, is that right, Mikhail Alexandrovich?"

"That's right."

"Well, who hires lawyers isn't up to us. Our job is only to fire them."

"You can suggest it to the person who hires lawyers."

"We'll tell them you asked."

"I'll tell them myself. Who is it?"

"That's not something you need to know, Mikhail Alexandrovich." Front Seat opened the opposite door and slid out into the night. The man in back pushed forward the back of the front seat and oozed out too, arching his shoulders back and his face skyward in relief—he had been sitting hunched over in the cramped back seat. The two of them made a vast black shape in the darkness, a single shape that vanished into the larger darkness of Moscow night.

# 15

FALL COULD NEVER WALK UNDER THE GREAT IRON AND GLASS ENTRANCE canopy of the Metropol without reflecting, with both sadness and keen hope, that if Russians had created such a wonder once, they would someday be able to do so again.

The Metropol Hotel represented at once the past and, in the hopes of many, the future of Moscow; but it hardly seemed part of the present. Once the grandest of Moscow's hotels, under Communism it had sunk through the course of years into a quiet decay of uneven floors, sagging beds, unwashed windows, and curtains that never quite closed. Perestroika had brought it back to life, or back at least toward life, to an existence in which it was *in* Moscow but not, presently, *of* it. The hotel's grimy walls had vanished one day behind a facade of scaffolding marked with the sign of a Finnish construction company. What emerged, several years later, in the last year of the Union—for nothing happened quickly in the years of the Union, not even the work of foreign construction companies—was still labeled with the words of Lenin—"Only the dictatorship of the proletariat can relieve mankind of the burden of capitalism"—in gray-green, shimmering, iridescent tiles along the length of Sverdlov Square. But the renewed building seemed hardly related to the gray lump that had long stood there, and hardly related to the gray city that continued around it. It might have been a capitalist luxury liner making a port call in the gray socialist sea—a ship that the passing citizen could envy, but not go aboard. Its newly clean pale walls with their elegant frescoed bands hovered above Sverdlov Square, which remained as grimy as ever. It was a mirage that those who had known Moscow for years could not help feeling might someday vanish as mysteriously as it had come.

For a long time it had been Fall's custom to breakfast at the Metropol—an expensive custom, but one that had more than paid for itself in clients. The Metropol was where wealthy Americans, or executives of wealthy American companies, stayed in Moscow. Most days Fall had breakfast meetings there; but when he didn't, he went there anyway to see who was in town.

Arriving at the hotel at seven-thirty, Fall was surprised to see Slavin's car in the crowded parking lot. He was even more surprised to see Slavin in it. The concept of breakfast as an occasion for business had not yet penetrated Moscow circles, and as for Slavin, Fall had never known him willingly to agree to a meeting before noon.

Slavin waved casually to Fall and got out and came over to him.

"I never thought you'd see this part of the day, Misha!"

"I need to have a couple of words with you. Can you spare some minutes?"

"An hour. Let's have breakfast."

The mention of food always brought Slavin a pensive look. "It's early . . . but still . . ." He shrugged.

From the breakfast buffet Slavin carried back to their table three plates at once. The first was for hot meats—bacon, crisp, six strips; ham, two slices; middle-size boiled sausages, three; small fried sausages, four; mustard on the side. The second contained an assortment of cold cuts, fish, and fresh vegetables— roast beef; salami liberally larded with, well, with lard, or at least with small round pieces of fat; fresh herring, a pile; and slices of cucumber and tomato. The third plate was dedicated to fruit, both fresh and canned, especially pineapple, but also pears and peaches in syrup, a banana, and a fresh apple. For want of hands, he had piled his breads atop the fruit: several slices of white bread with butter, a cinnamon roll, and a small *pirozhnoe,* a sweet cake with powdered sugar.

"Don't you want kasha, Mish?" Fall asked him. There was a large urn of the steaming hot cereal at one end of the buffet.

"I do," Slavin said seriously. "But I don't like to appear . . . immodest." He pondered. "Is it permitted to go back?"

"It's encouraged."

"Wonderful. I suppose they'll bring tea to the table," he added hopefully.

"I guarantee it."

As he arranged his plates and settled the order of things, Slavin stared around the room at the linen-clothed tables, the chandeliers hoisted on massive polished brass columns, the glistening interior balconies opening off rooms two stories above, and the huge stained-glass skylight far overhead. Although he had been born and raised in Moscow, he might have been a country bumpkin just in from Novosibirsk. Fall, amused, didn't notice that Slavin had also looked over everyone at nearby tables. "This is as it was before the Revolution, I suppose," Slavin said. The building was Bal'kot's masterpiece erected in the burst of art nouveau creativity just before the Revolution froze Russian arts. "Not just the building, I mean." He turned to his meal with no appearance of regret, but then appended a question: "This breakfast, now: how much will it cost us?"

"Twenty-two dollars."

"*Re*ally? So much, for two little meals?"

"That's for one little meal, Mish. Twenty-two apiece."

Slavin chewed a sausage thoughtfully. "About two months' wages, for a doctor or engineer. Not quite as much for a worker." With the last Five-Year Plan several years in its grave, blind momentum still carried forward the traditions of the planned economy: workers were paid more than intellectuals. Slavin put down his fork and knife. "I'd better go back for kasha, then."

It was hard to tell sometimes, with Slavin, when he was un-comprehending and when being clever.

Slavin did go back for kasha, and brought along some extra fruit and another cake.

"Don't forget you can go back again, Mish," Fall said.

Slavin sighed. "It's an unfair challenge. You know the Russian saying? 'It's better to burst our stomachs than let good things go to waste.' But I think there's too much here. Who'd have thought there were so many good things in the world?" He chewed medi-tatively on the sugared cake. "Well, another good thing come to an end. Now, to business?"

"When you're ready."

"I've been putting it off minute by minute. It's not an easy thing." Slavin slurped his tea loudly, as if the noise would cover his hesitation. "I had visitors last night."

"Anyone I know?"

"I hope not. They were the sort of people one doesn't want to know and hopes it is mutual. Unfortunately, although they were no one I thought I was acquainted with, they knew me."

"Who did they turn out to be?"

"They didn't say. But clearly they were part of our security services. Either now or in the past."

"The police?"

"No. MBR, I think." The Ministry of Security—the new name for the KGB.

"Why do you think so?"

"They knew some things about me . . . I'd rather not say what. It isn't flattering."

Fall smiled. "Your secret past, eh, Mish? Well, what did they want?"

"They wanted me to stop representing our client, Mr. Chap-man."

Fall stopped his cup halfway to his lips and set it down again. "Now *that's* interesting! What did they say when you refused?"

Slavin sucked again at his tea. "They used persuasion."

"What sort of 'persuasion'?"

"Very little physical. Mostly a reminder of the things they know about me."

"I could have told them it's a waste of time trying to persuade Slavin."

He smiled sadly. "They were quite eloquent."

"What did you do?"

"Eventually, I suggested that, instead of resigning, I'd keep on representing Mr. Chapman but make sure that the defense would—how did I put it?—'avoid mistakes that might free a guilty man.'"

Fall sat in shocked silence, staring at Slavin.

"I didn't have any choice, Alex."

"You could have told them to piss off."

"I've never believed in pursuing short-term satisfaction at the cost of long-term goals. And the satisfaction would have been *very* short-term. If I hadn't said what I did, our client would be without a Jew lawyer this morning, one way or another."

"Did they believe you?"

"Yes, of course."

"Why?"

Slavin didn't flinch, didn't look to one side or the other. A trained performer, he looked straight at his audience. "Because they think they know that I'm already their man. And they believe that once they make you their man, you're theirs forever."

"Why do they think you're their man?"

"Because I *was* once."

"Because you worked at the Militia Academy?"

"No. That shows an inclination to be on their side; but it doesn't mean they own you. They think they own me." When Fall said nothing, Slavin went on: "A long time ago there was a man accused of certain crimes. Treason was one of them. It was a common story, in those times. We needn't go into detail. The man had broken no laws, if the law is what is written in books; but anything can be a violation of law, if the law is whatever the authorities say it is. In those times, the law was whatever the authorities said it was. So the man was guilty. I was to defend him.

"Before the trial, two men came to me—there's always more than one. They came to me and said, 'Mikhail Alexandrovich, this man is a traitor to the Motherland. He doesn't deserve such a good lawyer as you.' They flattered my abilities. I wasn't such a good lawyer in those days. I was young. Young and foolish enough to think the man deserved an honest lawyer. I said as much. They said to me, 'Mikhail Alexandrovich, the kind of lawyer who would defend such a man is not the kind of lawyer who should be appearing in the People's Courts.' Well, I understood what they meant. I was young, but I wasn't stupid. I'd grown up in this country. My father had been a lawyer, and my mother too. No one would keep me from defending this man; but if I did, that would be the end of my career. And it wouldn't help him. He was already guilty. So, there was nothing to do. I resigned from the case. How innocent I was then!"

"I thought the law wouldn't let you resign."

"It won't. And also, the law presumes the defendant is innocent . . . if you read the law from a book. But I resigned. No one objected. The client didn't object: he was a kind man. He said to me . . . well, no matter what he said." Slavin's gaze had lowered as he spoke. Now he raised his eyes to Fall's. "So they knew then that I was their man. They preferred it that way, you see: first you resisted, and then you gave in. Then they knew they'd got you. Most people saved them the trouble—they never resisted from the first. That was easier, of course; but it was . . . uncertain. With someone who had never resisted, you could never know when he might start. So they preferred working with broken people. We are more reliable."

The bitterness in Slavin's voice swept over Fall's heart. He put a hand on his friend's sleeve. "I know you haven't given in, Misha."

"Thank you. You're right: I haven't. But we must be sure *they* don't find that out."

"Yes. You'd be in great danger."

"I'm *in* great danger. Worse than that. I'm a great danger to you now. To everyone."

"At least you're a danger we know. And maybe there's an advantage in this. Could you find out who these people were?"

"Maybe. I can try. But it won't help to know who *they* are. They weren't anyone. Just part of the system. I thought it was dead; but here it is, back again. But knowing *them* wouldn't help.

Knowing who sent them . . . maybe. But this does tell us one thing. It tells us I was wrong."

"About what?"

"I thought that all we were fighting was the law. That our client had got himself into trouble in spite of your good advice, or by ignoring it. Because, as I told you in the beginning, our laws were made to prevent business, not to regulate it. But now I don't think we're fighting only the law. We're fighting *people.* The two heavyweights they sent to visit me weren't supposed to tell me anything and probably weren't even supposed to know anything. But everyone knows something, even if he doesn't always know he knows it. So I learned one thing from them without their knowing I learned it." He paused for effect, waiting for the question—"What did you learn?" But Fall only smiled, recognizing Slavin's rhetorical training, appreciating it but not seeing any need to help it along. When the question didn't come, Slavin continued smoothly, "I learned that they think someone else is going to take over our client's company. And that means we shouldn't be looking just for a good defense. We should be looking for treason." He smiled, for the first time since the beginning of this conversation. "Anyone raised in this country—the old country, I should say: the Union—has a lot of experience in looking for treason."

The waiter came offering more tea. Slavin took a second cup, waited for the man to go away.

"I was quite concerned you might not trust me any longer."

"Of course I do! What reason would there be not to?"

"I'm an unknown to you, in many ways; just as you are to me. We grew up in different countries. Mine was so different I can hardly imagine myself, now, what it was like." He looked seriously at Fall. "I'm not going back."

"If you want to resign, I'd understand."

Slavin smiled. "Certainly I'm not resigning. How often does one get a second chance to do the right thing? *And* to be well paid for it!"

"Why do you think they want you off the case, Mish? I don't mean 'because you're a brilliant lawyer.' I mean, whoever's behind this, why do they want Brad to be convicted? What do they have to gain?"

"Power, of course. To shift the balance of political power—that's been the purpose of all anticorruption campaigns, ever since Lenin. I don't flatter myself that I'm important; neither is Brad Chapman. But we're a part of something bigger, and maybe an important part, to some people. Plenty of people in this country aren't excited about foreign ownership—'foreign domination,' they'd call it. Especially not foreign ownership of such an important business, ownership of a means of communication. They'd love to show that the foreigners got in by corruption. Plenty of people would try to build a career on that."

"Is the Prosecutor's office in on this game?" Fall wondered.

"Anybody could be in on this. It depends on how high up the campaign goes. In the old days, the Party's days, everything started at the top and everyone was in on it. No one had a choice but to be in on it or to be eaten by it."

"The Party's gone now," Fall said.

"The Party's gone now, but the people who were *in* the Party aren't gone."

"So; is the Prosecutor's office in on this game? You didn't get to be a prosecutor, in the old days, without being a Party member."

"Well"—Slavin smiled, a small, rueful smile—"nothing worked perfectly even in the old days. There were always people who didn't believe in the system. They took part if they had to, and if they didn't have to, they didn't. Now they don't have to. Anybody who participates would be a volunteer. But some people, of course, did believe in the system; and they're still there in their old jobs. They'll volunteer. But we won't necessarily know who they are."

"So the Prosecutor's office could be in on it."

"Or somebody working there could be. Certainly not everybody. But it wouldn't take everybody."

"Then we can't inform Volkov about the visit you had."

"I've known Volkov a long time. We're not enemies. We're not friends. I don't not trust him, but I don't trust him. Not in this."

"Do you still have friends in the militia?"

"A Russian never lets go of a friendship. Not that I'm really a Russian, in their eyes; but I'm really a Russian. Some people there will help me if they can."

"Maybe they'll have an idea who's behind this. Or how high it goes."

"I can ask," Slavin said. "Whether I can find out . . . ?" He shrugged.

# 16

CHAPMAN WAS INCREDULOUS. "TRUST HIM! HOW THE HELL CAN I TRUST him, Alex? Don't be so damned innocent! The man's said they've got something on him! He won't tell us what! How many games is he playing? Ours? Theirs? His own?"

"He's not playing any game, Brad," Fall said. "He's your lawyer, and he's going to work his little heart out to get you off. I'd stake my life on it."

"Sure! But it's not your life that's at stake. It's mine!"

"It's not your life," Fall corrected him. "Theft of state property and bribery get you fifteen years, at most." He was annoyed enough at Chapman to be precise.

"If their next prison is anything like Petrovka or Butyrka, I wouldn't survive fifteen years of it." But Chapman saw that he had pushed Fall too close to the edge of something, and he stepped back from it. "I'll keep him on if you think I should, Alex."

"If you don't, you're crazy."

"All right. All right! But be sure you know what he's up to! All the time!"

"He's up to keeping your rear end out of jail. All the time. And he's risking his own to do it."

"What makes him so noble, I'd like to know?"

"It's not noble. It's his job. But it isn't a free ride for the rest of us, either."

"What does that mean?"

"If someone wants you out of the way, they may use other tactics. And since you can't leave . . ."

"Why the hell can't I?" Chapman interrupted him. "I'm not in jail."

"You've given your undertaking not to leave Moscow. If you try to skip, they'll jail you for that alone."

"If they catch me."

"They'll catch you. And if they don't, Hawke Jordan isn't going to be happy. His manager skips town charged with theft of state property? His company will be up for grabs. And in this atmosphere, somebody's going to grab it.

"You can't leave," Fall went on, "but you ought to think about sending Joanna and Jennifer home."

"Why? Nobody's accused them of anything."

Fall was annoyed. "Because if they're here, they're hostages to fortune."

"Yes, of course you're right, Alex." Chapman sounded tired. "I'll send them."

It appeared, though, that Joanna didn't agree. Chapman called Fall the next day, inviting him to their house for added persuasion.

Joanna had set up lunch on the back patio. "If we're going to argue," she said, "let's do it outside so the neighbors can enjoy it. I'd certainly want them to do as much for me. We get so little pleasure here."

"I don't think we have anything to argue about," Fall said.

"I thought the purpose of this meeting was to try to pressure me into cutting out. And if that's the purpose, we're certainly going to argue."

"For Christ's sake, Joanna, you've been ready to leave since the day we got here!" Brad exploded. "Now that it makes sense to go, you want to stay?"

She got up from the table and walked over to the edge of the concrete patio slab, to the beginning of the close-cut Midwestern lawn that after two years was finally just beginning to fill in the edges of its assigned space. She looked at the grass, at the still birch trees with the log bench hidden among them. She turned back toward the table. "I'm not going," she said. "Alex says you've got to stay here; and if you're here, I'm here."

"Alex, tell her it doesn't make sense," Brad said.

"It doesn't make sense, Joanna," Alex said.

"In my opinion it didn't make sense for us to be here in the first place. But here we were. And here we are. And I'm not leaving my man behind." As she said this, she looked at Alex with something like sheer hate in her eyes. Gray eyes with a touch of gold, but in them a violence that startled him.

They lunched in uneasy silence, in unspoken agreement to let the matter lie there for now. They talked about nothing—about the weather: it was fine; about Jennifer: she was fine, she was gone for the afternoon, playing with Lyuba's daughter, Joanna hoped she wouldn't come home speaking Russian; about Farquhar, the new North American Mining representative, who had left his wife and moved in with his secretary: Joanna hoped he got the clap, if she hadn't already given it to him.

Joanna suggested a walk to the river. They lived on a peninsula hugged by an arm of the river Moskva, and the water lay glistening under the summer sun.

Brad begged off. "After three weeks in jail, I've got work to do. I'll stay here and make some calls."

"He thinks he's irreplaceable," Joanna said. "He'd do this job if the world was ending around him."

"Take her out and convince her, Alex," Brad said. "It's clear that I can't."

"Take me out and convince me, Alex," she said.

They walked along the street, suburban America on the edge of Moscow. The sky was blue; the houses were brick; the cars in the drives were Volvos and Mercedes. The contrast to Moscow irritated him. It was like being back on the edge of Chicago. It was what every Russian he knew scorned, and wanted.

"You don't like it out here, do you, Alex?" she said, watching him. "Out with the Americans."

"I like it," he said truthfully.

"Why don't you live out here? You can afford it."

"I don't know. It's inconvenient. And my job is interpreting Russia to Americans—and Europeans and Japanese and whatever other foreigners come here for business. It's easier from there." He waved in the direction of Moscow; but it was a wave in the direction of a foreign country.

"It's easier to keep in touch if you live among 'em?"

"Something like that."

"You've really gone native, haven't you."

That expression irritated him too. It was as if being too close to the Russians made you somehow unsanitary. It was a colonial point of view that he found grating. He told her so and was more irritated when she was unrepentant. "You're certainly touchy," she said. "As bad as Bradley. Maybe you don't fit in as well as I thought you did. Is your love life going badly?"

He said nothing.

"Haven't you found a replacement for little Innochka yet?"

"She's nobody's 'little Innochka.' She's the strongest woman I've ever met. Until you know her, don't talk about her."

She fell into an angry silence. That coldness in her eyes again. Finally, he asked, "Look, have I done something wrong? We used to be friends."

"Don't be stupid, Alex. You're perfect."

"Irony is the last refuge of scoundrels." He paused for effect and shook his head. "Did I get that right?"

"The last time I checked, it was 'patriotism.' "

"Irony is the last refuge of patriots?"

She didn't laugh, but the anger left her voice, and her eyes had melted. "All right, you aren't perfect. But I wasn't being ironic. You're too close to perfect. That's the only thing you've done wrong. That's what makes it hard to be friends with you."

"I could try to screw up more often."

"I think it's too late for that, Alex."

He said nothing, trying to head off what he saw was coming, but he didn't know how.

She said, "You'd have had to start long ago. Before we went to Belaya Gora, for sure."

Still he said nothing.

She said, "If you deny it, you're an asshole."

"I've always been a screw-up."

"That's not a denial."

"I deny it."

"Asshole."

They stopped walking. Neither one stopped the other. They just both stopped.

"Joanna, Brad's my client."

"Yes, and your client's wife is in love with you, and she doesn't even care if you're in love with someone else. How do you like *them* apples?"

They stood facing one another in the middle of a short Midwestern street dropped somewhere in the heart of Russia, a street where all the neighbors knew them; and he thought how unfair it was to be faced with this small-town dilemma so far from home. He hadn't come halfway around the world for personal ethical conflicts.

"So deny it," she said. She said it in the offhand way of a high-school beauty queen tormenting a sophomore. She said it smiling in a way that wasn't mockery, but mockery of mockery. "Maybe you don't love me; but you can't deny you struggled not to love me. Or if you can deny that, you can't deny you lusted after my body, you beast."

"Can I plead 'no contest'?"

"I can't leave you, Alex. I've busted my ass trying to get Bradley to send me away from here to save my marriage, not to mention my sanity; and now I find out I can't leave you anyway."

"If you loved me, why did you send me to someone else?"

"Stupidity. Sheer stupidity. I was so ... *innocent!* I thought once you had someone else I'd get over you. I thought you'd find out you couldn't love anyone else and would come crawling back to me. I don't know what I thought. I probably thought a lot of other things, all of them stupid. I cursed your name every way I knew how, and when that was all over, I still wanted you." She turned and walked on and, not knowing what else to do, he walked beside her. She spoke again, not looking at him: "Don't worry. I'm not going to try to make you do anything against your principles. That's one thing I liked about you from the beginning, your principles. They're the same as mine. I'm married to Bradley, and that's it. But at this point, if it's all I ever get out of this, at least I'm going to have the pleasure of knowing that you know that I know, and so on and so forth. I hope that doesn't make sense."

"Unfortunately, it does."

"That's certainly refreshing honesty from a lawyer."

"I guess so. What does it get me?"

"Nothing. What does any of this get either of us?"

"Nothing. Less than nothing."

They walked on in silence. The street ended at the riverbank, at the end of the peninsula. There was a small beach caught in the crook of the river's arm, and on it several small children were playing under the watch of a Russian nanny. One of them was Jennifer. She didn't look up. None of them did.

"So," Joanna said again, "how's your love life?"

"Going badly." For some reason he felt comfortable talking to her now. He felt nothing but an old-friend feeling.

"Inna's not coming back?"

"I don't know. She never said she wasn't. I thought she was. Then I thought she wasn't."

"So what are you going to do about that?"

"I don't know."

They turned and walked away, back up the Midwestern street. As they walked, he remembered Belaya Gora, and how different his life might have been, and how hard it was to kill love that had never had a chance to grow tiresome.

# 17

ALEX HAD ORGANIZED THE TRIP TO BELAYA GORA BECAUSE JOANNA asked. They flew to Simferopol and went by taxi over the mountains to the seaside, to the Black Sea and to the White Mountain, which is what Belaya Gora meant in Russian. With luggage they were too many for a single car, so Brad went in one with Jennifer, and Alex and Joanna went in another. The road climbed out of the haze and smoke of Simferopol up goat-gnawed mountains that grew more and more barren until, suddenly, as if poverty had been stretched past all endurance, the road broke out onto limestone cliffs hanging over an azure sea. As the car rushed down from switchback to switchback, Joanna clung to Alex's arm, terrified and delighted. By the time they reached Belaya Gora they were dizzy with air and sunlight.

They stayed in a government guesthouse. Alex had once done work as a favor for the director of a state enterprise that had access to it. They were the only foreigners there, or in the village. In the morning they took the elevator down the cliff to a private beach, unfortunately stony; in the afternoon they read in their rooms; and in the evening they left Jennifer asleep in the care of an old woman and walked to the village, an old fishing village spruced up in an attempt at Capri based on imagination and old magazines but no real resources. The village fathers had thought to lure foreign tourists with a late-night disco and a porn video salon. No foreign tourists came, but the mountain and the warm air and the sea endured. Alex and Brad and Joanna ate shashlik under a grape arbor in the courtyard of a small restaurant and then sat drinking white wine and breathing the sweet sea air.

On the second day, sitting on the stony beach, Brad made an

announcement. "I'm ready for the next event. Or the first," he corrected himself. "Nothing has really happened since we got here."

"Don't be silly," Joanna said. She had just come from the water and glistened with salt. "We've swum and we've sat in the sun and we've had a drink among friends."

"With a friend," Brad said. "There's just Alex."

"And there's you and there's me. That makes three. So it's 'friends.' "

"No. It's a drink with a friend. Ask Alex."

"All right. Alex?"

Alex was lying facedown in the sun wishing there were fewer stones but blessing the heat of the sun and the sight of Joanna's long legs close by his face. He had no inclination to enter the discussion and tried to pretend he was asleep. Joanna poked a foot into his ribs. Her toes were warm from the sand. "Alex, I know you're awake. You're always awake. Settle this."

He sighed. "Who's my client?"

"I am," Brad said.

"It's a drink with a friend."

"You don't get away with *that*, buddy." Joanna sat down beside Alex and looked into his face. "We go by reason here, not by privilege."

"He has reasons," Brad said. "He always has reasons. Ask him."

"Defend your judgment," she said.

"You and Brad are husband and wife, not friends. A husband and wife may be taken as one in the eyes of the law, and probably of God for all I know. So the two of you, taken as a couple, were having a drink with a friend. And conversely for me. Also, it is a maxim of equity that a ménage à trois doesn't count as friends."

She stuck out her tongue at him.

"See," Brad said. "He had reasons."

"Oh, Bradley Chapman, you don't even know what a ménage à trois is," Joanna said.

"I don't need to. That's what I hire lawyers for—to talk Latin at people who need to be put in their places."

"Well, you better be damn careful, or you'll find out what a ménage à trois is in Latin, and then see how you like it."

"If I ever want to know, I'll ask Alex."

She cleared stones from a strip of sand and lay down with her face close to Alex's. She was lying on her stomach with her chin on the backs of her hands, looking into his face from a foot away. She smiled.

Her eyes were as gray as the sea, and the gold in them a hint of sunlight.

"If he'll tell you," she said in a very, very low voice. "In Latin."

Alex closed his eyes.

"Fucking telephone doesn't work," Brad said. He came out to join Joanna and Jennifer and Alex sitting on the patio of the guesthouse, watching the sun sink behind the mountains across the bay, above the cliffs down which their cars had fallen.

"Why don't you curse in Russian instead of English when your daughter is listening," Joanna suggested.

"You're always saying she should concentrate on English. And she already knows the Russian words. Listen to this, Alex. What's the worst word you know in Russian, Jen?"

"*Yo*—" she started to say, but her mother clapped a hand over her mouth. "Don't you dare!" She said to Bradley, "You could clean up your act in two languages. Anyway, why are you trying to use the telephone *here?*"

"Just a couple of things I wanted to check on at the office."

"Christ, we didn't come here for your work, Bradley! We came to get away from work."

"Watch your language when your daughter is listening," he suggested, laughing.

They dined at the same restaurant. There was no other in the village and they did not want to sit at the guesthouse. The menu was again shashlik, but this surprised only Joanna, who had not traveled much in the former Soviet Union, and bothered only Brad, who knew the Union but was quickly tired of the same things over again. But it was good shashlik, and the bread was even better, long, flat, golden loaves of Georgian *lavash* warm from the oven. The wine, the same wine over again, offended no one. They sat and saw the stars bloom above the arbor and heard the distant pounding of the rock music from the open door of the disco down the street. "We could see what's playing at the video palace," Brad said, but no one moved.

Joanna said, "You've seen better at home."

"A fresh slant never hurts."

"It hurts when the wife finds out about it."

"Then it's best to be careful she doesn't find out."

Alex sipped his wine and watched the starswing of the sky.

On the stony path to the guesthouse Joanna, between them, slipped a hand through each of their arms.

"I thought the Union had dissolved," Brad said the next day. He had come down to the beach late and was waiting when the others came out of the sea. "But this is definitely the Soviet telephone system. You can't call Moscow, but Moscow can call you. At least you can call Simferopol," he added.

"Why are you trying to call Simferopol?" Joanna asked. She swished her long hair back over her shoulder with a swing of her whole body.

"To try to get an earlier return flight."

"To what?" She stopped dead still, a towel halfway to her hair.

"Something's come up at the office. I'm not much for sitting on beaches anyway, you know."

"What can be happening at the office that can't wait?"

"It's the Ministry license for a new service extension . . ."

"That's been going on for months. The office will run without you, Bradley. And Alex put a lot of work into arranging this trip for us. Have the kindness to be a little grateful."

"I don't have to be grateful to Alex. He's my lawyer."

"That's a horrible thing to say."

"Yeah, I guess, but it's true. Isn't it, Alex."

"No one has to be grateful to his or her lawyer," Alex confirmed.

"Well, he isn't *my* lawyer, and I'm grateful. If you go back early, you'll damn well go by yourself."

"Unless I want to take my lawyer. Right, Alex?"

"Is my meter running?"

"Turn it on while you answer."

"Okay. It's on. If I go back, my meter runs the whole trip. Door to door. Shall I turn it off now?"

"Yes, turn it off, damn it."

"I don't care about your damn meter, Alex," Joanna said. "I'm not staying here alone without someone who speaks Russian. And I *am* staying here."

Brad shrugged. "If you really want to . . . I don't want to spoil your vacation. I guess Alex can take care of you and Jen."

"Fine. We'll be a ménage à trois," Joanna said.

Brad left the next morning by taxi as the sky was turning from white to blue. After he was gone, Joanna cried a little, in a way that showed either she didn't want Alex to see, or that she wanted him to see that she didn't want him to see. He couldn't tell which.

They had breakfast on the guesthouse terrace looking out across the sea, waiting for the sun to heat the stony beach. It was an elegant guesthouse, by Soviet standards, which were what it had been built to. It had cavernous halls and lobby, all lined with fossiliferous limestone slabs, and this terrace floored with the same material. The guest rooms were small but well furnished in a dark way, with French doors that didn't quite fit opening onto balconies above the sea. Weeds more patient than gardeners cropped up between the slabs on the terrace.

"I hope there's nothing for him to do," Joanna said. "I hope he's bored out of his skull."

"There's always plenty for him to do," Alex said. "He loves his job."

"The company certainly got more than they deserved out of him. Well, we're not going to mention him again."

The beach seemed emptier without Brad—*was* emptier, for they had been the only ones on it and now were three instead of four. Jennifer ran up and down ahead of the low waves looking for shells. Alex watched her from the beach while Joanna swam along the shore.

When Joanna came back, she said, "You'll make somebody a good father one day."

"I'd rather make somebody a good baby."

"You could probably do that too. Go swim. I'll watch my kid."

He waded out waist deep and then swam slowly away from the shore. The beach sloped gently into the water, and he was a long way out before he could no longer touch bottom. He turned and swam slowly back, letting the waves do the work. When he reached the beach, she was knee-deep in the water with Jennifer. They were wrestling and laughing. Jennifer grabbed for a hold on her mother's bikini top, caught it but slipped, and pulled the top down on one side. Joanna's blush spread from her face down her neck and into her exposed breast. "*That* certainly was forward of you," she said to Jennifer. She turned away to readjust her top. She turned back and smiled at Alex, the blush fading from her cheeks.

"I saw your breast, Mom," Jennifer said.

"Yes, so did everyone else, dear."

"Not ever'one. Just Alex."

Joanna laughed. "Not ever'one. Just Alex."

They took Jennifer with them to the restaurant that night. She was proud to be out with big people. The restaurant was run by a family of Georgians who eventually all came out to inspect the little American girl and congratulate the couple on such a fine child. Jennifer translated for her mother. At the end of her translation she giggled: "They think Alex is my dad!" She drank grape juice and pretended it was the wine her mother would not let her taste and had a wonderful time. When they walked back up to the guesthouse, Alex in the middle, Jennifer took his hand, and then Joanna did too.

"Say good-night to Alex, Jen," Joanna said at their door.

She said it in Russian. "Good night, Uncle Alex," the natural way for a child to address a grown man in Russian.

"In English, Jen."

"Good night, Alex."

He shook her hand. "Good night, Jen. Good night, Joanna." Not hers.

\*    \*    \*

They had three days together. In the mornings they took the elevator down the cliff to the private beach, unfortunately stony; in the afternoons they read in their rooms—apart, the first day, but together after that—while Jennifer napped; and in the evenings they took Jennifer and walked to the village for dinner at the restaurant. Alex took to calling her Jenner-fur. She liked it. The Georgian family called her Jenochka and stuck flowers in her hair. She liked that too. Used to being spoiled by her mother, she accepted tributes unself-consciously. They stayed late that last night. The Georgians drank wine with them at their table, and before they left, Jennifer fell asleep at the table. Alex carried her back up to the guesthouse. "Bring her in," Joanna said at the door to their room. "Maybe she won't wake up."

He put her on her bed, and Joanna took off her shoes and socks and put a quilt over her. Alex started to leave, but Joanna said, "You don't have to go. It's nice out. We can sit on the balcony."

The balcony had two plastic chairs and a table. They sat across from each other, the moon on the sea lighting their faces on one side, the other side dark. She looked a harlequin, half her face chalk white, the other somber.

They sat a long time without speaking. Then she said, quietly, as suited the night, "Well, it's been a great ménage à trois, Alex. I'm grateful."

"Nobody has to be grateful to his or her lawyer."

"You're not my lawyer." She sounded annoyed, and he was sorry for having said it. But she added, no longer sounding annoyed, "But even if you've kept your damn meter running, it was worth it."

He laughed, quietly, as suited the night. "It's strictly pro bono."

"You *do* talk Latin at people who need to be put in their places, don't you!"

The night air stirred around them, and he could detect the scent of her hair. She had not worn perfume since Bradley left. He had noticed. This was just the scent of her hair, of her. He could have reached out and touched her. But after that, what?

His hands did not move. Nor did hers, but he could feel them, as though he *had* touched them.

After a while he got up and went back through their room to the hall. She came after him, but left the door open behind her. "I wish we could stay longer," she said.

"Yes. But probably it wouldn't be good for us."

"Probably. But I'll always remember this. Always remember you. Not ever'one. Just Alex."

When they returned to Moscow, Brad was waiting outside the terminal as they walked across the hardstand from the airplane. It was bitter cold, and a thin ground curtain of snow blew across the tarmac, glistening in the sun. The air was full of sparkles as fine snow sifted down from nowhere, from a blue sky.

"There's Daddy!" Jennifer said, and ran to him.

Joanna hesitated only a moment before she walked on quickly after her daughter, away from Alex.

He had never known Joanna well before Belaya Gora. At first she was just the wife of a client, and then when he became friends with Brad, she was Brad's wife. He knew that after Belaya Gora it was going to be different; but he didn't know how it would be.

He didn't see her for a week. Then she came by the office one afternoon with Brad. "Joanna was in town," Brad said. "We sent her car in for service, so we're going home together. Can you park her somewhere while we finish the comments on this contract?"

"She can have my office, and we'll take the conference room. Or vice versa."

"Or I could watch you work," she said. "Work fascinates me. I can watch it by the hour."

"Don't tell him that," Brad said. "He'll charge us double, by the hour."

"Can you run your meter twice at once?" she asked.

"For you it's on the house. For Brad, the meter runs."

As they did their work, she sat and listened and said nothing. When they had finished, she shook Alex's hand on parting.

\*     \*     \*

In another week he met her at a party given by her neighbors, the Millers.

"You have an interesting office," she said. "Do you believe you can tell a man's character by his office?"

"You can tell his work habits." Alex's office was stacked with papers filed by the visual system. "I don't know if you can tell his character. Do you think so?"

"If so, you're a monk."

"I?"

"You don't have any girl's picture in your office."

"I don't have a girl." It was something they had never discussed in Belaya Gora.

"How can you not have a girl in Moscow?"

"It isn't easy," he said.

He told the truth. Being an American man in Moscow at that time was like being a prince back from exile. An American man who was reasonably young and not physically repulsive got a reception that in the rest of the world was reserved, Alex supposed—without having any experience to prove it—for movie stars and royalty. In a country where the average salary was worth fifteen dollars a month, any American was rich, or would have been if he could live entirely on the ruble economy—which he couldn't. There were two parallel economies, one in rubles and one in dollars. Where they intersected, life became strange. Dinner at Pizza Hut cost twenty dollars. A 15 percent tip would give the waiter a fifth of an average month's wages on the ruble economy. To tip what he'd earned in rubles seemed ridiculous, given the price of the meal. But of course it was illegal to pay Russian citizens in anything but rubles, either because the government wanted its people kept pure or because, like governments everywhere, it wanted to control money. To control money was to control people. Consequently, although dollar earners didn't feel rich, they were superrich within the limits of things available to ruble earners. People became a little crazy to get into the dollar economy. Good-looking young women had the best chance. Plenty of them took it. Too many to make the sport interesting.

Unattached American men went through three phases on arriving in Moscow. The first was what one of Alex's friends described as being "tall dog in a meat market"—disbelief, shocked joy, determination to get plenty before the chance vanished. Some men never got past this phase. They tended to stay on in Moscow long after their first job obligation had ended.

Men who came to Moscow already attached, never having had a full chance at the first stage, could become seriously envious of unmarried men. They tended to become unattached before their tour of duty ended.

The second phase set in, for some men, when it became apparent that the chance wasn't going to vanish. Western men were not used to being pursued hard, with no tactics barred, including liberal applications of sex. The result was culture shock as they discovered that it's not easy being royalty, especially when you haven't been trained for it. Royalty have the advantage of being lied to from birth that they are superior to others. It is therefore only natural for them to accept their inherent desirability. Lacking this training, most men ultimately found it hard to believe that so many beautiful women really wanted them. The conclusion was obvious: she only wants me for my money. And generally this was true. Many men got stuck circling between phases one and two, enjoying the benefits but complaining about it.

The third phase, although not many reached it, was asceticism.

Alex had reached the third phase.

"You need a girl," Joanna said.

He was surprised she would think so, and hurt. "Do you have someone in mind?" He asked it lightly.

"No; but I'll keep an eye out. You're too good a man to waste, Alex." Joanna had decided that the only safe way for her was to get Alex out of her reach. She had a husband she loved—if he worked too hard, it was for her too—and a child she adored; and expatriate Moscow was too small a town to get involved with anyone, let alone her husband's best friend.

He couldn't even tell her how bitter it was to him that she would want him to want someone else. "Thank you. I generally try to make my own choices. But I'll certainly scrutinize any candidates you send my way."

"Scrutinize. Is *that* what they call it now?"

"Among the best families of London."

Fate saved Joanna her labor. *Fate, also known as Betsy Miller,* Alex liked to say later. "Alex, Joanna, excuse me." It was Betsy Miller. "I'd like to introduce you to someone. Inna?" She took by the arm a young woman.

He had often wondered, later, what direction their lives might have taken if Fate, aka Betsy Miller, had not come along just then. And he had often wondered if Joanna ever wondered. He had wondered if what they had started was a lovers' quarrel . . . no, not a quarrel, but the first steps of a dance, and who knew what came in the second movement, or if that was only his imagination. He had wondered if she ached inside the way he had, ever since Belaya Gora. He had wondered whether, without Inna, he—either of them—would have had the strength not to say more, not to say too much, even though it would be a long time before the ache had faded.

Joanna was annoyed at Fate for presenting exactly what she had said she wanted. *Who is* this? Joanna wondered. *And who the hell is Betsy Miller to bring her along* now?

Alex knew who Inna was. Anyone who read Russian newspapers or watched Russian newscasts knew who she was.

She accepted the introduction shyly, in the way of those not yet used to fame: *when will it all vanish?* "Inna's a member of the Russian *leg*islature!" Betsy said. "If you can believe that anyone so *young* could be an important politician! And so good-*look*ing!" And with that Betsy Miller, a good hostess, disappeared.

She was not so good-looking, he thought. Certainly she didn't compare with the Russian girls who would assault you any Saturday night at any restaurant. She had a too-square face and a too-determined jaw. But the eyes . . . her eyes were luminous, like one of those eighteenth-century paintings of aristocratic beauties dying fashionably of consumption.

"Have we met before?" she asked him, and he was first aware that he was staring at her.

She was afraid she had offended by not recognizing him. It had become her occupational hazard.

"No . . . no, I'm sorry. It's just that I've seen your face so many times. In the press, on television." He spoke in English, as she had, because Betsy had introduced them in that language.

"Excuse me, I do not speak English well." She spoke precisely but carefully, a beginner trying notes on a new instrument, missing only the music.

"Oh, you speak *very* well!" Joanna said with more enthusiasm than truthfulness.

"Thank you. I hope I will soon."

"I beg your pardon," Alex said in Russian. "We can speak Russian. I will translate."

"Will that be polite?" Inna asked in English.

"If you'll excuse me, you two will have an easier time without me," Joanna said with a fraudulent smile, and left them.

"I didn't mean to drive away your friend," Inna said in Russian.

"You didn't. I think we were finished."

Betsy Miller popped back again. "Inna, have you met the Canadian ambassador? Alex, you won't mind if I take her away again, will you? You can have her back, I promise you."

It was a promise Betsy failed to keep. When Fall next saw Inna, she was leaving early with the man she had come with, another member of the Russian legislature—Antipov, the head of the Democratic Orthodox party.

Alex did not think much about Inna in days to come. His mind was full of Joanna, and he was not a man to have many women on his mind.

Probably he would have forgotten her if he had not met her again soon after. It was at a conference on Western investment in Russia—one of hundreds of conferences Moscow was full of at that time, when it seemed that all that was needed to make the Evil Empire into a free-market democracy was liberal applications of hard currency and plenty of free advice. The format was the usual: Russian leaders told what help the country needed, and Western experts told them why they were wrong. Fall was a speaker on "The Need for a Law on Bankruptcy." Inna was on the same panel, representing the Russian legislature: she was a member of the Committee on Problems of Economic Reform and Property.

She greeted him before their panel was seated. "We *have* met before." She had a ready smile.

"I'll try not to stare, this time. I'm afraid I was rude."

"Oh, no woman minds that." But the way she said it was not encouragement. It sounded formulaic—something she had heard and adopted without thinking about it, not as encouragement, but as a defense. She was wary of him for much the same reason he was wary of Russian women—fear that she was of interest to him only for her position.

Those were the only words they exchanged. The program started. He was surprised at her presentation: she was a sensible, organized speaker, sure of herself and of what she thought. At the end of the formal program they were swept apart by questioners; but afterward there was a reception, and he found himself with her toward the end. On the spur of the moment, he asked, "Would you go to dinner with me?"

She glanced at her watch. "Someone is supposed to pick me up."

"Your friend Antipov?"

"Yes." It was a perfectly neutral answer.

"I'll take you both to dinner, if you have time. There's a very good restaurant here in the hotel."

"I'm afraid we'd be quite an expense."

"My law firm would love to pay." She was not only on the Supreme Soviet's Committee on Problems of Economic Reform and Property; she was also on another committee having to do with legislation, and chairman of a subcommittee. And Antipov, though prickly to foreigners, was head of a political party. It was one of those ephemeral splinter parties dedicated to the memory of a Russia that never existed; but in a fractious, divided legislature, any party head could become important. His law firm would certainly be happy to buy their dinners.

"Perhaps it wouldn't be appropriate."

It was a neutral refusal, with no appeal invited. Fall was surprised. Russian politicians ordinarily took their pleasures when they could get them.

"Anyway, Vasily Ivanovich and I"—she referred to Antipov

respectfully by his first name and patronymic—"are working on a project together. For the legislature. Time is quite pressing. Ah, here he is now. Have you met?"

They had, although there was no reason for Antipov to remember. Antipov was a famous writer, elected to the legislature from Nakhodka, his home district in the Russian Far East—although he had long resided in Moscow—on a platform of opposition to the corruption in the Center, and of Russia for the Russians. A movement had gathered around him in the legislature; he had become a small power. But he still spoke of himself as a fisherman's son. He shook Fall's hand—his own were large and powerful but not calloused—and affected to remember their previous introduction. He had a habit of closing his eyes slowly while talking, as if reading his words on some inner screen, which gave him an air of thoughtfulness. He was a handsome man in the solid Russian-peasant mold, barrel-chested, thick-boned, solid as the earth. He spared only three sentences of chat about the conference—he hadn't heard it, thought it was a waste of time, Russia should take care of herself—and turned to Inna: "So, Inna, are you ready to quit this den of thieves?"

Antipov was proud of his well-known bluntness, but Inna blushed. "I'm sure you don't include Mr. Fall in that category."

"I'll tell you when I know him better," Antipov said. He said to Fall, "We Russians are notoriously cautious of strangers. Not without reason."

"Well, I have my own opinion," Inna said.

Antipov laughed. "I would be surprised if you did not."

She shook Fall's hand. "Perhaps in the future, then," she said.

It was no commitment; but when he called her several days after that and invited her to a concert, she accepted. She confirmed later, when they knew each other better, that she had been put off by his readiness to spend his company's money on her—she did not care to be counted part of a commercial transaction—and had accepted his second invitation only because she felt ashamed of Antipov's rudeness to a foreigner.

So he owed to Antipov his real introduction to Inna.

# 18

FALL STOOD UP AND RUBBED HIS BACK, ACHING FROM HOURS ON A HARD wooden chair.

Fall and Slavin had now spent half the week in the Department of Investigations at Butyrskaya Prison, reviewing the complete record of the case. At this stage, although their client was free, they were prisoners of the record. All the evidence that had been collected against Chapman Bradley Allen had been gathered into twelve large bound volumes of paper that would be transferred from the Investigator to the court before the case was set for trial. It was a numbing mass: financial records, property descriptions, experts' opinions on value.

Brad Chapman, although he had a right to be present, wasn't there. He had seen enough of the evidence in jail, he said. He knew what was in the case. He had more important things to do at the office.

"If I'd known we were going to read this record *here*," Fall said, "I'd have resigned from this case the first time Brad bitched about our work. A defense lawyer in the States would tell you he'd give a critical part of his anatomy for a chance to read the Prosecutor's complete case. But that's only because he's never had to do it. This is torture."

"If I were you, I'd hold my anatomy sacred," Slavin said. "It isn't the procedure that matters in the end: it's the judgment."

Fall settled back into his chair to stare at the bound volume he had been reading. "There's something wrong."

"Tomorrow I'll bring you a pillow. You'll need a functioning anatomy in court, when we get there."

"I appreciate your thoughtfulness. But it's not just my anatomy that's out of whack."

"What else?"

"These financial records—or Brad's story about them. About the payments to Turbin. He says he was making a file of them. Who believes that? There were only two payments. Why make a file of two payments? Or why make it by throwing away all the rest of the whole year's accounts?"

"Do you think our client would lie to us?"

"I've never thought so before."

"My father told me once, 'A guilty client always lies. Especially to his lawyer.' " Slavin's father had also been a prominent criminal defense lawyer. "But that was Russians. I thought Americans were probably different."

"Why would anyone lie to his lawyer?" Fall had spent his career as a corporate lawyer, not defending criminals. But he knew from law school that a client's only hope of an adequate defense was to tell his lawyer the truth and let the lawyer decide what to do with it.

"The reasons are sometimes different," Slavin said. "Often they don't want to admit even to themselves that they were wicked, or stupid, or whatever the reason was they committed the crime. But also they know, by intuition, that a lawyer works hardest for a client who is not guilty. Most persons charged with a crime, unfortunately, are guilty. Even here in Russia. So they lie."

"So you think Brad is guilty?"

"Oh, no. It's not a reversible proposition. Or at least, I don't think he's guilty of a *crime*."

"But you think he lied to us."

"Yes, of course."

"But why would he lie about a stupid thing like this?"

"There is only one reason to lie," Slavin said. "And that is to conceal the truth."

"Probably this is a profound statement," Fall said.

Slavin ignored his remark. "The truth he was seeking to conceal can't be that he paid Turbin. We already know that he did. And so does Investigator Volkov. Yet this file shows that Turbin had *not* been paid. How can that be? The file itself is a lie. Our client was lying, then, to conceal why this file exists—or who created it."

"He says he created it himself."

"But how likely is that? As you said yourself, there were only two payments to Turbin. Why create a file for two payments only? And Volkov's people found no such file. No, the only sensible conclusion is that he said so to draw our attention away from the other file—the one with the payments to Turbin removed."

"Why would he make that file, either? He believed the payments were legal, and he knew that Volkov knew about them."

"Yes. So the only natural conclusion is that someone else made the file."

"But who? And why?"

"Let's think first about who. Who else could have?"

"The accountant?"

"This was on Chapman's personal computer. Password protected. Did the accountant know his password?"

"I doubt it. We can find out."

"If not the accountant, who did?"

"Turbin?"

Slavin looked doubtful. "It seems unlikely to me. Turbin was a bureaucrat. Russian bureaucrats do not use computers themselves. They have women to use computers for them."

"Women?"

"Well . . . it could be anyone. But women, usually. You've seen how our enterprises work. Ideas are hatched by men. Papers are made by women."

"Alexandra," Fall said.

"Who is Alexandra?"

"Alexandra Shubina. Brad's secretary. And Turbin's secretary too."

"Would she know Chapman's password?"

"She shouldn't."

"But would she?"

"We can ask her. But if we think Brad's lying to us, we shouldn't let him know we're asking her."

Alexandra Shubina lived in a sixth-floor apartment on 1812 Street, not far from the Victory Arch commemorating Napoleon's defeat in that year, when he captured Moscow but abandoned it in the face of the Russian winter.

Fall had not telephoned to tell Alexandra he was coming. He did not want her to have a chance to talk with Brad before he arrived. He came in the late evening, expecting to find her at home. But no one answered the door, so he went back to his car and moved it to the next street, in case she might recognize it and wonder. He walked back slowly through the back courtyards of the apartment buildings, almost empty now in the gray twilight.

When he reemerged onto 1812 Street, he recognized Brad Chapman's car stopped at the entrance to Alexandra's building. Two people were in the car, talking with animation, if not happiness. The passenger door opened. The light showed them to be Brad Chapman and Alexandra Shubina. She started to get out, turned—or was pulled—back; the door closed; they blended into one shape. The door opened, and she got out.

Suddenly everything was clear.

As she walked from the car to the apartment building door, her white knit dress was a clear brushstroke on the twilight. Brad waited until she entered the building with a little wave toward his car. Then he drove away, and Fall crossed the street to the building and waited in the dark hall for the elevator to clank back down in its wire cage. All the lights were out on the sixth-floor landing, but having fumbled along the wall once before, now he knew where the bell was and pushed the button.

She must have thought it was Chapman, unable really to go; for she didn't ask who it was, but opened the door, saying, "You know your wife's going to . . ." She bit her lip.

The light behind her pronounced her figure, which Fall already knew to be very fine in any light. Her dress clung to all of her. "Alex!" she said, as if this were the most wonderful surprise. "I thought you were someone else."

"Yes, so I understood. He's gone."

"You were spying on me," she accused. It was a gentle accusation.

"No. But I was waiting to talk with you."

"You must certainly be eager! It's late, Alex. Can't I come to your office tomorrow?"

He wondered why was she offering to come to him. To make it easier than going to her, so that he'd be more likely to go away now, so she could talk to Brad first? "I think we should talk now."

She leaned against the door, as if to close it, but he had stepped half inside at the beginning to prevent that. She shrugged. "All right. Would you like some tea?"

"Yes, thank you."

"Or would you prefer vodka?"

"Tea," he said.

"Come in. We'll talk in the kitchen. Please, sit down." The only place to sit was on an L-shaped bench in the corner behind a low, square table. Instead he lingered in the kitchen door. She rinsed the teakettle. "Sit down," she said, smiling. "I'm not going to run out." She added, "You aren't going to attack me, are you, Alex?"

"No. I'm not going to attack you."

"Then why should I run out?"

"You might not want to talk about what I want to talk about."

"Tell me what it is, please, and we'll see. Do you want English tea or Russian? The English is good; but the Russian is from Azerbaijan, handpicked. The highest sort."

"Russian."

He watched her move about the kitchen. She was a fine-looking woman, graceful in motion, and if he had not known Joanna, he would have understood Brad's position perfectly.

The kettle boiled and she set the teapot on the table to brew and set out some small cakes. "Now, sit down," she said, again indicating a place on the bench. "I'll sit back here so you can catch me." She took the place farthest from the door, where she would have to pass him to get out. "Now, what do you want to talk about? It isn't Bradley, is it? That kiss tonight, that was just friendliness. Just silliness."

"Let's talk about Turbin."

Her smile was replaced by a look of pain. "Poor Vladilen Viktorovich." She glanced down at her hands, shifted her eyes back to Fall. "What do you want?"

"I want to know how JorSov records came to show that he had never been paid in dollars, when I know he had."

"*Had* he been?" She affected surprise.

"You know he had."

"I don't know accounting. You had better go over to Marina's apartment." Marina was JorSov's accountant. "Shall I call and tell her you're coming? Or do you want to surprise her too?"

"Does Marina know the password for Brad's computer?"

"She shouldn't. Whether she does, I don't know."

"Do *you* know it?"

She studied his face for a long while, and the smile came back to her lips. "You must *think* I do, now, don't you?"

"Do you know it?"

"Yes. I know it. It was necessary, sometimes, when he was out, to get information from his computer."

"Do all the computers at your office have passwords?"

"Yes; but they were all the same except Bradley's. His had a different one."

"Were you there when the police took the computers?"

"Yes. I couldn't stop them."

"Did you give them the passwords?"

"I gave them the main one. I could hardly deny knowing it."

"And Brad's?"

"I told them I didn't know it."

"Why?"

She looked at him as if he were a little dense. "I didn't want to help them find whatever they were looking for."

"They had a record from his computer. How would they have got the password?"

"I don't know. I suppose they asked him."

"Have you ever changed any records on his computer?"

She looked in the teapot and then poured two cups of tea. "I've changed many things, when he told me to. I'm his secretary."

"Has he ever told you to change records of payments to Vladilen Viktorovich?"

"No. He never did that."

"Have you ever changed any records of payments to Vladilen Viktorovich?"

She put a sugar cube in her mouth and sipped tea around it. "No."

"Have you ever made a record of payments to Vladilen Viktorovich?"

"No."

"Has Brad?"

"Not that I know of. He might have. He's always playing with the financial records. He doesn't tell me what he's doing."

"Aren't you his secretary?"

"Yes, of course. But some things he does himself. 'Reports to the home office.' I think the 'home office' doesn't like to trust Russian secretaries." She smiled again as she said this, as if amused at this sign of home-office foolishness.

"Did you ever see those reports after he made them?"

"They were in the files."

"And you see what is in the files."

She didn't bother to answer. There was no need to comment again on the curiosity of Russian secretaries.

"Did he give those reports to Turbin?"

"I don't know. But Vladilen Viktorovich didn't read a lot of reports. His business was to keep friendly relations with the Ministry."

"Did he do that?"

"Of course. He was a deputy minister." She glanced at his cup. "Drink your tea. It's not poisoned." She said this with friendly irony.

Fall took his first drink of the tea. It was strong, smoke-tasting, demanding to be sweetened in the Russian fashion. He followed her example, put a sugar cube in his mouth, and sucked the tea around it.

He tried again: "Do you know whether Turbin ever received payments in dollars?"

"I don't know."

"Did you ever see any record or hear anything to indicate that he had been? Was there any record like that on Brad's computer?"

"I think I should tell you what I told the police, or they might think I wasn't telling them the truth."

"What did you tell the police, then?"

"I told them I don't work on Brad's computer."

"But you do have the password."

"I told you so."

"And the other part of my question: did you ever see any record or hear anything to indicate that Turbin was paid in hard currency?"

"You are persistent, aren't you." She laid a hand on his arm, a kind of congratulation.

"Lawyers are paid to be." He waited for her answer.

She left her hand where it was. "I told the police I didn't know."

"I'm not the police. I'm Brad's lawyer. They're not allowed to question me about what I know."

"Maybe not according to the law," she said.

"Did you ever see any record or hear anything to indicate that Turbin was paid in hard currency?"

"Of course I did. You know how we work here. Everyone knows everybody's business."

"What records did you see?"

"Not any."

"What did you hear?"

"Everything."

"What exactly?"

"I'm not going to talk about every rumor I ever heard. If you want to know what was paid to whom, you really should go see Marina. Although"—she glanced at her watch, and when she did, her hand squeezed his arm—"I doubt she's still awake. She goes to bed early. Although maybe you wouldn't mind catching her in bed."

"I'm looking for truth. Getting a woman into bed doesn't necessarily make her truthful, does it?"

She pouted, or pretended to. "Do you know," she said, "you're the first man who's ever come here and refused vodka?"

"That's quite surprising."

"Why is it surprising?"

"Vodka affects the judgment. Any man here would want his judgment intact. Also, it affects performance, and I suspect that any man here would need all the performance he can muster."

She laughed. "I always thought you were just a stuffy lawyer, Alex!"

"I always was."

"Would you like some vodka now?"

She looked steadily into his eyes. A little smile came and went on her lips.

"What do you know about Turbin's death?" he asked.

He thought he had surprised something in her eyes, for an instant. Then she pouted and released his arm with an emphatic gesture. "You *are* a stuffy lawyer."

"I guess I am. But I don't sleep with a woman who's sleeping with my client."

"Does that include his wife?" she said crossly.

Taken aback, he said nothing for an instant. "Certainly it does."

"Remember, I hear everything."

"Who did you hear *that* from?" He was instantly sorry he had asked, but it was too late. She smiled, a different sort of smile now, but said nothing.

"It doesn't matter who you heard it from," he said, "since there's no truth in it. Now: what do you know about Turbin's death?" But it was too late.

"I know what everyone else knows. He was found dead on the ground outside his apartment."

"Did *he* ever come here for vodka?"

She answered, "My friends are my own business."

"Unless they relate to your employer's defense."

"I wasn't having an affair with Vladilen Viktorovich. I never did have, and I never would. He wasn't my type."

"Where were you the night he died?"

"I was at home. Here. In my apartment."

"Was Brad with you?"

She sipped the dregs of her tea and didn't answer.

"You know the police want to make it a case of murder. They can't, yet. But they want to. And their prime suspect is Brad.

Because he has no alibi for where he was. He says he was at the office alone. But he was here with you, wasn't he?"

"I was home alone," she said.

"If I'm going to defend Brad, I need to know the truth."

"Why don't you get it from him?"

"It's taken me until now to understand why I don't get it from him. He won't admit where he really was the night Turbin died. He won't admit how the company's financial records got changed. I couldn't understand why until tonight. Until I saw that 'silliness.' Passionate silliness."

"You have a very American view of passion," she said scornfully, "if you think *that* was passion. You need a Russian woman to teach you something."

"I need a Russian woman to tell me the truth."

She shrugged. "Ask me something."

"Was Brad here the night Turbin died?"

"That's a question for him to answer."

# 19

As FALL RETURNED TO HIS CAR THROUGH THE SILENT BACK LOTS OF Muscovite apartments, a lot of things made sense that hadn't before. He knew now Brad had lied about where he was when Turbin had died or was killed; but now Brad had an alibi, if he would admit it. But maybe he wouldn't admit it. The price of that could be losing his wife, and who would want to lose a wife like Joanna? And Fall knew why Brad had lied about the record of payments to Turbin: Brad had realized that only Alexandra could have changed the records, and he was protecting her by saying he had done it himself. And, as he said, what did it matter? The payments weren't illegal. Except that now the Investigator had concluded he was hiding bribes to Turbin.

But although a lot of old things now made sense, something new didn't make sense at all: since the payments weren't illegal, why had Alexandra faked the records? Fall was sure she had, although she wouldn't admit it. And the way she "hid" them, the payments were sure to be found. All the police had to do was review the company's bank records, as they were sure to do. Or even to cross-check other financial records in the computer.

Or was that the point? That the way she "hid" them, they were sure to be found?

It was barely past midnight. Fall knew Slavin would be awake, and he was. Fall explained about the computers. "Is there any chance we can get access to Brad's computer, Misha?"

"We can if Investigator Volkov is done with it. And since he's concluded his preliminary investigation, he should be done with it. He's either found what he's looking for or is sure it isn't there. I'll try him early in the morning." Knowing that for Slavin anything before noon qualified as "early," Fall got a promise that he would hear from Slavin before ten in the morning.

Slavin kept his word, although at nine fifty-four he still sounded only half-awake. "Send a car to the Central Police Station," he said. "Your driver can pick up the equipment. I'll come to your office. Is noon early enough?"

"You're a miracle worker, Misha! How about eleven?"

"For a miracle, I should get to go back to bed until noon. How about one o'clock? Anyway, your car won't be back by eleven."

"All right, noon. In honor of the miracle. How did you get them to release the computer?"

"It's early. We can talk when I come to your office."

As it was, the car barely beat Slavin to Fall's office. Fall's driver came in complaining, "If I'd known what I was collecting, I'd have gone for a truck! Come and see this!" He had in the Volvo sedan four computers with monitors and keyboards, plus a large metal cube that was the backup hard drive that kept a copy of all documents created on JorSov's computers. Each monitor occupied a passenger seat, with its computer on the nearest piece of floor. The keyboards were stashed behind the monitors. Three large boxes of paper documents filled the trunk space not taken by the backup hard drive.

They finished unloading just as Slavin drove up.

"I thought we were getting one computer," Fall said. "What's this?"

"This is everything," Slavin told him. "Four computers. Chapman's, Turbin's, the secretary's, and the bookkeeper's. The police took them all in for questioning, and now they're done. Plus three boxes of documents they took, God knows why."

"How can they be done? Don't they want the computers for evidence?"

"To quote Investigator Major Volkov, 'You can throw these away, for all we care. We've got a copy of everything on them.' He said they made their copy *before* they moved the computers, just in case. That may have been a hint, but I didn't think we were ready to take it. Should I have got someone to come copy the disks before moving these?"

"It beats me, Misha. I hope not, because I sincerely don't want to lose whatever's on these things. Volkov didn't make any remarks about Westerners thinking they're so goddamn smart, did he?"

"He did, but I didn't think you needed to hear that part. He also said, 'We've got smart computer guys of our own.' "

"These guys are going all out, aren't they? I wonder what they think is on these computers."

"The answer to all their questions, maybe."

"Maybe. I'd settle for one good answer, right now."

"To what question?"

"How do we get onto Brad's computer without the password?"

They stood looking at each other for several seconds before they simultaneously burst out laughing, at the realization that they didn't have the password either. "I never thought about it until this second," Fall admitted. "I was so busy finding out whether Alexandra knew it, that I didn't ask her what it is, and we surely don't want to ask Volkov."

"We could ask our client," Slavin said, but his tone showed that he knew they couldn't.

"No, if Brad knows we've got these, he'll want them back, and before we poke through them. He certainly won't help us."

"Will Alexandra tell you now?"

"It's hard to know. Maybe, if she thinks that otherwise I'll tell Brad about our talk last night." Fall had already briefed Slavin about that. "If she hasn't told him herself."

"Well, there's always Anatoly," Slavin said.

"Who is Anatoly?"

"He's the son of a friend of mine. He's said to be quite expert on computers. In fact, his father told me he worked for Apple Computer in Cupertino last summer. I think I was supposed to know what Cupertino is."

"That's where Apple Computer is headquartered. How long would it take to get Anatoly down here?"

"Not long if he's at home. His family lives just near Patriarch's Pond. I'll telephone. And while we wait, we could have lunch, I suppose."

"Yes, Misha; we could have lunch." Fall's office, like most Moscow businesses, served lunch for the staff. There was no real alternative. The old state cafeterias, *blynnaya*s and *shaslichnaya*s, hung on, no longer cheap, but as dingy and unpleasant as ever; a restaurant meal took two hours; even McDonald's—there was only one in the entire city—had a thirty-minute line and cost a day's wages for a Russian worker. Fall's office of three lawyers had its own full-time Russian cook, Sveta, who served a huge lunch—the day's main meal for most Russians—in the conference room for the entire staff: lawyers, secretaries, drivers, and all.

When they telephoned, Anatoly was at home. Anatoly was delighted to have new computers to tinker with. Anatoly arrived before lunch was half over and joined in to dispatch his share.

Fall had not expected Anatoly to be quite so young, and when asked, Anatoly was even younger than he looked. Fall took him for sixteen—a thin but soft-faced young man with large Slavic eyes and a wisp of mustache wasting its time trying to make him look eighteen—but he gave his age as fifteen.

"You say Apple Computer hired you last summer?" Fall asked him. "What did they have you doing?" He supposed Anatoly had gone for training of some sort.

"They were interested in a program I had developed," Anatoly said. "A mathematical algorithm for simplifying certain calculations. Breaking codes, for example. There are some codes that can't be broken even in principle; but others can be with sufficient computing power—the only problem is that the time required is longer than the life of the universe. My algorithm shortens the calculation. Now it would take only a hundred thousand years. But with the steady increase in power of real-world computers, eventually the computing time will come down to, say, a few days. Then the algorithm will be the basis of a marketable product. Apple wanted me to come back this summer, but I'm working on my entrance examinations for the university."

While explaining this, Anatoly finished a carrot salad, a bowl of *soup kharcho,* and a pork cutlet. He was a match even for Slavin in capacity and speed of consumption of food and made short work of Sveta's chocolate cake as well. But before the tea arrived, he was eager to get at the computers, and so for tea he and Slavin and Fall adjourned to the spare office where the driver and Fall's secretary had got all the computers and the backup hard drive together. There were enough extension cords and cables to get all the machines running, but they refused to talk to each other or to take any commands. Sveta brought tea and cookies while Anatoly settled down at a machine.

He said to Fall, "You say three of them have the same password, and one different. Do you know which one is which?" Fall did not know. "Well, no matter. Let's see what happens. Do you have a hard disc big enough to copy everything onto? That way we won't lose things like dates documents were last worked on, if we accidentally make some changes."

"We have our own backup hard drive," Fall said; "but it's probably smaller than JorSov's. But if there's any chance of making accidental changes, stop now. If we change anything, the records are useless to us."

"I wouldn't make any changes in the contents," Anatoly said patiently; "but if we were to open a file and accidentally hit the space bar, for instance, if we save that extra space when we close the file, the computer will assign today's date to the file as the date it was last worked on. So we'd no longer have a record of the last date it was *really* worked on. Still, if we're careful, we shouldn't have a problem."

"Is there any way to tell whether the police did that while they had the computers?" Fall asked.

"In principle, no. But Mikhail Alexandrovich told me the police had taken the computers into custody on June ninth, so we know that any dates after that show that something was done by the police, and any before that were done at JorSov—although we don't know by whom. The only ambiguous date is the day the computers were seized. But the computer will automatically label all records with not only the date but the time they were closed after they were last changed. So if you know the time of seizure, you know who made the last change. But maybe that question won't arise."

"It won't if we can't make the computers work," Fall said.

Anatoly smiled. "Let's see."

"By the way," Slavin said, "you understand, Anatoly, that you are employed by me as legal counsel to Bradley Chapman, so that any information you gain here is privileged as lawyer-client information and can't be divulged to anyone other than Mr. Chapman's lawyers without Mr. Chapman's consent?"

"Cool," Anatoly said, in English.

Fall said, "Let the record show that Anatoly has indicated his assent in Californian."

The computers, in the event, kindly identified themselves. When turned on, each gave the name of its assigned user and a space for a password. "That's nice," said Anatoly.

"How do we start?" Fall asked, generously including himself in the task, although he knew he wasn't going to contribute much.

"The best way probably is to start by guessing," Anatoly said. "Most people are very sloppy about passwords. What we're looking for is on Mr. Chapman's computer, we think? Let's start there. If people would do what they're supposed to, and assign a random word as password and change it regularly, this could be hard. Do you think they did?"

"Chapman's secretary said she knew 'the password,' " Fall said. "So I'd guess they never changed it."

"That's nice." Anatoly flexed his fingers in imitation of a pianist beginning a performance. "Let's try names. Names are popular." In the space the computer had left for a password, he typed "Chapman" and pressed RETURN. In a moment the computer notified him that the password was incorrect. Next he tried "CHAPMAN" with the same result. "First name?" he asked.

"Bradley. Or Brad."

Those didn't work either.

"Is he married?" Anatoly asked.

"Joanna." No luck, with or without capitalization.

"Try Jo."

"Too short," Anatoly said; but he tried it anyway, with no result.

"His daughter is Jennifer," Fall said. "Or Jenny, or Jen."

Nothing. Anatoly tried the company name, JorSov, in various capitalized and uncapitalized combinations, but it didn't work either.

"Do you know his mother's family name?" Anatoly asked. "That was a popular item at Apple, among the really security-conscious people. Nobody ever forgets it."

"I don't know," Fall said; "but that's one I could ask Brad without tipping off what we're doing—unless it really is the password. But then if he won't tell me, we know we should try to find it out somehow. We could ask Joanna."

"Do you think Joanna might know the password?" Slavin asked.

"That would be too easy," Fall said. "But I can ask her."

"Can you think of any other names I might try?" Anatoly asked. "Friends, so forth? If not, we can go on to more sophisticated methods. But sophistication can take a while. Guessing is less elegant, but it's usually quicker. I'm disappointed."

"Wait," Fall said. "Try Sasha."

"You think he's named it after you?" Slavin said, smiling. Sasha was the Russian nickname for Alexander.

"We're close personal acquaintances," Fall said. He didn't bother to say, although of course Slavin knew it, that Sasha was also a Russian nickname for Alexandra.

Anatoly typed in "Sasha" and hit the return key. A little clock appeared on the monitor, its hands spinning; and in a few seconds a new screen came up.

"The son of a bitch," Fall said.

Slavin smiled his small sardonic smile. "The she-fox kissed the rooster," he said, "right down to his tail feathers."

"That was certainly easy," Anatoly said. "Hardly something you needed a consultant for, eh?"

Fall, who had just been thinking the same thing, was embarrassed.

"Well," Anatoly said, "let's see if I can earn my fee." He continued to type. "Have we talked about fees, incidentally? One mistake now could do very bad things to the information on this hard disc." For a fifteen-year-old, Fall saw, Anatoly was sophisticated. He had become a comedian in California.

"Let's see what's in here," Anatoly said. The screen was full of file names. He selected one and instructed the computer to open it. A little box came up on the screen: "This file is password protected. Please type in your password."

"Hey, clever," Anatoly said. "Two levels of password protection. I hope the second is no better than the first. Do you know any more friends' names?"

They tried words at random for a few minutes, but then Anatoly began to look bored. "Time to get serious," he said.

Anatoly had arrived with a small case of computer discs. He took one out and inserted it in the disc drive of Chapman's machine.

"What's that?" Fall asked.

"Tools," Anatoly said. "This one's a tool to unscramble a computer's brains. They've probably encrypted this thing by scrambling the driver. I'll try installing a new driver to bypass the one that's on there. This could take a little while. Would it be possible to have Sveta send in more cookies now?"

Fall went to the kitchen to relay the order, stopped in his office to check for messages, returned one phone call, and by the time he got back to the room, Anatoly was smiling again.

"You got it?" Fall asked.

"I've got it."

"What next."

"More tools," Anatoly said, flipping through his box of discs. "This time, a tool to bring back the past."

"A nice trick if you can do it."

"Well, we'll see." Anatoly kept working at the keyboard as he talked. "The nice thing about a hard drive," he said, "is that the past isn't necessarily gone. You said that Mr. Chapman told you he had thrown away his old file. But casual users of computers often don't understand that when they delete a file from a disc, the file does not in fact vanish. The computer simply marks it as something no longer to be used, but it remains on the disc until it's written over during the creation of subsequent files. By the use of tools—programs—designed for the purpose, it can still be retrieved until written over. The nice thing about this case, if what you say is true, is that the police seized the computers. If they weren't totally ham-handed, they won't have written anything to disc—they shouldn't have. And the seizure will have kept anyone else from adding files. So what we should have here is a snapshot of the last changes made to the JorSov files."

At the end of the day, Anatoly had developed that snapshot.

# 20

INNA'S APARTMENT WAS ON THE WAY TO ALEXANDRA'S, AND THE CAR almost took Fall there out of habit, trying to turn at the corner where he had always turned, for he could not help thinking of her as he drove down that street. But he recalled himself and went on, over the river and out Kutuzovsky Prospect.

Before leaving for Alexandra's, Fall had telephoned Brad to make sure he was at home. He did not want any surprises, such as walking in on Brad at Alexandra's apartment. And even though he had telephoned Brad at home a half hour before, he again parked a block away and walked to her building. Lights showed in two of her windows—the kitchen and the living room.

After only an instant of surprise, she seemed perfectly happy that he was at her door. "You're becoming a regular," she said. "Tea again?"

"I brought something more to the point." He put down the bulky plastic bag he was carrying and took two bottles from it. Finlandia. He couldn't tell the difference in vodkas, if there was any, but it wouldn't do for a foreigner to come with a domestic gift.

She smiled. "You're not afraid for your judgment today?"

"I've decided to be bold and take risks. Starting today."

They sat again in the kitchen, old friends. She was dressed in a fuzzy gown and slippers, and she had her makeup off. She was the better for it, he thought. Her skin, without makeup, was like milk. Like Inna's. He cut that thought off.

They drank vodka from her kitchen glasses. They both drank the first glass warily, relying on polite conventional toasts.

As he poured the second, she wondered, "Did you come to get me drunk?"

"No. But to have a friendly conversation."

"Does this make it easier?"

"We'll see."

"Sometimes it's easier to have a friendly conversation lying down."

"But then the alcohol goes to your brain too easily. No, I need you to remember, Sasha."

He had never called her anything but Alexandra before, and she noticed. "Are we being friends now?"

"I hope so. I need your help."

"How can I help you?"

He had brought the bottles in a plastic bag. He put the bag on the table. It was still heavy. There was a stack of papers in it. Anatoly's snapshot. "I want to show you a picture," he said.

"I love looking at pictures. But this must be a lot of pictures!"

"No, it's all one." He spread out several pages on the table. "This is the desktop on Brad's computer." She knew the Macintosh operating system: he didn't have to explain what she was seeing. He had printed out what the screen showed. "And this is yours; and this is the backup hard drive's."

She bit her lip. "Where did you get these?"

"From the computers, of course."

"But . . ."

He would take no questions. "These"—he pointed to other document names on the printout—"are the financial records that the police found. The same on each computer. I won't show you the printouts—I'm sure you know what's in them. They're just duplicates, anyway. The original was on Brad's computer. In this file." He pointed to a file name on the picture Anatoly had printed from the screen of Brad's machine. "There's an interesting thing about this file."

"I'm sure you'll tell me what it is." She worked on her glass of vodka.

"I'm sure you already know."

"Tell me what you think it is."

"It's the date. The computer, as you know, records the date every file was created or last modified. Brad told the investigator, Volkov, that he made this file by accident while he was working on a file of payments the company had made to Turbin. But of course, he didn't. Because on the date this file was made, Brad was in jail. This file was in fact made in the evening on the day before the police seized the computers, when Brad had been in jail for ten days; and it was never modified. And what's more, there is no file of payments to Turbin on any of the hard disks in the JorSov computers, nor on the backup hard drive. But what there is, is this." He drew from the sack a thick printout. "This is a copy of the real financial records of JorSov. It's the same as the one that appears on the list of files on Brad's computer and all the others. Except for one difference. This record shows that dollar payments were made to V. V. Turbin. Except for two differences, actually. The second difference is that this file does *not* appear on the list of files that are on the computer. Why not? Because this file, you see, had been thrown away. It was thrown away immediately after the creation of the other file, the one without payments to Turbin."

Alexandra was brassy. "If it was thrown away, how did you get it? If it wasn't on the computer."

"I didn't say it wasn't on the computer. I said it had been thrown away. Most people don't realize that when they throw away a computer file, it still is on the computer." He explained, without mentioning Anatoly, about recovering records from a computer hard disc.

After a moment, she said, "You're smarter than I thought you were."

It could be nice being a computer nerd. He thought he might take it up in the future.

"Now," he said, "did you change that record?"

She said it hesitantly, but she said it: "Yes. I did."

"When?"

"You've already discovered when. When Bradley was in jail."

"Why did you do it?"

She took a deep breath. "Because I knew that if the police learned that Vladilen Viktorovich was being paid dollars—and so many dollars!—they would be able to think of no reason other than a bribe. And if they thought he was being bribed, they would think that Bradley murdered him to keep him from talking." She shrugged. "So, you see, I had to do it."

"Nice try. But I don't believe you."

"Why do you not?"

"Because as a financial record this document makes no sense. It couldn't possibly be used to hide payments to Turbin. There are too many other places where those payments can be found. The bank records, for one. Marina Ivanovna's brain, for another. If the police are thinking about financial misdeeds, they're bound to question the bookkeeper. They *have* questioned the bookkeeper—her testimony is in the record of the case right now. No, this record really could do only one thing—make the police think that someone made a clumsy attempt to hide payments to Turbin. And who would they think tried to hide the payments? Well, this clumsy attempt appears on a computer that only Brad had the password to—or so he testified. And that's the way it should have been. It's company policy. JorSov is a little company, but Jordan Enterprises is a big company. Big companies write things like that down. I found the Jordan Enterprises policy manual in the documents the police had borrowed. In foreign stations, the office manager's computer contains some records that are not to be accessible to anyone but him. No one is to have his password. So Brad wouldn't have admitted that he gave you the password. Even if the main password weren't Sasha."

She blushed, and then he knew he was right, even though she responded, "But why would anyone want to do that—to make the police think Brad was trying to hide something?"

"Why? Maybe to make them think about JorSov's financial records in a new light—that maybe this *was* a business with something to hide. Or maybe to make them think Brad really was connected with Turbin's death. But you tell me. I believe you have a better impression than I do, on the question of *why*."

She said nothing. The blush was fading from her milk white skin. She had colored down her neck and even into her breasts, where her gown was a little open. She followed his eyes and snapped the gown closed.

"Why, Sasha?" he demanded.

She said nothing.

"Do you want me to have Brad ask you? I'm sure he'll want to know why."

She recovered her composure. "Brad knows why. I told you why already; and I told him the same thing I just told you. I thought the payments were illegal, and I was afraid for him."

"I've told you I don't believe it."

"He does."

"Then we'll have to let Volkov decide what *he* thinks of it."

"No!"

"No? That's his job."

"You don't know what you're doing if you get me into this."

"I'm protecting my client, is what I'm doing."

"No, you're not! You're asking to have Brad killed! If you want to protect him, get him out of the country!"

Fall was taken aback by the force of her words. "I can't get him out of the country until these charges are dropped."

"Don't be stupid. He still has a passport. He has money. He can get out. Nothing else is going to save him."

"But he's innocent." *Or at least, guilty of nothing indictable,* he thought. *But I'm only Brad's lawyer, not his confessor.*

"He's guilty of owning a company someone else wants."

"What? *He* doesn't own anything."

Suddenly Alexandra changed: her shoulders fell; she lowered her eyes, and in a voice suddenly lower, too, she said, "I wish I'd never got into this. No, he doesn't own the company, but it's the same as if he did. Jordan Enterprises owns the foreign part of JorSov. But Bradley *is* Jordan Enterprises, here. And he is the co–General Director of JorSov. And if he is found guilty of something—not Turbin's death, that's nothing, but of some economic crime that a company would benefit from—then JorSov and Jordan Enterprises are guilty of it. And then the state will have to take over the foreign interest in JorSov, to protect the company from criminals. And then maybe somebody else will 'inherit' that piece of the company. Do you understand?"

He did understand. "So you changed the books to make it look as if JorSov was hiding something. Something they weren't really hiding at all."

She said nothing, but she didn't deny it.

"For whom?" he asked her. "Who is behind this?"

"Do you think I know? I'm no one. I'm just a person who works for Bradley and has a chance to help get him out of the way."

"The way Turbin was got out of the way?"

"I don't know anything about Turbin. But that way won't help, with Bradley. They don't want him dead: they want him convicted. Or else made to run. If he runs, it's like being guilty."

"Then the state would step in and take over JorSov."

"Yes."

"And who are 'they'? The 'they' who don't want him dead?"

"I don't know. Nobody I would ever see, I'm sure. I've only seen their seven-by-eights."

"Their what?"

"Their muscular employees. Two of them. They came to see me. They sat right here at this table. One of them sat where you're sitting. They talked about the corruption of good Russian companies by foreigners, and how it was important to have the country's communications in Russian hands, and how I could help to achieve that."

"When was this?"

"The first day Bradley was in jail."

"There was money in it for you, I suppose?"

She bit her lip. "Yes. Why lie about it? It wouldn't have been safe to refuse it. But the money wasn't the reason I did it."

"No?"

"No. I wanted Bradley safe. To get him out of the country—that was the best thing."

"How were you helping to get him out of the country?"

"By making him see that he couldn't win."

Her glass was empty. She took the vodka bottle and poured herself half a glass and drank it.

"Go easy on that," he said, a little ashamed that he had come with the idea of loosening her tongue with it.

"Don't worry, dear guest. *I* know what you've been up to! But in Russia we take vodka with our mothers' milk." She poured another half glass.

"The two men who came to see you: can you describe them?"

She could. And he thought he recognized the description: Slavin had met them too. Or maybe all seven-by-eights fit the same description.

"The other chance," he said, "is not that Brad runs away, but that he wins."

"How can he win? That's stupid."

"You could testify for him."

"And if I did, then what?"

"Then he doesn't have to run."

"But *I* do. Except I've nowhere to run to. You haven't lived in this country, have you? You're such an innocent, Alex, you're like a rabbit! You've *been* in this country, but you haven't *lived* in it. You're a foreigner. If you don't like the conditions, you can always leave. Or if you feel like it, you can stay. You can stay because you can always leave. If I testify and Brad wins, maybe Brad could stay: he's a foreigner. Or Jordan Enterprises could send somebody else in his place. They were ready to do that anyway. But I'm just a Russian. I don't have anywhere to go. And anything could happen to me."

"Jordan Enterprises will get you out," Fall said. "They'll send you to America."

She had been about to pour herself another glass. She stopped. "Would they really do that? How?"

"You could have a job in Houston. With JorSov going well, they need Russian speakers there."

He knew she had been to Houston once, to the Jordan Enterprises headquarters. That was the first trip Turbin made as a co–General Director. Alexandra was his translator.

He could almost see her mind working, balancing hopes and fears. He wondered if Brad Chapman was on the hopes side.

"Are you sure they would take me? And take me before I jump out of my window with someone's help?"

"I'll get you an invitation from Hawke Jordan himself." It was an easy promise. It was just words. But he had got Hawke Jordan into this once. He could do it again, if he had to. "If I arrange to get you out, will you testify to what you've told me?"

"Arrange to get me out, and then I'll decide."

# 21

ON HIS WAY HOME, THE URGE TO SEE INNA STRUCK AGAIN. IT WAS NOT just reflex, this time. He was thinking about her. He was feeling good about himself. He had done something good for a client today, in spite of the client's obstruction. He wanted to tell someone about it. He would tell Slavin, of course. But that was just professional. He wanted to tell Inna. To have her know he was doing good work. To have her know he was doing something useful.

She came to her door dressed in blue jeans and a man's old

work shirt. In the photos he saw of her in the newspapers, she was always conservatively well-dressed these days, as a people's deputy should be; but at home she could still revert to dissidence.

She smiled. She had said to him once, smiling, "When I look at you, Alex, my heart just blossoms." Now she had the same smile, but only for an instant; then it was gone. "It's too late, Alex," she said. She leaned against the edge of the open door—not opening it, not closing it.

"Too late for a visit? Or too late for us?"

"I don't know."

"*I* know. I caught that smile."

"I can't hide anything from you."

"I was passing by. I wondered how you're living."

"Not better than yesterday."

"I hope you don't miss me as desperately as I miss you." *My love.*

"I guess I probably do."

"May I come in?"

Several seconds passed before she stepped back from the door. She closed it behind them. She leaned back against it. "Your slippers are in the closet." Russians never wore shoes at home.

"I'm glad you haven't thrown them out."

"You know I couldn't."

He put on his slippers—old, worn-out Russian cloth *tapochki* that he had bought when he was first a student here, years gone now. He had kept them as a memento back in the States, all those years when he thought he would never return to Russia, a sort of inverse status symbol as they grew shabbier by the year. He had never parted with them until he came to Inna those few days of their honeymoon; and then he had left them here, not wanting to take them back even when she moved to his apartment. They were, he realized now, a claim on her.

He wondered if she thought that too.

"I'll put on the kettle," she said.

Her table was covered with papers. It was the only work surface she had. It was a one-room apartment, counted Russian fashion: one room plus a kitchen and bathroom. There was no space for a desk. Her bed was a pull-out sofa, and the room also held her garderobe and an armchair for visitors and nothing else. It didn't seem small to her. She had grown up living here with her mother, and with both parents when her father wasn't in prison. But at least they had their own kitchen, one not shared with the neighbors.

He glanced at her papers as she made tea. She didn't object, although he could see that some of them were official. None were marked secret. But he didn't suppose she was a likely person to receive secret materials even now—if indeed any People's Deputy was.

"What have you been working on?" he asked, wanting her to ask him the same.

"Still corruption."

"We're comrades-in-arms, then."

"That's a pleasure. What do you mean?"

"The Mafia are trying to steal my client's company." *Mafia* was the Russian word, but it was a word broader than the English equivalent, taking in corruption in government as well as other organized crime.

"Tell me."

He told her—a brief version, without mentioning Alexandra.

"It's terrible," she said. "It's what we've got to stop: what we're going to stop, somehow. Antipov is alarmed about the foreigners stealing the country from the people, and he's right; but stealing from foreigners is no better. We can't arrive at justice through injustice. We've tried enough years of that."

"Is Antipov still a part of what you're doing?"

"Yes, certainly he's involved. I know you don't like him"—it was true that Fall had never liked Vasily Ivanovich Antipov from the day he first saw him with Inna—"but he's a true patriot of Russia."

"Patriotism is the last refuge of scoundrels," Fall said. But she didn't understand. What he had said wasn't a saying in Russian, and in Russian there was simply no way to be ironic about patriotism; so saying it left Inna puzzling over the words and left him feeling guilty—and more so because he thought of that day with Joanna when he said it.

"Vasily is no scoundrel," she said.

"I didn't mean anything against him personally."

"You shouldn't speak against good men. There are enough bad ones in the world."

"I'm sorry, Innochka. I didn't come to quarrel." They had never actually quarreled. Even when she had broken off with him, it had been in anguish on both sides, and not recrimination. He tried to catch her arm, to pull her to him with the idea of kissing her, but she evaded his hand. That she did it without saying anything was the hardest part. And it meant he could say nothing either.

They drank their tea with little talk. When it's over, there is nothing to say. He had never accepted, until then, that it was over.

He left soon, cursing Antipov in his heart, even though he knew Antipov had nothing to do with it.

# 22

FALL SLEPT UNEASILY, TO WILD DREAMS OF LOSS AND ABANDONMENT. Then he fell into heavy sleep, and it was light in his bedroom when a dream of his telephone woke him and became real. His room was bright with morning sun, but darkness in his brain kept him from finding the telephone for a long time. When he found the handset, he recognized Brad's voice long before he could find his ear. "Alex, Alex, are you there?" Brad kept saying.

Fall tried to say yes, without much success at first. At length he croaked out a response. "What time is it, for God's sake, Brad?"

"I don't know what time it is. Alex, you've got to get over here."

"Over where?"

"I don't know. I'm on . . . I'm at a pay phone on Kalinin Prospect. Just get over here, will you?"

Fall grumbled sleepily, "Why don't you come here, Brad?

You're not that far away." Kalinin was only a few minutes walk from Fall's apartment off Arbat Street.

"I don't want to come there. Just get over here, will you?"

Fall finally recognized the panic in Chapman's voice. "What's wrong?"

"I don't want to talk. Meet me on Kalinin at . . . No, you can come to my office. No . . . what the hell, meet me at the Arbat Restaurant." The Arbat was on Kalinin Prospect. Brad's office was twenty minutes' drive from there.

"All right. The Arbat. I'll be there in ten minutes. Do I need to wear a tie?"

He thought he might relax Brad a little; but he didn't. "God damn it, Alex, this is serious! Be there!"

Kalinin Prospect ran straight as a ruler from the Moscow River to Arbat Square. It had been smashed through the winding old streets of the Arbat district at Khrushchev's order. At eight in the morning its whole length was bathed in sunlight, barred by the evenly spaced shadows of the evenly spaced modern office buildings that marched along its southern side in good Socialist array. The lower floors of the office buildings contained shops, department stores, and the Arbat Restaurant.

Fall had come out onto the street a little way east of the restaurant, and he began walking toward it. The sidewalk was crowded and so was the street—even the old limousine lane in the center, formerly kept empty by evenly spaced traffic policemen for the use of Party officials whose limos boomed into the west gate of the Kremlin from their apartments or country dachas. The change was always startling to Fall, even after a year of seeing it daily— ordinary cars driving in the lanes reserved for the rulers.

A car swerved to the curb beside Fall. "Alex! Get in!" It was Chapman. He drove on again as soon as Fall was in the car. "I don't want to be seen here."

"So, why didn't you come to my apartment?"

"I didn't want to be seen there either. You've still got that doorman, don't you?"

"We've 'got' him when he's not asleep. What's wrong with you, Brad?"

"Nothing's wrong with me. I've . . ." He was on the edge of tears, then over the edge. "She's dead, Alex!"

Fall's heart leaped. "Who? Joanna!"

"Joanna! No, for Christ's sake! It's Sasha! She's dead!"

"Pull over." He was afraid Chapman was going to crash the car. He was surprised Chapman obeyed, but he did. "Sasha? Sasha Shubina?" Chapman nodded, unable to speak. "But how can she be? I just saw her . . . not ten hours ago."

Chapman stared at him. "*You* saw her? Where? How?"

"I saw her at her apartment. I was there"—Fall looked at his watch—"yes, ten hours ago."

"Why were *you* there?"

"I was there to find out why she doctored the JorSov financial records, about payments to Turbin."

Chapman ignored this, or didn't hear it. "*You* were there. She was alive?"

"Of course she was alive!"

Chapman seemed half in a trance. "Ten hours ago. She was alive."

"Brad, are you sure she's dead? How did you find out? Did the police call you?"

Chapman looked at him strangely. "Police? No. No police. I found her. She's there . . . in her apartment. She's dead."

Fall was sorry that his first thought was *there goes my case.* But it was. His second was even worse. It was *did you kill her?* But why would he?

Fall didn't think Brad would, but he could think of reasons why Volkov might think so.

"You were there," Brad said. "What were you there for?"

"I just told you."

"You could have killed her."

"Are you crazy, Brad? Why would I kill her?"

"Because she wouldn't do what you wanted. She told me how you were after her."

"She told you *what?*"

He did cry now. "She was there on her bed. . . . Poor Sasha. What am I going to do now?"

"We're going to have to tell the police."

"Tell the police! How can we do that! You know what they're going to think."

Fall did know, unfortunately. They were going to think Brad had killed her.

"They're going to think one of us killed her," Chapman said.

"One of us? One of us?"

"We were both there, last night, this morning. You found her alive; I found her dead. Who's the better suspect?" Chapman was suddenly tearless, and rational in a crazy sort of way.

"We'd better see Slavin," Fall said.

Slavin greeted them with large sleepy eyes and mutters about tea and the hour of the morning. Fall made tea in the kitchen while Slavin dressed. All the shades were drawn in his apartment. He left them that way. They sat in semidarkness, a lamp glowing dimly in the corner of the kitchen, talking in tones of conspiracy.

"Yes, all right, she was my . . . I slept with her," Brad said. "You didn't know her; you can't judge. She was a wonderful woman."

"So is your wife," Fall said.

"Yes, so is my wife, in her own way."

"In her own way? You can't mean you preferred Sasha to Joanna?"

"What I mean about either of them is none of your business."

"We had better talk about what we have to do right now," Slavin said. "As I understand it, we have a dead person to deal with. We have to notify the police."

Chapman seemed astounded. "What? Why do we have to do that?"

"Well, for at least three reasons. One, it's the law. Two, we can't just leave her lying there, can we, until the neighbors begin to wonder? And three, this is Russia. Someone almost certainly noticed one or the other of you being there, so eventually the police are going to know about it."

"No one noticed anyone being at *Turbin's* apartment," Chapman said.

"If there was anyone. But if there was anyone, he or they

were professionals. It's their job not to be noticed. You two aren't professionals; not in that profession."

"I was careful," Fall said. But even as he said it, he knew he hadn't been careful enough. Dozens of people could have seen him, a foreigner visiting a citizens' apartment building. And, more suspicious yet, parking a block away and walking up.

"You haven't said why you were there," Chapman said.

"Yes, I have. You weren't listening. I was there to find out why she changed the JorSov financial records about Turbin's dollar payments."

"She didn't change them. I told you that was just a mistake I made working on the records."

"Yes; but you lied."

"You son of a bitch, don't call me a liar! You think I can't fire you?"

"Fire me. You think you can find another lawyer who'll keep your ass out of prison?"

"We have more a important question to discuss right now," Slavin said firmly. "What to do about Alexandra. Now why don't you tell me what you know, so that we can be ready before you have to talk to the Investigator."

Chapman leaned forward, his elbows on the table, his face in his hands, as if still to keep his part in this hidden. "I went to pick her up on the way to work," he said.

"You called me at seven, or not long after," Fall said. Slavin laid a hand on his arm to stop him from saying more.

"We start early," Chapman said, recognizing the implicit accusation.

"Start *what* early?" Fall asked.

"Just tell us what happened," Slavin said. "We can discuss philosophical issues later."

"I found her on the bed—"

Slavin interrupted him. "How did you get into the apartment?"

Chapman stopped, bit his lip, thought for a moment but didn't answer.

"Did you ring the bell?"

"No. I had ... I have a key."

"Do you still have it?"

"Yes."

"Give it to me." Chapman took out a set of keys in a leather keyholder. He extracted one and handed it to Slavin. "Did you see anyone outside the building or on the stairs, on your way in?" Slavin asked.

"No. No one."

"Did you leave your car outside the building?"

"Yes. I parked it on the street, just at the end of the building."

"Do you park there frequently?"

"What the hell does that have to do with anything?" But Slavin only looked at him with a slow owl-blink of his eyes. "Yes."

"Were there any other cars there?"

"No, except for an old Zil under a cover. It's always there. I guess somebody's restoring it, or trying to get it to run."

"She was on the bed," Slavin prompted him.

"I thought she was asleep. I said to her, 'Sasha,' and then when she didn't wake, I shook her shoulder, and then . . ." He started to say something else but couldn't say it. He moved his hands down his face, wiping tears from his eyes with his fingertips. "Her eyes didn't open. She was dead."

"Was her body rigid?"

"I . . . No. No, she was just like life; but she was cold."

"Could you tell how she died? Were there any marks on her? Any bruises? Any signs of a struggle?"

"I told you: I thought she was asleep. God, she looked so beautiful!"

It was some time before he could answer the next question. "What did you do then?"

He said at length, "I didn't know what to do. The only thing I could think of was to call Alex. I didn't want to do it from there. I thought the phones . . . you don't know who's listening, do you? I left."

"You called Alex. Where from?"

"A pay phone on Kalinin."

"When you left, did you see anyone?"

"There was an old woman, between Sasha's building the next one. An old woman with a dog."

"Had you ever seen her before?"

"Yes. I think she lives in the next building. I'd seen her outside with the dog."

"Did you touch anything in the apartment?"

"I don't remember. I touched *her*. I don't think so."

"His fingerprints will be everywhere anyway," Fall said.

Slavin ignored Fall. "Did you wipe the doorknob as you left?"

Chapman flashed a dark glance at him, as if caught in a shameful secret. "Yes."

"Do you have any idea what she might have died of?"

"No. She looked like she was asleep."

"Was there anything else you saw that caught your attention? Anything at all?"

"No." Then he paused, as if physically seeing something, seeing it for the first time. "There was a vodka bottle beside the bed. A bottle and a glass. I never saw her drink vodka. I think they were empty."

Fall suddenly felt empty himself.

Slavin said to Chapman, "I'm going to talk with Alex about his visit with Sasha. I don't want you to hear it."

"I want to hear it."

"I know you do. And it would be fair for you to hear it. But there's a good reason you can't. He's your consular representative. So the police aren't likely to ask him any questions about what you said, and even if they do, he can refuse to answer, and there's nothing they can do about it. It's a gray area, what right they might have to ask him questions as a witness; but in practice they're not going to press him. But *you're* not *his* representative. So the police have a right to learn from you anything he says to you about his own actions. If there's more you should know, and it's safe for you to know, we'll tell you."

"Lawyers always stick together," Chapman said.

Slavin was not offended. "Good lawyers do what's in the interest of their client, whether the client likes it or not. Why don't you wait in my bedroom."

They sat in silence until the bedroom door closed. Then Slavin asked, "May I safely assume she was alive when you last saw her?"

"Nobody likes a wiseass, Misha."

"Sorry. But thoroughness is a virtue in a lawyer. May I safely assume . . . ?"

"She was alive when I last saw her. She was sitting in her kitchen drinking vodka."

"Might it have been the same bottle that was beside her bed?"

"It might have. You didn't ask what brand it was."

"That's correct. Maybe it's better not to focus our client on things he didn't notice for himself. You were taking something along to loosen her up a little, as we discussed?"

"That's correct. Also, it's very likely my fingerprints will be on the bottle, and on the glass beside her bed: I poured her a drink. And even if they're not, they'll be on another glass in the kitchen, unless she washed the dishes before she went to bed. I doubt she was that precise a housekeeper."

"So, what did you learn from her last night?"

"I learned that she cooked the books to make it look as if JorSov was hiding payments to Turbin. I learned that someone is trying to take over the foreign-owned part of JorSov by having Brad convicted of some economic crime so the government will seize Jordan's interest in the company; or else they want to scare him into skipping out of the country, which would have the same result without their having to convict him. I learned that she claimed not to know who was behind the scheme. Probably she was telling the truth. I learned she had ideas of marrying Brad herself, and getting herself out of the country too. I learned that she started drinking vodka with her mother's milk, and that she'd have got into bed with me in a second if she thought it would help her get any of what she wants without endangering any bigger part of what she wants. Sasha was quite an operator. What did *you* learn about her? Were your old friends from the Militia Academy any help?"

"You know how this country operates," Slavin said. "Friends are always useful. Yes, I learned some things. Nothing so much to the point as what you've discovered. But some things." He sat for a moment as if listening to the past. "Sasha Shubina was an ambitious person. She always wanted what the people had who are on the List of Names. But she didn't have family connections, so what she got, she got by her wits and her beauty. She was allowed to go to the English School with the children of the *Nomenklatura* because she was smart; and she married the otherwise useless son of the director of an institute of the Academy of Sciences because she was beautiful and smart enough not to show how smart she was. She divorced him when she couldn't stand him anymore, but she was smart enough to get a good apartment of her own out of the divorce, and by that time she probably had her eyes on something bigger. You already know she was smart enough to get a job with a foreign company, which gave her a chance really to escape her past. She might have had hopes of marrying her boss, as you suggest. She was beautiful enough for that to be a plausible ambition. But then she found herself forced to choose. We don't know what the terms were— maybe a piece of JorSov for herself. Probably not. But the choice is clear: them or us. 'You can help us get control of this company and expect our gratefulness; or you can refuse and take your chances.' The same choice I've been offered. Probably she thought that she might have it both ways: help them by scaring Chapman out of the country and have a chance to go with him too. Instead she got neither. Possibly the outcome I'll be faced with too." Behind his glasses, his eyes were large as owls' in the dim light. As large, and as unintimidated. He seemed neither frightened nor excited, but only analytic.

"So what do we do now?" Fall asked.

"As I said before, we call the police. And we prepare you and Mr. Chapman to answer some hard questions."

"Couldn't we go clean up the apartment first?"

Slavin shook his head. "Your fingerprints? No."

Fall started to protest: he suddenly had a much keener understanding of his client Bradley Chapman than he had ever had before.

Slavin interrupted him. "It would only make things worse. We couldn't get in and out without being seen. We couldn't be certain of getting everything clean. And, most important of all, I am an officer of the court, and arguably you are too. It is not ethical for us to hide evidence from the Investigator."

"But what happened was not at all what it's going to look like."

"Then it will be our job to convince the Investigator of that."

"Who will investigate? Volkov?"

Slavin thought a moment. "If we report it to 02"—the police emergency number—"whatever investigator is on duty will get the job. When he learns of the connection with JorSov—with Turbin and with Chapman—he'll have to contact Volkov. Probably then Volkov would take over. But it will be better to report it to Volkov directly, I think. He's the devil we know. At least we won't have to educate anyone. And it will make him look good, to be the one who hears it first. If you want a friend, help someone look good."

"We can certainly use a friend," Fall said.

# 23

IT WAS NOT YET MIDMORNING WHEN VOLKOV SENT A NOTICE TO HAVE Chapman come to his office immediately. Fall had expected to receive one too; but he didn't. Instead, he had a telephone call from Murchison, the United States Consul. "Get your butt over here," Murchison said.

"Any reason?"

"Yes. You're using the name of my office. I want to know who you've killed."

"My master's voice," Fall said to Slavin, covering the phone with his hand. "You're going to have to get Brad ready for Volkov yourself."

"What do I tell Volkov?" Chapman asked.

"You tell him the truth," Slavin said. "It's too hard to keep track of lies. They've done us enough damage already."

Volkov interviewed Chapman without counsel present: he was a witness, not a suspect. Slavin objected on the ground that Chap-

man was already charged in another case and so was entitled to
have his lawyer present anytime an investigator interviewed him;
but Volkov was not moved. He said, "If this *is* a related case, I
might agree with you, Comrade Advocate. But Citizen Shubina
might have died in any number of ways. Until we know more,
do you really want me to assume that her death is related to the
troubles at the JorSov joint venture? I would think not."

Slavin, of course, thought not too, however much he wanted
to be present for the questioning.

Murchison kept Fall waiting outside his office, a show of
power that did not amuse Fall.

When he was finally shown in, the greeting was, "Why are the
police after you?"

"It's not the police. It's the Prosecutor's office."

"Is there a difference?"

"Yes. The police police, the Prosecutor prosecutes."

"Why does he want to prosecute you?"

"I hope he doesn't. An investigator wants to talk to me about
a dead woman. But you know that already."

"Yeah. This Russian sent me a note." He tossed the note across
the desk to Fall. "It's in Russian."

"It's a request for your permission to interview me."

"I know that. We do have translators." Murchison was looking at a typed page of English, apparently the translation of
the request. "You natives just can't stay away from the Russki
girls, can you." Life as a consul had left Murchison ignorant
of the real Moscow and fearful of it, and envious of those
who weren't.

"I was doing my job," Fall said. "She was a potential witness."
He didn't want to tell Murchison more than he had to: who knew
whom he'd talk to?

But Murchison wasn't interested in that anyway. He leaned
back in his chair as he scanned the translation.

" 'Believed to be the last person to see her, late last night.' You
work long hours, Fall."

"It's an occupational hazard."

"Sure. How was she?"

"I didn't know her personally."

"Did you kill her?"

"Don't be stupid."

Murchison dropped the front legs of his chair back to the floor and leaned across the desk. "I'm going to *stop* being stupid, at least. I'm going to terminate your representation of Mr. Chapman and replace you with one of my people. And then Volkov won't have to ask my permission to interview you." He looked at the translation again. " 'Interrogate' you. You said 'interview,' but this says 'interrogate.' "

"They're the same in Russian," Fall said, although he knew they weren't. He had been trying to soften the situation in his own mind, using the word *interview*. "But whatever it is, I don't mind talking to Volkov. And of course you can do what you want about replacing me. But I don't know what Mr. Jordan will think about it. He's indicated that he wants Chapman to have an American lawyer. I suppose it wouldn't have to be me, although I've been representing JorSov for a long time. Are any of your people lawyers, Murchison?"

"You're an insufferable, arrogant asshole, Fall."

Fall shrugged. "I don't think those who know me well consider me arrogant. But two out of three ain't bad."

"I expect you to answer every question this investigator puts to you. It's our policy to cooperate with local authorities here."

"Mine too."

"And I expect a full report from you. I haven't tried to keep up with what you're doing, for two reasons. One, I assume you report to Jordan Enterprises, since they're paying you. And two, I don't like you. I don't like talking with you, and I want to see as little of you as possible."

"You should speak your mind freely, Ira. Don't hold back. Just release your feelings. It'll make you feel better. Like relief from constipation."

"Get out."

"Just what I had in mind, Ira. Nice talking to you."

After Murchison, it was almost a relief to be interrogated by Volkov.

The interrogation took place in an interview room of the Department of Investigations, next door to Butyrskaya Prison. Both
buildings were built from the same buff brick, and it gave Fall a
chill to walk inside on a personal basis. He wished Slavin could
be with him; but at least, if they didn't offer him a lawyer, he
wasn't a suspect. Yet.

Volkov opened his black leather notebook, wrote the date on
a ruled page, and began: "So, you talked with Shubina in her
apartment last night. Tell me about it."

Fall declined this invitation to ramble. He said, "I went there
about nine-thirty and left there about ten-thirty." Then he waited
for a question.

"What was the purpose of your visit?"

"I wanted to ask her some questions concerning my client, Mr.
Chapman. They arose out of a discussion I'd had with her the
previous night." Fall wanted to be sure that, without giving away
more than he had to, he made Volkov aware of both nights'
meetings. It would not be good to have the Investigator discover
the earlier meeting for himself.

"You talked with her the night before as well?"

"Yes, I did."

"You are not an investigator. Nothing in the law gives you the
right to contact witnesses in a criminal investigation."

"So far as I was aware—in fact, so far as I *am* aware—she was
not a witness. Her name hasn't appeared in any of the evidence
which has been shown to us. I believed she had information that
was relevant, and I thought it was my duty to see if I was right,
and to present that information to the Investigator."

"Did you obtain any information?"

"I did. I was going to suggest that Advocate Slavin ask for
Shubina to be added as a witness in the trial of Mr. Chapman.
But we've lost that chance now."

"That chance, if not more. What information did she have?"
Before Fall could answer, Volkov added, "Did this have anything
to do with Slavin's request for the return of JorSov's computers?"

Asking a second question before the first was answered was
bad technique, by conventional standards; but in fact Volkov's
guess put Fall off-balance. Fall did not want to have to admit—

not yet—that Chapman had lied about the computer records. Not without a witness to the truth, and the witness was dead. Fall said, "Shubina admitted that she was the one who changed the computer records to delete dollar payments that had been made to Turbin."

"Why would she change the records?"

Fall was not ready to tell Volkov what he had finally got out of Shubina—that she had changed the records under orders, as part of a plot to take over JorSov. He did not know if it was true; but if it was, he also didn't know who was in on it. There was no reason to think that Volkov was; there also was no reason to think that he—or someone above him—wasn't. Finally, Fall settled for telling a half-truth, by passing on Shubina's first version of her reasons: "She told me that she was afraid that if the records showed dollar payments to Turbin, the police would think that was evidence of bribery. So she erased those payments."

Volkov's response made Fall afraid, for a moment, that Volkov already knew more than Fall had told him. "Who ordered her to change the records?" Volkov asked.

Fall tried to equivocate. "I don't know. She wouldn't tell me. Or not yet. Not *then*," he corrected himself. "Yet" implied that she might do it in the future. Sasha Shubina had no future. The only remaining reference to her was "then."

"At Mr. Chapman's order, surely," Volkov said. "He was her direct superior."

Fall relaxed then: Volkov was still trying to tie the changes to Chapman. Fall proceeded in the opposite direction; "No, not at Mr. Chapman's order. When she made the change, he was in Butyrskaya Prison. He had no way to contact her; you made sure of that yourself."

"It *is* unfortunate you have no witness to this."

"There is a witness, in a way."

"Yes? And what witness is this?"

"The computers themselves are witnesses."

"The computers?"

Fall explained about the record of transactions on the computer discs.

"But you took the computers yesterday," Volkov said. "You could have changed them."

"You told Slavin you have a copy of everything on them. We couldn't have changed that. And if the files still on the computers match your copy, that will prove we didn't change the originals. I don't object to your checking."

"Objection would not be effective," Volkov said dryly. "I'll send an officer for the computers. They're at your office?"

"Yes."

Volkov went to a telephone in the corner, called someone, and then returned to the table. He resumed, "So there was a reason you might have wanted to see Citizen Shubina dead."

"That's ridiculous. She was going to free my client."

"So you say. But let us begin again at the beginning. You arrived at her apartment when?"

"About nine-thirty."

"What happened first?"

"She asked me in. I had brought some vodka as a gift, so we opened it and had a toast."

"Why had you brought vodka?"

"She had offered me vodka the night before. She seemed disappointed when I refused. I thought it might make things more comfortable—a friendly gesture."

"Do you habitually refuse drinks offered by women?"

"Is that relevant?"

"No. What sort of vodka was it?"

"Finlandia. Two bottles."

"Did you know Shubina to drink large quantities of vodka?"

"Is two liters a large quantity in Russia?"

"One hears many stories about Russian consumption of vodka. As to Americans . . . have you ever drunk a liter in one evening yourself?"

"No. I hope I never do."

"How much did you drink with Shubina?"

"A hundred grams. A hundred and fifty."

"And she?"

"She drank two and a half, maybe three glasses while I was there. Two hundred and fifty grams."

"And what was her condition when you left her?"

He thought carefully. "Relaxed, but not drunk."

"Did she express any intention to continue drinking?"

"No."

"Was she despondent?"

"No."

"Worried?"

"I'd say hopeful." Fall could have made out a case for either, but he didn't want Volkov to get into questions about what might have been worrying Shubina.

"What was she hopeful about?"

"Getting Bradley Chapman acquitted."

"When you left her apartment, you left the second, unopened, bottle of vodka behind?"

"Yes."

"Why?"

"You don't take away a bottle you brought to someone's house."

"A Russian doesn't leave without finishing a bottle he brought to someone's house."

"Well, it takes a difference of opinion to make a horse race."

"You drank a hundred fifty grams, and she drank two hundred fifty; so when you left, there was six hundred grams left in the first bottle, plus another liter. Correct?"

"Plus whatever she had at home. She offered me vodka the night before." Volkov was writing notes. Fall said, "Why is it so important how much we drank? You aren't thinking of charging me with drunk driving, are you?"

Volkov continued to write. "I hadn't considered it, but very clever. I will keep it in mind for some other opportunity." He finished writing and looked up at Fall. "We've had the report back from the pathology laboratory. Shubina died of alcohol poisoning."

"Good God!"

"Also, a search of the apartment found one empty vodka bottle, Finlandia brand, beside her bed. There was a half-empty bottle of Stolichnaya in a kitchen cabinet. A second bottle of imported vodka was not found. The Finlandia bottle bore two different kinds of fingerprints, mostly rather smeared. But one was definitely Shubina's. The second type is unidentified. Possibly unidentifiable; but we will want to take your fingerprints."

"I'm sure the second will be mine. I carried the bottle and poured from it. My fingerprints should also be on a glass that I drank from."

Volkov frowned and flipped through his sheaf of papers. "Where did you leave the glass?"

"On the kitchen table. She might have moved it."

Volkov said nothing; but from that nothing, Fall knew that the police had not found a glass with fingerprints.

When he met Slavin after the interrogation, Fall was depressed—depressed at even being thought of as a possible suspect in a murder, but more depressed at the loss of his witness. But he was most depressed at the thought of Sasha Shubina lying dead beside an empty vodka bottle that he had brought to her. Whatever her shortcomings, she had been an energetic and resourceful and beautiful woman.

"We'll meet our client at your office in an hour to debrief him," Slavin said. "I didn't want him hanging around the Department of Investigations. He's not cheerful."

"I wonder why."

Slavin started to explain why, until Fall pointed out that his remark was ironic.

"Ah. American irony. Well. It's a wonderful thing. I hope I can learn to use it." After that, as they drove, Slavin settled for questioning Fall about the interrogation.

Slavin expressed no dissatisfaction with Fall's report, but he gave no compliments either. Mainly he went back over details. The drinking glass was one of them.

"I wouldn't have believed she'd wash the glasses after I left," Fall said.

"Is this irony?"

"No. It's an invitation to a discussion."

"Ah. Good. Well, I wouldn't have either," Slavin said.

"But the police didn't find it."

"Then that leaves three possibilities: either it wasn't there, or they simply overlooked it—"

"Look out!" Fall grabbed the steering wheel with one hand and swerved the car out of the path of a bus coming out from the curb. When he was thinking hard, Slavin tended to lose track of the world.

"Thank you," Slavin said, unperturbed.

"My pleasure. As for the glass, it's not likely the police overlooked it, whether it was on the table or she moved it to the sink."

"Or its condition was changed."

"What does that mean?"

"Someone removed the fingerprints, although not Shubina. Someone possibly even put the glass away, although not Shubina."

"Who would have done that?"

"The only answer that makes sense to me is, someone who knew her. Someone came after you left, had a drink with her, and washed the glasses—including the one you had left, if indeed they didn't use the same one. Not everyone is fastidious. But why would unfastidious people, or any other midnight guest, wash the glasses and put them away, leaving their hostess dead drunk? Either they were very tidy—that is, not Russian—or they wanted to destroy any evidence that they had been there. To remove fingerprints, in short. Perhaps they had used your glass, perhaps they inadvertently mixed them up and therefore washed yours to be certain. Let's assume they did it to remove fingerprints. Why would they want to do that? Only one reason comes to mind: that after drinking with her, they killed Shubina.

"Who might have done that? If we think like Investigator Volkov for a moment, unfortunately, there is one easy answer: our client. He saw you leave, went to Shubina's apartment, accepted her offer of a drink, interrogated her about what you had been doing there so late at night and why did it involve imported vodka, and dissatisfied with the answer, killed her in a jealous rage. Then he destroyed the evidence of his own presence as best he could, carefully leaving the evidence of yours—the bottle you had opened and used before he arrived. The only thing inconsistent with the story he told you is the time of his arrival at her apartment. Otherwise, there are many differences—mostly omissions—but no inconsistencies."

"I'm glad you're not the investigator, Misha," Fall said. "I don't think he's got that far yet. I hope he never does. But I don't believe any of it."

"No? I don't either. Why don't you?"

"First, because I know Brad. Even if he would kill someone in a fit of rage, I'll never believe he'd poison a woman by forcing alcohol down her throat. Second, because he wasn't faking when he called me this morning and when I brought him here. He had really gone to pieces, and he hadn't been holding that in since late last night. And third, because he should have been at home at that time last night; and if he was, his wife can vouch for it."

"Wouldn't she lie for him?"

"Jo?" Fall couldn't imagine it. But then . . . of course she would, to save her husband, Jen's father. But then . . . to save a husband who had been with his mistress instead of at home?

"Volkov would certainly expect it of any wife," Slavin said. "But if not our client, then who?"

"The 'muscular employees' she told me about," Fall said. "The employees of whoever is after JorSov. They came to see her here before, she said. They sat at this table and talked, she said. If they did it before, why not again? And when they didn't like what she said, or didn't believe it, they killed her. Brad's not the kind of guy who would do it; but they are, if they're anything like the two you told me about. And since they had taken a drink with her, they washed up the glasses to remove any fingerprints."

"It's a plausible hypothesis," Slavin said.

"But Volkov seems inclined to think that I made up a story for her and then killed her to keep her from denying it."

"No, I don't think he could really believe that. There would be no point in your killing her to keep her from contradicting a story you say she told only to you. With her dead, her story won't get into evidence. There's nothing she could contradict. No, if we want her story in evidence, we'll have to prove it all over again."

"The only way I can see to get there is to find out who killed Shubina."

"It's possible, of course, that she simply drank too much by herself, without intervening force."

"You can't believe that."

"I'm thinking for Volkov again. Here is a woman whose life has fallen apart. Her lover, whom she hoped would be her ticket to America, was separated from her by the force of the law and now has been released and has returned to a wife who has stood by him valiantly. He is going to be tried for economic crimes. If he is found guilty, he goes to prison—so the woman loses him. If he is found not guilty, he goes home to America with his wife—so the woman loses him. The future of the company which employs her is in doubt. No matter what she does, there will be questions about her part in the mess. In short, she has bet on all of the wrong horses. She had abundant reasons to drink. It's not necessary to think that she intended to drink herself to death. The death would have been an accident. It would certainly not be the first accidental death by alcohol that Volkov has seen in his career. I've seen more than one myself."

"You could almost convince me, Misha. But there are still some troubling details: if Alexandra drank herself to death, who washed the glasses?"

"She might have washed them herself, before she climbed into bed with the remainder of the vodka."

"But you don't believe it, and neither do I. But even more troubling: if she drank herself to death, where is the second bottle?"

"If she finished it, I suppose she threw it away," Slavin said.

"Why didn't the police find it in her trash?"

"She dropped it in the trash chute, of course. Or if she was drinking with someone who killed her, that person dropped it in the trash chute."

"Trash chute?"

It took Slavin a moment to understand Fall's puzzled look. "Ah, you live in one of those old Arbat-district buildings, don't you. You have to carry out your trash. Out where Shubina lives the buildings are all Khrushchev's era. There's a trash chute in every kitchen. The trash falls straight to the basement."

"Turn around," Fall said.

"Turn around? I can't. I'm driving."

"Turn the car around, Misha."

"Turn the . . ." His face lit up. "Of course! To Shubina's building!"

It took them twenty minutes to find the caretaker of Shubina's building where she was sleeping in a chair down behind the elevator cage in the basement of another staircase. She woke grudgingly—a thick-legged, old woman dragged from dreams of her youth. "What do you want? What?" she demanded out of her sleep.

"We want the key to the trash room for the north corner apartments on Staircase One," Fall said.

"Staircase One. Where poor Alexandra Ivanovna lived. What do you want? Are you more police?"

"No. We're friends of hers."

"Friends! Fancy friends *she's* got. Too many of them. Go away."

Fall took out his wallet, extracted a hundred-ruble note, and with the note in his hand repeated his request for the key to the trash room. The changed circumstances had a powerful effect on the old woman's mind and on her tone of voice. "You should have *said* you were friends," she murmured. She took the note, stuffed it into a pocket in her dress under her gray apron, and reached out a hand to be helped to her feet. "Any friend of poor Alexandra Ivanovna's, friend of mine." From a nail on the wall she took a wire ring with several dozen keys jammed onto it. Fall and Slavin helped her up the short flight of stairs to ground level and followed as she shuffled out the door, up the sidewalk, and into Staircase One, and again down the stairs beside the elevator. At a door in the damp block wall she stood trying keys and muttering under her breath.

"Police," she said. "Police were everywhere."

"Did they come down here too?" Fall asked.

"Down here? No. What for? Poor Sasha's apartment is up there, not down here."

She found the right key at last and swung the door aside.

A single incandescent bulb was burning in the trash room. It threw a circle of light across one side of a mound of kitchen garbage, papers, trash of all descriptions that formed a pinnacle under the aperture of the trash chute in the ceiling and sloped away in all directions to an alluvium of trash that covered almost the entire floor. As they stood at the door, a rattling sound heralded a new arrival: a bottle dropped from the opening, bounced from the top of the pinnacle, rolled down the alluvial slope, and ended at their feet. The woman kicked it off into a corner outside the room.

"How often do you clear this out?" Slavin asked.

"Every three days," the woman said. "But not me. Borya does it."

Slavin looked doubtful of her facts. "Was all this done in the last three days?"

"Sometimes Borya misses a day," she admitted.

"Sometimes two?"

She inclined her head, a kind of shrug of the shoulders. "Sometimes."

"Don't you have a trash container?" Fall asked.

"Sure, of course we do! Right outside there in the alley. Borya takes this right out there. There's his shovel." She pointed to a battered instrument leaning against the wall just inside the door.

Fall and Slavin looked at each other.

They started with the top layer, assuming that nothing from the previous night would yet be covered. They found vodka bottles in plenty, but no Finlandia. They found Rossiiskaya, Gorkaya, Limonnaya, and Stolichnaya; but no Finlandia.

Then, because they had to be sure, they began moving trash. The old woman wandered away, muttering about insanity, as with Borya's shovel they scraped a layer at a time into the far corners and up against the walls, until the pinnacle was gone and in its place was a Dead Sea of stagnant air surrounded by barren hills of trash.

They had more bottles—plenty of vodka and wine and some beer and one Armenian cognac—but no Finlandia.

Fall threw down the shovel in disgust. He had tried to be tidy, but his trousers were filthy to the knees. He wiped his hands on them. He said, "Education is a great leveler." He sympathized with Borya, now that he knew more.

"I'm certainly learning a lot from you about Western ways of representing a client," Slavin said.

"We're a full-service law firm, Misha." Fall looked around at their handiwork and, struck by the absurdity of it, began to laugh, and Slavin did too.

"Well, we did what we had to," Fall said. "At least we know she didn't throw it away."

"Then someone took it," Slavin said. "Which means someone was there after you and before Brad."

# 24

BRAD CHAPMAN HAD ALWAYS BEEN AN IDEAL CLIENT. SOME LAWYERS would have defined the ideal client as one who always followed his lawyer's advice, but Fall didn't. Brad Chapman was a man who asked for advice, considered it, made up his mind what to do, and never worried about a done decision.

That was before Volkov. Before Turbin's death. Before Alexandra's.

Now Brad Chapman was a man who didn't know what to do, didn't want advice, and didn't want to talk about it.

They went through his interrogation once—or at least his interrogation as he reported it—but he balked at any follow-up questions. "I have had it with talking about this," he said finally. "Volkov has been looking for any charge he can throw at me. Now he's got a big one. And I just don't feel like talking about it. Okay?"

"Volkov didn't spend half the time with you that he did with me," Fall said. "If you go by that, he should be twice as suspicious of me as he is of you."

"You're just fresh meat," Chapman said. "He needs a diversion. But he'll get back to me soon enough."

"I don't see why you think so, if you told him what you told us."

"What else would I tell him?"

"Don't be hostile. But if all you said was you went there at seven this morning . . ." Chapman suddenly looked sick. Fall said, "You didn't go there last night, did you, Brad?"

"No. I didn't go there last night."

"Then what's wrong?"

But Chapman would say no more.

When Fall got home, she was waiting in the hall, outside the door of his apartment. She was leaning against the wall, her arms crossed under her breasts, her long Minnesota legs crossed below the hem of her yellow dress. The dress glowed in what was left of evening in the hallway. "Hello, sailor," she said.

"Jo! How did you get here?" He had thought it was Inna, at first.

"The KGB brought me," she said.

"The KGB?"

"Or whoever that was that I've been talking to."

"Who have you been talking to?"

"The Investigator. Volkov. He's cute. You didn't tell me he's cute."

"Volkov brought you here?"

"No. His driver did. A man with a badge, in a plain white car. Was it the KGB?"

"The KGB doesn't exist anymore, by that name. It's the Ministry of Security now. The MBR. But . . ."

"Whoever. Aren't you going to invite me in?"

"Yes. Sure. Come in. But Volkov? Why would he . . . ?"

Through the door, as he opened it, the last evening light from his windows illuminated her face. She had been crying. She saw her face in his hall mirror. "Sorry for this mess," she said. Her mascara had made slender sorrowful trails on her cheeks. She took a tissue from her purse and wiped at her eyes.

"Volkov came to question you?"

She continued to wipe carefully at her eyes and cheeks. "Had me brought in. Is that how they say it in the movies? 'Haf Joanna Chapman brought in for kvestioning.'" She folded the tissue carefully, dropped it back into her black purse, and closed the purse.

She continued to look into the mirror. In her yellow dress, she looked like a spring flower. The reflection of a spring flower. A tall spring flower.

"What did he ask you?"

"Where my husband was last night. Whether he—"

He interrupted her: "What did you tell him?"

"Oh, he was home. We went to bed early. He got up early. He had an 'early meeting at the office.' Then Volkov asked me, 'Was your husband in the habit of picking up his secretary on his way to work?' I said, 'I don't know.' I'd never thought about it. 'But he had an early meeting at the office,' I said, 'so I don't think he was picking her up this morning.'" She turned to face Fall. "Have you ever seen one of those puzzles—optical illusions I guess—where there's an hourglass shape or a birdbath or something, just a black shape on a white background, and suddenly it changes and suddenly it's a white shape on a black background, and it's not a birdbath, it's two faces looking at each other? Everything is just the opposite of what it was before. Well, Volkov showed me one of those puzzles. And it was my life." She bit at her lip and wouldn't look at him. "How long have you known, Alex?"

"Known what?"

"Don't give me that crap. I don't deserve it from you. How long have you known Brad was cheating on me? All those late nights at the office. All those out-of-town trips. Coming back early from Belaya Gora, for God's sake!"

"I didn't—" he started to speak, but she interrupted him.

"And why didn't you tell me? My God, I even told you that I loved you, but there I was still being the faithful little wife in spite of that, and *still* you didn't tell me! I guess you were laughing at me the whole time, weren't you."

"I wasn't laughing at you, Jo. I'd never laugh at you. And I didn't know about Brad until this morning. I hadn't even guessed anything until . . ."

"Until when?"

"It doesn't matter. I'm not going to talk about it. He's my client."

"Screw your attorney-client privileges. If I mean anything at all to you, you're not going to hide behind that crap. Until when?"

"A couple of days ago."

"Why then?"

"I saw him with her."

"Doing what?"

"It's not going to help to know about it."

"It must have been hot stuff, if you won't tell me."

"I was going to her apartment to ask her some questions. Brad dropped her off. She kissed him—outside in the car. Then he left. It was nothing." He thought of Alexandra's words: *it was just silliness.* Words he hadn't believed either.

"It was enough to make you know something was going on."

"I didn't know."

"It was enough to make you suspect."

"All right."

"And you didn't tell me."

"Tell you that I suspect your husband of playing around? How could I? Leave out that he's my client. Could I break up your marriage? You wouldn't thank me for that."

"I might. I might be damn glad you did. It's something I've thought about often enough. Ever since we were in Belaya Gora." She stepped forward and put her arms around him, dropping her purse on the floor. " 'I couldn't do that to my husband,' I thought. 'I have to be a good wife.' Well, I've been a good wife; but he didn't mind doing it to *me*. So let him live with it. The funny thing is, here I am grilling you about Brad, and I don't even care that much what he's been up to. Except for my pride."

She kissed him. She was almost as tall as he was. He thought, for an instant, of Inna, standing on tiptoe to kiss him. Only for an instant.

"Can I stay tonight?" she asked.

"Stay? Here?"

"Do you have a hideout someplace else? Of course here."

"What about Jen?"

"She's staying with Lyuba and her daughter. She's all right. She's stayed with them before."

"You know you can't stay."

"You don't want me?"

"You know I do."

"Who are you being true to? Your client? Your lady friend?" When he didn't answer, she tried a couple of others. "Your dog-gone attorney ethics? Yourself?"

"I don't know. All of the above, I guess. I was never good at multiple-choice tests."

"Are you afraid it's malpractice to sleep with your client's wife?"

"I suppose that depends on how good I am in bed?"

"I've always been a pushover for a sense of humor." She kissed him again. "I want to sleep with you, Alex. Not ever'one. Just Alex."

"I won't sleep with you just to get you even with Brad."

"I didn't say I want to get even with Brad. I want to sleep with you, Alex. You're the first man I've ever had to ask twice."

"Hard to believe you've ever had to ask a man at all."

"I haven't. Why the hell am I asking *you* at all?"

"Maybe because you know I won't accept."

"Yeah, maybe." She leaned against him, her chin on his shoulder. "Maybe that's why." She stepped back from him to arm's length, then let go. "All right, I'm going." She picked up her purse.

"I'll take you home."

"No, you won't. It's going to be a bad enough scene, without you there. Besides, I don't know how long your virtue will last. What happens if you change your mind on the way to my house? I'd hate to lose you as a buddy."

"Then I'll get you a cab."

"All right."

They walked down the dark stairs and into an evening that had almost gone into night. He would walk with her to Kalinin Prospect to find a cab. But before they left the darkness of this street he stopped, swung her toward him, and kissed her hard. She broke away from him with a gasp or a sob, but then turned back and hugged him fiercely.

As they clung together on the sidewalk, from a car parked halfway up the block a dark, slender metal cylinder protruded from the passenger's window. It swung in an arc, then settled pointing straight toward their darker shape in the darkness.

At that moment they released each other and walked, hand in hand, toward the bright arch of the passageway through to Arbat Street and toward Kalinin.

The metal cylinder swung back and was withdrawn into the car.

# 25

IF THERE WERE TWO SEVEN-BY-EIGHTS OUT THERE IN MOSCOW KILLING witnesses, no one knew of them. Slavin had once before tried asking his old contacts from his days at the Militia Academy, but no one had been able to tell him anything. Now he tried again, even more cautiously. The descriptions matched a hundred musclemen from the militia and the KGB—so many that it was useless to try to check them all. But he was afraid to try to narrow the field by giving more information, for fear that the information would get there ahead of him and alert someone that he was looking.

Eventually he gave it up. Trial was coming. It was all he could do to prepare.

But one night, working late at home, he received a telephone call.

"Mikhail Alexandrovich."

"Yes? I'm listening."

"Good evening, Mikhail Alexandrovich. I just wanted you to know we'd not forgotten you."

"Who is this?"

"A friend. A friend who remembers Kornev." Slavin dropped into a chair. "You haven't forgotten me, have you, Mikhail Alexandrovich?"

"No. No, I haven't forgotten you."

"And our bargain. Are you remembering our bargain?"

"I remember."

"That's good. We were afraid you had forgotten. You've been working so hard on the case."

"And how do you know that?"

"Never mind. We know."

"It wouldn't do not to work on it. It would look suspicious."

"Certainly use your own judgment, Mikhail Alexandrovich. That's why we have a smart lawyer. Just be sure to lose." There was a click: the caller was gone.

The unfortunate part, Slavin thought, was that it would be a hard case *not* to lose. He tried not to discourage Chapman; but as trial came on, he began to fear that their client would feel sold out in the end, in spite of all he or Fall could do.

# 26

JUDGE PSKOVA, PRESIDENT OF THE MEETING OF THE MOSCOW CITY Court, turned to the People's Assessors on either side of her and murmured, "Are you ready, comrades?" Although the Party was years gone, the habits of a lifetime had not gone with it. Law was a conservative business, and judging was the most conservative part of it. Anyone connected with the functioning of Pskova's courtroom was still addressed as "comrade."

The two People's Assessors were new; this was their first case and she could see that they were nervous, being at the center of attention. She wished the Chairman of the court would adopt her suggestion of letting lay judges break in on small cases, a simple murder or a rape, before being thrown into a major case. But to the Chairman, procedure was Procedure: the People's Assessors were chosen by the organization they worked for, and that was that. They started on whatever case was starting when they arrived. So the two good citizens at her left and right, workers from the Lenin Young Communist League Automobile Factory (still going under that name), fidgeted under the eyes of a crowd they had never expected to find paying attention to them: not only the People's Prosecutor, the defendant and his counsel and his Consular Representative—even Judge Pskova had never seen one of those at a trial—the defendant's wife, the Secretary of the Court, all of the usual paraphernalia of a trial in the Moscow City Court.

The People's Assessors murmured back that they were ready: Tushin on her left and Bitova on her right. She noted that Tushin's voice was a little unsteady. He needed watching.

"The Court Collegium on Criminal Cases of the Moscow City Court will hear the case of Chapman, Bradley Allen," Judge Pskova announced, "charged with violation of Articles Ninety-three Prime and One Seventy-four of the Criminal Code. Secretary of the Court, please report on the readiness of the case."

The Secretary, a young woman with thick glasses that magnified her heavy eye makeup, read from her checksheet the persons who were present or expected for the case: the defendant, the attorneys, the witnesses, the experts. Chapman was to be the only witness that day. The lawyers saw that Pskova expected to make a job of this case.

"All right. Defendant . . ." Slavin signaled Chapman to rise. "Defendant Chapman—is that how you pronounce it? Good. Do you need a translator, Defendant?"

"No, I understand Russian."

"All right. State your name, date of birth, and residence."

He did.

"Your Russian's very good, Defendant. You're American, are you? I didn't think Americans bothered to learn Russian."

"I studied it in college, and then I kept on until I learned really to understand it."

"Well, I'm sure you're glad you took the trouble, since it brought you here today. Did you receive the Prosecutor's Conclusion on the accusation in this case?"

"I did."

"On thirteen July, correct?"

"Yes."

"All right. You can sit down. Comrade Lawyers, are there any petitions to disqualify this court, myself, or the People's Assessors Bitova and Tushin on the grounds of nonobjectivity?"

The Prosecutor rose—Yuri Alexandrovich Kol'tsov, long and lean, looking as if he had recently been on starvation rations. But he had been that way all his life. Slavin knew him from law school. Kol'tsov, one of two deputy prosecutors for the city, supervised the Department of Courts in the office of the Moscow City Prosecutor. The other department, the Department of Investigations, investigated cases; Kol'tsov's department tried them. His personal presence here showed that the justice system viewed this as no ordinary case. He wouldn't stir from his office for an ordinary case. "No petitions, Comrade President." He sat.

Slavin rose. "We are satisfied with the court."

"Thank you, Comrade Advocate. Defendant, it is my duty to inform you of your rights as defendant in this case. You have the right to know the content of the accusations against you and to give explanations regarding them. You have the right to present petitions to the court, including to ask for disqualification of the judge or the People's Assessors"—she glanced at the citizens on her left and her right—"the Prosecutor or any expert witnesses. You have the right to appeal the decision in this case." She didn't tell him, but Slavin already had, that he had the right not to answer questions from the judge or anyone else and not to testify. She concluded and turned again to the lawyers: "Are there any petitions from counsel on other issues?" Her look said there had better not be, not at this stage. Judge Pskova was well known for keeping a case moving.

"No petitions," Kol'tsov said. Slavin agreed.

"All right. Defendant, do you acknowledge your guilt on the charges that have been brought against you?"

Chapman stood again. "I am not guilty of any of the charges."

Pskova took the first of the volumes of the case that were spread on the desk in front of her and the lay judges. "Since you understand Russian, you knew what you were signing when you signed the protocols of charges, I guess." She opened the volume. "Did you? Not that your esteemed counsel, Advocate Slavin, would have let you sign without understanding."

Slavin nodded to acknowledge the compliment. He had tried a lot of cases in Judge Pskova's courtroom. He wished that made him feel better about trying this one in her courtroom.

"I understood the charges," Chapman said.

"I am going to ask you some questions." Judge Pskova flipped her hand at the books on her desk. "This is the evidence, Defendant. I've read it. Not much fun, but it's my job. What it all adds up to is, somehow your company got state property and money ended up in the pocket of a state official. A state official who also worked for your company. We may not be as sophisticated as you are in New York, but a peasant can shovel away manure if you give her enough time." Pskova came from a peasant family in the village of Pskov. It had been a politically correct background for a judge, in her day.

"I'm not from New York," Chapman said. "I'm from Minnesota. We're all farmers there."

"You've come a long way from your farm, Defendant. Is that your wife in the back?"

"Yes."

"You don't look like a Russian farmer's wife," the judge said to Joanna.

"Mrs. Chapman speaks only a little Russian," Slavin said.

"Is that so? Why don't you have a translator for her? How's she to know what's going on?"

"We didn't want to interfere with the business of the court," Slavin said. "A translator talking . . ."

"They can sit in the back row and hold down their voices. It's up to you, but I'm sure she'll feel better knowing what's going on. A woman should be more than just a decoration."

Slavin released his breath. One never knew about Pskova. She could be a sweet old woman, but at the judicial desk she had a core of steel. "We'll get her a translator," he said.

"It's up to you, Counsel; it's up to you." Pskova turned her attention back to Chapman. "So, if I've scared you enough about what's in these books, why don't you tell me your story. What's going on here?"

It was Pskova's favorite opening question: tell me everything connected with this investigation. Later the Prosecutor and then the defense counsel would get their chances to ask questions—but by then they would be questions around the edges of the story. Pskova wanted the story itself from the defendant, and she wanted to control the pace and the details of it. Not all judges like to interrogate witnesses themselves; Pskova did.

Slavin and Fall had coached Chapman on how to respond to Judge Pskova: tell her your story, make it convincing, and keep it simple. But be ready for questions, and remember, she won't forget anything you've said.

Brad began as they had rehearsed: "This is the story of a company trying to improve a basic and important service for the Russian people—a postal system. It is a joint effort by Russian and American enterprises. We joined to form a new company, JorSov, which received property both from the Russian side and the American side to use in the business. I am the co–General Director of the company."

"It's too bad the Russian co–General Director can't be here today," Pskova observed. "I guess no one's saying you had anything to do with that." She looked at Kol'tsov as she said this, but Kol'tsov held his peace.

"My codirector was V. V. Turbin. He's dead. I don't know anything about that."

"Well, you're not charged with his death, certainly, and this court is only concerned with the charges before it. So tell us about this property your company received from both sides."

Joanna did not try to follow the Russian. It was a long, tangled story. Brad tried to keep it simple, but the line of his narrative kept weaving and shifting to follow the questions that Judge Pskova threw out. Joanna knew all the shifts and tangles of the story already, or thought she did, so her mind drifted through the courtroom. Pskova—she seemed such a nice old woman. Hard to imagine that she deserved the reputation Slavin said she had: a hanging judge. Not literally: they didn't hang people in Russia. Shot them, when they got the death penalty, but few crimes carried the death penalty, Slavin said. Not bribery, not theft of state property. Pskova couldn't hang people, but she gave them a lot of years at hard labor. Not a hanging judge—a lot-of-years judge.

The courtroom had a lot of years on it. Looked as if it had done hard labor for a lifetime. Typical Russian decoration, or lack of it. Blond plywood paneling. One yellowing fluorescent light to brighten up the daylight. Dirty windows and not enough of them. Stamped metal chairs. The judges got better chairs, high-backed, but even they didn't get a decent bench, just a blond plywood desk with a front so you couldn't see their legs under it. Saw them when they came in, though. Judge Pskova's were like pine trees, thick and untapered. She wore a beige skirt and a kind of flowered-print blouse. Not even a robe to mark her as a judge: just a person. A person with the power to send Brad away for years. Making chairs like these, probably. And the lay judges: a man and a woman. Wonder if they always do that, one of each? A man in a dirty gray jacket and brown trousers. A woman in a dress. Her legs like pine trees too. Or birches. Whiter than the judge's. Not hairy. Not shaved; just not hairy. Being sent to prison by a woman with hairy legs.

The judge asks all the questions. Not like TV courtroom dramas at home, the lawyers getting all the lines and the judge sitting there. She asks all the questions. Not much life in the lawyers. Shouldn't Misha and Alex be objecting? Could they? She's the judge.

How long would this last? Days of it. Maybe weeks, Misha said. The judge would hear the witnesses: Brad; the bookkeeper; the millmen who raided the office; the experts on property values; the whomever. The judge reads the testimony of Turbin out loud: he can't be here himself. They interrogated him before whatever happened, happened. Brad, too, though he hadn't told her. Not the only thing he hadn't told her, the bastard. But no use thinking of that. Can't take days of this. Not days of looking at that cage.

Ugliest thing in the courtroom, the cage. She tried to keep her mind away from it; but it sat there at one side of the front, behind the defendant's lawyer, drawing her eyes. Every time she looked at Misha, she had to look at it—a bear's cage, all cold iron and uncaring. For the defendant, Misha had said. A Russian's idea of a joke, she had thought at first. But it wasn't a joke. For Brad? she asked. For defendants who are in jail, he told her. A defendant who's in jail hears his case from the cage.

Who would believe in the innocence of a man in a cage?

It was another reason Slavin had wanted Brad out before trial.

Instead Brad sat in the first row of seats. Not even with his lawyer. Like a special guest, not a defendant. Alex sat with him. Consular Representative—another special guest.

She watched Alex talking to Brad. Talking to her husband.

# 27

ON THE SECOND DAY OF TRIAL, THE FIRST WITNESS AFTER BRAD WAS THE state's expert on property values.

The Chief Investigator had found his witness deep within the bowels of the Institute of Court Expertise, where he had spent a lifetime learning the value of everything and the price of nothing. His name was Schotov.

Judge Pskova asked him, "Did you prepare this analysis of the value of property contributed to the JorSov joint venture?"

"I supervised it." Schotov spoke loudly. He was a man proud of his ability and not afraid to show it. "This was a complex case. It involves three different kinds of values: buildings, equipment, and technology. When I received the Investigator's questions, I put together a team to answer them. But I supervised it all. I stand behind it."

"Well, I can't make heads or tails of it. Explain it to me."

Schotov was not offended. This was, as he had said, a complex case. He didn't expect the judge to understand it, unaided. He was a friendly guide, leading the judge by her hand through thickets of thought to the plain facts at the end of the path.

"What we did, you see, Comrade Judge," he said, "was to find comparably sized cities in the rest of the world, comparable to those where the properties contributed to JorSov are actually located in Russia. And we had our embassy staffs abroad compile information on the value of commercial buildings in those cities. We wanted to be fair. We could have taken New York as a basis, or London, or Paris; but these buildings aren't in the capital city, not in Moscow, so we said, 'Let's be fair. Provincial city for provincial city. Analyze them by size of population.' And we did. That's for buildings and other immovable property. And for equipment we acquired the catalogs of manufacturers of similar equipment in the West and took their prices."

"I see," said Pskova. "So if a building in—what's a city: Dallas? If a building in Dallas was worth a thousand rubles a square meter, you'd say a building in Sverdlovsk, whatever, is worth the same?"

"Yes, in principle. Although of course the value you suggest is really not comparable. A building in . . . well, let's take a real example. Cedar Rapids, Iowa. A commercial building in good condition ought to be worth a thousand dollars a square meter, not a thousand rubles. That's according to public records, actual sales, gathered by our embassy staff in Washington. They keep a record of these things in America, how much buildings sell for. These are all sales in or before 1990, but within three years or less, nothing older."

"That's great," Brad muttered to Fall, "for anybody who thinks a building in Sverdlovsk is worth as much as one in Dallas."

"So if you add the value of all the buildings contributed to the JorSov joint venture," Judge Pskova said, "you get this number at the bottom of the table? What is this, rubles?"

"Yes, Comrade Judge. We calculated the value in dollars, and then we converted it at the 1990 official exchange rate, which is what was applied at the time the company was created. To be fair."

"This is fantastic," Pskova said. "The original value on the balance of the joint venture for all buildings and equipment was around seventeen million rubles; but you're showing buildings alone worth hundreds of millions!"

"At a thousand bucks a square meter, why wouldn't they?" Chapman hissed to Fall. "If they can find anyone to pay that for a building in Sverdlovsk, I've got a lot of buildings I'd love to sell him! Is Slavin going to let him get away with this?"

Fall put a hand on Chapman's arm. "He'll get a chance at the witness later."

"And as for technology," the Judge was saying. "How did you value that?"

"Technology of course is more of a challenge," the witness said, leaving no doubt that it was a challenge he was equal to. "Every case is different. But we have a long history in Russia and in the former Soviet Union, in the acquisition of technology; and we have a long filing system. We selected cases we believe are comparable, where technology was purchased abroad; and we even asked for some commercial bids from Western companies, for some of the very items of technology contributed to JorSov by the Ministry of Posts and Communications. Just to test our conclusions. The request wasn't real, of course, but the bidders didn't know that, and so the bids were real. The results are quite illuminating."

Chapman groaned. "The chickens come home to roost."

"Meaning what?" Fall asked.

"The Soviets have overpaid for every technology known to Western man," Chapman said. "Not to mention that they're comparing real technology to all the crap they forced on us in this deal!"

"The results," Schotov said to the judge, "are at the bottom of page twelve of our report, which you have there. The combined value of all the technology transferred to JorSov by the Russian side was over a hundred million rubles."

"And it was valued at what, for the transfer to JorSov?" Pskova asked.

"Well, about fourteen million rubles. The number's here . . ."

"Yes, I see it," the Judge said. "I see it very well."

"Do you really think," Slavin asked Schotov when his turn came, "that the value of a building in Sverdlovsk, to use the judge's example, is as great in dollars as the value of a building in Dallas?"

"Yes," Schotov said. "If they're the same kind of building, why not? First-quality construction, comparable age . . . why not?"

"Would a buyer pay as much for a building in Sverdlovsk as for one in Dallas?" Slavin asked.

Schotov shrugged. "Same purpose, same quality, same age: why not?"

"Is there a market for buildings in Sverdlovsk? Has anyone ever actually bought a building there?"

"Well, of course not. That's why we had to perform this analysis!"

"Do you agree that the price of a building in Sverdlovsk might be affected by the ability of the people there to pay for it?"

"Yes, of course."

"Then how can you determine the value of a building in Sverdlovsk by the price of a building in Dallas when people in Dallas are paid salaries much higher than people in Sverdlovsk?"

"But the value in Sverdlovsk doesn't matter. We were asked by the Investigator to determine the value of buildings—and other property—based on 'world market value.' That's how the law requires contributions to joint ventures to be established, as I understand it. So Sverdlovsk doesn't matter. It's the *world* market that matters. So we looked around the world."

And Schotov would not be budged from his position.

It was late afternoon before Pskova reached the next witness. Another judge would have let her go until Monday and start the weekend a little early. Pskova was relentless.

"Now, witness, how much is it that the company's records show was paid to the dead man, Turbin?"

The witness was Marina, the bookkeeper for Chapman's company.

"There were two payments," Marina said. "In July and September 1991. The total value was twenty thousand dollars."

"And Turbin's official salary at that time was how much?"

"Oh, I don't remember. His salary most recently was thirty thousand rubles a month."

"Thirty thousand rubles! That's a lot of money!" Pskova seemed amazed that there could be so much money in the world. Her own salary was barely seven thousand rubles; but she recalled the day—the days, for they had been most of her life—when two hundred rubles a month was riches. But after a moment she asked, "How much is thirty thousand rubles in dollars?" Perhaps she only seemed amazed.

"In dollars?" Marina hesitated. "I don't know. The value changes so fast, with inflation . . . It's about three hundred."

"Three hundred dollars? It doesn't sound like as much that way, does it? Did it seem odd to you, as bookkeeper, that the company was paying twenty thousand dollars to someone whose salary was only three hundred dollars?"

Marina said nothing.

Pskova said, all gentleness, "Do you have hearing troubles, dear?"

"No." Marina's eyes were cast down.

"Well, so did it seem odd to you. . . . ?"

"It wasn't my job to determine how much was paid to Vladilen Viktorovich," Marina said, suddenly stubborn. "And Mr. Chapman was being paid eight thousand dollars a month."

"Eight thousand! Really! What do they expect you to do for that much money, Defendant Chapman? Kill someone?" Pskova's smile invited the courtroom to laugh—although when they did, she called for order. She said to Slavin, "I didn't mean it personally, Counsel. I was just surprised by the number. Eight thousand dollars. Right now that's . . ." Judge Pskova didn't finish the sentence; she didn't need to. Right then, eight thousand dollars was a lot of rubles.

"It's over eight hundred thousand rubles a month," Marina said helpfully.

"And the capital contribution of the Russian side to this joint venture was how much?" Pskova asked.

"Well, about thirty million rubles."

"So Defendant Chapman is being paid . . . oh, two and a half to three percent of the Russian contribution every month."

"Well . . ." Marina struggled. She was used to numbers on paper, not in her head.

Slavin interrupted. "The contributions were valued in 1990, not in 1992. They aren't the same rubles."

"Not the same rubles?" Pskova asked. "I was paid last week with some rubles that must have been around in 1990. They certainly looked it."

"But you got more of them than you would have in 1990, Comrade Judge," Slavin said. "I certainly hope you've got a raise since then."

"Yes, but there's a difference, Comrade Advocate," Pskova said. "The company didn't get a raise. It's still got the same thirty million rubles in capital from the Russian side. That's what the books show. Don't they, witness?"

Marina nodded. "Yes. They do."

"But that's just a bookkeeper's entry," Slavin objected. "The company actually has buildings and other property, and not a stack of thirty million one-ruble notes. The property is worth what it's worth, whatever the bookkeepers said in 1990. And it's worth far more now than it was then."

"Well, I'd say the company's going to have to sell some of that property if it keeps on paying Mr. Chapman at the rate it's paying him. In three years, that property will be all gone."

Pskova was a smart enough woman, and good at arithmetic, but market economics had never been on the curriculum at her law school.

When the case adjourned for the day, Chapman asked Fall as they left the courtroom, "How long does this go on?"

"As long as the judge wants to know more."

"Tough old bitch," Chapman said. "How do you think it's going, Slavin?"

"It's too early to know." But they all knew from Slavin's tone that he wasn't happy.

"It's enough for today," Fall said. "Let's meet tomorrow to go over today's testimony and strategize. Thank God tomorrow's Saturday. Ten in the morning, Brad?"

"How about if I call you? Being tried as a criminal is hard work. I'm going to try to sleep in."

"All right. I'll be home. I'll call Misha when I hear from you."

The JorSov driver was waiting with a car. Brad and Joanna walked together to the car, but not touching, and got into the back seat on separate sides.

As the car moved away, she glanced back at Fall and raised a hand.

# 28

INNA WAS SICK OF CORRUPTION.

She had lived with it all her life, but it had been secret and unheard from. Living with it that way was unpleasant, but it wasn't hard. The people at the top got theirs, and you didn't; but your nose wasn't rubbed in it.

Living with the story of corruption was harder. She was sick of the story of it. She was sick of hearing, from day to day and all day, of bribes and thefts and swindles, of misappropriations and malfeasances. The woman who couldn't get a heart operation. She had a congenital bad heart but no bottle of cognac for the surgeon, and no way to get one. The restaurant owner who had to bribe the health inspectors to keep his kitchen open, although his kitchen was spotless and the state-owned *stolovaya* it had replaced had been a slough of despond where people sickened daily from unreported food poisoning. The official of the Moscow State Property Committee who denied that anyone in *his* operation—himself included—took bribes to release state buildings into private hands; but he had somehow built an eight-room country house on the Moscow River—a house worth tens of millions of rubles, built on the foundation of a salary never greater than twelve thousand rubles a month.

Inna was tired of them all. An honest girl could take only so many problems, only so many grafters.

She was, perhaps, a one-person microcosm of Russia: desperate for honesty, overwhelmed with dishonesty, and about ready to stop her ears.

But she was like Russia in another way too: having started down this road, she was on it to the end, and people who thought otherwise didn't know her.

The subcommittee's last witness of the day was ready, and Inna was glad. The deputies and staffers in the back seats were mostly gone. Calm fell like evening over the hearing room.

Her subcommittee's hearings were the talk of Moscow, and where most Supreme Soviet business went on out of sight, unremarked, nearly every day her hearings drew a crowd—not only the public and the press, but deputies and their aides. Public hearings were a new thing—possibly dangerous, possibly useful, certainly to be watched. They had raised Inna Korneva from obscurity to stardom, and her colleagues saw suddenly, as politicians must everywhere, that politics is publicity. But by now it had been a long day, and the reporters were gone to make their deadlines, and most of the deputies had gone after them.

The current witness was Nikolai Kulagin, an economist from Moscow State University. She had known him a little, in the old days. He could not be friends then with the daughter of a dangerous dissident, for his job would have been in danger; but he sympathized, and she knew he did. He had come out during the nominations for the first elections to the Congress of People's Deputies of the USSR. He had run as a democrat—at a time when it was still possibly dangerous to do that—and had nearly won. Two democratic candidates had split 60 percent of the vote, and an old-guard factory manager had got 40 percent. Under the Russian system, the two leading vote-getters entered a runoff. Kulagin had come in third, with a fraction under 30 percent of the vote to his democratic opponent's fraction over 30. The democratic opponent had won the runoff, 60 percent to 40 percent. He was now a fixture in the legislature, and Kulagin was still an economics professor. It was Kulagin's brush with fame. He was intelligent, honest, hardworking, kind to the unfortunate, handsome (a ladies' man of some repute on the economics faculty) . . . a fraction of a percent more, a mere few hundred votes, and he would have been on his way to being a world statesman.

But that train was gone. He was still a member of the economics faculty of Moscow State University, still a ladies' man, although of progressively less repute with each year that passed. His name had been rumored in connection with several high government offices immediately after the coup attempt; but no appointment had followed, and now he was in decline without ever having actually ascended.

But Kulagin had not lost his taste for national issues. What he wanted to warn the subcommittee of was the danger to foreign investment resulting from corruption. "If foreigners must bribe officials for things they have a right to receive, there is that much less money to invest in business that benefits the rest of the nation. If they are asked to pay too much, they simply will not come. The mere reputation for corruption can cause some foreigners to stay away. But worst of all, there have been rumors of some attempts by so-called 'nationalists' to have foreign ownership in Russian businesses taken over by Russians. There is no surer road to ruin for all of us."

This was a stone thrown into Antipov's garden, and he was not a man to sit still for it. He seized his microphone. "You talk as if all foreigners are honest," he growled. "Well, they aren't. And it takes two to transfer a bribe—one to get and one to give. If they weren't giving, no one would be getting. If they give bribes, their property interests *should* be forfeit. We've given foreigners protection. Some say we've given them too much protection! Our laws say that if their property is seized, they have to be paid for it. Why should they be? And besides that, our laws now practically invite companies to pay bribes; because bribes are always given by somebody, and that somebody can be sent to prison, but a company can't be sent to prison. So they've got every interest to get some dimwit to do their dirty work for them—let him go to jail, what do they care?—and get what they want. It shouldn't be that way. One thing we'll see out of this process, I say, is a law that states not only can a person go to prison and his property be confiscated, but if he's acting for a company, the company's property can be confiscated too. And this isn't antiforeigner. This is for everybody. And as for 'so-called' nationalists, there's nothing 'so-called' about this one. I'm a nationalist, sure, and I'm proud of it. Russian companies should be run by Russians."

Kulagin was not intimidated: "Russian companies should be run by whoever can run them best. Do you think in the United States they only let Americans run companies? No. They let in whoever can do the job best."

"There are plenty of companies that the Americans won't let any foreigners own," Antipov answered. "I've studied this. You can't fool me. Airlines. Banks. Some places in America, foreigners can't even own farmland! Did you know that, Mr. Economist?"

Antipov's use of the term *mister* to a Russian citizen was intended as an insult, and Kulagin knew it. He, too, was not a man to have a stone thrown into his garden. "And what about postal service companies?" he fired back.

"What about postal service companies? Why should foreigners be able to control our communications?"

"The question isn't whether foreigners should be able to own them," Kulagin insisted. "The question is whether, once we've let them own a company, we can afford to sit back and let corrupt elements steal it from them under the disguise of 'fighting corruption.' "

Antipov turned red. Inna knew Antipov well. He had the Russian peasant's endurance and craft; but he had the violence of his temper, too, and was proud of it—as proud as he was of his nationalism. She interrupted. "If the witness is finished," she said, leaving no doubt that he was, "we will recess until tomorrow."

Antipov had a habit of running his fingers through his hair when he was excited. He did so now. It left him looking like a badly built haystack after a high wind.

After the hearing Kulagin came toward the platform. Seeing him coming, Antipov stormed off.

"It seems I wounded your friend, Inna Romanovna," Kulagin said.

"I hope you haven't made an enemy for your own cause. He doesn't forget easily."

"Your cause too, surely."

"Yes, and Antipov's too, in spite of a different emphasis. It's good to have his energy on our side."

"Rather like a friendship with a hurricane," Kulagin replied.

"What was it you said that made him so excited?"

Kulagin was thoughtful a moment. He looked around the chamber. As they talked, the chamber had slowly cleared, until they were almost the only ones left in the room. No one was near them, only a group of three deputies loudly swapping jokes twenty meters away at the back of the chamber. They were on the one about the boy who wanted to be absolved of the sin of fornication. They had all heard it before, but it was still good, and so they all laughed all the way through, teller and listener alike.

Kulagin said in a lower voice, "Antipov was excited about communications. You've heard about the express-delivery company?"

"Yes, of course. It's in all the papers. The trial of that American." Chapman's trial was the moment's sensation in the Moscow press. She didn't mention what else she knew about it, through Alex Fall.

"You know about Turbin, then."

She said cautiously, "Poor old Turbin, fell from his balcony." It was what the papers had said. But Turbin had been well known, among his friends, for immoderation in spiritual matters. The papers had said that too. Inna had never been one of his friends, but many of her fellow deputies had been, and she still heard Turbin stories.

"I wouldn't talk about him so loudly, Inna Romanovna. Turbin didn't fall, and he didn't commit suicide." Kulagin paused before going on: "He was murdered."

"What? How do you know this?"

He laid a hand on her arm in warning to lower her voice. The laughter at the back of the hall had broken off for a moment. But it resumed; somebody was telling the one about the man caught waiting for a train in the closet of his best friend's wife.

"I thought everybody knew. I wouldn't talk quite so openly about it in this chamber, if I were you."

"You're the one who brought it up!"

"I was antagonized by Antipov," Kulagin said. "I've known Antipov half my life, and he's always been an ass."

Inna was exasperated. Moscow was constantly swept by rumors that everybody "knew" to be true; but if you asked for evidence, none ever came. "How do you know?" she demanded again.

"I know by listening. It's a useful skill. But if you really want to know more, you should ask your friend Antipov. Isn't he the one who has demanded for so long that foreigners get out of the country?"

"Vasily Ivanovich has his own ideas about what's best for Russia."

"As well as what's best for him. Be careful."

"Do you want to give additional testimony? I can recall you next week."

"No. No, thank you, I said enough." He shook her hand. "The work you are doing is important, Inna Romanova. Don't let anyone stop you from doing it."

What Kulagin had said left Inna shaken with a feeling of helpless outrage. What he implied was slanderous of Antipov, but she could do nothing about it. It was a feeling she knew well and had hoped never to feel again, for it had been a part of her all throughout her youth—the helpless knowledge that something terrible was being done to someone who mattered to her, and she could do absolutely nothing about it.

Mixed with it was the feeling that she knew her father must have had—that, hopeless or not, she was going to do what she could about it.

And yet—she recalled what Alex had told her: someone was trying to steal his client's company. What could Antipov have to do with that?

She decided to sort it out then and there.

She found Antipov in the deputies' cafeteria. He was alone at a table, glaring at a cup of tea.

"So," he growled at her, "you've heard all your blue friend had to say?" Kulagin had been wearing a blue suit, but that wasn't what he meant. *Blue* was a reference to homosexuals. She ignored it. She knew it was baseless. It was just Antipov being purposely crude.

"I don't think I heard all he had to say. He didn't want to talk about some things."

"Then he's wiser than I ever thought he'd be."

"He didn't want to say any more about postal service companies. He said that I should ask you."

"Me? Do I look like a postman?"

"You certainly became angry when he mentioned it. What did he mean about stealing companies?"

"Who knows what Kulagin means? I've known Kulagin half my life, and he's always been an ass."

Some foreboding kept Inna from repeating what Kulagin had said about Turbin. Instead, she said, to see how he would reply, "I asked him to testify again next week."

"Then you're a fool."

"I am what I am, Vasily Ivanovich." She didn't say that Kulagin had refused to come back, or that he knew nothing, really.

He looked hard at her. His eyes were dark under heavy brows. She thought for an instant of Rasputin, the dark mad monk who helped the last czar to his doom. Antipov carried all the doomed passions of Russia. "You're your father's daughter," he said at length. "He never knew when to quit either. Sit down, Inna Romanovna." It was years since he had addressed her so formally. By using her patronymic now, he was being ironic, emphasizing just how much she was connected to her father.

She sat down.

Antipov glared at his teacup, perhaps instead of glaring at her. "You don't see what's happening, do you?" he said angrily toward the teacup. "We're trying to kill corruption in Russia. But you're letting our goal become confused. People like Kulagin, they come along and say, 'But we've got to be nice to foreigners.' Well, we *don't* have to be nice to foreigners. That's something else altogether. We've got to stick to our own goals. Otherwise we'll become a river that runs in a hundred channels and disappears into the sand." He looked up at her. "We must not confuse our goals. The chorus won't sing if not everyone agrees on the tune."

He ran his fingers through his hair again, and now it stood almost on end.

"Our goal," she said, "is to build a nation governed by laws. Laws that everyone has to follow. Whether they're Russians or foreigners."

"No," he contradicted her, "that's just a step. Our goal is to build a nation where the Russian people can live in peace and happiness. We don't need foreigners. And it's no start toward that goal to invite foreigners into our house to steal our silver and china."

"When did the Russian people ever have silver and china to steal? Not since before the Revolution."

"The Revolution was stupidity," Antipov agreed. "Seventy years on a road to nowhere, and nobody wants back on *that* road. But it wasn't Russian stupidity: it was foreign. Lenin and all the rest; all of them Jews. Now we're off that road at last, but still people want to follow foreigners. 'This way! This way!' they say. 'Here's where the foreigners are going.' But we don't have to go that way. We *shouldn't* go that way! We are the great Russian nation, and we should go the way a great nation goes—our own way. We don't let anyone steal from us. We don't have silver and china, you say? True, we don't now. But we should have. This should be a rich country, Inna! This *would* be a rich country, if it followed its own destiny and stopped whoring for foreign trinkets. This *will* be a rich country!"

"It will never be rich if so much of our money goes into the pockets of dishonest officials, Vasily Ivanovich."

He grasped her hand with both of his—huge, rough hands like bears' paws. "On this, you and I agree completely, Inna. And that's why the work we are doing is so important. We can't let squabbles about foreigners divide us."

" 'We should go the way a great nation goes,' you say. 'We don't let anyone steal from us.' But does a great nation steal from anyone, even from foreigners? This isn't a squabble about foreigners. It's a debate about ourselves."

He let go of her hand, slammed a huge palm on the table. The bang rattled his cup and saucer and startled two deputies at a far table, the only other people in the room. "I don't know how

I'm going to convince you!" Antipov roared. The two deputies laughed, seeing it was just Antipov.

"Maybe you should tell me about this company Kulagin mentioned. How does that help Russia become a great nation?"

Antipov pursed his lips. His hand went to his head, and his thick fingers began to smooth his tangled hair. After a moment he said, "The post office isn't my business, Inna. But I'll do more than tell you about it. I'll let you talk to the people whose business it is. Then you'll see how important it is."

# 29

THE COUNTRY OUTSIDE MOSCOW WAS FEATURELESS, BUT INNA KNEW the region well enough to know generally where they were although she had not taken this road before. The road wound among trees and some fields and more trees—sometimes passing a high-rise apartment building with nothing near it, dropped into the woods as if from a spaceship; sometimes a cluster of uniform square cottages, the weekend dachas that Muscovites prized so much, packed together like a military encampment within a cleared square, the outermost cottages shouldered right up to the first tree branches.

The car passed a cemetery, then pitched across a set of railroad tracks. On the far side was a low concrete building, unlit, with a sign: PRODUKTY. Groceries. Behind this store the lit windows of an old village straggled off on both sides of the road.

The road wound through trees again, and then Antipov's car stopped at a solid-steel gate in a high, white wall topped by three strands of barbed wire. They had not turned off the road. It seemed that this was the destination to which the road had been built. Villages and dachas and apartments were but incidents along the way.

A policeman stepped out from a small gate cut into the large gate. He approached the driver's window, saluted as Antipov rolled the window down.

Antipov held up his identification card. The policeman studied it, handed it back, saluted again, and disappeared again through the small gate. In a moment the large gate rolled open across the road.

The wall outlined a compound perhaps a half kilometer square. Around the edges of the compound were scattered solidly built log houses, far different from the tiny dachas and sagging peasant houses just passed. The compound climbed a hillside through which a stream fell, dammed at the bottom end to form a pond. On the far side of the pond from the gate, near the top of the hillside and discreetly separate from any of the houses, stood a larger building, painted white and too large for a house. It had three stories and a central bank of vertical windows that stretched clear to the roof. The evening was growing dark. The inside of the building was lit, and Inna could see that the tall windows opened into a single central space.

"Where are we?" she asked.

He didn't give a name, but said only, "It belonged to the Party." But she had recognized that already. Whom else could it have belonged to?

"Who does it belong to now?" she asked.

He shrugged.

It might have been that he didn't want to say; or it might have been just a hard question to answer. Some questions were like that now, in Russia. Things belonged to who could hold them.

The drive curved around and ended behind the large building in a parking lot of a dozen spaces. Three of them were occupied. There were a red Lada, two black Volgas with government motor-pool plates, and a huge black Zil limousine, twice as long as the other cars, that almost blocked the drive. Antipov edged around the Zil and parked beyond the other cars.

She had thought they would go into the central building; but instead Antipov went along an asphalt walk that led down to the houses. The air was still: the only sound was an argument of ducks on the dark water of the pond.

He knocked at the door of the second house. The door was opened after a moment by a lean-faced man with dark hair parted in the middle of his head. That and his wire-rimmed glasses made him look like a 1930s musical conductor. He said, "Ha, Antipov. You're here at last."

"Hello, Anton. You're all here?"

"Even the General." Anton turned his attention to Inna. "Generals are always late. But who's to tell them otherwise? Except deputies, of course." He took her hand. "Welcome, Inna Romanovna. Your fame has preceded you. Since mine probably hasn't, I'll tell you my name is Minin. Anton Antonovich." Minin's breath smelled of alcohol. He raised her hand and kissed it. "Let me get you a drink. You can get your own, Antipov."

"I'm capable," Antipov said.

"Who doubted it? Inna Romanovna, what are you drinking?"

"I can't drink. Doctor's orders." It was a formula she always used. She did not like alcohol, but in Russia not drinking required an excuse, and "doctor's orders" was the only one acceptable. When she was first elected to the legislature, she had great difficulty knowing what to say. It was Antipov, in fact, who had suggested this response to her, but he said nothing about it now.

"It's a pity," Minin said. "You look healthy. But welcome anyway. This is a place that women of all different behaviors have been known to frequent."

Minin led the way into the next room, a large room that a few lamps failed to illuminate completely. It was lit mainly by a large fire in a fireplace at one end. Its light glowed golden on the log walls.

A sofa and some armchairs faced the fireplace. Behind them was a rustic dining table and around it some heavy wooden chairs. Vodka bottles and glasses were scattered over the table amid a profusion of plates and dishes of *zakuski*, Russian appetizers—slices of ham, beef, sturgeon, and herring; a dish of cucumbers and tomatoes and onions; a salad of eggs and potatoes with meat; pickled garlic cloves and shoots; sliced sausage; sardines; cheeses. No one was at the table, but at the fireplace, two men were sitting with glasses in hand. An open bottle stood on the floor in front of them within reach of the sofa, where someone was lying.

"Your best behavior, everyone!" Minin commanded. "A lady has arrived. And Antipov, of course, but we won't change our behavior for anyone of his character."

The men looked around lazily, but one of them jumped up from his chair. "Inna Romanovna! How wonderful to see you here! Hello, Antipov. Good of you to bring her." Inna recognized him: Valentin Ivanovich Sidorov, one of the faces on the dry hillside of the Supreme Soviet, but it comforted her to see him there. Sidorov was an old man, with a sweet old face set off by floating white hair that would never lie still: when he spoke, it made a moving halo around his head. Now the firelight gilded it and made him look almost young again. A garrulous old man given to talk of the days of building Communism in Dnepropetrovsk in his youth, he was friendly with everyone in the legislature, although he came from a crowd who prided themselves on bluntness. His office was not far from hers, and often a crowd of older deputies was there, men like him who had been heads of important industrial enterprises or provincial Party staff people. All names from the List of Names. "Nobody important," as Sidorov liked to say in self-deprecation, but they had been members of the club that ran the Union. They were used to power. Not fame, but that quiet power that ran a nation. They were people who could be called on the white telephone.

"Come, sit down with us, Innochka," Sidorov called, motioning toward a chair next to him. "The fire feels good. It's going to be an early winter. Wake up Oblonsky there," he said to no one in particular. "Our guest is here." But Oblonsky did not wake up, and the other man there did not rise to greet her. Sidorov introduced him from where he sat: "Perhaps you know the General already. General Marchenko. Or Grigory Artyomovich. You may call him however you please."

The General did not second this invitation, but looked at her carefully over the top of a half-empty glass. Inna did not know him already, but it was clear from the introduction that General Marchenko was not a man Sidorov would describe as "nobody important." She could not tell what he was a general of: the

General was not in uniform, except to the extent that his gray suit and tie were the uniform of the *Nomenklatura*. Inna nodded to him and curved her lips in a smile.

"Sit down, Innochka, sit down," Sidorov said, patting the chair next to him. "Minin, where's this lady's drink?"

Minin arrived with a glass of vodka for her in spite of her instructions to him. "Just one small taste," he said. "For friendship." She smiled at the words. "For friendship" was one of a hundred phrases Russian had—"for peace," "for the motherland," "for those in the field"—for the useful purpose of getting vodka started down the throat.

"Yes, for friendship!" Sidorov said with enthusiasm. He took the bottle from the floor and refilled glasses all around, even that of the supine Oblonsky. "For friendship!" he proposed. Everyone knocked back their glasses, except for Inna, who only tasted hers, the General, who drank his back again to half-full, and Oblonsky, who did not stir.

Antipov stood with his back to the fire, squeezing his vodka glass as if he would crush it, and looking like a thunderstorm. "Give the woman something to eat," he grumbled; he didn't offer to do it himself.

"The food is good here," the General said. "The herring are delicious. The tomatoes are excellent this time of year, of course." But he didn't offer to help her either.

When no one else offered, she concluded that she could get her own food. She found a clean plate and wandered around the table and returned to her seat.

Sidorov said, "The General has been following the work of your subcommittee, Innochka. And Antipov's, of course." He paused to refill the glasses all around. He overflowed Inna's and offered her his handkerchief, already somewhat used. "We should have a toast to your work. Gentlemen, to the work of this lady—and of course Antipov—who is striving to excise the ill effects of these cursed times from our nation!" He drank enthusiastically. Antipov drained his glass according to duty. The General tasted his to match Inna, while Oblonsky let out a snore. "Another country heard from!" Sidorov chortled.

"I *have* been very interested in the work of your subcommittee," the General affirmed. "Antipov has kept us all closely informed. And Sidorov has too, of course." Sidorov nodded in acknowledgment. "It's necessary work, and we support it fully."

"When you say 'we,' whom do you mean?" Inna asked.

"He means the organs of state security, of course," Sidorov said. *The organs* was a classic Soviet term for the KGB, the Committee on State Security, now renamed the Ministry of Security but still the same organization.

So Marchenko was a general officer of the KGB.

"I mean the members of this small group you see here, no one else," Marchenko said. "The state security organs would not presume to take a position on any activity of the Supreme Soviet. The organs are subject to whatever the Supreme Soviet decides, and they obey its commands. But as citizens, it is of course our right and our responsibility to form opinions, and to express them. Those are the conditions of democracy, are they not? And we here are nothing but a group of citizens, concerned about the future of our country. That, I think, is why Antipov was so kind as to bring you to us—his feeling that the discussion you were having was important to the future of the nation, and that perhaps we could influence it for the good of the nation."

"You are a debating society, then?" Inna asked innocently.

Minin laughed; Antipov scowled; Sidorov seemed flustered; but the General smiled for the first time. "Yes, in a way we are," the General said. "And very much so, in our origin. We came together in different ways, just as you see us, a group of citizens thrown together by the chance of friendship, but concerned, each in his own way, about the direction our country is taking or may take. We voiced our concerns to one another, as friends will, and we found that we had some ideas in common. But in these days we need fluffy phrases less than plain deeds." Inna recognized the last words, as any Soviet schoolchild should have. They were a quotation from Lenin, although Marchenko did not credit him.

"'A word is also a deed,'" she said, quoting Lenin back to him. The General smiled. "But what deeds have you done then, General, beyond your words?"

"We simply do, within our own capabilities, what our principles demand of us. Antipov's actions you know of. Indeed, you may deserve more credit than he does. Action to give the police and the security forces more tools with which to combat the corruption that is eating the heart out of our society. Comrade Sidorov works along the same lines within the Supreme Soviet. He will bring a large number of votes in support of proper legislation that we hope will result from your efforts and Antipov's."

"What do you mean by 'proper' legislation?"

"He means," Antipov growled, "laws to put the crooks in jail and keep the foreigners out."

The General smiled again. "Put in Antipov's true earthy style, but that will do for a basic description."

"But why 'foreigners out'?" Inna demanded.

"I had thought you agreed with us about the importance of controlling our own destiny, Inna Romanovna," the General said. "I understood you had some connection once with a young American lawyer—the same lawyer who is involved in this bribery case I read of in the papers. But you turned from him out of principle—at least in part. And correct principle, in my view— that Russian politicians should be seen to represent Russia and Russia only."

Inna blushed. "That has nothing to do with excluding foreign investment. It's a question of my personal dedication. I don't want even to appear to have any higher interest."

"And it's very commendable. I wish more politicians had the same personal dedication."

"But I don't apply the point to foreign investment. Money has no personal feelings. And we need foreign money. We need money from any source. This country is dying for lack of investment. Under the Party, we wasted all we had. We ate our seed corn. Now we don't have the capital to rebuild the country. We are going to have to rely on foreigners."

"We cannot rely on foreigners!" Antipov interrupted. "No great nation can afford to do so. None ever has."

"America was built with foreign capital," Inna said. "You know the information our experts collected. In the last century, America built itself with money from Europe. The foreigners didn't take *them* over."

"But Russia is different," Antipov said. "Russia—"

205

Minin interrupted. "Antipov proves too much. Maybe we need some foreign investment, for a time. All right, let's have it. Let the foreign capitalists come in and get things moving again; but then let them take their money and leave."

"And especially let them take their money out of *your* industry," Antipov said sourly.

"Or let them *leave* their money and leave!" Sidorov suggested. "Just so they leave! Eh, Vasya?" He poured another round, unsteadily, but the General covered his glass with his hand.

"And what is your business?" Inna asked Minin.

"I'm in a number of businesses, Inna Romanovna," Minin answered.

"He's a vulture," Antipov said. "All *biznesmen* are vultures." Antipov said the word *biznesmen* as if it tasted bad. "Vultures feeding on the people. They buy goods cheap from the state and sell them dear to the people."

"If we were all philosophers, we'd all starve," Minin said. "But I'll agree with you this far, Antipov. Some businessmen *are* vultures. But they're not feeding on the people; they're feeding on the bloated carcass of a dead economy. But you shouldn't think that they killed it: it was dead when they found it. And even vultures provide a service: they get rid of the carcass. You can write your fine heroic tales about the people and the nation; but real people won't be able to breathe freely until that carcass is gone and a live economy takes its place."

Inna saw that, although Minin's vodka had been going somewhere, it probably had not been going into Minin. He was animated, but he wasn't drunk. Whether he was animated by the vodka's spirits or his own, or whether he was acting, it was hard to tell.

Minin turned to Inna again. "Not all of my businesses feed on the old state economy. Some do; I'll admit it. I buy lumber cheap from a state mill and I sell it for a little more to people who want to build houses but can't find lumber. The state mill won't take the lumber to the people who want it, and they don't have a way to go get it. The state mill isn't a real business. A real business would find a way to get its products to the people who want them. But lumber isn't my real business either. I have some restaurants. I have a bank."

"He's a postman," Sidorov said.

Minin shrugged. "It was my start."

"Minin," Sidorov said, "was Vladik Turbin's deputy, back in the Ministry of Posts and Communications." He used a nickname for Turbin that would have applied to a small boy, so Inna knew they must have been friends for a long time. "And then he became head of Mespost. He had all the postal system in Russia west of the Urals under his thumb." Sidorov repeated the words, almost singing them: "All the postal system . . . under his thumb."

*And then,* Inna thought, but didn't say it, *Turbin took Mespost's business to the foreigners in JorSov.*

"Some industries," Minin said, "are too important to be controlled by foreigners."

"There are some industries too important to be controlled by foreigners," the General agreed.

"Then," Inna said, "we need a law that says 'foreigners may not control delivery companies.' We can't invite them in and then simply steal their investment."

"It was a mistake to give any of the postal system to the foreigners," Sidorov said gaily, as if taunting someone by quoting him, "and if mistakes have been made, they must be corrected."

"But if foreigners have obtained their share unjustly, then they deserve no more protection than anyone else," Marchenko said, ignoring Sidorov, fastening his eyes on Inna. "Don't you agree, Inna Romanovna?"

"Of course. But if mistakes have been made, who made them? And who will pay?" Three traditional Russian questions followed any failure: "Whose mistake?" "Who will pay?" and "Who gains?" She didn't need to remind Marchenko of these. And although she had asked only two, the third was implicit when she asked the first two.

"Vladik made them," Sidorov said, "and Vladik paid. Nobody else ought to pay."

"Valentin Ivan'ich, you've had too much to drink." Minin said it as one drunk chiding another, or tried to.

"How do you mean, Turbin made them?" Inna asked. She

couldn't refer to a dead man as "Vladik," even if she had known him that well in life.

"Turbin's mistake was taking money from foreigners," Antipov said.

"Turbin's mistake, as I understand, was accepting bribes for state property," Marchenko corrected him. "But I'm not fully familiar with the case."

"And how did he pay for his mistake?" Inna asked this of Sidorov, but Marchenko answered instead:

"It appears that Turbin escaped payment for his crime, to call it what it was. He received payment of bribes, and he escaped payment for bribery. The penalties for bribery are clearly prescribed by law, but Vladilen's life ended before the penalty could be exacted."

Inna smiled at Marchenko's choice of words. His life ended. Third-person singular, past tense, intransitive. No one else had anything to do with such an ending.

But she also noted how Marchenko momentarily referred to Turbin as "Vladilen," someone he had known, not as "Turbin," a stranger.

Sidorov sighed. "Poor Vladik. He was always careless. I always warned him, vodka is won'erful, but if he wanted to drink, he shouldn't live so high up."

"We've heard rumors about Turbin." Inna said it with conviction and hoped that saying "we" conveyed a sense that there was someone standing behind her—the members of her subcommittee, even the power of the Supreme Soviet itself. She had never felt more alone.

There was a profound silence. She heard the wind sigh around the dacha as evening turned to night.

Minin was the first to speak: "What sort of rumors?"

"Idiotic rumors," Antipov said.

"Rumors that Turbin's life didn't just 'end'—that it was stopped."

"That dimwit Kulagin," Antipov said. "He's like a donkey. Sucks up every tale he hears and pisses it back out. With color added."

"Kulagin?" Minin asked.

Antipov waved a hand downward, as if putting down a dog that was trying to jump on him. "The economist. He testified today. She's invited him back." He took the bottle from Sidorov and poured himself another vodka and knocked it back.

"How interesting. What more do you expect Kulagin to say?" General Marchenko asked.

"Probably nothing. I don't think we will have him back," Inna said. She had begun to be concerned about the weight Kulagin was being asked to bear without his knowing it. She did not want to be the cause of making the Ministry of Security interested in anyone. She had seen too much of that already for one lifetime.

"So, what if people do say Turbin might have killed himself?" Minin said. "Turbin was depressed. He was about to be arrested, and he knew it. So the rumors might be right. He might have ended his own life."

"How do you know he was about to be arrested?" Inna asked.

"It's common knowledge."

"Your rumor's as good as anyone else's," Antipov said with a scornful laugh.

The General said nothing. "General Marchenko," Inna asked him, "do you know anything of V. V. Turbin's death? You said you read of this case in the papers. It would be disappointing if our state security service got *all* of its information from the newspapers. Did your organization investigate it?"

"My organization does not investigate slips and falls, whether accidental or suicidal. We are concerned only with the security of the state. But it's our duty to cooperate with the law-enforcement authorities. I understand that the police investigator concluded that Turbin died by accident—although I can well understand that he would be depressed, facing a charge of bribery. I can't relate the details to you, of course. I'm sure you understand."

"Maybe our committee will ask you to testify," she said. "Then it would be your duty to cooperate with *us*. And then maybe *we'll* understand the details too."

He looked at her with anger. "My organization could not consent to disclosure of secret matters. The interests of the state have to be protected."

"Probably the Supreme Soviet can decide what the interests of the state are," Inna said, "as well as what matters are to be kept secret."

"The Supreme Soviet," Marchenko said, looking at Sidorov, "is full of people who couldn't keep a secret if their tongues were tied to their neckties. With all due respect to the deputies present," he added, moving his eyes from Sidorov to Inna and then to Antipov.

There was a knock at the outer door of the dacha. "I'll go," Antipov said. He came back in a moment with a young woman dressed in white—even her hair was put up under a white cap. She hugged a serving tray to her chest, a kind of armor, but she relaxed a little when she saw Inna. "I'll take your dinner orders," she said. She seemed doubtful of her mission, seeing the *zakuski* almost untouched.

"Good. This talk is too serious," Minin said.

Inna took advantage of the interruption to ask the girl where she could wash her hands.

It was in a separate part of the cottage, past two bedrooms down a long hall opening off one side of the entry hall. As she was washing her hands, there was a thump at the door. When she opened it, Sidorov was leaning against the wall a little way from the door, breathing heavily. " 'Scuze me," he said. "Ol' legs aren't what they used to be. Misjudged the distance."

"You need to be careful of your health, Valentin Ivanovich." She started to squeeze past him in the narrow hall. He put a hand on her arm.

"Vladik too," he said in a low voice. "Needed to be careful of his h . . . h . . . health." He breathed heavily, releasing a cloud of alcohol vapor that she expected could be dangerous near an open flame. "They killed 'im."

"Who killed him?"

"H . . . he wouldn't share. Wanted it all for h . . . himself. Wasn't fair. Shouldn't h . . . have killed him, though."

"Who killed him?"

"People. People who know how. He would have turned us in, otherwise. You un'erstand, don't you?"

The door at the far end of the hall opened and Minin came in. "Waiting turns?" he called. "You're next, Valentin Ivan'ich."

Sidorov, startled, shuddered. "No, not me!" Then he seemed to recall where he was. He looked around, released Inna's arm, and laughed. "The old pisseroo. Yes, I'm next for the old pisseroo." He went into the toilet and closed the door. It sounded as if he had leaned back against the door from the inside.

Minin had gone back into the big room and the door was closed. Inna put a hand on the knob, then let it go and went to the outside door. She opened it and stepped out.

"Good evening," a voice said. Inna jumped and nearly fell from the step.

# 30

A LARGE MAN WAS SITTING ON A CHAIR IN THE WALKWAY FACING THE door.

"I . . . I didn't expect anyone," she said.

"No. I see that. Well, but here I am." He didn't move from his chair.

"I'm going out for a walk."

"Oh, you shouldn't do that. It's dangerous, in the dark. You might step in a hole, or . . . who knows what. No, I can't let you do that. Not alone. But I'll go with you."

"I can certainly take care of myself."

"I can't let you, though. It's my job to take care of guests. If I don't do it, I'll lose my job. You wouldn't want that, would you?"

She said nothing.

"Work's hard to find," he said.

"Well, I'm going."

She started along the walk, away from the cars, toward the pond. She heard the chair creak. Heavy, slow footsteps followed her.

It was clear she was not going to be allowed to leave. She walked as far as the end of the pond, to show her independence, and stopped there looking out over the water. The ducks had fallen silent.

The man stopped a little way from her. He was huge—not just high, but broad. Voluminous. His eyes looked out from a vast head, like a small barrel of beer set on top of a larger barrel. She could tell that he was watching her, but he said nothing.

When she started back to the dacha, she passed him without looking at him. He said nothing, but followed slowly behind her. He sighed as he sat down again on his chair.

A heated conversation stopped when she opened the door to the big room. ". . . stupid to bring her here!" Minin was accusing Antipov, while Antipov, waving a vodka bottle, had his teeth bared like a baited bear.

"I'm ready to go," she said to Antipov.

"You can't go yet!" Minin objected, instantly hearty. "Dinner's ordered!"

"I'm not very hungry, and I have a busy day tomorrow, starting early."

Antipov said, " 'F she wants t' go, I'll take 'er." His face was flushed.

"You're in no shape to drive," Minin said. "You'll run in a ditch and kill you both. Then where will our anticorruption law be? Dead in a ditch too."

"I c'n drive. Vodka helps th' reflexes."

"I'll drive us," Inna said.

"*You* never drove before," Antipov said.

"It can't be that hard. You manage."

Minin and Marchenko laughed. "Stay for dinner, Inna," Marchenko coaxed her. "I know we're hard cases; but with you our discussion has been stimulating."

"Then," she said, "you won't mind if I continue it."

"Not at all. In fact, I think it's important that we continue it and come to some understandings. After all, you've become an influential person. It's important your influence be for the good of the country."

"Meaning that it isn't now?"

212

"Not meaning anything at all, except that it will be pleasant to continue our discussion."

The door banged. Sidorov came back into the room. He weaved among the furniture and paused, swaying, in front of the sofa where Oblonsky was still snoring, although now lying on his face. "There," Sidorov said, "the represen'ative of our aristoc'cy. Still useless as ever." Oblonsky was the name of an old aristocratic Russian family.

"Who is he?" Inna asked.

"Plans to be a duke," Sidorov said. "Again. Out of his share."

"Share?"

"Of the post office." Two steps seemed to take Sidorov by surprise, but at the end of them he did a neat pirouette and fell backward into his original chair. "Whee!" He struggled to sit up, couldn't, but went on talking from where he reclined. "Our 'ristocrats. Turbin and Oblonsky." Turbin was the name of another aristocratic family, before the Revolution. " 'Cept Turbin wanted it all."

"You've said enough, Valentin Ivan'ich," Minin said.

Sidorov made an obscene gesture to Minin. "No matter. Give 'er a share too. She'll keep quiet. Same as us."

"Be quiet," Minin said ominously.

"Vladik wasn't one of us," Sidorov said. " 'Ivanov, Petrov, and Sidorov.' That's us." It was the Russian way of referring to "everybody"—Ivanov, Petrov, and Sidorov were like Smith, Jones, and Johnson: they were Everybody. "We're all in it. But not Vladik. Ivanov, Petrov, and Sidorov . . . and Korneva."

Antipov sank down on a chair by the fire, facing out into the room. He had a blank, hopeless look on his face.

"You've had too much to drink, old man," Minin said. "You're saying stupid, ridiculous things."

" 'N that woman," Sidorov said.

"What woman?" Antipov asked.

"What woman?" Inna asked, but she knew what woman.

"That woman. Should've known when not to talk. But 's okay. We've got a smart lawyer. Smart Jew lawyer on our side." He gave Inna a slow wink. The eye stayed closed. "We get our shares, 'cause we got a smart Jew lawyer." Sidorov's head fell forward, and he snored.

"He's raving," Minin said.

"He's talking about personal matters," General Marchenko said. "Matters important to him, but unimportant in the larger arena. Unimportant to Ivanov, Petrov, and Sidorov, except for this particular Sidorov. What we should be talking about is principle. There is a battle under way, Inna Romanovna—a battle for the soul of the Russian nation. In every battle some soldiers fall. We grieve for them, but we do not turn aside from the battle because of it. This is a battle you are already a part of, and an important part. But it's a battle you have wandered into, without knowing quite who is on your right side and who on your left, who attacks under what banner and who defends. But now you have to choose. You've shown that your heart is in the right place by choosing the needs of Mother Russia over personal desires. But you must choose further. You are in the middle of battle, you have to choose. When my troops took the Kabul airport, there was a key instant when we could have gone this way or that. One way or another, men were going to die; but I could not say how many or for what end. Was this way better or that? I didn't know. Perhaps neither way was good. But I had to take one.

"That's what's before us now. A choice of the way for our nation. Will it be foreign domination, the way Turbin wanted; or will it be Russia free and strong on its own feet, the way your friend Antipov wants it, the way we want it."

"One man's greed can't be 'llowed t' determine a nation's fate," Antipov said.

Inna looked at him coldly. "And the woman?"

"I don't know any woman."

"Not everyone needs to know everything," Marchenko said. "If we have to discuss all the details with all the soldiers, the battle will be over while we still are talking. In this life, someone has to take charge of events. To take charge of events is to take responsibility for the lives of people. Not everyone is capable of that. But someone has to do it."

The General was an impressive man—handsome and straight and well-spoken. And she knew he was lying.

"You say it's a battle for the soul of the nation," Inna said. "It seems to me a battle for the assets of the nation. Oblonsky will be a duke again with his share. What will you do with yours?"

Marchenko merely smiled, although without any sign of amusement; the man who had won the Kabul airport was not a man who gave up easily, even under an insult. "In every struggle, different people are spurred to action by different causes," Marchenko said. "In the abstract we can say that one cause is better or worse than another; but we should never lose sight of the goal—to win the struggle. With clear vision, one cause is not better or worse than another, except as it contributes to reaching the goal.

"You and I are much alike, Inna Romanovna. I know you aren't motivated by personal gain. It is insulting to you to offer you a share of spoils. Your reward is the proper performance of your duty. There are others less blessed who still have abilities that are needed. If the cost of those abilities is within our power to pay, why should we not? The goal is the main thing, not the cost.

"Join us. We need your vision. We need your dedication. We need your help."

"And if I don't?"

He shrugged. "It will be our loss. We'll still admire you. It will have to be from afar."

But she didn't believe him. Now, she feared, the question was how to escape Turbin's fate, and Shubina's. Her father's example showed her that good people did not necessarily come to a good end. She supposed the only hope was not to show fear. "I'll consider your arguments, General. Take me home, Vasily Ivanovich," she said to Antipov.

Antipov struggled to his feet. It was clear that he would indeed have them in the ditch within minutes, if not seconds. But she meant to learn to drive tonight, if necessary. If she got the chance.

"It's not safe to let you go," Minin said.

"Not safe for whom?" she asked.

The General put an end to the discussion. "Of course Inna Romanovna can go anytime she wants to. If Antipov can't drive, someone can take her. Someone can take both of them. Take my car, Inna Romanovna."

"Take mine," Minin said. "It's bigger. My driver will take you both. And my guard can drive Antipov's car home at the same time. I'll go tell them."

"You'll find at least one of them right outside the door," Inna said.

Minin flashed a smile at her. "They're very attentive."

She had thought the Zil was the General's limousine, but the General had one of the black Volgas. The Zil belonged to Minin. One of his companies had absorbed a Party motor pool after the Party went out of commission, and now he moved around Moscow in a vehicle meant for a head of state.

Inna had never ridden in a Zil. It had a back seat big enough for three wide Communists to ride without touching, and two jump seats that her feet would not reach with her legs stretched out. The seats were upholstered in green velour. The trim was Circassian walnut. A glass divider separated the rear and front compartments.

Minin's guard, the man who had been posted to watch at the door of the dacha, squeezed himself behind the steering wheel of Antipov's car. He did not offer any chat as Inna and Antipov were being seen aboard the limousine by Minin, but he grinned at her, as if they shared a secret.

The limousine driver was his twin in size.

At the gate the cars stopped while the policeman saluted and rolled the barrier aside. When they had left it behind, Antipov blurted, "I'm sorry, Inna."

It made her angry. "What are you sorry for, Vasily Ivanovich? You're getting Russian control of an important communications company. You're getting to control it yourself, as I understand."

"I don' want it. Tha's all just talk. Ever'one says when this foreigner's convicted of bribery, the company'll go back to Mespost."

"Minin's company."

"Yes."

"And then Minin will remember his friends."

"I don' want any of it. I didn' know 'bout Turbin. I swear to God." Antipov had never been a Communist, so she didn't laugh at his oath. "And I never heard of this woman."

"She was just a soldier in a battle." Inna had a sudden overwhelming urge just to sink back into the soft seat of the limousine and go to sleep and to wake up safe at home.

Instead, she looked back to see how far behind Antipov's car was following and then studied the roadside ahead in the limo's lights. She was looking for deep, dark places where she could bail out of the car and have a chance to get off the road before the guard, in Antipov's car, could hit her, and into the forest before either of the seven-by-eights could get back to her. Gray late evening had almost reached the edge of the short Moscow summer night. It would be dark in the forest. She wondered if the seven-by-eights had a spotlight. Certainly they had guns.

But the Zil was moving fast. If she jumped at this speed, probably she wouldn't move at all for a while.

If she didn't jump, probably she wouldn't move for a very long time.

The limousine slowed a little at the village, and Antipov's car closed up behind it. There was nowhere to go here. It was too open. The dogs would make a racket. And nobody would take her in late at night, this close to Moscow.

The cars slowed further for the railroad crossing. Easier to get out now, but easier for them to stop, too.

Red lights flashed ahead. The metal arm of the crossing gate began to come down. The driver speeded up the Zil for an instant, hoping to beat the train, but then thought better of it and came to a stop, the big car panting like a great animal on the unlit road.

The light of the engine flashed onto the crossing gates, and then she could see the train up through the scattered village trees. It was coming slowly—a heavy freight train. She could hear the rumble.

She found the door latch and squeezed it and held it as the rumble grew louder.

She pushed the door.

The light in the back compartment flashed on. The driver turned to look into the back, but by then she was running for the crossing. It was only ten yards to the tracks. She hoped she had guessed the train's speed right. If it was too slow, one of them might get across the tracks after her. If it was too fast, she would be cut off. She heard car doors opening. She heard a shout behind her.

The blast of the train's whistle seemed a physical force pushing her off the track. She stepped into a void between the rail and the boards of the crossing. She almost fell, caught herself on both hands, and pushed up again; but her foot stuck. The whistle bore down on her, frantic, screaming. She yanked at her leg and her foot came free, leaving her shoe in the crevice. She fell and rolled free, onto the road on the other side.

Lying there she could see under the train. Beyond its wheels, silhouetted by the headlights of the limousine, were a pair of legs, then a hand with a gun, and then a head. She could not make out a face against the lights. Then a second pair of legs were coming up from the car.

She rolled into the ditch and began to crawl. As she rolled, she looked for the end of the train. It was a long freight, and it was slowing.

Probably the engineer thought he had hit her.

She crawled in the dirt and cinders to the first building, a crossing shack alongside the tracks, thanking God it was on this side of the tracks and not the other. It would have been a long crawl to the next safe spot.

She crawled behind the shack, got to her feet, and ran.

The cemetery began a hundred meters from the shack. She was not an athlete. She was a politician. She regretted it now. After ten meters she threw away her other shoe, and then she ran easier; but still she had to slow before she reached the fence. Her lungs burned. Her stockings were torn and her feet were cut by the cinders.

She thought she could still hear the train rumbling behind her, but maybe it was her heart pounding in her ears. If the train stopped, the seven-by-eights could get under it. But they'd have to abandon their car completely, and they weren't athletes either, from the look of them. Were once, maybe.

The cemetery fence was of close-spaced iron pickets, as high as her shoulders. She tried to squeeze between, couldn't. There was no time to search for a gate. She turned sideways and rolled facedown onto the top of the pickets, trying to get as many of them as possible under her body to spread the pressure, like an Indian fakir. She felt something catch near her knees, heard a ripping sound. She fell from the fence, got to her feet, and holding her torn skirt, stumbled into the cemetery.

It was an old burial ground, over the years grown dense with tombstones. Some she could barely squeeze between. There were bare nameplates on steel pickets; there were marble monuments of old village families, towering above her head. She looked for a path, found one, lost it.

She heard the train moaning behind her. She could not tell if it had stopped. She thought it had. She heard shouting. She plunged on.

Behind her, her guards were faced with a dilemma. The train had stopped. The train crew were running back along the track. Her guards could abandon the cars, leaving Antipov to explain, while they crawled under the train and tried to catch Inna. Or they could get the cars away from there before anyone arrived to ask embarrassing questions.

They compromised. The driver spun the limousine around and shot off down the road toward the compound. As he did so, Antipov fell out of a half-open back door, which slammed closed again as the big car slewed sideways. Antipov picked himself up unsteadily and tottered toward the village in the direction the car had gone.

The guard, leaving Antipov's car standing, its lights on and its motor still running, crawled under the train and panted off up the road toward the cemetery, feeling increasingly unfriendly toward a certain People's Deputy. He was thirsty. He thought about how nice it would be to have a little taste of vodka. But the bottle was in the trunk of the Zil.

*    *    *

The cemetery was a maze. Wide paths wound through it, but they all seemed eventually to branch into narrower paths and then still narrower until they ran out into dead ends surrounded by clusters of graves. Most of the graves were surrounded by fences of low iron pickets or wire, some of them little courtyards with benches and flowerpots, and there was no way between them. But if going back led to a wider path, that path led only to another branching network and another dead end.

It was too dark to read the names on the gravestones, although sometimes she could make out faces—photographs that had been transferred somehow to stone, in the Russian custom. They were dark, serious faces, all of them.

She tried at last climbing the fences whenever she reached a dead end, and then she was able to continue. She took her direction from the train's, moving as directly away from it as possible. It whistled and complained for a long time, but then it started a slow, steady rumble that grew in pitch and intensity for a few minutes and then died away and was gone, and she was alone in the silent dark.

She sat down to rest. Her feet were painful. When she touched them, her hand came away sticky with blood. Her mouth was cottony. She found a little water caught in a monument carved into a bowl shape. She was able to get her face into the bowl far enough to suck a drink, and then she washed her hands and her face and felt better.

As she was climbing down, she heard footsteps.

She slid behind the monument and watched and listened.

She saw nothing; but someone was walking cautiously on a path perhaps two rows of monuments over. The footsteps stopped.

She waited. Eventually the steps began again, and then she moved. Trying to go as directly away from the steps as she could, she tripped over something and fell against a fence. A loose gate in the fence swung and clanged shut.

As she lay in wet grass, she heard the sound of someone climbing fences, coming toward her.

She got up and stumbled forward, ignoring silence now. She came to a path, ran up it, and found that it was curving back the way she had come. She heard an iron fence crash down and than a curse in a man's voice: *"Blyad!"* She came to a fork in the path and took the branch that led away from the man. It ended in a tangle of waist-high weeds and untended graves and broken fences. Beyond was the forest. Out of the tangle here and there rose dark monuments of stone. She could not get through in silence. Maybe she could not get through at all. Behind her the footsteps had reached the path.

# 31

GENERAL MARCHENKO AND MININ WERE OUTSIDE THE DACHA WHEN the driver returned. The Zil's headlights flashed across them. The driver left the car running and hurried along the walk to them.

"Done so soon?" Minin said. When the driver didn't answer, he asked, "Antipov didn't make trouble about it, did he?"

*"She's* the one who'd make trouble," Marchenko said.

"Something went wrong," the driver said.

"We'll talk about it somewhere else," Marchenko said. He glanced through the open door at Sidorov and Oblonsky. The two of them were sleeping peacefully. Sidorov was still in his chair, but Oblonsky had somehow got onto the floor, where he was snoring in unbroken rhythm.

Marchenko closed the door and led Minin and the driver away from the dacha.

"What went wrong?" Minin asked. "Where's Joker?"

"He went after the woman."

"Went after her? Where did she go?"

"She got across ahead of the train, and before it stopped—"

"Wait. What train?"

But the driver had his story ready and didn't know how to change it. "—she got out of sight; and then it stopped and we

couldn't get the car across, and the train crew were coming back . . ."
When he spoke, there was a faint bloom of alcohol odor.

"Wait."

". . . and so Joker went after her and sent me back here so they wouldn't ask any questions."

"So you didn't crash Antipov's car."

"We didn't get a chance!"

"And where is Antipov's car?"

"I left it there. What else could I do? I can't drive two cars at once."

"And Antipov?"

"He's in the limo."

"You're sure?"

"He was."

But when they looked, the limo was there but Antipov was not.

"He was here a minute ago!" the driver insisted.

"Then he's got to be in the grounds. Get the militiaman and start looking." The driver aimed a look of appeal at Marchenko.

"It's a waste of time to search the grounds," Marchenko said. "Antipov's not our problem. That woman's our problem." He said to the driver, "Turn the car around and follow me. I'll take my car." He said to Minin, "You'll come with me."

In the car, Minin shook his head. "God, the people I have to work with! Now I know why they call him Brick."

"Maybe he isn't the world's brightest," General Marchenko said, wheeling the Volga out onto the curving driveway, "but he's a steady man under fire." The Brick had been a sergeant under his command, when Marchenko was a junior officer. The Joker had been first sergeant. It was a long time ago, though it seemed like yesterday. Marchenko had got them both jobs with Minin during the reduction in force at the Ministry of Security after the August coup. Marchenko didn't like Minin's comment about Brick. Brick was loyal: he carried out his orders to the end. Marchenko wondered if Minin was a man who understood what loyalty meant.

"What were they going to do?" he asked Minin. He hadn't wanted to know, before. Now he had to.

"Joker said they'd smash Antipov's car off the road and then put the bodies into it. As if they'd died in the accident."

"And burn it for good measure, I suppose," Marchenko said.

"We didn't talk about that."

"Some things you don't have to talk about."

He was sorry, now, that he had lined up Brick and Joker with Minin. It was like leaving good tools to someone who didn't know how to use them. Minin swaggered around Moscow in that limousine and bragged that he had KGB men as his personal guards. But they weren't KGB men anymore. They had rusted from lack of use. From lack of care. Drinking on the job—he'd never have expected to find the Brick drinking on the job.

When they approached the village, Marchenko slowed and turned his lights off. In midsummer Moscow, the nights were not black dark under the open sky, and he was able to stay on the road driving slowly. Brick in the Zil behind him did the same.

Running that way, they were almost at the railroad crossing before Marchenko saw it. The lights were not flashing. The train was gone. And Antipov's car was gone too.

He stopped and got out of the car in the middle of the road. He could hear the train then, a long way to the east, moving away.

The driver came up from the limousine. "Where's the other car?" Marchenko asked. Minin had got out too, but Marchenko ignored him.

"We left it here," the driver said. "It was right here in the road." He pointed toward his feet to emphasize the placement.

"Maybe Joker took it," Minin said.

"Maybe. Where were you going to dispose of it?" Marchenko asked the driver.

"There's a place where the road curves in another kilometer or so. There's a long drop on the outside of the curve. It's a good place to put a car over. Block the accelerator and aim it straight at the start of the curve. But he wouldn't have come back for the car unless he caught the woman; and he wouldn't take her there without People's Deputy Antipov. That wouldn't make sense. Why would she be in People's Deputy Antipov's car alone? It'd raise questions."

"Quite right, Sergeant," Marchenko said, extending the title as a courtesy. "You've got a good head on your shoulders." He pointedly ignored Minin as he said this. "No, if Joker took the car, we'd have met him on his way back to the dacha—whether he caught her or whether he didn't. So someone else took it. And since we didn't meet Joker on foot, he's still somewhere ahead of us. Where was the woman when you saw her last?"

"She was on the far side of the tracks, crawling away up the ditch. And then she got up and ran behind that building. We couldn't get a fair shot at her."

"We'll go on and see what we can learn."

They drove the cars across the tracks. Marchenko stopped there, and they all got out and inspected the ground. Marchenko looked toward the dark under the trees a hundred meters away behind the cemetery fence. "They've got a twenty-minute head start," he said. "They could be a kilometer away by now." It would take a sizable search party to find them, even in daylight. Marchenko silently cursed his luck, that he knew what to do but lacked the resources to do it. "Well, there's no point in looking for him: it's a big country. Best to leave him to what he's doing and hope he does it well. Meanwhile, we'll have to assume that he'll fail."

"That don't seem fair to Joker," Brick said. He was careful not to seem too critical.

"It's not a question of 'fair,' Sergeant. It's a question of being prepared for the worst. It's no fault of Joker's, but if he finds her in the dark, it'll be sheer luck."

"Her bad luck," the Brick said.

Marchenko sent the driver back to the limousine while he talked with Minin. "You were a fool to let Antipov bring her tonight," he said.

"It's Antipov's fault," Minin said. "He was convinced that she'd join us, once she understood the importance of it."

"We already knew that Antipov's a fool. But I didn't know you were one. Only a fool listens to a fool."

"You were willing enough to try to convince her," Minin said.

"That was our only chance, once Antipov decided to bring her in."

"One chance out of two. The other was to get rid of her."

"If you call that a chance." It made Marchenko angry, to hear civilians chatter about "getting rid of" people. What did they know about killing and dying? They talked about it as if it were nothing. It wasn't nothing. Soldiers knew.

"None of this would have happened if you hadn't been so quick to 'get rid of' Turbin," Minin said.

"That was different. Turbin sold us out. He was willing to turn over the company to the Americans, just so he got his piece of bread. But I don't have time to waste on this now. There are things that have to be done if she's got away, and we won't know if she's got away until Joker comes back. You take that limo back to the dacha. We can't have it standing around here inviting questions. Leave Brick here to wait for Joker, with instructions to find a way to telephone you the minute he shows up. Then you telephone my office. No message—just ask to have me telephone you." Marchenko opened the door of his car and got in.

"What if he doesn't show up?"

"He will."

"He could get lost in those woods at night."

"He's been in worse places than this and come back." Marchenko slammed his car door in disgust at civilians.

# 32

WITH NO OTHER CHOICE BEFORE HER, INNA PUSHED INTO THE TANGLE of weeds. One foot caught on something, and she fell to one knee. Her other foot landed on cold iron. The chill of it went through her, went to her heart.

When she felt the iron, she knew she was at the very end.

When she knew that, the fear left her.

She reached down and groped for the iron under her foot. She found it, pried her fingers under it, and it came up out of the earth. It was a fallen grave marker, an iron rod as thick as two fingers and as long as her leg. Near one end was a metal plate with a picture on it, the picture of a young girl. Above the picture was a Russian cross.

"All right, you bastard," Inna said under her breath, "let's see if you can kill me."

The steps came along the path, cautiously now, stopping every few seconds to listen.

They became a heavy man, breathing heavily.

He waited a long time at the edge of the weeds.

"Come out," he said. "Come out, I won't hurt you. We've just got to get you home."

Nothing.

From somewhere far off came the sound of a car door slamming. He turned his head to catch the sound. Nothing followed it. He turned back.

"Look," he complained, "this is crazy! If I don't get you home, I'll lose my job. Jobs are hard to find these days!"

She might have been sympathetic, but for the gun in his hand, held beside his ear, pointing skyward. She saw the glint of it when he turned his head.

Still nothing.

"Aw, for—! Get my damn *feet* muddy?" He pushed into the weeds, holding his arms up like a man wading a stream.

As he passed, Inna stepped out from behind a monument and brained him with the grave marker.

It was too heavy for her to hold up long, but she rested its tip on the ground and swung it with both hands from the ground up and aimed it at the back of his head, right beside the pistol. The impact knocked him three steps forward, and then he fell and didn't move.

He lay facedown in the weeds. She scrambled around for his gun, found it, and backed away from him. He was still not moving. She listened for ten seconds, heard nothing, turned, and pushed on through the weeds toward the forest.

It was pine forest, black as hell under the trees, but open and carpeted with a deep layer of fallen needles. She stood feeling the edges of the needles under her feet as she wondered which way to go, and she was suddenly without force. The needles lay in every direction on the forest floor, like a million small signposts pointing everywhere at once, and she thought that her feet could tell the direction of each one of them; but none pointed a way forward. But as she stood uncertain, she thought that she heard far off another train. The sound jolted her from her reverie. She started toward it.

After a long time she came out of the forest onto the railroad track. She did not know where she was or what direction was Moscow, so she turned right and began walking, stepping carefully from one tie to another, trying to keep her feet off the rocks of the roadbed. She didn't limp, because both feet hurt equally, but after a little way she stopped and tore the rest of her skirt into strips and tied them around her feet.

For a long time there was nothing but forest on both sides of the track. She had no idea how long she had been walking, but she was deadly tired. Finally there was a break in the forest on one side, and when she reached it, she saw that it was a suburban train station at a road crossing, a concrete, one-room building behind an open boarding platform. The station was closed and dark. But there was a sign on it: SOSNOVAYA.

Now she knew where she was: not half an hour by train from Moscow's Kiev Railway Station, and from there within walking distance of her home.

It might as well have been the moon.

She looked at her reflection in a window of the station. It was too dark for her to see much detail, but from what she saw she didn't long for more light.

No passenger trains would stop here until near dawn, but she wouldn't be getting on a train in this condition. The conductor might take her for just another drunk coming home from a great party. But he might also call the police, and the General had said his organization cooperated with the law-enforcement authorities.

Anyway, she had no money for a ticket. Her purse was in the Zil.

There was a pay phone on the station wall facing the platform, but she still had no money. Not even two kopecks.

She went back to the window and raised her hands over her brows to shade a space to see better inside, and then she saw she was still carrying the pistol in her hand.

She thought about waiting at the crossing for a car to come and, pistol in hand, demanding a ride into Moscow. But that was only an amusement.

She stepped back, covered her face with her left arm, and punched the pistol through the station window. She knocked out the remaining shards of glass, felt inside for the latch, opened the window, and crawled through.

She groped in the dark until she found a desk and then a telephone. She dialed Alex Fall's number.

# 33

FALL WOULD HAVE MISSED THE STATION IF THE ROAD HADN'T CROSSED the tracks. There was nothing around it but forest, although over the hill was one of those isolated apartment buildings that the planners had decreed be dropped out here, with a footpath from it through the forest to the station. As it was, he came over the hill, crossed the tracks before he saw the station, and then had to back up.

As he was looking toward the station for Inna, she came out of the forest on the opposite side of the road and got into the car.

"Innochka," he said, "you don't have to go to this length to keep our meetings secret." Then he really looked at her, and stopped joking. "What happened to you?"

"I took a shortcut home through the forest."

"You what? From where?"

"I don't want to talk on the road, Alex."

"What happened to your face? What happened to your dress?"

"Will you find someplace we can get off the road?"

He drove slowly, looking for turnoffs glancing from time to time to the side to see if she was really there. They came to a place where the car could be run off the road up among some trees, and he pulled up there and stopped and turned off the lights. He reached in the back and found the bundle of clothes she had asked for.

"I knew there was some reason I left these things at your place," she said.

"I thought it was so you'd have an excuse to come back."

"No, I just wanted to be prepared for tonight. Excuse me while I change." She looked away so he wouldn't see her face under the dome light when she got out.

He had brought her jeans and a shirt and sweater and a hat. She tried to put on her shoes he had brought, but she couldn't get her swollen feet into them, so she just put on the socks and got back into the car. "All right!" she said. "There's nothing like a change of clothes to make a girl feel good!"

"You forgot to take this with you." He was holding the pistol. She had left it on the seat.

She took it and stuck it into her belt.

"Innochka, what's this about?"

"I wanted to teach people about corruption. I learned some things I didn't want to know."

"Tell me."

When she had finished talking, he said, "I'm going to kill the sons of bitches."

"That's sweet of you, Alex." She kissed him on the cheek.

"My sweet love . . . your poor face!"

"It's just scratches, Alex. If you want to feel sorry for me, feel sorry for my feet."

"I'll kill them if it's the last thing I do!"

"Can it wait until morning, then?"

"Sure. Revenge is best served cold." He thought for a moment. "We'd better call Slavin."

"Slavin? Why?"

"To get his advice on what to do. This is a dangerous mess

we're in now. We need all the brains we can muster to get out of it. I don't know any better brains than Slavin's."

"Let's not tell Slavin."

He was touched that she thought he could handle something like this himself. He knew he couldn't. He doubted that they could all together, but at least they had a better chance. "Slavin's got a lot of connections," he said. "I know you do too, but his go back farther. And he knows the system, and where to go for help. We're going to need him."

"His connections are the problem."

"What do you mean?"

"There's a 'smart Jew lawyer' on the other side, and I think they meant Slavin."

Fall studied her face. "He's not. But the best lies are built on a grain of truth. Somebody tried to push him out of this a long time ago. We couldn't find out who. Now I think we know. Maybe it was these same two animals—the description fits. He pretended to go along, but he told me about it instead."

Her eyes were steady on his. "I still believe it."

"Why? On the strength of some rumor?"

"No. Because there's more than a grain of truth in it. I don't know if we can trust him for hard business. He failed my father."

"Slavin did?"

"Yes, Slavin. He agreed to defend my father, but when they pressed him, he dropped the case. My father forgave him. But he's not a man I want to save me from drowning. I'd rather swim for myself."

Fall did not know what to say. "He told me," he said at length, in wonderment, like someone telling of a dream.

"He told you? About my father?"

"He didn't tell me it was your father. He said he had been pushed once to give up a case, and he did it. He seemed glad they were trying to push him out of this case, Chapman's. He saw it as a way to make it up."

"He's a clever man, Slavin. It's not safe to believe him."

"I have to believe him. No . . . I don't have to. But I do." He turned to her. "Give him a chance, Inna."

She said nothing for a long them. Then: "All right. If you say I should."

Slavin slept lightly in the middle of the night. It was morning that he found hard to face. He went to bed late and grudgingly, and in the morning he woke the same way. But when his telephone rang at three A.M., he answered it instantly although he had been in bed for an hour. "Hello. . . . Yes, hello, Alex. . . . No, it's not too late, that's nothing. Of course I want to discuss strategy. The usual place? . . . I'll be there in half an hour." As soon as he learned that someone wanted him off the case, he and Fall had agreed on a place to meet if they ever needed to talk and were concerned about surveillance. They had never used the meeting place. He wondered what had happened, that Fall wanted to meet now.

Fall stopped his Volvo on a dark side street not far off the main road to Sheremetyevo Airport. He shut off the engine but left the radio on. Peggy Lee was singing "These Foolish Things." He had been singing along with it, but with the engine off, his voice suddenly sounded loud, and he faltered, embarrassed. "American music at three in the morning," he said to cover his embarrassment. "Who'd have expected it, in the old days? Even old American music? Or *any* music? When I was a student here, the radios died at midnight."

"You have a nice voice," Inna said. "Don't stop."

He looked in the rearview mirror and suddenly pulled her to him and kissed her fiercely.

She tried to push free after a moment, and he said, "Milliman," and kissed her again.

There was a soft double tap at the back fender of the car on the curb side, and then the policeman walked on past, strolling in the direction the car was facing. He had tapped on the car. As he left, he waved one finger back toward them: naughty.

"Sorry," Fall said. "Protective cover. I hope I didn't hurt your face."

"You didn't."

231

He kissed her again. "Cops always travel in pairs, at least."
Her arms went around him. And again.

"Do you see another one?"

"No, but we'd better be careful." And again.

"Oh, Alex, I've missed you so much!"

A car driving on parking lights came up slowly behind them
and stopped.

"Damn the militia," she said.

He looked back carefully through the headrest. "It's Misha."

"Damn Misha."

Slavin got out of his car and came up to the driver's door of
Fall's Volvo. He stood there without touching the car. Fall rolled
down the window.

"Ah . . . Alex?"

"Yeah, Mish. We were just watching out for militia. We'll be
right there."

"All right." He started to walk back to his car, then turned
again. "Take your time."

Fall helped Inna back to Slavin's car. She walked tenderly.

When they got into his car, Slavin said nothing at first. Then
he said, "I'm sorry. I thought you were going to be alone. You
didn't tell me . . ."

"Never mind. Misha, have you met Inna Romanovna?"

Slavin glanced into the rearview mirror—she had got into the
back of the Zhiguli. It was a moment before he said anything:
"It's been a very long time."

"I was just a girl. But of course I know all about the famous
lawyer."

"Not all of it bad, I hope."

"Not all of it. I'm very happy to meet you again, Mikhail
Alexandrovich."

"Well, you do me too much honor. You know I knew your
father."

"I know."

"We've talked about it, Misha," Fall said.

"Oh. Well." Slavin turned his attention to getting the Zhiguli
under way. The starter ground, the engine fired, died, fired again.
"To the place we agreed, then?"

"Let's go."

They drove to a gas station on the main road to the airport. It was the only station in this part of Moscow that worked late at night, and even past three A.M. a line of cars an hour long crawled toward the one working pump.

They talked in the car in the gas line. Two lovers in a car on the street were acceptable, but three would have been a target for any passing policeman. Here any number were just that many more people in a gas station line wishing to be somewhere else.

Slavin listened to Inna's tale intently. He interrupted her only once—when she named General Marchenko.

"Marchenko?" Slavin said. "Are you sure? What was his name and patronymic?"

"I think his name was Grigory. I'm not sure. He said he had something to do with the Kabul airport."

"Marchenko. Yes." Slavin waved for her to proceed.

When she had finished, he restarted the car, inched it forward in line, shut it off again. "I'm sorry you got caught in this, Inna Romanovna."

"Are you sorry *you* did?"

He thought about that. "No."

"Then why be sorry for me?"

"This is very dangerous."

"Of course it's dangerous," she said. "But what is there to do? 'We make our life with our own hands,' my father said. Do we drop everything now because it's dangerous? What does that do to our lives, if we drop all the things we stand for?"

"It's always hard to be sure what's the right thing to do," Slavin said. "But in any event we have to get you to the court. What you say may save our client. But it may save you, too—if you say it soon enough. Once your story is in evidence, then there's no longer a reason for them to silence you." Slavin sighed. "I hope Judge Pskova won't mind hearing a surprise witness. Judges hate surprise witnesses. And the Criminal Procedure Code doesn't require a judge to hear any witness not listed in the investigator's case."

"Today is Friday," Fall said. "No, Saturday, now. Can we take Inna to the judge today?"

Slavin smiled. "Madame Pskova would find that quite surprising. No, the Criminal Procedure Code is definite. Witnesses can be heard only in court. Everyone will have to be there—the defendant, the Prosecutor, defendant's counsel, the judge, the People's Assessors, the Court Secretary . . . the public, if anyone's interested."

"We know who's interested," Fall said. "Can't we at least get a hearing closed to the public?"

"No. We don't have all this witness-protection business they say you have in America. There are only two possible reasons for closing a hearing—testimony on state secrets and testimony on 'intimacy.' "

" 'Intimacy' sounds interesting," Inna said. She was holding Fall's hand behind the seat back.

"Intimacy would not be interesting in Madame Pskova's court," Slavin said.

"What do we do with Inna until Monday?" Fall asked. "She can't go home. And certainly they'll look for her at my apartment, and probably yours too, Misha. I don't think we can go home either."

"Isn't there anything we can do today?" Inna asked. "Shouldn't we go to the police?"

"We considered going to Volkov before," Fall told her, "but we decided we weren't sure we could trust him. But Inna's story puts a new color on the case, Misha. Don't you have any friends who could help? Your old buddies from the Militia Academy?"

"There's only one. Although we've never thought of ourselves as 'buddies.' "

"Who is it?"

"Investigator Volkov."

"Volkov!"

Slavin's smile glowed briefly. Slavin loved effects, and he had obviously used the name for effect. "Don't look so startled, Alex. You yourself said that Inna's story puts a new color on the case. Going to Volkov always had its dangers. We still must be cautious. But now I think we can be sure that he's only the investigator, and not part of the story."

"How can you be sure?"

"I've told you I've known Volkov for a long time."

"You've told me you were both on the staff of the Militia Academy."

"Yes. Under General Krylov, Chairman of the Academy."

"I had forgotten Krylov."

"Volkov hasn't. Neither has anyone else who worked for Krylov."

"I remember. You told me he died in disgrace."

Slavin bumped the car forward and shut it off again. He looked out the side window, away from Fall and Inna. "General Krylov was a fine, honest man," he said, continuing to look away from them. "But his time was not a good time for fine, honest men." He turned his face back toward the front of the car and began to speak, in the way of someone telling a tale long rehearsed— the way of a lawyer summarizing evidence yet to be presented. "Krylov was the closest friend of Shcholokov, the Minister of Internal Affairs under Brezhnev. Shcholokov was corrupt, and under him the police became corrupt. But Krylov was not. He was a General of Militia, but he was also a lawyer and a scientist. He stressed a scientific approach to criminal matters—prevention, not just chasing lawbreakers. He believed in child-care programs, for example, as a way of preventing juvenile crime. And he insisted on keeping records of real crime rates, not the sanitized records that the Party wanted, with all crimes ever-decreasing to the vanishing point. It was a brave thing, at the time.

"At the same time, you may remember, General Andropov headed the KGB. Andropov, who later became General Secretary of the Party, and in effect the head of the Soviet state.

"The KGB was more powerful than the Ministry of Internal Affairs, but Shcholokov was closer to Brezhnev. He had come up with Brezhnev through the Party ranks in Moldavia, where Brezhnev came from.

"The KGB, I might also say, was and is the least corrupt branch of the state. But it had its own defects. It saw no bounds to its duty to protect the Party and the state. It was self-centered in its zeal.

"Andropov, maybe, was jealous of Shcholokov's friendly relations with Brezhnev. Or maybe he just wanted to see justice done. Whatever he wanted, he was unable to attack Brezhnev's friend; but he was not unable to attack the friend of Brezhnev's friend. Perhaps I give Andropov too much responsibility in this. It doesn't matter whether I do: what matters is that the staff of the Militia Academy—Krylov's staff—believed this. Volkov believes it.

"However it happened, Brezhnev's son-in-law, Churbanov, was appointed as First Deputy Minister of Internal Affairs. You probably remember that he was later arrested and found guilty of corruption—after his father-in-law died, of course. His sentence was twelve years in prison, with confiscation of all his property. But that was much later. At this time, Churbanov was atop the Soviet world.

"Now Churbanov, as First Deputy Minister, could not live in a world where one of his subordinates was the closest friend of the Minister himself. So it was necessary for him to be rid of General Krylov. Churbanov treated Krylov with increasing disrespect, including public insults. But General Krylov went on doing his honest work.

"Eventually certain information came to Churbanov indicating that the activities of the Militia Academy and its Director should be investigated. Those who knew Krylov knew the information came from the KGB.

"Churbanov had himself appointed as head of the committee of investigation. The direction of things from that point was clear to Krylov. In protest, he killed himself in his office. Shot himself twice through the heart with his service pistol. He was found in his office by his personal assistant. He was still alive, but he died in the ambulance on the way to the hospital.

"It was recommended to the officers of the Academy that they not attend the funeral, but a few did. Volkov was there."

"How do you know?" Inna asked.

"I saw him there." After a while, Slavin added, "In fact, it was the last time I saw him before this case. The whole staff of the Academy was 'put out of draft,' as the saying is—that is, they could remain in their jobs only if reappointed. Most were not. Volkov became a police investigator. And I, as you know, became an Advocate."

Slavin started his car, moved it forward, shut it off again. They were almost at the gasoline pumps.

"I don't see why this would mean we can trust Volkov more now than we could before," Fall said.

"This goes deeper than you know," Slavin said. "The Russian memory of wrongs never fades. There are many old feuds unsettled between the police and the KGB. This is one. But in addition to that, to Krylov's friends, this is personal."

"Who was Krylov's personal assistant?" Fall asked. He guessed from Slavin's suppressed emotion as he told the story that it had been Slavin himself.

Slavin said, "Maxim Volkov was Krylov's personal assistant. It was he who found Krylov dying in his office." He stared at the instruments of his car, as if there were something to read there, something about the past or about what made life the way it was.

He said, "If I know Volkov, he'll pursue this case even to his own grave, because a young KGB officer on Andropov's staff was responsible for the investigation of General Krylov. His name was Grigory Marchenko."

"General Marchenko," Inna said softly.

"General Marchenko," Slavin said. He started the car roughly and lunged it up to the pump. He sat a moment and took a deep breath before he opened his door. "This is wonderful efficiency, preserving a client and refueling my car at the same time. And being given the chance to settle an old, old score."

When Slavin got back into the car, Inna asked him, "What do we do now?"

"I've got to see Volkov as soon as I can. But first we'll find a place to put you, Inna, in case it occurs to our opponents that you may go to the police."

"First let's get something to eat," Inna said. "I'm starved. I didn't get dinner last night."

"How about the Metropol for breakfast?" Slavin suggested. He was joking, but wished he weren't. The idea of revenge had given him an appetite. He began dreaming of sausages and fried eggs and Danish pastries.

They settled for bread and soft cheese from women waiting for a farmers' market to open as the sun rose at four in the morning. One of the women was brewing tea in a samovar. A fire of small sticks glowed in the metal chimney that ran through the center of the samovar's water chamber. "Tea for your wife, my sweet?" she said to Fall, glancing toward Inna, who had stayed in the car. "She does look tired." She seemed to know that Inna was with Fall and not with Slavin. What could she have seen from this distance? he wondered. Were their feelings so transparent? The woman gave them glasses of tea and would take no payment except the return of the glasses.

As Slavin drove them back to Fall's car, Inna fell asleep in the cramped back seat of the Zhiguli.

"A remarkable woman," Slavin said.

Fall answered, "If she can sleep through your driving, Misha, she's a truly remarkable woman."

Slavin laughed. "But now we have to preserve this remarkable woman, to make sure that she becomes a remarkable witness." His face lit up; he grinned to his ears. "I can hardly wait to hear Kol'tsov's objection when I ask Madame Pskova to hear an additional witness."

"Where do we hide this remarkable woman, to keep her alive for Judge Pskova?"

Slavin became thoughtful, although he continued to smile. "I have a cousin. Every Jew has a cousin, of course. But I have a cousin. And this cousin has a dacha."

# 34

GENERAL MARCHENKO ARRIVED AT HIS OFFICE AS THE SUN WAS RISING. His arrival put the hall guards in a flutter, a hawk startling a flock of dozing chickens.

But he only passed through the hall and closed the door to his office.

Marchenko sat down to think. His chair was a chair General Andropov had once used, before he left the Committee on State Security to become General Secretary of the Party. It was where Marchenko thought best. He had died too soon, Andropov. If he had lived, Gorbachev would never have come to office, and then the Union would have survived, and the Committee on State Security . . . well, it was no time for history. History was what people do here and now. And here and now was a problem. Marchenko did not know whether the woman People's Deputy was dead or alive. Joker had not returned and had not telephoned anyone. It could mean he was still on the track, too occupied to make contact. It could mean that he had got lost in the forest. The only safe course was to assume that the woman had escaped in the night; if she had, steps had to be taken immediately. But they were steps that he would not take at all if he had any choice. They would burn a lot of favors owed to him, whether they got results or not. When you set out down an unknown road, who knew what would be at the end of it?

And one wrong step now would make Marchenko look like a fool. The worst error a man could make was looking like a fool. A strong man was forgiven anything, but fools were not forgiven. That fool Gorbachev.

Marchenko decided to use his own resources first. There were men he could command without having to ask favors.

They couldn't arrest the woman, of course, even if they found her. She was a People's Deputy, immune from arrest for any reason. That would have meant nothing in the old days, in the days of the real KGB. But today, even the best men wouldn't risk an unauthorized arrest. Maybe especially the best men. But they wouldn't have to arrest her. They could watch her. No law against that. It was the job of the Ministry of Security. And if anything else had to be done, there were other people who would still do it. People who knew that Stalin had it right: "Where there's a person, there's a problem. No person, no problem."

If she was still in the forest, she wouldn't be there much longer, now that the sun was up. There were no big stretches of unbroken forest so close to Moscow. She'd find a road or a railroad and be gone to the city. If she was going to be found, she'd have to be found in the city. Not easy, but not impossible. It was a big city, if you thought of it as a collection of ten million people, and all the places they might be; but most of those people and most of those places were irrelevant. The world grew suddenly small to someone needing help, and this Korneva woman was someone in need of help.

Where would she go? Home or to friends. That was where people went: home. Her apartment, or her office at the Supreme Soviet. If she spread her story around the Supreme Soviet, it would be bad. She'd have to be stopped from going there. She might go to the police. Impossible to watch all police stations, though. Not enough men. There were never enough men. That lawyer, the American she had been in love with. She might see him as protection. His apartment and his office, then. And Antipov's apartment too. Where had Antipov got to?

He picked up his telephone.

# 35

THE SUN ON HIS FACE WOKE ANTIPOV. HIS EYES WERE STILL CLOSED, BUT he could see the sunlight through his eyelids. Shadows moved on them. His neck hurt. He shook his head, moved his lips tentatively to see that they still operated, then opened his eyes.

He found himself looking up and out of a car window, looking at the sun shining through treetops far above. His neck hurt because his head was bent back over the back of the car seat, as well as being turned sideways. He thought he should move his head, but he didn't. He closed his eyes again and watched the shadows move across his eyelids. Light and dark. Light and dark.

Suddenly he sat bolt upright, banged his head on the inside of the car roof, swore, found someone's hands clutching the steering wheel. They were his hands.

Suddenly he saw everything, remembered everything.

He was in his car at the side of a forest road. If this was sunrise, the road ran easterly. It was a dirt road, tan clay, and sunlight fell through high trees onto the tan clay in bars and dapples.

Inna.

Inna should have been with him. He looked around. She was not with him.

She should have been here with him, in the back of Minin's limousine, in the darkness. She was not.

Perhaps he didn't remember everything.

He looked around again, took inventory of his sensory impressions, confirmed them.

He was in the driver's seat of his own car, on a clay road in daylight, not in the back seat of a limousine on a paved road in darkness. Inna was not here. There was no railroad. The car was out of gas.

Railroad. Something about a railroad. What was that? There had been a railroad.

Out of gas. How did he know?

He turned the switch, tried the starter. It worked, but nothing answered in the engine. He read the gauges. The gas gauge said empty. How did he know?

He swore off drink again, meant it. He'd done it a thousand times before. Meant it then too. Much drink not good for a public man. Not even one in disgrace.

Disgrace? What was that about?

He remembered more, then. Remembered too much.

Inna. *Innochka, run! Did you get away?*

He remembered then. Finding himself alone by the road. A car running. His own car. Driving to look for Innochka. Not finding her on the road. Driving on then. Driving east. Driving home. Had anyone ever driven to Siberia?

He had to go back. He knew it at once, when he remembered. Inna in danger. He had to go back. She knew too much. It was his fault. He hadn't known so much himself. Hadn't wanted to. Now maybe he knew too much.

He got out of the car. He felt the clay road soft under his feet. He turned back west, the way he had come, seeing the car tracks deep in the soft early-morning clay of the road, his own car tracks and no others. He locked the car, took a few steps, stopped, felt the sun warm on his back. He stood awhile, feeling the warmth of the sun.

He knew too much.

He turned to face the sun, stood awhile that way, letting his eyes close and the sun shine through his eyelids. Then he opened his eyes and walked eastward up the clean, clear road ahead.

# 36

Minin's associates were not people who rose early, although he was, but he woke them early this morning. When the Brick came in without Joker, just after sunrise, Minin saw at once what had to be done, and he started telephoning. The Brick wanted to go tramping through forests looking for his friend, but there was no point in it. Joker would come back sometime. Or else he'd just keep on going, in shame at not being able to deal with one helpless woman. Either way, it was a waste of manpower to go looking for him. The one they needed to look for was the woman, before she got to the police.

Marchenko had said he would handle it. Let him think so. He was full of himself, Marchenko, but he hadn't shown much on this operation yet. The real work had been done by Minin's people, and if there were any problems, they were caused by these parasites he'd got from Marchenko.

Minin was sorry now that he had left such important work to two old Committee castoffs. He should have known, when the KGB let them go, that it had a reason. The KGB had never given the country anything worth having. As for these two rotten apples, he should have got rid of them before they spoiled the whole barrel. He could tell Brick had been drinking again during the night. Probably why the KGB let him go.

"If you do a thing yourself, you'll know it's done right," Minin's father always told him. He lived by that. The hell with Marchenko. Here was something that had to get done, and done right, and quickly. Minin wasn't about to wait and see whether Marchenko got it done.

Minin knew what was needed now: the power of the competitive market. In these last few years, Minin had developed great faith in the power of the competitive market, and the power of cash to settle any situation in Moscow. If only one had enough of it and knew how to apply it. Minin had enough of it, and he knew better than anyone how to apply it. The Ministry of Security, for all its authority, was just a big, stupid monopoly, no better than any of the other big, stupid monopolies the Soviet state had engendered. But the market was infinite. Offer a large enough incentive, and the market would find eyes to watch any place this woman was likely to go. Offer a large enough incentive, and the market would sell her silence.

Minin had been on the telephone for some time now arranging payments, waking people with the agreeable news that today they had a chance to become rich. Minin liked to bring people good news. It was a satisfying feeling.

And if they couldn't do it themselves, let them find someone else to do it for them. Spread the news and take a commission. That was the way to get rich in the new world of the market. A little commission on a big transaction.

The only problem was time. What if the woman got to the police or to the Supreme Soviet and testified before making anyone wealthy?

In that case, life would be better somewhere else.

Minin was a man of foresight. He had always supposed there might come a time when his life would be better somewhere else. There was nothing unusual in that. Everyone he knew, everyone he had ever known all his life, had talked constantly about how much better life must be somewhere else. Everyone who was not a Party idiot. Some said one place, some said another: Germany, Italy, Brazil. The consensus was America. That was where life must be best, because otherwise why would the government propaganda always have been saying what a hellhole America was?

The difference Minin saw between himself and everyone else he had known all his life was that while they were talking about how much better life must be somewhere else, he was preparing to do something about it. First he made his life better here, where he was; and second he prepared for the time when life really had better be better somewhere else.

No, he wasn't actually the only one. The Party people, the

really big people, the ones who controlled the Party's funds, they had been preparing too. The difference was, they did it with the people's money, and Minin did it with his own.

Now, Minin thought, maybe the time had come when life would be better somewhere else.

He wasn't sure. He had never been outside of Russia and wasn't sure he would really like life anywhere else. But suddenly this seemed an appropriate time to find out. For the next few days, or the next few weeks or months, whatever it took, he might like to sample other parts of the world and see what life was like there. God loved Holy Russia, but the sun shone elsewhere too.

He had made the arrangements he needed to make about this woman; he didn't have to be here to carry them out. If the arrangements worked, he could come back anytime; if they didn't— well, the world was a big world, for a person who didn't have to ask anyone for help.

He stood up from telephone and looked around the room. Although the sun was up, the drawn shades left the room still dark. He could just make out the bottles, the food on the table, the last embers of last night's fire winking in the ashes on the grate. He went to the table and made a sandwich from slices of roast beef and ham and black bread. He washed it down with vodka from a bottle still standing on the floor.

Sidorov was still in the chair, his head tilted back, his mouth a trap for flies. He was going to have a stiff neck in the morning.

And Oblonsky, the last of the Russian nobility, lay snoozing sweetly on the floor. His kind had slept out one Revolution and looked certain to sleep out another.

Minin took a last swig, in a friendly gesture put the bottle back on the floor where Oblonsky could reach it without getting up, stepped over the recumbent Duke, and went quietly out the door.

# 37

SLAVIN'S COUSIN'S DACHA WAS AN ANCIENT, DECREPIT FARMHOUSE surrounded by apple trees on the bank of the Moscow River. They put the Volvo in a shed behind the house. Inna still couldn't get her feet into her shoes, so Fall carried her into the house. He put her on a chair in the kitchen and found a basin and drew water from the pump outside to wash her feet. She bit her lip but said nothing as he peeled the socks away from her. "We'd better get you to a doctor," he said. "How did you walk on this mess, Innochka?"

"Lightly," she said. "Very lightly."

He kissed her knees.

When he turned his head, he found Slavin staring at him. Slavin switched his eyes hastily away and coughed into his palm. "We don't want Inna out on the streets," Slavin said. "But I know a doctor. I'll go for her. There's a telephone here, but don't answer it unless you know who's calling."

Fall smiled. "And how will I know that?"

"If it's me, I'll let it ring three times and then hang up and call again."

"You come prepared for everything, Misha."

"It's part of the service."

While Slavin was gone, Fall left Inna in the kitchen and inspected the house. In a narrow upstairs bedroom, sun was falling through an east window onto a double bed. No bedding was on the mattress, but he found sheets and blankets in a chest of drawers and made up the bed. When he returned to the kitchen, he found her asleep in the chair. He carried her up to the bedroom and laid her on the bed. He considered for a moment, then turned the bed down on one side and began to undress her. Under her sweater, he found the pistol still tucked into her belt. It was a Russian service pistol, but with the state crest of the Soviet Union deeply engraved on one side of the slide, and a shape of some kind—apparently a map—engraved on the other. He laid it on the windowsill in the sun. He finished undressing her, put her under the covers, and went to the door. He started to close it softly behind him, but she said, "Alex."

He turned back into the room.

"Alex, come to bed with me, please."

Brad Chapman sat in the sun on the deck behind his house, facing the birch grove. A week's mail had collected unread while he was getting ready for trial. Now he had read it and was letting the midsummer Moscow sun warm him while he thought about his life.

He picked up the extension phone and tried again to call Fall. Fall's voice on the answering machine at his apartment again invited him to leave a message, so he did, even though he'd done it before. The last one was, "Alex, this is Brad. What about our strategy meeting? I'm here. Where are you?" This one was, "Alex, goddammit, call me."

He had already called Fall's office, and the weekend guard had told him that Fall had gone. Gone where? The guard didn't know. Mr. Fall had left a message to say that he was "gone."

Brad sighed and leaned back in his chair, holding in his hand one envelope that had come in the mail. He thought about how things had been when he came here, two years ago. Nobody had believed he could make this company work. For Houston, for Minneapolis, it was a posting to Siberia. They joked about that in Minneapolis: "Brad's going to Siberia." But one of his friends had taken him aside seriously: "Don't do this, Brad. It can't work. It'll kill your career." But he had made it work.

And now it all depended on one old woman, one old Russian woman, one tough old bitch of a Russian woman who didn't even understand accounting.

He flapped the envelope against his leg. He was wearing shorts. The birch grove cut the wind, and it was warm here except when the wind veered around and a gust slipped between the grove and the house.

All down to one tough old bitch, and no matter what she decided now, there was still Turbin and there was still Sasha. The police hadn't closed those cases. Volkov could be letting them wait, just to see what the old bitch was going to do. He had nothing to do with Turbin or Sasha, with whatever had happened to them, but Volkov wouldn't care about that. Volkov had a career to make.

And Joanna knew about Sasha.

He wiped away a tear. It was the wind gust.

Joanna came out the back door. "Do you want something to drink, Bradley?"

"No, thanks."

"Something hot? Something cold?"

"No, I'm all right."

She came and sat down on the front of the next chair and put a hand on his leg next to the envelope. "Don't worry about the meeting. Something must have come up. Alex will call."

"I'm not worried about the meeting. I have better worries than that."

"Don't worry about the trial, either. You're innocent, and Alex and Misha will prove it."

"And if they don't, why, it's only eight to fifteen years until you see me again."

She had never known him to fall into self-pity, and so she took it for irony. "I'll be waiting, sweetie," she said. "What was in the mail?"

He thought he might hand her the envelope then, but he didn't. "Nothing much. A bill that's come due."

"It can wait."

"Yeah. It can wait."

When she went back into the house, he thought it all through again; but he couldn't come to any conclusion other than the one he had come to already.

He opened the envelope again and took out what was in it. He looked it all over for messages again, but he still couldn't find any. He wished he could find some words, but he couldn't. Only the pictures.

It was a film strip, six photos apparently taken a few seconds apart. They looked as if they had been taken on infrared film, like one of those Gulf War pictures through night-vision goggles, except they weren't of soldiers. They were of Fall and Joanna. Standing close to each other. Standing closer. Kissing—two frames. And drawing back. He could even see the expressions on both their faces. In the last frame, pain.

He got up and went into the house. "Jo," he said, "get Jen's things together. We're leaving."

Fall woke with a start, hearing a car drive up. He sat up, and his hand fell on the pistol on the windowsill. It was warm from the sun, but the sun had moved. The time seemed to be close to noon.

He looked out the window. There was a strange car. A woman was getting out.

Fall dressed quickly and went downstairs. Inna was still asleep.

He answered the woman's knock at the door. "Are you Alex?" she asked. "I'm Clara. Mikhail Alexandrovich sent me." She was a plump Jewish woman of about forty carrying a black leather bag and a string shopping bag with several plastic packages in it.

"Are you the doctor?"

"His cousin the doctor. He told me to say those magic words."

"If you're his cousin, this must be your dacha."

"I'm not really his cousin. But I'm really a doctor."

He invited her in. "Where's Misha?"

"He said he had someone important to see. He'll be back. Where's the victim?"

"She's upstairs asleep."

"I'll see her there."

"Don't wake her."

"Who's the doctor? Anyway, feet don't sleep." She put the shopping bag on the floor and went up the stairs carrying her black doctor's bag.

She came down after ten minutes. "Nasty cuts," she said, not waiting for Fall to ask. "If we're lucky, they won't be infected. I have some solution that will help for now, but you'd better try to get her some antibiotic ointment from the American Medical Center. You're not likely to find anything worth using in a Russian pharmacy. She needs to keep off of her feet. If she does have to walk, she'll need bigger shoes. She won't get into any she has. Now for part two of the therapy." She put her doctor's kit in the corner and took the shopping bag into the kitchen. She hunted through cupboards until she found a frying pan and started working on fried potatoes and onions. "You're probably starved, Alex," she said with a knowing look.

He realized that he was.

The smell of food brought a call from Inna. "Alex?" Fall went to get her. He helped her dress and carried her down. "You're getting lighter," he said. "Time to fatten you up."

The three of them sat in the kitchen and ate fried potatoes and onions as the sun moved toward noon in a clear sky.

Inna was the first to move. She started to get up, but Fall caught her arm. He didn't want her walking. "I've got work to do," she said. "I'll need to find paper and a pen, Alex."

"Don't worry about writing your memoirs. There'll be plenty of time."

"I've got to prepare a report on this for my committee, and plan whom to call to testify to us. My life doesn't stop after I appear in court on Monday."

Clara knocked on the wooden table. In Russia, even doctors could be superstitious.

"Who do you think you'll call?" Fall asked.

"Everyone who was at the dacha, of course. Even Sidorov. *Especially* Sidorov. And Antipov. How could a member of the legislature get mixed up in a thing like this?"

"And General Marchenko, I suppose," Fall said.

"Marchenko of course."

"You really are a glutton for punishment, aren't you?" Fall said. "What makes you think any of them will show up?"

"That's not my problem. If we're going to be a country of laws, I have to do my part, whatever other people may do."

She was an admirable woman, Fall thought, but he didn't tell her so.

# 38

A TRANSPARENT GLAZE OF SUNLIGHT COVERED THE STREETS OF MOSCOW, and for a while even the grime on the walls glistened.

Slavin stopped his car before an old building not far outside the Garden Ring. It was obvious that it had once been a mansion and, like many Moscow mansions, converted after the Revolution into housing for a number of families; now most of the windows were blank, uncurtained. No children's voices rang in the courtyard.

The staircase smelled of fermented cabbage, the last residue of years of housewives's thrift: readiness against winter. But the landings were bare. In most old Moscow apartment buildings, things flowed out into the staircases: sleds in winter, toys in summer, tools and tires and building materials, all the gathered provisions of a too cramped life in too cramped quarters. But here the landings were bare, up to the fourth floor, where Slavin found the door he was seeking. Outside this door a child's carriage stood by one wall, dusty, as if it had not moved in years. Behind it, a rolled-up floral carpet, shy wallflower, huddled in the corner.

He rang the bell.

Feet shuffled inside, but no answer came. He rang again. A woman's voice responded, "Who is it?" A high-pitched voice, hard-edged, but without force.

"Mikhail Alexandrovich Slavin. Is Maxim Nikolayevich at home?"

The feet shuffled away again. In a moment, footsteps. Hard-heeled footsteps. Volkov opened the door. He was wearing blue jeans and a white T-shirt, and police-uniform shoes.

"Hello, Maxim," Slavin said.

"Hello, Misha." It was a neutral response: not formal, not friendly. A greeting for someone Volkov had known once, when they were young.

"I have some information about the Chapman case," Slavin said.

"I heard you'd gone to trial. If you need a postponement, Kol'tsov is your man, not me. Won't he be in court on Monday?"

"Kol'tsov isn't the man for this, Maxim. And it won't wait until Monday."

Volkov had not let go of the doorknob. "What do you expect me to do? This has already gone to the City Prosecutor and the court. I'm signed off. It's out of my hands."

"It could come back to your hands. If it doesn't, it will be because somebody above you managed to keep it quiet—to keep it from coming back to the militia."

"The more reason for me to keep out of it. I don't want to be part of any deals. There's too much politics in this country already, and too little police work. That's what this case is all about, isn't it? Somebody's political deals. If you need a political deal, Misha, you'd better go to the people who do them. Go to the people who *can* do them. I can't imagine why you'd even think I'm one of them. You know I don't have any connections."

"This isn't about political deals, Maxim. It's about police work. Police work still to be done. But you're wrong about one thing: you do have connections."

Volkov stiffened, uncertainly angry, scornful: "What kind of connections do *I* have?"

"You worked for Sergei Mikhailovich. You went to his funeral."

Volkov flushed with anger at the memory, even after twenty years. Then his color faded. "Yes, I did." He added, not sure how to take what Slavin had said, whether as accusation or something else, "I saw you there."

"There weren't many of us."

"Not a goddamned tenth of those who should have been!" Volkov's anger passed. He said coolly, "What does this have to do with your deal, Misha? What kind of connection is that?"

"Do you remember Grigory Marchenko?"

"I didn't forget General Krylov. Am I likely to have forgotten

Marchenko? I tell you as a good Communist that I wish I believed in God, so that I could believe Marchenko would rot in hell."

"What if I tell you I have a witness who'll testify that Marchenko and others had Turbin killed, and the woman Shubina, too, to get control of JorSov?"

Volkov looked from Slavin out into the stairway as if looking for something far away, or long past. Only after several seconds did he look back at Slavin. He said, "Come in, Misha."

They went into the kitchen. It was a large room, high-ceilinged; but the walls that cut across old ceiling decorations showed that it was only part of a room that had once been much larger. There were two plates on the table, the remains of lunch—black bread, cabbage salad. He pushed them aside. A Russian should have offered tea, but Volkov was too agitated. "Tell me what you know," he said.

From where he sat, Slavin could see a woman in the opposite room. She was standing facing partly away from him, brushing her hair—in front of a mirror, he supposed, although he couldn't see it. She was dressed in a shabby dressing gown and slippers, but her figure was slender and her hair was long and golden and her hands were elegant. He wished he could see her face. He had never met Volkov's wife, but he had heard she was a great beauty. That was twenty years ago, but a Russian woman who hadn't put on weight could be beautiful still.

Slavin took his eyes off the woman and outlined his story, without naming his witness.

"Some investigators say you'd sell your mother's soul to get a client off, Misha. There's no other explanation, they say, for some of the cases you've won. They'd say I should ask what this witness cost you."

Anger flooded Slavin. He forced it to pass. When he answered, it was with unforced calm. "No price could buy a witness like this, Maxim. A People's Deputy. A darling of the journalists."

"Korneva."

"Yes."

Volkov sat silent for a long while. Then he looked at Slavin and said, "No, I never believed you'd sell the General's name. When can you bring your witness for questioning?"

"I won't bring her in. There are too many dangers. Too many eyes, at any police station. Who knows whose pay they are in?"

"You were always a nervous person, Misha."

"It's what clients pay me for."

"Do I have to arrest her?"

"She's a People's Deputy." Slavin knew Volkov would understand what he meant: People's Deputies were immune from arrest. "You'll have to go where she is."

"I'll go where she is. I'd go to hell to interview this witness." Volkov began to laugh softly.

The footsteps shuffled into the kitchen beside Slavin. He turned his head. The woman was standing just inside the door, holding a hairbrush in one hand. Long, blond, lustrous hair fell over an emaciated face—sunken cheeks and a sharp nose, a crooked face that had something wild in it. A few gold strands were still tangled in the brush.

"Krylov!" she cried. "Krylov again? When will we be rid of that old man?"

"Ella," Volkov said, "this doesn't concern you."

"Doesn't concern me? When you gave up your career once for a dead man, and I see you about to do it again? Just when we're about to move from this pigpen, to get a decent place to live for once in our lives, and get your poor daughter a room of her own to sleep in? What if they take that away from us? You know they can do it!"

"The world doesn't work that way anymore, Ellochka," Volkov said gently. "The state doesn't control apartments now." He said to Slavin, "We've been offered a trade, an apartment in a new building on the edge of the city for our place here. We're one of the last. You could see the building's mostly empty."

"And finally our poor daughter will have a place to sleep!" the woman insisted. "If only you don't mix it up with this Krylov business!"

"It's already agreed that we'll move, Ellochka. We don't need any permission. Whatever I do won't affect that."

"With a KGB general on the other side? How can that be?

Don't think I don't know who he is, this Grigory Marchenko. 'General Marchenko!' I've seen him on television, and seen *you* when you've seen him on television. Don't think I don't have eyes! Well, let him go, I say! That's another world. He's gone into it and we haven't, but we still need a room for my baby. Take that, and let him go, and finally let go of your old dead man."

Volkov got up from the table.

"Where are you going?" his wife demanded.

"I'm going to get dressed, Ellochka. I've got to interview a witness."

"God damn you!" She lunged at him with the brush, trying to scar his face with it; he caught her wrist and easily twisted her hand aside.

"Please, Ellochka," he said softly, "not in front of company."

She subsided into tears, and he released her wrist. She slumped into the chair he had got up from, crying softly.

"Will you behave now?" Volkov asked. She did not answer. In a moment he said to Slavin, "I'll be only a few minutes." He said to the woman, "Come with me," and led her into the other room and closed the door.

Behind the door, the woman continued to sob softly; but if she said anything more, Slavin couldn't hear it. He tried not to listen. He looked at the clock on the wall and waited for it to move its minute hand only a few minutes.

Apparently God hadn't poured honey into everyone's wife.

Volkov came out of the other room and closed the door behind him. He was dressed in the gray uniform of a Major of Militia. Slavin had not seen Volkov in uniform throughout the investigation—and not for twenty years before that, he supposed. Not since he had last worn a uniform himself. He realized that he must have looked startled—he hated to look startled—for Volkov said, "I thought I should dress. This is the Militia against the KGB now. Even if you and I are the only ones who know it." He added, "I'll have to call for a car. I should have done it before. My wife put my mind off of business. I'm sorry."

"We can take mine," Slavin said. "As few people as possible should know about this."

Volkov considered this. He seemed undecided. "I should wait until Ella's mother comes. She lives with us. She's just gone out to the store."

"How long will you wait for Marchenko to give you another chance?" Slavin asked.

"Yes. All right. Let's go." Volkov took his hat from a shelf in the hall and closed the door to his apartment behind them without saying good-bye to his wife. He and Slavin walked in silence down the stairs and to Slavin's car.

In the car, after they had driven a few blocks, Volkov said, "Forgive my wife. She's a good woman, but sometimes she can't control what she says."

Slavin shrugged. "It's the way women are, isn't it? I understand how she wants your daughter to have a room of her own."

Volkov stared out the side window. "We have no daughter."

Slavin, unable to think of anything to say, said nothing.

"We have plenty of room," Volkov said. "It's a big apartment—three rooms. But we have no daughter. Our daughter died five years ago, when she was nine. It drove my wife a little crazy. I'm sorry to have it inflicted on you." He added, "She had her own room, even then."

"I'm sorry to hear of it, Maxim. Forgive me for what I said—about waiting for your wife's mother. I didn't know."

"Never mind. You couldn't know. We don't talk about it. But that's why we're moving, you see. The building's being traded to speculators. Almost everyone else is gone. We could stay, but my wife wants to go. The apartment was my father's. And his father's. I grew up there. But it's a question whether to go, and leave our memories behind, or to stay and live with them. I don't know which is harder. It's different for her, of course, than for me. I grew up there. For her, the memories are . . . more concentrated. I think that's what it is that makes her this way." He turned toward Slavin. "What do you think I should do?"

The question struck Slavin dumb. He was used to advising clients on their most important and most personal decisions, sometimes literally questions of life and death. When he was a young lawyer, he had sometimes felt it was more than he could bear, the emotional responsibility for the lives of others. But he had learned to bear it. Now people leaned on him, and they found him strong. But their questions were always of the law's impact on their lives. Volkov's question was different. His question was, how do I reconcile what's done with what is to come? No one could answer that without knowing what was to come. At length, Slavin said, "I wish I were wise enough to tell you, Maxim. Maybe you need a prophet, not a lawyer."

"I tried a priest." It was a strong admission for a former Party member—a good Communist who didn't believe in God, as Volkov had said. "But what do they know, these priests? The old ones, they all worked for the Committee"—he meant the KGB, the Committee on State Security—"and the young ones are just children."

From there they drove on in silence.

# 39

MARCHENKO WAS BURIED IN HIS OFFICE.

In summer he always worked with the windows open, but today he had them closed and the blinds drawn.

The world outside oppressed him.

At midmorning, it had been clear that the woman must have escaped. As soon as he decided that, he picked up the white telephone and began burning favors. He regretted every one; but if he failed now, he would never have a chance to use them anyway. He wished he could be everywhere at once, in person, but he was only one man. Good help was always hard to find. There were two less now: two good men ruined by that fool Minin. He wondered what could have happened to Joker.

He spent the morning on the white telephone. What he was going to do needed support. He should have built it sooner, he knew; but doing without it was a risk he had decided he should take, then. He knew everyone supported what he was doing, at heart, but few would dare support it openly. Better to let them sit on the side and scramble to applaud him when it was done.

Who could have known that this woman would come from nowhere?

But the support was not there, now that he needed it. He dared not ask directly—only hints. But no one was willing to understand hints. He knew they all agreed with him, but only if their voices could not be heard. They all agreed, all had said so more than once: if one highly visible foreign investment could be shaken, they would all be shaken. Capitalists were like sheep. They all came running, or none did. Cripple one important foreign-owned company, and you would cripple the foreigners' plans to take over the economy. Visibility—that was the key. It was his plan's strength, and it was its weakness. Communists were like sheep too. No one dared support him in the light of day.

Most men were sheep.

He should have got that woman on his side in the beginning. She had more balls than anyone else he'd seen. To walk right in like that—she must have known what danger she was in. But she did it.

The kind of woman that came from good Slavic stock.

It was time to get the Slavs back together again. Damned Russians, some of them still acted superior to a man with a Ukrainian name, no matter that his family had been four generations in Russia. He was as Russian as any of them. But it was just as good to be Ukrainian. Only that fool Gorbachev let the Slavs be divided. Once a thing was broken, it was so hard to put it back together.

He was sorry now that he hadn't got the case under Ministry of Security control when he had had the chance. It had all been ready. The other woman, the dead one, could have planted the documents anytime, to make this a case of espionage. But it had seemed better to keep this strictly a militia investigation. If anything went wrong, there would be no Ministry of Security fingerprints on the case. A fool's reasoning, that. Or a weakling's. None the better because it was his own. But at least he could face his own mistakes. Not many men could do that.

Probably that damn woman could.

There'd been no word from the teams sent to watch for her. No word from Minin either, and no one answered the telephone at the dacha. The fog of war had descended.

Well, on to the last call. No favors to burn here. The Moscow City Prosecutor wouldn't piss on a KGB man if he was on fire. No favors. Just old-fashioned bluffing.

He reached for the white telephone with the crest of the USSR on it, but before he could pick it up, another telephone on his desk rang. Who the devil knew he was here?

He answered, "Marchenko."

"General, it's Brick, sir."

"Who?" He had concentrated all his attention on what he was about to do. It took him an instant to shift his concentration. "Oh. What word is there from Minin?" Before Brick could answer, Marchenko added, "What are you still doing here? Didn't Minin tell you to get yourself and that car out of town?"

"He told me. But I had to check on Joker. He's not back. I need help finding him, sir."

"Forget Joker, he can take care of himself. Just do it, Sergeant!"

A long silence. "Yes, sir." The line went dead.

Marchenko rubbed his face with one hand. Brick was tenacious, but he wasn't the world's brightest. Right now he was another thing to worry about, and you could only worry about so many at one time. The mission before the men: that was the soldier's way. You did what you could for the men, but eventually the mission came first.

He picked up the white telephone with the crest of the USSR on it and dialed. As the telephone rang, he leaned forward, trying to get his concentration back, his left elbow propped on the green leather of his desktop and his left palm supporting his forehead, shading his eyes, as if it were not dark enough in the room already. He tried the Prosecutor's home first: it was Saturday noon, after all. He got no answer. No surprise. Who wanted to be at home on a fine July afternoon? He dialed the Prosecutor's office, not with any hope of finding the Prosecutor there, but just for the sake of completeness.

"Linnik." A rasping voice.

What a treasure this prosecutor was! Actually in his office on a Saturday! "General Marchenko here. Ministry of Security. I'm calling about an investigation."

"I'm listening." Marchenko had never met the City Prosecutor, but he knew Linnik was an old Party man, with a Party man's instincts: always cover your backside; never say anything until you understand what's going on; and then agree with the strong man.

Marchenko said, "It's been determined that this case involves national security. It's to be transferred to our jurisdiction immediately. I'm sending some men to pick up the files."

"What case is this we're talking about?"

"An American who's stolen state property."

"The *JorSov* case?" Linnik's question had a "can you believe this" quality to it that raised Marchenko's caution level.

"That's right."

Linnik was indignant. "That's already gone to court! One of my Deputies is trying it himself. If the Ministry of Security had evidence of a national security concern, why the devil didn't you show it to us before this?"

In the old days the Prosecutor wouldn't have dared to question a State Security request, but now Marchenko saw he would have to sugarcoat his demand. He couldn't afford any needless fights. He had enough real problems already. "We've just received the evidence," he said. "We're analyzing it. It can't be released, of course, but we'll do whatever we can to help you with the judge. What do you think would be best?"

"We'll have to petition the court to send the case back. You'll be wasting your time sending anyone to *our* offices to pick up files: the court has them all. Send me a letter with your evidence attached, and I'll pass it to my Deputy. He can petition the court if he thinks it's merited."

"If *he* thinks it's merited? I've told you this is a matter of national security! And I've told you I can't release the evidence now."

"You've told me that, General. But I'm the City Prosecutor, and this office decides how cases are prosecuted."

It was clear that Linnik did not relish the idea of having a major case sent back for further investigation. But Marchenko was on the edge of desperation. "I'll send your letter," he said. "I'll have it to you yourself today. But it's vital that this be concluded at once."

"I gathered that it was. This is the first time I've had the honor of a telephone call from a Ministry of Security general at my office on a Saturday. Better to send it to my deputy Kol'tsov, though. He's the one who's going to have to petition the court on Monday. You can have it delivered to his office. He'll see it first thing Monday morning."

"Monday? Monday is too late. I tell you, this is a case of the highest urgency, Comrade!" Marchenko slipped unconsciously into the old jargon, the words of a time when a City Prosecutor would have swooned to be called comrade by a KGB general.

"Well, I can tell you that the court isn't in session until Monday. We've got a judge and two People's Assessors to convince, and we haven't even seen your evidence yet. And I don't know where Kol'tsov is—probably gone to his dacha for the weekend."

*People's Assessors!* Marchenko thought. People's Assessors were nothing but workers brought in from a factory floor to rubber-stamp court decisions. How could the fate of Russian industry depend on the whim of people like that? *Not in session until Monday!* He felt for an instant the immense weight of Soviet bureaucracy leaning against him, resisting more the harder he pushed. Oh, for a squad of handpicked men and an airfield to take!

"It has been decided at the highest levels that this case must not proceed in public," Marchenko said in the voice that had given commands at the Kabul airfield. Once you started playing this hand, there was no hope but to play it all the way. He added for good measure, "It has also been decided that, until our investigation is completed, the evidence we have received cannot go beyond those people who have already reviewed it—and been satisfied with it, I might add. I am going to bring this letter to your deputy myself, and I expect him to take me to the judge in person. I expect to have the court hearings terminated and have all files delivered to me. Those are the orders I've received."

There was new caution in Linnik's voice. "My deputy will look at your letter, General."

"He'll have it shortly."

"I'll have someone try to locate him. Have your aide call my office for the address."

"I said I'd see your deputy myself. I'll make the call myself too. That's how important this is." Marchenko was not accustomed to placing his own calls, and he regretted not having someone to unload such black work on. But since he couldn't trust anyone with the details, he decided to make a virtue of necessity and impress Linnik with the seriousness of the matter.

"We will of course do everything that we are authorized to do," Linnik said. "It's our purpose to assist the organs of state security."

*The Organs of State Security.* Marchenko could tell there were no capitals on the words when Linnik said them. It did not leave him happy.

Linnik was not happy when he hung up the telephone. He thought for half an hour about the telephone call from General Marchenko of the Ministry of Security; and the more he thought, the less he liked it. At length he picked up the telephone and dialed his deputy Yuri Kol'stov. He had lied to Marchenko when he said he didn't know where Kol'tsov was, but Marchenko wouldn't have to know that.

"Yura," he said, "you're going to be receiving a letter today."

"The postman's already been here," Kol'tsov said, "and I didn't see a letter."

"This one has a higher-level delivery boy—a Ministry of Security general."

"The devil! What's this about?"

Linnik smiled—he thought he could almost hear skinny Yuri's bones knocking over the telephone. Yuri Alexandrovich was a good man, but not yet fully formed. A few more years would do him good. "Why, State Security wants your case, Yura. The case of this foreigner. New evidence, they say. Matters of national security. Looks like they think he's a spy."

"A spy? New evidence? What new evidence, Pavel Ivanovich? Why didn't the investigator have it?"

"Ha. The General wouldn't tell me. 'State secret,' he says. Not fit for the eyes of mere members of the *Prokuratura* like you and me."

"What am I supposed to do about it?"

"You're supposed to run off with this general to the judge and convince her to send the case back for further investigation. And then we turn it over to the Ministry of Security. End of the case, for us."

"Send the case back for further investigation? At this stage? A case this important? We'll look like fools!" Kol'tsov had asked to try this case himself. It was the biggest case in the City Prosecutor's office. He had been interviewed about it on television. If it were sent back now, what kind of questions would the television reporters ask?

"I have a feeling this general doesn't care about that, Yura."

"Anyway, I've never heard of a judge hearing a petition during the weekend. And she'd have to find the People's Assessors . . ."

"They're going to do whatever the judge decides, of course."

"Yes, of course, Pavel Ivanovich. But the People's Assessors are part of the court. Pskova can't just send the case back on her own. She hasn't the authority. And then, to send it back without seeing any new evidence . . . even if the court agrees to do it, why should *we* agree? We'd be cutting our own throats. What's going on here, Pavel Ivanovich?"

Linnik laughed. "You ask a very good question, Yura. We'll make a lawyer of you yet. The answer is, we don't know what's going on here. But when this general shows up, have a good look at his letter of request, and then you call me."

Producing the letter was no problem for Marchenko. It would have his signature on it, and he knew the required style. "On account of newly discovered evidence, the Ministry of Security requests that the case of Chapman Bradley Allen, charged with violations of laws of the Russian Federation, be sent back for further investigation of additional charges, including violation of Article 65 of the Criminal Code of the Russian Federation. This request is based on reports of investigators that are classified Absolutely Secret and that are therefore not attached to this letter. The reports contain evidence that Chapman Bradley Allen through his position as co–General Director of the joint venture JorSov has been collecting State secret information and sending it abroad."

Marchenko was sorry to be violating the secret operative's first rule—always work through someone else. But there was no one else he could trust. He was going to have to leave some fingerprints on the case now, and they would be his own.

He was glad he had a typewriter in his office. Damn few generals did. It wouldn't do to have the hall guards see him typing. That was something they'd be sure to remember, if asked later. There was not enough time to get the document perfect, but it was too late to worry. It was ironic—all the resources that the Ministry had to carry out document forgeries, experts available day and night, and he couldn't use any of them. Just do what he could do now, and leave the details to be straightened out tomorrow, if tomorrow came.

# 40

FALL WAS STILL SITTING WITH INNA AND CLARA AT THE TABLE IN THE big kitchen of the dacha when they heard a car drive up. Fall was sitting with his back to the driveway. Inna was facing it. When Inna gasped, he turned to see a policeman cross outside the window.

He had left the pistol lying on the table. He grabbed for it, found it, and turned to face Slavin coming in the door with Volkov, in uniform, behind him.

There was an awkward silence.

"You're protected, I see, Mr. Fall," Volkov said. "Do you have a license for that?" It was a question that answered itself. Only very important civilians could get pistol licenses.

"It's not his," Slavin said. "It's evidence. Alex was just about to turn it over to you. Here." He took the pistol from Fall and handed it to Volkov. "A service pistol, isn't it? It's not likely to be registered; but if it is, it could identify the person she took it from last night."

Volkov studied the pistol, then looked Inna over. "If you took this from the kind of man who'd be carrying it these days, Deputy, I wouldn't want to meet you in a dark alley." He looked around the dacha. "Can we go into the other room, the two of us? I'll want to interview you alone."

"I want to be with her," Fall said.

"I'm sure. But I want to do my job, Mr. Fall, and I know you know the rules by now. The People's Deputy is not suspected of any crime, so there's no call for her to have counsel. And you don't actually qualify as counsel anyway. Besides that, I don't want there to be any questions about whether the proper procedure was followed in this case. And I'd guess that, after you think about it, you don't either."

"There's a bigger problem with her going into the other room," Clara said.

"What's that?" Volkov asked.

"She shouldn't walk. Her feet are in terrible condition. And there are no shoes in this dacha to fit her. We've already looked."

Volkov went around the table and looked down at Inna's feet, with evident sympathy once he had seen them. "Then we'll stay here," he said, "and you can all go. In the other room or outside: it doesn't matter."

"If she does need to walk, probably I can help," Slavin said. He went outside, and from the trunk of the Zhiguli he produced a pair of rubber galoshes. "I have very small feet. It runs in the family. These might not be too large."

"Pad them with a lot of socks," Clara said.

The three of them went outside, but Fall would not go far. They sat under the apple trees. Flies buzzed over unripe fruit already fallen. "I'd better call Brad," Fall said, "and give him the good news—as much of it as I can tell over the phone. I completely forgot that we agreed to have a strategy meeting today. He'll be looking for us. He's probably going bananas."

"He'll be glad to hear the strategy has changed," Slavin said.

"I'd better not call from here. Probably they haven't tapped Brad's telephone. But if they have, we don't want any calls traced here."

"Go up to the village," Clara said. "There's a public phone outside the store."

"I'll wait until Volkov's done with Inna," Fall said.

"Volkov's not going to bite her," Clara said. "Or if he does, we'll make him stop."

"I'll wait," Fall said.

If it was a long wait, probably it was not as long as it seemed to Fall. Volkov and Inna came out of the dacha. Clara looked at Inna closely. "No bite marks," she said. "At least, not in my professional opinion. It's just a friendly joke," she said to Volkov.

"How soon will you start making arrests?" Fall asked Volkov.

"Who is there to arrest? People's Deputy Korneva gave me a complaint"—he held out a piece of writing paper with a short note in Inna's hand—"and I can base an investigation on it; but the only one I could surely arrest is the man who followed her with a gun. And even he said he just wanted to take her home. We know he had a gun"—he patted his uniform pocket, which bulged with the pistol wrapped in a handkerchief—"but we can't yet prove what he intended to do with it. As for the others . . . on her own testimony, there were some words from a drunk man about two people being killed, but no identification of who did it. There was talk of a conspiracy to take over the company of your client, Mr. Chapman, and no one denied that; but it's not clear that the conspiracy was a criminal one." When Fall started to protest, Volkov went on, "You know and I know that it was a criminal act, Mr. Fall, but on the facts I have now, there's just not enough for criminal charges. If these people were no one, I'd just detain them for questioning. And if these people were no one, detaining them would go a long way toward keeping Deputy Korneva safe until she can testify for your client on Monday. But these people aren't no one: they're powerful people. And so

I can't just drag them in from their homes. Even if I could, it wouldn't keep Deputy Korneva alive until Monday. These people can get others to do their work for them. You want to get your client off, and you want to keep Deputy Korneva safe. Well, so do I. But I also want to succeed in prosecuting crimes that I have reason to believe have been committed. But I don't have the proof now. If this investigation is to succeed, it has to be done carefully. And protecting Deputy Korneva is going to have to be done carefully. I offered police guards for her. She said to ask you and Mikhail Alexandrovich."

"Misha said we should trust you," Fall said, "but he also said the KGB has always had informers in the Militia."

Slavin said nothing. After a moment, Volkov said, "I can choose men for you. Not many. One or two."

"I say the less contact, the better," Fall said. "We can't know who's watching, at the police station."

"Then keep her here." Volkov did not appear happy.

"All right," Fall said. "But what are you going to do?"

"I'm not going to tell you my plans. It's against the law, for one thing. But I'm going to try to make enough progress before Monday that by the time you have to produce Deputy Korneva in court, I'll be in a position to start questioning the people she's told me about. I can't open an investigation without telling the chief of the Investigations Department. Just to file the form is going to be dangerous to Deputy Korneva. I have to tell my chief, but maybe I don't have to tell him until Monday.

"But now," Volkov said, "I need a ride to a telephone and then to my office. I'm going to have to start some men working on this. But I don't want them to come for me here. You're right not to want anyone else to know I've been here—it would be too easy for someone to understand the connection between my visit here and the questions I'll be asking. I hate to say it, but the KGB *has* always had informers in the Militia."

"I'll give you a ride," Clara said. "I'm the least visible person here."

# 41

Yuri Kol'tsov looked at the letter and then looked back at the messenger who had brought it—a general of the Ministry of Security, in full uniform.

Kol'tsov had come to the position of Deputy City Prosecutor in the usual way. He had been a police investigator, a minor Party official, a deputy district prosecutor, a district prosecutor. He had seen plenty of strange things and heard plenty of stories, and he had learned to be suspicious of all of them. But he had never seen anything like this, nor been as suspicious. He wouldn't have needed Linnik's telephone call to raise his doubts. A Ministry of Security general arriving without a driver?

Still, there was no doubt that this was a Ministry of Security general. Kol'tsov had seen him on television: Marchenko, the hero of the attack on the Kabul airport.

And there was no doubt that it didn't pay to seem doubtful of a Ministry of Security general.

But there was also no doubt that no judge was going to send back a case for further investigation on a weekend, without a full hearing before all the parties and their lawyers. It was against the law. And Kol'tsov did not want to be the deputy prosecutor who tried to convince Judge Pskova otherwise.

He looked at the letter again.

"Is something wrong?" the General asked in a voice that left no doubt that there had better not be.

"Well, actually . . ."

"We haven't got any time to waste."

"Well, actually, this letter doesn't have the registration number on it."

"Why should it? It has my signature on it."

"It's nothing to me, of course. I personally don't object in the least. But an official request from the Ministry of Security to the City Prosecutor should have a registration number of the department that issues the request. This letter doesn't have one."

Marchenko knew the letter didn't have a number. He knew it should have one. He had stood outside the office of the chief of the department, pondering whether to concoct a story that would get a hall guard to find a key that would let him into the office to try to find the record of numbers. If the letter ever came back to the department, a wrong number—or lack of one—might lead to an inquiry. But if the letter ever came back to the department, a right number might lead to an inquiry too. And so might a missing number, if no copy were found in the records. He had concluded that it wasn't worth the effort. Who would expect a deputy prosecutor to quibble over an internal registration number of the Ministry of Security?

"Of course the letter doesn't have a number," Marchenko said. "Who's going to bother the chief of a department to open the records on a weekend? We'll get it on Monday." Bureaucracy annoyed Marchenko—annoyed him even aside from the need for a number on this letter. Bureaucracy was what had killed the Union and looked likely to kill Russia too. It was a tyranny of little people. Friendship with a records clerk was worth more sometimes than the friendship of the President.

He had never been so keenly aware how hard it was to do anything alone.

Kol'tsov supposed there was no way he was going to get out of going to Judge Pskova with this letter in his hand, number or no number.

Anna Ivanovna Pskova, Judge of the Moscow City Court, in cotton dress and bare feet, was picking beetles from the potato plants in the patch behind her dacha. In one hand she had a small tin can with a little kerosene in it, and with the other she turned up each leaf of each plant, exposing the hiding places of the little devils she knew were in there. Nearsighted, she bent with her nose almost into the plants as she sought out the destroyers of her sustenance, and when she found one, she muttered with satisfaction as she cast it squirming into the kerosene. It was satisfying work, more satisfying than the bench. There, a complex world pressed in on you. It was hard sometimes to know what was right, to *do* what was right. She had seen the bad go free and the good punished, no matter how much she tried to avoid that. Here, one was always right—always *justified*—and justice was swift and deserved.

When Pskova bent over, an immodest amount of judicial behind could sometimes be seen from the road, but the neighbors rarely looked. They had seen all of this before, and there were better sights to behold in the neighborhood. The new bride of that young lawyer up the way, rich from working for a Western law firm, for instance. Old men who wouldn't stop for Pskova would come out to see *her*, gardening in a French bikini. There were some ways, everyone could agree, that new times had improved the country.

Pskova paid no attention to the sound of car doors closing. She knew they must be at the neighbors': she never accepted visitors at her dacha. It was her place of escape from people. She saw enough of them during the week, and the worst sorts too.

Kol'tsov, confronted with Judge Pskova's barely covered backside, retreated, but Marchenko did not. Marchenko was a man with a mission, and he had faced worse at the Kabul airfield.

Marchenko cleared his throat.

Pskova straightened up slowly, turned around, and wiped the sweat from her brow with the back of one thick forearm, pushing the sweaty strands of hair back from her face. Her kerosene can was still in her other hand. "Who the devil are you?" she demanded.

"Marchenko." Ministry of Security."

On each shoulder he wore a single star.

Pskova was a judge, but she had also been a Party member and a Soviet woman. To any Soviet person of her age, a general of the KGB was no one to trifle with. On the other hand, she was a woman at her dacha, her sacred soil; and her potatoes had beetles.

"What do you want?" she asked, not entirely kindly.

"I've brought a request to have a case sent back for further investigation. The case you're trying just now."

270

She shaded her eye with one hand, the better to see the General against the sun. She squinted. She did not have her glasses. "You came all the way out here . . ." Words failed her.

Marchenko held the request out to her.

"It's up to the Prosecutor to submit a petition," she said.

"He's here." Marchenko groped behind him with one hand, then turned to see where Kol'tsov had got to. Kol'tsov was standing, sheepish, just by the corner of the dacha, looking as if he were trying to be there without quite being there, or not to be there while still being there.

"Yuri Alexandrovich, is that you hiding back there? Pskova demanded. "Do you have a petition in your pocket?"

Kol'tsov shrugged and came forward. He handed her a paper. She looked at it. Then she took the paper from Marchenko and read that. Then she looked back at Kol'tsov. "What kind of foolishness is this?" she demanded. "You know I don't have the power to sign orders on my own. That's a power of the court, not of the judge. I'd have to consult with the People's Assessors assigned to the case. God knows where *they* are on a weekend." Although she had been a Party member, Pskova had begun life as a village girl, and in these new times anyone could use a villager's reference to God, even in the presence of a general of the Ministry of Security. "And even if we found them, what are we supposed to do standing out here in a field? Send this case back from a potato patch? You know the Code of Criminal Procedure as well as I do—or if you don't, you're not qualified for your job. The court only hears petitions in the courtroom in the presence of all the parties."

Kol'tsov did his best to back away from his position. "W-well of course, Judge, I didn't think you'd send the case back from here; but I thought we might discuss p-p-procedure, for Monday morning, and I knew you'd want to hear . . ."

Pskova ignored him completely, as if she didn't hear him. She looked down at her cotton dress, a threadbare red print with large yellow flowers. "Am I fit to manage a courtroom, dressed as I am? Is this a way to dispense Russian justice?" She shook both papers at Kol'tsov and pushed them back at him. "If you have evidence to present in support of this petition, you present it in court on Monday morning, Comrade Lawyer! And until then, get your feet off of my potatoes!'' She said nothing to Marchenko. She turned and bent over the plant she had been working on, exposing a wide swath of judicial physique to the interlopers.

Marchenko drove away from the judge's dacha without saying a word. It was all he could do to keep from taking out his rage on the Deputy Prosecutor, who rode in silence in the passenger's seat of the General's black Volga, staring straight ahead. But there was nothing for Marchenko to gain by attacking someone whose help he might still need. And he might need this deputy prosecutor on Monday morning, if that woman was still at large.

It was hard to be alone in the world.

He pondered how alone that woman had been, there at the dacha.

That woman. Was he really going to have to take ultimate measures against her? It would be a pity. Mother Russia needed all of her children now, and She hadn't many like that one.

# 42

AFTER VOLKOV LEFT WITH CLARA, FALL DROVE SLAVIN'S CAR TO THE store with a public telephone that Clara had suggested as a place to call Chapman. The store was the usual Soviet village store, a one-room, crumbling concrete building with the word UNIVERMAG painted on it, short for "universal magazine"—a department store. All of this store's departments were in its one room, together with two customers and a dozen clerks and a cashier. The telephone was in its customary place too, outside on a wall.

Fall let Brad's telephone ring for a long time, but no one answered.

Fall became a little worried. He knew Brad hadn't planned anything for the weekend except to work on the case; and he was surprised that Brad would have gone anywhere before hearing from him.

He decided to try calling Ed and Betsy Miller. They were next-door neighbors.

"No, Brad's not over here," Ed Miller told him. "I don't think he's come back yet. I didn't see the car."

"Back? Where did he go, Ed?"

"I don't know. They left maybe an hour ago. Maybe two hours."

"They?" Fall's heart sank. "Was someone with him?"

"Oh, they all left. Brad and Joanna and Jen."

"Was anyone else with them?"

"No—I don't think they had company. Brad was gone for a while late this morning, and then he came back, and they all left again. I think they may have gone for the night. I thought he may have wanted to get out of the house, with all this pressure on him."

"Why do you think so?"

"Well, he put a couple of suitcases in the car. Not enough to go anywhere serious. I thought maybe they'd go to a hotel for a change of air. Is anything wrong, Alex?"

"Oh . . . I was trying to reach him to arrange to talk about the trial."

"Yeah, I'm sure you guys must be busy. How did it go, the first days?"

"It's just been preliminaries so far." Fall didn't want to talk about the trial.

"Yeah, it takes the Russkies a while to get warmed up. Well, but if there's anything at all I can do, Alex . . ."

"You'll be the first to know, Ed." *You already* were *the first to know, once,* Fall thought, *and you refused.* But he didn't say it.

"Do you want me to have Brad call you if I see him?"

"I'll be a little hard to reach, Ed. Tell him to leave a message at my office and I'll call him back."

He called his office then and got the message that Brad had called and asked how to find him, but that had been at noon. Nothing since then.

273

Fall drove fast back to the dacha. Slavin and Inna were sitting at the kitchen table.

Slavin said, "We were just discussing ways of getting Inna into the courtroom on Monday. Someone's sure to try to stop her. Even if they can't find her here, they know she has to show up in court Monday morning."

"If she's safe here, we can worry about Monday later," Fall said. "We've got a problem right now, Misha. We've got to find our client."

"You couldn't reach him? We can call him in the morning and meet somewhere. There's not even much to talk about now, with Inna as a witness. It's easy."

"I don't think it's so easy. I think he's gone."

"What?"

"He put his family and some luggage in his car and left the house. He's decided to get out."

Slavin bowed his head and put his hands over his ears.

# 43

VOLKOV HAD CLARA DROP HIM AT THE SOUTHWEST METRO STATION, AN easy place for a patrol car to pick him up. He telephoned his office from the station. Ordinarily he would have walked from the station until he found a policeman on foot and used the policeman's radio to call for a car; but he didn't want his message on the air. Agencies other than the police were known to listen to police radios.

The telephone was answered by Alexander Parnov. Parnov had already been in the Department of Investigations when Volkov was assigned there from the Academy. He was an old professional assistant investigator whose life was the Militia. He had known Krylov.

"Shura," Volkov said, "I want you to think about cemeteries."

"You know how to make your workers happy, Maxim Nikolaye-vich. I was just saying to Shumsky here, 'Nikitka, what I'd like to do today is spend the afternoon thinking about cemeteries.' Is there anything in particular about cemeteries that you'd like me to focus my thoughts on, Maxim Nikolayevich?"

"Somewhere in the southwest Moscow suburbs there's a ceme-tery next to one of the main rail lines—possibly between two main lines. It's not far from the Sosnovaya passenger station— maybe an hour on foot. Maybe closer, if you're not tired and your feet don't hurt. It's also not far from a Party sanitorium, or rest area, or hotel of some kind—something that only real high-ups would have used. There's a compound—a main building, some dachas, and a pond. Probably it's privately operated now. I need to know the location of the cemetery and of the Party facility. Get out the maps and have a look."

"Think about cemeteries *and* party places for the Party. Any-thing else, Chief?"

"Yes. Check with the Ministry of Railroads for incident reports. Some train inbound to Moscow last night was delayed by a near miss on a pedestrian adjacent to that same cemetery. Ask the Regional Police if they had any reports of that kind too."

Over the telephone Volkov could hear the creak of Parnov's chair, and he imagined Parnov, a moment ago leaning back in his swivel chair, now leaning closer to his desk. Parnov loved police work. Volkov heard the scratch of a pencil in a notebook.

"Anything else?"

"Check for registrations on privately owned Zils. Find out who the owners are and where they live. If it's a company, find the company address."

"Private Zils! Can't be many of those. What've we got going?" More pencil scratching as he talked.

"I'll tell you when we talk in person. Also see if you can find coordinates for Minin, Anton Antonovich, a big-shot capitalist; a people's deputy named Sidorov—should be easy; and some bureau-crat in the Ministry of Communications, family name Oblonsky. Send a car to pick me up at Southwest metro station. When he gets here, I'll call to see if you know where the cemetery and the hotel are. If you have to talk about this with anybody, talk with Shumsky. Nobody else."

"Sure! Wow, a hot one! We got a hot one!" Parnov hummed happily into the phone as his pencil scratch, scratch, scratched.

Volkov's next call was to his apartment. A woman answered, a voice so like Ella's but not. An older woman. Once their voices had been quite different, but Ella's sounded older now too. She was catching up to her mother.

"Hello, Maria Ivanovna." Volkov was always glad to hear his mother-in-law's voice. "How's your daughter?"

"As bad as she's ever been. Why did you leave her alone?"

"I had to go out. I knew you'd be back soon. Didn't you find my note?"

"I did. But you shouldn't have left her like this."

"I had to go out, Maria Ivanovna. I'm sorry, but I had to."

"All right. I know. Can you be home soon?"

"I don't think so. There's an important case. I'll be home when I can."

"Ella's feeling very bad for what she said to you. I don't know what she said, but she needs to see you. You know how she gets."

He wondered if he could go by his apartment on the way to the Sosnovaya area. It would be far out of the way. The day was going fast—too fast. "I don't think I can come now. I'll call later."

"All right."

He wondered if his mother-in-law's voice had ever been like her daughter's. As her daughter's was before.

When the car arrived and Volkov made his telephone call to his office, Parnov already had the name of the cemetery and of the Party compound. Volkov left other instructions he'd thought of in the meantime and started for the suburbs.

The road came to the cemetery first. Volkov would have stopped, but there seemed to be a lot of people going in and out—probably a funeral—so it would be hard to see anything worthwhile. Because of that, and because it was late in the day, Volkov ordered the driver to go on past the cemetery and take him to the compound first.

He worried a little about getting into the compound. If it was a private operation, he should have a search warrant; but then he'd have to explain why he wanted one, and he didn't want to do that. As an officer in uniform, he thought he could get in without a warrant, and if he did find anything that could be used as evidence, he could always argue that he had needed to act quickly to preserve it. The Prosecutor wasn't going to throw away perfectly good evidence on a technicality. Better for an investigator to get what he could while the getting was good.

A guard stepped out of a sentry box beside the gate, but when he saw Volkov's uniform, he waved the car through.

Following Inna's description, Volkov had the driver follow the road up to the main building. No one was about. Volkov went inside and found himself in a large, empty lobby. There was what appeared to be a registration desk but no one behind it. A door was open into an office behind the desk, and a light was on in the office. Women's voices eddied out through the open door. He banged on the desk. Nothing happened, so he banged again. After he had banged the third time, a woman's voice called from the office, "This office is not working. Come back in thirty minutes."

He walked down to the end of the desk from where he could see into the office. Two women were drinking tea.

Seeing his uniform, they both stood up suddenly. One of them came out, nervously smoothing her dress down over her legs. "I'm sorry," she said, "I didn't realize . . . I thought it was just a guest."

Volkov smiled. "You needn't worry, it's nothing official. But there was a party here last night, in one of the dachas. I need to find someone who attended."

"I wasn't on duty yesterday," the woman said hesitantly, but the other woman's voice came from the office, annoyed: "There wasn't but one party last night, and they're still in the place. We couldn't even get in to clean." She had sat down again and poured another cup of tea and was stirring it in loud annoyance. Hotel work would be bearable if it weren't for guests.

"They're still here?" Volkov said, surprised.

"Part of 'em. The cars left, but not all the people left with the cars."

"Well, if they pay, what's that to us?" the first woman asked. Standing closer to Volkov, she seemed to feel a need to be kinder to the guests.

"*If* they pay," the other woman said; "but we still won't get our work done on time. Well, *I'm* not staying late. I can promise you that."

"Well, if they were the only party, they must be who I'm looking for," Volkov said. "Where are they?"

"Cabin Three," the woman in the office said. "If you talk to 'em, ask 'em what time they're leaving."

The door to Cabin Three was closed, and no one answered his knock, so Volkov opened the door and went in.

He stepped into an entryway, heard nothing, stepped across through an open door into the main room. The room was full of the smell of a burned-out fire. The shades were drawn, and the room was dark, for the cabin sat under deep trees, and the sun was low in the west, although it would not set for hours.

At first he thought the women were wrong: he saw no one in the room. Then he saw that he was wrong: as his eyes adjusted to the darkness, he saw an old man reclining in an armchair. His head was cocked back at an angle over the chair back, and his mouth gaped.

Volkov walked over to the reclining man and stood watching him for a moment. Then he reached down and put a finger under the jaw to close the mouth. The mouth did not close. When Volkov pushed harder, the jaw, and then the whole head, resisted.

Now he was going to have to bring more people in on the case. He was sorry for it, but he had no choice. Corpses had to be reported. He located a telephone at the far end of the room and called his office.

It would take an hour for the police pathologist and the technicians to arrive. After calling for their support, Volkov went around the room for a little while looking but not touching. The technicians would come for fingerprints and other physical evidence of who had been here. There should be plenty of fingerprints. There were plenty of bottles, and where there were bottles, there were fingerprints, as Shura Parnov liked to say. Parnov loved bottles. They had such broad lovely surfaces, so attractive to the essential oils from human fingertips.

Sidorov's death was a blow to Volkov. He regretted it as if his own grandfather had died. Ever since he parted from Inna at the dacha, he had been composing the plan of this investigation in his mind; and in it, Valentin Ivanovich Sidorov, People's Deputy, had featured as the leading songbird.

Sidorov was the perfect candidate. He was, according to Inna, remorseful, and as a People's Deputy, he was immune from arrest. The Supreme Soviet could of course cancel that immunity, but it would take a political struggle to do it, and by not pressing too hard, the Prosecutor could ensure that the attempt would fail. So Sidorov could have been assured he had little to fear personally from assuaging his remorse. That was always a powerful combination.

While he waited for support, Volkov questioned the women at the office; he expected them to know nothing, and they did, except for the name of the person who had rented the cabin and the identity of the staff who had been on duty the night before. The cabin had been in the name of Minin.

Volkov gave instructions for the staff to be called in for questioning the next day.

By the time he was finished writing up the women's statements, the pathologist had arrived.

While his hopes for Sidorov's confession had died, Sidorov's corpse still kept a little candle burning in Volkov, a candle of hope that maybe someone had killed him to keep him from talking. But Volkov couldn't really believe in it. Would they be so stupid as not to dispose of the body?

The little candle went out when the pathologist gave his preliminary opinion. "Ten to one it's a heart attack."

"Could someone have induced it?"

The pathologist shrugged. "He'd probably drunk well." He waved a hand around the room at the bottles. "You could argue either way about what that means. Did someone hold him down and pour it down him? Did someone excite him with dancing girls? You'll have to work out the background, Major. A pathologist can only tell you so much. But if you want to know what I think . . . an old geezer like this? He was just old."

"All right. Call me with the final results. If I'm not there, talk to Parnov."

"I won't autopsy him until tomorrow. I've been on duty all day as it is."

"Why don't you do him tonight and take tomorrow off." Volkov knew it was useless to suggest, but he did it anyway.

"That's not my shift. Besides, I've done one stiff already today. There's a limit to the work one can do and still be accurate. It's not like cutting a hog, you know. This is medicine, not butchery." Pathologists, used to being condescended to by other physicians, protected their fragile egos by taking no grief from anyone else.

On the way back to Moscow, people were still coming and going at the cemetery gate. Volkov had his driver stop.

Just inside the gate was a middle-aged man wearing a red armband on one sleeve of his black jacket, the mark of the civilian volunteers who assisted with police duties. Seeing Volkov in uniform, the man made a kind of half salute and said, "It's back there." He waved the end of the salute toward the back of the cemetery, along the mainstream of the foot traffic.

Volkov did not like looking around with so many people here. "What is it, a funeral?" But the crowd seemed to be both coming and going. At a funeral, everyone came and went together.

The man looked at him. "Well . . . they're here to see where the body was." Then he laughed. "Oh, I see. It was a joke. Well, I'll take you up there myself. We put a rope around the spot, to keep people off, thinking you might want to come back for more investigation." He marched off up the path, physically moving people out of the way but careful not to get ahead of Volkov.

"It was Tomsky that found 'im," the man said. "But you probably know that."

"Pretend I don't. Tell me what *you* know about it. Who is Tomsky?"

"Tomsky is the grandson of his grandfather, who was buried here many years ago. Lived here in the village all his life. There's folk still alive who knew him, though I didn't. My dad, he was one; but he's gone now, of course. Well, old Tomsky's son—the son of the grandfather, that is—he was ordered to Leningrad during the war, and he died there, they say, during the siege, but not before he'd got a child. The child was a boy, and he grew up in Leningrad and never could take proper care of the grave. So some people here in the village did it for him, although not as well as I would have liked them to, I have to say. Not since so many people are here to see the place now. But it was that Tomsky, the grandson, who found the body. He decided to come down to the home village to see his grandfather's grave. And what a sight he did find."

"Tell me about it."

"Why, here was Tomsky with his fine city wife, down from Peter to visit his grandpa's grave for the first time"—the volunteer had previously used the old Soviet name, Leningrad, for the city, but now he used the familiar slang term, Peter, which had survived through all the Leningrad years and still referred to St. Petersburg—"and what does he find but a man stretched out on the gravesite. They thought it was a drunk fallen asleep from the night before, and it's said that Tomsky got a bit sore and put his foot into the man—not to kick him, of course, but to stir him up—and found that he was stiff as a board. And then they saw, of course, that the back of his head was cracked open. The police investigator this morning said somebody really big and really strong had hit him in the back of the head with a grave marker."

They had angled back and across the cemetery, onto narrower and narrower paths, and now they had come to a back plot where old grave markers rose from a tangle of weeds. The crowd was all on the same path, and it was hard to move, for they were hemmed in by fences—iron pickets in some places, wire in others—on both sides, except at one point where a section of fence had been knocked down. Opposite this, at the very back of the cemetery, the crowd flowed out into an open space where the weeds had been trampled flat. The man pushed through the crowd, his red armband his authority, to reach a rope tied to several grave markers. The rope kept sacred a small clearing around a tall stone memorial. "That's Grandad Tomsky's grave," the man said. "And that's where he was." He lowered the rope, inviting Volkov to step inside. It appeared that the crowd expected it of him, so Volkov did. The man did not follow, but raised the rope again, respecting the loneliness of Volkov's expertise.

There was nothing to see but the marks of a thousand feet, but Volkov knew he was looking at the place that Inna had described.

Volkov was saddened. Not for the departed: from Deputy Korneva's account, he'd had it coming. But this was another witness dead. It was a waste. It was going to take live witnesses to nail a general of the Ministry of Security.

Volkov used a coin telephone outside the village store to call Parnov. "Shura, check for reports concerning that cemetery whose name you gave me. Supposedly there was a murder there last night. I want to know who it was."

"A murder? This is definitely a hot one, Chief. Promise you'll let me in on it?"

"You'll get more of it than you want before it's over. Get me the details."

"Hold on." Parnov put the phone down on his desk and went across the room. Volkov could hear him using a different phone on the next desk but couldn't understand the words. He waited without impatience. There was no hurrying telephone calls in Moscow, not even police calls.

After a while Parnov's steps approached the phone again and he picked it up. "You sure there was a murder there, Chief? We don't have anything."

"There's a big crowd here who seem pretty sure. A volunteer policeman here says a police investigator looked at the body. Who would the investigator be?"

"Hold on."

It was a longer wait this time. Then Parnov came back. "I found him. The Regional Police had the case, not us. We might never have known about it. You know, this is a *very* interesting case, Chief."

"Who's the deceased, Shura?"

"That's what's so interesting. He had his papers on him. The Regionals didn't bother to look him up, but I did. If he's who his papers say he is, this is very interesting."

"Who do his papers say he is, Shura?"

"They say his name is Shutnov; but it's not so much who he is, but what. The papers are for an old KGB bad-face who went off to work for private business sometime back."

"Yes, that is interesting. Shura, find this corpse's address and let's go have a look at his apartment. I'll call you from on the road into the city."

"Can I use your name to ask the Prosecutor for a search warrant?"

"I thought I heard someone say no one was to know what you're working on."

"I heard that too. Just checking."

"We'll ask for a search warrant when we know we need it."

# 44

PARNOV WAS WAITING IN AN UNMARKED CAR AT WARSAW EXPRESSWAY on the Moscow Ring Road. The car was a white Zhiguli with civilian plates. "It ain't comfortable," Parnov said, "but if you don't want people to know what we're working on . . . Of course, I didn't know you were in uniform, Chief, or I'd have asked for one of the BMWs."

"My day started in a different direction," Volkov said.

"Yeah, isn't that a cop's life? Well, our departed colleague's place is in a Khrushchev slum out on Nagatinskaya Street. Now that we're not on the telephone, can you tell me what this case is about? Not that I'll quit working on it if I don't know."

"This case, Shura, is about justice. Delayed justice, but justice."

Parnov was silent for a while. "Well, thanks," he said at last.

Volkov waited a little while. "This one's for the General, Shura."

Parnov knew whom Volkov meant when he said "the General," even after twenty years. Parnov had gone through the Militia Academy too.

They had no key to the apartment, but Parnov had ways of persuading doors. While Parnov was doing that, Volkov visited the building superintendent. He asked her, "Has anyone else been here looking for the owner of this apartment recently?"

She was a woman who knew what she knew. "No. Definitely not. Except his friend, of course." A woman who knew what she knew, but didn't always know what it was.

"His friend?"

"With the big limousine. I don't know his name. They were in the you-know-what together."

In Moscow, where people lived all their lives in the same building, it was impossible for a building superintendent not to know who worked where, including for the you-know-what, even if she did think the security of the state depended on her not saying that name even to the police.

"What time was his friend here?"

"It was just after ten o'clock this morning."

"What did he do?"

"I don't know. I saw the car, and him getting out of it and coming in the building and then leaving again. But I don't live on this staircase, so I don't know what he did. Nothing but knock, I'd guess. He was here less than three minutes."

When he had closed the entry door behind them, Volkov said, "We'd better send a man to watch this place, Shura."

"Who's it going to be?" Parnov asked. "Major Zaitsev's got practically everybody tied up on that drug stakeout he's working on. We don't want any strangers sitting on this place."

"No. But we want to find Shutnov's friend. Well, we can't call from here anyway. Let's see what we find, and worry about his friend later."

The apartment was a typical *Khrushchevka*—one room plus an entry hall and a kitchen. They started in the entry hall and worked into the main room, leaving the kitchen for last.

"What are we looking for, Chief?"

"Evidence that was in danger of disappearing if we didn't act promptly to secure it." It was the formula necessary to explain why he'd acted without a search warrant.

Volkov didn't expect to find much in an old Committee man's apartment, and so he wasn't disappointed at the main room—basic ugly furniture (two chairs, a desk, a sofa that made into a bed; no personal photos, no letters, no papers of any kind). Parnov did the hall, then went into the kitchen. "You've got to see this, Chief," he called. "Our departed colleague was a collector."

"What is it? Child pornography?"

"No, that would be typical KGB. This is unique."

Volkov found Parnov standing just inside the door of the kitchen, staring at the opposite corner.

The opposite corner of the kitchen—almost half the room, really—was occupied by a half-pyramid, two sides jutting into the room, with the peak in the very corner where the two walls of the room met, up almost at the ceiling.

It was a pyramid of stacked dead bottles.

They were all open, empty, set neatly in rows sorted by size, and sometimes by genus—wine here, champagne there; a few were Scotch or bourbon, but mostly they were vodka.

"That must have been a life's work," Parnov said reverently.

"Now we know what they do at the Committee."

"How many do you suppose are in it? Must be hundreds." Parnov started to count the tiers, starting from the top down, to estimate the number of bottles; but he stopped suddenly. "I'll be damned!"

"What is it?"

But Parnov had pulled a chair over to the base of the pyramid and was climbing on the chair, reaching. "You remember when we did that workup on the bottle from 1812 Street, Chief?" Then Volkov saw it too.

Up near the top, right in the front—even from the chair Parnov could barely reach it—was a Finlandia bottle.

"Where do you suppose he got it?" Volkov asked, hoping he knew.

Parnov put a finger inside the open neck to pull the bottle down without touching the outside. "Where there's a bottle, there's a fingerprint."

# 45

THEIR TICKETS WERE FOR CAR NUMBER THREE, JUST BEHIND THE ENGINE. Carrying overnight luggage, they pushed their way out through the crowd in the front of the station. Jen complained, overwhelmed by the crowd, but even overnight luggage was too much for Brad to carry with her too. He had suitcases in both hands and a small backpack slung over his right shoulder. Joanna carried his briefcase in one hand; in the other she clutched Jen's sleeve. Brad turned aside the offers of porters; he did not want to leave any memories in the station.

Out on the platform under the high steel-framed shed roof the crowd was less dense. The family wound their way among travelers gathering early. The roof ended before they reached car twenty, and beyond that they were under the open sky, with almost no one else on the platform. Brad looked around, uneasy. He had wanted to be one of the last aboard; but to be late would be a disaster, and compromise had made him early.

It was a long walk to car three. The train was nearly a half mile long, and it seemed longer because the track had a slight curve so that the engine could not be seen from the station. The train blocked their view of anything on the right. But on the left the other tracks were empty, and they could see for miles in the still evening air, all the way to the university towering above the distant Lenin Hills. From apartments beyond the tracks in that direction the voices of children playing rang clear through the evening.

The visibility was oppressive: anyone might be watching. They walked quickly. They passed no one.

Jen, though, was happier here outside, where she could see distance instead of legs and belt buckles. She shook loose her mother's hand. As a game she counted down the car numbers—in Russian, until Joanna asked what she was doing and made her switch to English.

The shades were pulled down in all the car windows.

Five, four, three. "We're here, Daddy, Mommy, we're here!" The shades were down in car number three too.

Brad tried the door. It was locked. A light was on in the conductor's compartment next to the entrance, but no one responded when he knocked on its window. He left the bags on the platform with Joanna and walked with Jen up to the first two cars and then to the engine. Those cars were locked too; but there was a crew on the engine. One of them waved at Jen, who waved back and cried hello in Russian.

When they came back to car three, someone was moving inside. As the motion shifted back toward the conductor's compartment, Brad banged on the window again, and after a moment the door to the car opened. It was a young woman, partly dressed in a conductor's uniform but not wearing her jacket. "What is it?" she asked in an annoyed voice.

"We have seats in this car."

"Well, they'll still be here at boarding time. It's now still thirty minutes, and we don't open the car until twenty minutes before departure."

"We have a little girl with us," Brad said, an appeal that often softened Russian hearts.

"It's a fine evening for her to be out. Call me if it rains." The woman closed the door.

Brad and Joanna stood beside their bags, not talking, while Jen ran back and forth along the edge of the platform looking for unusual rocks, crying out whenever she saw one until Joanna made her come back.

A few other passengers drifted around the curve of the train. A man came along lugging a huge leather suitcase closed with two buckled straps. He carried it sometimes in one hand, sometimes the other, mostly in both, banging it forward with one leg. He tried the door of car three. "Its closed," he announced—not to them especially, although no one else was nearby. He was a tall, lean-faced man with his hair parted in the middle and wearing wire-framed glasses. Joanna assumed he was a musician, or maybe an orchestra conductor. He put the suitcase down and sat on it. "So, now you support me for a while," he said to it. He took out a cigarette. The sour smell of Russian tobacco drifted around Brad and Joanna. Joanna coughed and moved farther away. The man looked at her with polite interest but said nothing.

"Look, Daddy, there's a milliman coming!" Jennifer had drifted away again up the track. She was looking back at them but pointing toward the station.

A man in the familiar gray uniform was walking rapidly toward them. He was saying something into the two-way radio clipped to the shoulder of his jacket.

"Come back here, Jennifer!" Joanna called. But she did not come back. Joanna ran to her, took her by the hand, and brought her back, as if there were some charmed radius around the baggage.

The policeman came on, marching fast but looking all around.

The man sitting on the suitcase watched the policeman come, but without turning his face quite toward him. He held his cigarette at his lips with one hand. The policeman walked past the man on the suitcase, who turned his head to watch the policeman's back, but without turning his face quite toward the policeman.

When the policeman was a few meters away, Jennifer addressed him in Russian: "Hello, Uncle Militiaman!"

The policeman stopped and looked at her seriously. He was a young man with the potato nose of the Russian peasant. "Hello, girl," he said firmly. "Where are you going?"

"We're going home," she said.

"Oh? And where is home?"

" 'Merika."

The policeman laughed. "You won't get there on *this* train."

"Yes, I will! My dad and my mom said so! We're going to Kiev, and then going to 'Merika."

"Is that so? Is this your dad and your mom?"

"Yes. And they said so."

The policeman looked at Brad. "You're Americans?"

"Yes."

"Show me your passports."

Brad freed his hand from Jennifer's, realizing only as he did so how tightly he was clutching hers. He reached for his briefcase, fumbled at the latches, but finally got them open. He handed over the three passports.

The policeman looked at the pictures inside the front of each passport. Jen's had been taken almost three years ago. He held it up beside her. "Is that you?"

She was scornful. "No. That's a *baby!*"

"It's an old picture," Joanna said in English, realizing what the policeman had asked without understanding the words.

"It's an old picture," Brad repeated in Russian. "Look at the date."

The policeman ignored him. He asked Jennifer, "Weren't you a baby once?"

She laughed. "Yes. That was when I was a baby! Don't you know *anything?*"

He smiled. "Not very much, sometimes." He said to Brad, "Where are your visas?"

"They're in the back of the passports." Each passport was in a clear plastic cover, with the visa in a pocket in the back. The policeman took out each one and read them, Brad's last.

"You all have multiple entry visas," he observed.

"Yes. We live here."

"Business?"

"Yes."

"What business?"

"I work for a joint venture."

The next question was obvious: "What joint venture?" Brad's mind was already racing for answers. If he said JorSov, any policeman who read the newspapers would think hard about what to do next.

The question never came. "You don't have Ukraine visas," the policeman said.

"When these were issued, Ukraine didn't have visas. They used Russian ones. These are supposed to still be good. I checked with the Ukraine office here in Moscow. They said I was supposed to have a visa, but they don't issue them and don't know how to get them, so we should just go."

The policeman shook his head. "Crazy Ukrainians. How are they ever going to run a country?" He handed the passports back to Brad. "Good luck. I hope they let you in."

"Thanks. I hope so."

The policeman started to walk away, then turned back. "That's a strange way to get to America—taking the train to Kiev."

"Well, we always wanted to see Kiev. I've been there, but the family never had the chance." He saw that Joanna had her nails dug into Jennifer's arm.

"I have a cousin there. She always says it's a beautiful city." The policeman turned away, then turned back again. "Is that all the baggage you have? You aren't carrying much, for a trip to America."

"We sent most of it ahead," Brad said. "This is just for Kiev."

"Ah. Yes, that's a good plan. So, have a good trip." He turned and walked briskly on his way.

After the policeman was out of earshot, the man sitting on the leather bag cleared his throat and spat. "Nosy bastard," he said.

A few more people gathered, dropped their bags, tried the door. At length the conductor opened the door. "All right, then. You can board." She said this to the Chapmans, in recognition that they had been first.

They had a two-berth compartment. This left Jen to sleep with one of them or the other; the only other choice was a four-person compartment, with the risk that the fourth would be taken even if they bought a ticket for the extra place. Brad bundled their things into the compartment and closed the door. While Jen acquainted herself with the luggage compartment above the door, he and Joanna had a quiet conversation about whether to warn her not to tell anyone what they were doing. They had had this conversation before, and they came to the same conclusion again: it was probably more dangerous to warn her, and impress it on her mind as something unusual, than to let her talk as she happened to. But the policeman had put them both on edge, and it was an unpleasant conversation, one that left Brad rearranging the luggage to avoid saying anything more.

He was standing on one berth hoisting the suitcases into the luggage space, having coaxed Jen down from it, when the door shot open. Startled, he jerked back, almost bringing a suitcase down on top of himself. A man in a military uniform was standing in the door inspecting the compartment.

No one said anything.

The officer looked from Brad to Joanna to Jennifer and back to Brad. At length he said, "There are three of you."

"Yes. My wife and daughter."

"There won't be room."

"What?"

"I have a place in this compartment."

"Well, it'll be damned cozy," Brad said.

"What?"

Brad had spoken in English without realizing it. He switched back to Russian. "We have this compartment. Look." He hunted for his briefcase, for the tickets.

Before he found them, the conductress appeared. "What's the matter?"

"This officer says . . . ," Brad began.

"I have a ticket . . . ," the officer said simultaneously.

"Let me see your tickets. All of them." She took the tickets and read through them slowly. "Well, there's been a mistake. You all have tickets for the same compartment. It's no surprise. Nothing has worked well since the Union vanished."

"Well, since we're already here," Brad suggested, "why don't you just give him another berth?"

"The train is full." This was said in the voice Russian bureaucrats reserved for official pronouncements—emphatic and final sounding.

"I stood in line for two hours this afternoon to get these tickets," Brad said. Brad never bought tickets himself, but he had not dared ask anyone else to do it today.

"Bradley, what is going on?" The quaver in Joanna's voice made Brad conscious for the first time that she didn't understand anything.

"It's nothing," he said. "This officer has a ticket for our compartment."

"You call that *nothing*? Oh, God!"

"Maybe we can take turns sleeping."

"Bradley, this is no time for fucking jokes!" She began to cry, cursing at the same time because she didn't want to be crying but couldn't help it just now.

The officer and the conductress were meanwhile having an earnest conversation. "If I give you a place in this compartment," she was saying, "then I'll have to move *all* of *them*. You know I can't put foreigners in with citizens. You of all people must know that! And there's nowhere in this car I can put two foreigners. Not to mention the child . . ."

The child decided the issue. Russians could be narrow-minded, bureaucratic, procedure-ridden idiots; but at the same time, they were likely to be soft at heart if they could find a way to square softheartedness with the demands of the rules—or if they could be sure no one would be the wiser. "So what do you want me to do?" the conductress demanded—rhetorically, for she clearly had no intention of doing anything but what she wanted. "Is it my fault that the authorities can't do their work properly? Shall I make this child sleep in the passageway? Or do you want to come in here and sleep with her and her mother in the same compartment? See, you've already made this woman cry."

The officer sighed. Seeing what he was going to have to do, he was prepared to be magnanimous about it: "Perhaps you could find another place for me."

"I've told you this car is full. The whole train is full, if it's anything like the usual day. But I'll see what I can do."

"I don't think I can stand it," Joanna said as the door closed behind the officer. But she had too much Minnesota in her: she had already stopped crying. She made Brad get a suitcase back down and got out Jen's pajamas and got on with the practical business of the night ahead.

With two sharp jolts the train started to roll. They all liked to stand in the corridor on trains. On Russian trains the corridor ran down one side of the car, and on that side the windows opened, so you could stand and look out with nothing between you and the world. In the compartments, the windows didn't open, and they always had a grimy film to obscure the view. But tonight the Chapmans all stayed in their compartment with the door closed and, now, locked.

The conductress returned, after a time, to take their tickets officially and to ask if they wanted tea. Brad declined for them.

"Doesn't this torture ever stop?" Joanna asked. "Why can't they all just leave us alone?" The train was rolling with aching slowness through the Moscow suburbs.

"They'll stop," Brad said. But he felt the same.

Joanna read to Jen until she fell asleep. Then she turned out the light, and she and Brad lay on their separate berths—Jen with Joanna—in the gray light of their final Russian evening. They did not talk.

Brad listened to the wheels hitting the joints between rails. *Ka-chonk. Ka-chonk.*
*Ka-chonk, ka-chonk, ka-chonk.*

The rhythm worked itself into his brain, and somewhere between waking and sleep a scrap of a poem popped into his mind. He didn't know where it came from, whether he had heard or read it or made it up. He didn't like poetry. He didn't like this poem, but it came anyway:

> The city slept,
> and there
> was no
> pursuit.

> *Ka-chonk, ka-chonk.*
> *ka-chonk*
> *ka-chonk*
> *ka-chonk*

Slowly the tension of the past days drained from his muscles. He reached out a hand, found Joanna's arm dangling from her berth. When he found her hand, she squeezed his. He did not know if she was awake. She said nothing. But her hand squeezed his.

He woke somewhere in the countryside to the bright early dawn. He sat up and looked out. A deep belt of trees bordered the track, as almost everywhere in the former Union, but the occasional break in the shelterbelt showed broad, rolling fields, some with grain nearing ripeness. They could have been any-where. But he looked at his watch, and from the time he knew the train must have crossed into Ukraine.

The city slept, and there was no pursuit.

# 46

WHILE THE TECHNICIANS WERE TREATING THE VODKA BOTTLE, VOLKOV first telephoned home to check on Eleanora and to tell his mother-in-law that he would not be home that night, and then he met with Parnov and Shumsky for an hour to prepare the next steps.

Shumsky had got Oblonsky's address and Antipov's but had no other information about them. The department had too few men to send anyone on surveillance. A trusted officer had gone to Minin's apartment and to his company office. Minin's neighbors reported that he had come home that morning in his limousine, not early, not late, and that the driver had taken the limousine away and had not come back. An hour or two later, Minin had left in a taxicab. No one was at his office. The limousine was not there.

Volkov was stone tired. The excitement of the chase had worn away. There had been too many events, too many conflicting emotions. When the discussion wore on without conclusion, he broke it off and told Parnov to leave orders to wake him at three A.M. He took off his boots and lay down on the wooden bench in his office to sleep.

Parnov and Shumsky left him there. They were already eight hours over the end of their shift, but they didn't expect to leave their posts until this investigation ended. Volkov had told them about Marchenko.

No one, of course, had been sent to check on General Marchenko. An event so extraordinary would have been the talk of the department instantly. For the moment, Marchenko had to be taken on faith.

In an hour of troubled sleep that night, Volkov dreamed of his daughter, and of Eleanora young and radiant. But when he woke, the dream had vanished, all but the barest memory, nothing he could hold.

He found Parnov already awake. They took the white Zhiguli and drove south.

Volkov ordinarily would never have gone to a witness's home to interrogate him; but he did not want any witness in this case to be seen in a police station or the Department of Investigations. Sidorov had caused enough talk by himself, and he was dead. Shutnov, the Joker, fortunately, was only in the files of the Regional Police, and in far-off Court Medicine Morgue Number 5. Nothing tied them together for anyone else, unless someone was either well-informed or very, very curious.

Volkov did not rule out either of those possibilities.

Oblonsky's apartment was high up in a twenty-story block not far off Leninsky Prospect, one of the last acts of the socialism that had vanished, an unremembered dream.

Oblonsky answered the knock at his door after a long time. His eyes were mere slits, but they opened wide, seeing two policemen in uniform. He started to slam the door but thought better of it.

"Arkady Arkadievich Oblonsky?" Volkov asked.

"Y . . . yes."

"We'd like to ask you some questions. May we come in?"

"At this hour?"

"I'm afraid the questions won't wait."

"It's about Sidorov, isn't it."

Volkov said nothing.

"I didn't kill him! I just woke up and he was there! I tried calling the others, but no one's answering!"

"Maybe we'd better go inside," Volkov said. "The neighbors."

"Yes. Yes, come in."

It was not the apartment of an aristocrat. It was a new, faceless three-roomer, the kind of place every bureaucrat aspired to, and those with connections eventually got. Three rooms with clean walls and your own kitchen in a building where the plumbing and the elevator worked. The kind of place Eleanora wanted. It was the home of a person with no history.

The only other aristocrat Volkov had known was an old woman who, when he was a child, had lived in a corner of the building he still lived in. She had grown up in it, as he had, and so she seemed to feel some affinity for him and invited him in for tea and cookies. She wanted to tell him stories about the place, but his father had warned him to be cautious in listening to her. Her stories were dangerous. Volkov had privately thought she was a frightful liar. Her single room was filled with things she said were from her family's history, and she told him about them: a serving dish, part of a set once numbering in hundreds, she said—but how could that be?—no one had hundreds of dishes, or even ten; a folding metal icon that had protected her great-uncle in the war, until he was shot—it was much later before he understood what war she meant, and that it was the Civil War and her great-uncle was shot as an enemy of the people; paintings of an ancestor or two; this one, she claimed, had known the Czar, that one had married a son of the builder of the Trans-Siberian Railway. She told him about her childhood home, how wonderful it was, the lights, the grand staircase, the tree at Christmas; but it was years after she had died that he understood that the home she was talking about was *this* home, the building he lived in, *his* home.

She was only an old woman, and so she was allowed to live out her history, but in the Union, having a history at all was dangerous. Volkov understood why Oblonsky lived as he did. A child of a noble family making his way in the System could not afford to presume to a history.

"Why do you think we're here about Sidorov?" Volkov asked Oblonsky as Parnov made himself ostentatiously comfortable on the couch without being asked.

"Well . . . aren't you?"

"Actually, as I said, we've come to ask *you* questions, and not the other way around. So would you please answer that one?''

Oblonsky sat down on a chair, as far from Volkov as possible. He seemed not to know how to answer.

Volkov was too tired to stretch out the interrogation. He said, as a way of getting started, ''You assumed that we knew Sidorov is dead. Is that right?''

''Yes. Yes, of course. I . . .''

Volkov sat down in a chair near Oblonsky and began taking notes in a bound notebook. ''You said you tried calling 'the others.' Who are they?''

''The other people who were there.''

''Who are they?''

''Minin and . . . Marchenko.'' The second name came out of him carefully, as if after a struggle.

''Their full names, please, and their positions.''

Oblonsky told him.

''Was anyone else there?''

''No. No one.''

''Was anyone else expected?''

''Yes. Antipov—the Supreme Soviet Deputy. Vasily Ivanovich.''

''Anyone else?''

''No.''

''Was Antipov bringing anyone?''

''No. Not that I know of.''

''Why were you trying to call the others?''

''I told you. I woke up and . . . Sidorov was in the chair. I thought it was funny, our both sleeping it off, and I tried to wake him. But he wouldn't wake. And then I saw that he wasn't ever going to wake.''

''What time was it?''

''It was just thirty minutes short of one. There was a clock.''

''So you tried calling Minin and Marchenko. Where?''

''At their apartments, first; then their dachas and then their offices.''

''The numbers?''

''I'll have to look.''

''Do so.''

Oblonsky went to a desk and took a notebook from beside the telephone. He came back, sat down, turned a few pages, and read out the telephone numbers. He started to take the book back to the desk, but Volkov said, "May I see that?"

Oblonsky gave it to him, clearly afraid to refuse. Volkov looked through it and tossed it to Parnov. "Will I get it back?" Oblonsky asked. Volkov didn't answer, and Oblonsky didn't ask again.

"Where do you think Minin and Marchenko have gone?" Volkov asked.

"I don't know. They hadn't talked of going anywhere."

"Why were you calling them?"

"Why, because . . ." On reflection, Oblonsky seemed not to be sure why he had tried to call them.

"Was it because you thought they killed Sidorov?"

"No! Why would they kill Sidorov?"

"Why did they kill Turbin, or that woman Shubina?"

Oblonsky's mouth opened and shut twice before he was able to squeak, "I didn't have anything to do with that!"

"Listen to the question. Why did *they* kill Turbin and Shubina?"

Still Oblonsky's mouth moved, but his vocal cords didn't operate.

Volkov said, while making a note, "Turbin, because he wasn't going to share the ownership of JorSov with the rest of you. With you and Minin and Marchenko and Antipov." He looked up at Oblonsky. "And Sidorov, but of course he doesn't get a share either, now that he's dead. Were you afraid they were going to kill *you*, Arkady Arkadievich?"

Oblonsky's jaw flapped.

"I'm curious," Volkov said. "Why did they have you in the group at all? The others I can understand, but what did you bring to the project?"

"I'm . . . I'm an assistant to the Deputy Minister. I can get things signed."

"Ah." Volkov made a note. "You mean, such things as reassignment of administrative accountability for state organizations?" One couldn't give away state property without going through the established—and public—privatization procedure; but one could move the control of a state organization from one state agency to another, and the public need never know. And who often ended up owning the property of a state organization when it was privatized? The managers of the state organization, and the officials of the agency that controlled it. "But why you?" Volkov asked. "Why not the Deputy Minister or the Minister? Or"—he knew he would have to make it easy for Oblonsky—"were you just standing in their shoes?"

"They don't know anything!" Oblonsky blurted, suddenly aware of the depth of the waters around him. "They don't know about Turbin and the woman!"

"They'll have to testify about that for themselves, of course."

"Oh, God!"

"But the more you tell me now, the less I'll have to ask them."

"Oh, God!"

"You'll be safer with me than with Marchenko."

"Oh, God!"

"How were they carried out, these murders?"

"I don't know. We never discussed it. I know with Turbin, it was agreed it had to be done." The impersonal passive, the true voice of the bureaucracy.

"Who agreed?"

"Marchenko said it had to be done."

"Who did it? How?"

"I don't know how. Minin had two guards. He was always bragging about his ex-KGB bodyguards. 'I'll send them to do it,' he said. 'This is what they're trained for.' Marchenko knew them. They'd been with him at Kabul. He didn't say that, Minin did. Minin complained about them once: they always stuck together, and they always acted like they were still at Kabul, working for Marchenko."

"And the woman?"

"I don't know. I never knew anything about her, except I heard Minin telling Marchenko that she'd been taken care of."

"What are the names of the two bodyguards?"

"I never knew their names. Just their nicknames. Cover names. Trade names. Whatever they are. Joker and Brick."

" 'Joker.' That's good," Parnov said. The family name on Joker's papers, Shutnov, came from the word for "joke."

"Where do these two live?" Volkov asked Oblonsky.

"I don't know. I don't know anything else about them."

It took another two hours of going back and forth over the ground before Volkov was sure he had got everything that could be got out of Oblonsky. Oblonsky seemed to believe that he was under arrest, and so Volkov followed Oblonsky's inclinations and wrote up an order to detain him for three days as a suspect in the death of Valentin Ivanovich Sidorov, Member of the Congress of People's Deputies. The order might bring Volkov trouble later, but it would keep Oblonsky from talking to anyone for a few days. And however much interest it might arouse in Volkov's office, if the interested persons were unfriendly, it might lead them to conclude that Volkov was following a different track from the one he was actually on.

When Volkov and Parnov got back to the office, Shumsky was there before they could sit down.

"Did you get him, Chief?" They all knew whom Shumsky meant: Marchenko.

"I can't arrest him yet. I can get him for questioning. But so far, we don't have a case, nothing but talk around the edges. Strong talk, but nothing to tie it all together. And Marchenko's not going to admit anything."

"This will help." Shumsky held out a file report. Volkov could see the copies of fingerprints attached to it.

"Where there's a bottle, there's fingerprints," Parnov said, his incantation.

"This bottle had gone the rounds," Shumsky said. "It was covered with prints, at least four different sets of them."

"Four? Who?"

"One was unidentified."

"A great start."

"Wait. The second was the owner of the apartment, our colleague the bottle collector, formerly of the KGB."

"No help there."

"The third was that American lawyer, Fall."

Parnov leaned forward. "I love you, Shumsky. And the fourth . . ."

"Wait for it. And the fourth was a dead woman, Alexandra Shubina, who had died in her apartment on 1812 Street of an overdose of vodka."

"*Yolki motalki!*" Parnov murmured, almost to himself. "Joker got that bottle from her apartment!"

"It's too bad he's deceased," Volkov said. "If he were alive, he could lead us where we want to go. To the people above him." He was suddenly deadly tired. Would they ever get to the end of this? He wanted to go home and sleep in his own bed. With his own wife. Even as she was.

"Somebody else can get us there, Chief," Parnov said. "You *know* whose the fourth print is. It's got to be the Joker's buddy, the Brick!"

"No, I don't know," Volkov said. "It could be anybody's print."

"Come on! It's got to be his buddy's!"

"If it were the buddy's," Volkov said, "then the buddy would have to be suspected of murder. But if he were suspected of murder, then when we find him, he'd have a right to a lawyer before I could question him. If and when we find the buddy, do you want the first thing I say to him to be, 'You have a right to a lawyer before you answer any questions'?"

Parnov sat silent.

"Me either. So, as for me, I don't have any idea whose print it is. Anyway, if it is his, it won't help us find him. We don't know who he is. We don't have access to fingerprints of Committee people. We could ask the Committee, 'You guys got any ex-operatives nicknamed Brick who used to work for Marchenko? You want to send us their fingerprints?'"

Parnov and Shumsky laughed at the idea of asking the MBR for anything.

"But if anyone in that bunch has any brains," Volkov continued, "they'll have got their Brick out of town. And you know Marchenko's got brains. Minin, too, from the sound of him, or he wouldn't own a private Zil limo."

"Didn't Oblonsky say Minin's two guards were always together?" Parnov objected. "What's Brick going to do? Maybe he knows his buddy's dead, maybe he doesn't. If he does, then it's too bad for us. But if he doesn't, he's going to look for him. And if he's going to, he's gonna check at the buddy's apartment, and probably he's going to do it first thing in the morning, because he'll be real nervous and won't want to wait until later. The building superintendent told us he's already been there once, yesterday morning. Send somebody out there now."

"It's a good idea, except that Shumsky told us last night there is nobody we can send."

"I'll go," Parnov and Shumsky said together.

Shumsky went.

# 47

THE GOLDEN DOMES OF MONASTERIES ALONG THE HILLS ABOVE THE Dnieper River once again greet travelers approaching Kiev from the east, as they did for centuries. The traveler comes by rail now, over a bridge that crosses high above the river. The track rises slowly out of a morass of railyards on the river's east bank, to a brief depressing vista of slag heaps, decrepit buildings, the rotting industry of Communism; but it goes on rising to soar above the powerful river, still not quite tamed, and to meet the high green hills that form the west bank of the river. The monasteries for many years lived cautiously, in danger of extinction, turning inward like old priests hunched in their cassocks, dreaming secrets of eternity. They let their domes go gray with corrosion and blended with the trees on the hillsides.

New thinking brought with it a great rebirth of old thinking. From somewhere a people too poor for bread found gifts for their God. Churches were restored, their domes again gilded, and the domes winked out welcome to those coming from the east.

It was Sunday. If the train had stopped just then, Chapman would have gone down to one of the monasteries and lit a candle of thanks.

\*     \*     \*

Although they kept the door to their compartment closed, the Chapman family were ready to debark long before the train halted at the Moscow station in the center of Kiev. Before they opened the door of their compartment, Joanna embraced Brad. They were safe in a foreign land.

He returned her embrace.

"We still have to get tickets out of here," Brad said in the cab on the way to the airport. He hadn't dared to try to buy tickets for a Western country in Moscow."But for dollars we can get anything." He was talking mostly to himself, out of relief. "Or even if we have to wait a few days, it's a free country, isn't it?"

"Let's go home," Joanna said. "Let's go today."

# 48

BY NOON, PARNOV WAS READY TO CONCEDE THAT HIS HYPOTHESIS WAS wrong. He told Volkov, "I'll bring Shumsky back next time he calls in."

At twelve-fifteen, Shumsky called. "Got 'im."

Parnov had answered. "Where are you calling from?" He waved frantically to Volkov, who was out in the anteroom. "Did you leave him? Don't let him get away!"

"Don't worry. He's in sight. He came and went into the building and came right back out and I followed him. He's driving the fucking Zil. How could I miss?"

"Where is he now?"

"He stopped at a kiosk for a bottle of vodka, and now he's gone in a restaurant. Took the bottle with him. I'd say he plans to drink it."

"I hope it's Finlandia. Where are you? We'll be right there."

At first Volkov hadn't believed that Parnov had got the right place from Shumsky. "That's right on the Garden Ring!" he objected. The Garden Ring was the major thoroughfare encircling central Moscow. "Why would they let him park a limo the size of a billboard right on the Garden Ring?" But when they got there, the Zil was parked, not on the Ring, but on a side street opening from it and visible from it. Shumsky was in his car just up the street, parked where he could see the limo and the restaurant and only a few steps from a pay telephone.

"He's still in there," Shumsky said.

It was a tiny Georgian restaurant, entered from the back of a building that faced the Garden Ring.

Shumsky stayed outside while Volkov and Parnov went in.

It was dark in the restaurant. Only two tables were occupied, and one was by five Georgian men—apparently the owner and waiters.

The Brick was sitting by a window, facing the door, but he was not watching the door. He was watching a mostly empty glass between his hands, next to a mostly empty vodka bottle.

Volkov and Parnov walked back to him. Volkov sat down across from him. Parnov went to the other table, flashed a police credential at the waiters and waved them out of the room, then came back and sat down next to Brick, close in so he couldn't move his arms quickly. The waiters left for the kitchen quickly, experienced.

Volkov took his credential from the inner pocket of his jacket and laid it, open, next to the bottle. "Police."

"Mmf." Brick nodded, looked at the credential, but didn't look up at either of them.

"Can we buy you a drink?"

" 'Ve got mine."

"Then I'll ask you some questions."

"Don't know anything."

"Is that your Zil outside?"

"Look like I own a Zil?"

"You look like you might drive one."

"Gettin' a parkin' ticket? Piss on it. I'll leave the damn car there. Buy another one t'morrow. You want it, you c'n have it." Brick went to move his right hand under the table, but Parnov grabbed the wrist. Brick looked at Parnov for the first time and smirked. "Keys." Although Parnov tried with both hands to stop him, he forced his hand into his trousers pocket and came out with a set of car keys. He tossed them onto the table.

Volkov scooped up the keys and dropped them into his jacket pocket. "Actually, we want to ask you some questions about Joker."

This time they both caught his wrist, Parnov with both hands and Volkov with his left hand; and Volkov, seeing that Brick was reaching into his jacket and not under the table, thrust his right hand inside the left side of Brick's jacket and stripped away the pistol from the shoulder holster there. Then Parnov had his own pistol out and had moved back two steps from the table.

Volkov slid back from the table but stayed sitting.

"I want to see your identification papers, please. If you have another weapon, don't bring it out, or Parnov will have to kill you."

Brick took a passport wallet from the inside pocket on the same side of his jacket and slid it across to Volkov.

Volkov read the identification. "Durov. Is that your real name?"

"Yes. What of it?"

Volkov dropped the passport wallet into his outside jacket pocket. He turned Brick's pistol in his hands. "Service pistol, nine millimeter. But with the state crest of the Soviet Union engraved on one side of the slide, and a map of Afghanistan on the other. Was it a retirement present from the Committee? Or did you get it in Kabul, when you were under Marchenko?"

Brick didn't answer.

"If it's not registered, you'll get five years for possession of it. And here's another one like it." With his left hand Volkov took Joker's pistol from his belt and laid it on the table. "Maybe you've seen it before."

Brick stared at the pistol on the table. He had seen it before.

"You arrested him for an unregistered pistol?" Brick said, surly. "Pussy cops. He protected this country abroad while you were jerkin' off back here in Moscow."

"We didn't arrest him," Volkov said.

"Well, he didn' just hand *that* to somebody."

"No. Somebody took it from him."

"From Joker? Don't make me laugh."

"Well, could be we have a misidentification. Let's go see. You can come voluntarily, or you can make me arrest you."

Brick shrugged. "I'll go with you." To Brick it seemed a better choice than arrest. He had had experience with law-enforcement agencies; his experience was that under arrest you were in their power, and once you were in their power, you were unlikely to get out of it.

Volkov was happy with the choice too. If he had arrested Brick, he would have had to tell him of his right to have a lawyer before questioning him.

"You don't mind if we cuff you, do you? Just to prevent any misunderstandings?" The Brick refused to answer. Volkov took it for consent. Before leaving the table, he made a note of it in his notebook. He didn't want any part of this investigation thrown out by the court on technicalities such as a defendant's lack of counsel.

Volkov intended to leave the Zil and Shumsky's car there. He tried to get the Brick in the back seat of the other car between himself and Parnov while Shumsky drove, but the Volga's back seat wasn't wide enough for three men including the Brick.

"You know, Chief, I've always wanted to ride in a Zil," Parnov said.

"That's strange," Shumsky said. "I've always wanted to drive a Zil."

Volkov shrugged. He said to Brick, "Do you mind if we take your car?"

Brick didn't answer.

They took the Zil, with the Brick handcuffed to a jump seat facing Volkov and Parnov. Shumsky drove.

"Just as in the best of families of London," Parnov said as the Zil rolled out onto the Garden Ring.

Court Medicine Morgue Number 5 was a pale yellow building with the Moskva River embankment in sight at the end of the street.

The policemen led Brick through the front hall and along a corridor to the rear of the building. A door opened and an attendant stepped into the corridor. Volkov and the others went into the room the attendant had come from, and Volkov closed the door. The room was empty except for a half dozen wooden tables. On one table a figure lay under a sheet. Volkov went to that table and pulled the sheet down to expose a man's face. It was a round, jowly face, looking vaguely dissatisfied, as if deciding whether to pout.

The Brick collapsed like a house falling.

"I guess it's him," Parnov said.

"I never seen a man faint before," Shumsky said. He sounded embarrassed.

They left Brick on the floor until he started to come around, and then Volkov and Shumsky loaded him onto the table next to the one his companion lay on. Parnov stood at a distance with his weapon ready, in case the faint was only a feint. Brick lay on the morgue table for some minutes, as large and as pale as his friend, and then he began to mutter; all he said was, "Joker. Joker." He seemed hesitant to awake, but at last he opened his eyes; and when he did, he saw three policemen still watching him, Parnov and Shumsky on one side of him and Volkov on the other, standing between him and the body of his friend. He started to sit up, but Volkov ordered him to lie back down, and he did.

"Tell me about Turbin," Volkov said.

"Fuck you," Brick said.

"All right, then tell me about the woman Shubina."

"Fuck your mother."

"Your answers are consistent, but incomplete. Let me tell you what I know, just to help you along. I know that Shubina died of an alcohol overdose, and I know that your friend Joker had a

307

vodka bottle in his apartment with her fingerprints on it. A bottle of a brand of vodka that I can prove was in her apartment on the night she was murdered and *only* on the night she was murdered. So, I can prove that he murdered her. I don't know what your part was in that. As far as I know now, you didn't have any. I'm not asking about you. I'm not asking about your friend either. But I want you to tell me everything else about her death and Turbin's, who gave the orders and why. If you do, I will see to it that your friend's name doesn't appear in this case as the murderer of a defenseless woman."

Brick bit his lip. He bit it until blood ran. He turned his head and spat on the floor. "Minin ordered it. For both of them. We worked for Minin."

"And for Marchenko?"

"Not Marchenko. Minin."

"Did Marchenko order Turbin killed? Or Shubina?"

Brick said nothing.

"It's no deal if I don't have the whole truth."

Brick thought again about his telephone conversation yesterday morning: the only telephone call he had ever made to the General. The only time he had ever spoken to him without being spoken to first. It was what he had been thinking of all morning. He hadn't asked for anything when he and Joker were sent down in the reduction in force. The General had sent them to that asshole Minin, but how could the General have known what it would be like? But yesterday morning Brick had asked for help finding Joker, and all the General had said was, "Forget Joker, he can take care of himself. Didn't Minin tell you to get yourself and that car out of town? Just do it, Sergeant!"

Brick had always known that loyalty in the Union went only one way, had known it with a part of his mind—the way you knew things in the Union—while denying it with another. They preached to you about loyalty to the Motherland and loyalty to the leaders; but when the shells were falling, then where was the loyalty of the Motherland and the leaders to the men in the field?

You didn't think about it.

But the General was different. When the shells were falling, he was there.

Had been different.

*Forget Joker, he can take care of himself.*

But Joker hadn't taken care of himself. He'd taken care of the General's business. And now here he lay alone, on a cold slab in a police morgue.

"How did he die?" Brick asked.

"He died trying to kill someone," Volkov said. "On somebody's orders."

*Forget Joker, he can take care of himself.*

"The General ordered Turbin killed. And the woman. It was Minin who told us to do it. But he said the General wanted them gone." Brick added, "Some things you don't do for civilians."

"When you say 'the General,' do you mean Grigory Artyomovich Marchenko who is a general officer of the Ministry of Security of the Russian Federation?"

"Yes."

Volkov could see Parnov and Shumsky, out of Brick's sight, begin to smile.

There were many more questions. Volkov wrote them all down and asked them and wrote down the answers. How long had Brick known Marchenko, in what capacities? What did he know of a conspiracy to gain ownership of the joint venture JorSov? What had he been ordered to do about a certain People's Deputy, Inna Romanovna Korneva? Who had given the orders?

Sometimes the Brick refused to answer. Then Volkov would stop asking questions and let him look at the face of his friend Joker until he began talking again.

At the end, Volkov handed Brick the written questions and answers, and Brick signed it.

# 49

BRAD CHAPMAN, WAITING IN LINE FOR TICKETS AT THE KIEV AIRPORT, was a happy man. He felt ethereal. He felt like a balloon tugging at its tether, about to be released and float away. He looked around at his fellow would-be travelers with affection.

The scene at the Kiev Airport was a duplicate of the scene in the railway station in Moscow—practically a duplicate of every travel station throughout the former empire of the Union: people waiting. But Chapman, anxious as he was to get tickets, was happy to be just a part of the scene, no longer an object of special interest. And with dollars in his pocket, it was not likely to be a long wait, only the time necessary for proper Socialist formalities—the completion and filing of multiple forms, the inspection of visas, the sales clerk's tea breaks.

"So," someone said to him in Russian, "you are going to America after all." Beside Chapman in the next line was the man with the leather suitcase who had boarded their train in Moscow. The suitcase was still at his heels. It startled Chapman to see him there. The man seemed in very good humor—much better than on the platform in Moscow. He appeared to have some vodka in him. Or perhaps he, too, was a balloon loosed from its tether. "After your few days in Kiev, I suppose," the man said.

"Sorry?"

"You're going on after your few days in Kiev. You mentioned your vacation, on the platform in Moscow."

"We decided to go on." Chapman turned away. If this man was supposed to stop them, he could certainly have done it earlier. But Chapman didn't want any public discussions of his travel plans.

"I'm going to America too," the man said. "Maybe I'll see you there."

"Maybe. It's a big country."

"I've heard life is pleasant there."

"Yes. Yes, life is certainly pleasant there."

"I've never been there. I look forward to it."

Chapman's line was moving faster. They drifted apart. Chapman bought his tickets and left quickly, without looking again at the man. He returned, tickets in hand, to Joanna and Jennifer where he had left them on a bench in the corner of the terminal.

While Brad was gone, Joanna spent the time trying to keep Jennifer occupied. With a part of her mind she knew that Jennifer could do that just as well by herself: she spoke Russian and was unafraid of challenging the strange Ukrainian accents of other girls and boys her own size—and there were plenty of them in the terminal. But keeping Jennifer occupied also kept Joanna occupied, so she kept at it.

She was uneasy with Brad gone. She was doubly uneasy whenever a Ukrainian militiaman walked by, for they wore the same gray, the same military hat with a dull red band, as the Moscow police. Brad acted as if he were free already; but she could not completely rid herself of the fear of being taken back—not in a country where the policemen looked the same as in Moscow.

As she sat looking across the terminal at the back of a militiaman going away, she had a vision that Alex Fall had come for her. It struck her with uncanny force. For an instant she recalled him—seemed really to see him—as he had looked at her that night in Belaya Gora when he left her room and she regretted that she had let him go. She heard Jennifer's voice: "Look, Mommy, it's Uncle Alex!" She supposed she must have seen someone who looked like him in the crowd.

Then she realized that Jennifer was shaking her arm, and it really was Alex who was coming to her, picking his way across the crowded terminal.

She stood up, stunned beyond words. All she could say, as he came to her, was "Alex."

"Joanna, thank God I've found you."

311

"How? How did you find me?"

"Uncle Alex!" Jennifer said. "Are you going to 'Merika with us?"

He picked her up. "Not yet, Jenner-fur. Not yet. Joanna, where's Brad?"

"He went to get tickets." She realized only then that Alex hadn't come for *her* after all. He had come for *them.* Or, even, he had come for Brad. He had come for his client.

Brad, across the hall, saw Fall talking to his wife, holding his daughter. He jammed the tickets into the inside pocket of his coat, next to the envelope he was carrying there, and pushed his way past the benches, around bags and boxes and parcels, stepping over people sitting on the floor.

"What the hell are you doing here, Alex?" he demanded.

"Just what I was going to ask you," Fall said. "As for me, I came to keep you from ruining your life."

"That's rich! The guy who got me a lawyer who's going to sell me to Siberia! The guy who's trying to steal my wife from me! Put down my daughter, you son of a bitch! She's my kid, not yours!"

"Daddy, *don't* fight with Alex," Jennifer said.

Fall set Jennifer down so she wouldn't be between them. It was easier to pretend she wasn't there if he could look over the top of her head. It was as close as he could come to keeping her out of it. "If you believe any of that," he said, "you're too dumb to be worth saving. If you weren't going to ruin your wife's and kid's lives, too, I'd let you go."

"Keep my wife and kid out of it!"

"Who brought them into it, if not you?"

Chapman's hand went to his inside pocket, to the envelope that was burning his heart. It was as close as he ever came to destroying his life. But in the end, he couldn't do it. When he looked at Joanna, he couldn't do it. He knew that if he got out the envelope, if he said anything about Fall, she would have to say something about Sasha Shubina. Then there would be no going back. She hadn't said a word about Sasha, even after she came back from Volkov's questioning. But even if there hadn't been Sasha, he couldn't have done it. He couldn't let her go. If it meant accepting that there was something between her and Fall, he'd accept it. He dropped his hand. He asked, "Why did you come, Alex?"

"I came to tell you we've won your case. We've found our witness."

When Fall had told them Inna's story, Chapman sank back on the bench next to his wife. "Why should I go back?" he asked. "I'm out now."

"You know why," Fall said. "We can win this case now. If you don't go back, the judge will put out an order for your arrest and adjourn the case. You turn the win to a loss. Hawke Jordan won't be happy. He may or may not lose his company, but you'll lose your job and any chance of another one like it."

"Yeah, but I won't be in a Russian prison. There's something to say for that, Alex." Chapman turned to his wife. "Jo, what do you think we should do?"

It was the first time he had ever asked her what they should do.

"We've got to go back, Brad," she said.

"When do we go to 'Merika, Daddy?" Jennifer asked.

Before he answered, Chapman looked around the terminal. All the happy people, waiting to go somewhere. Waiting to go to the West. Waiting to go home. He looked for the man with the leather suitcase, but didn't see him. "Later, sweetie. Later."

He wondered, looking at his wife, how much of her readiness to go back was due to the fact she would still be close to Fall. But he didn't ask. He knew he would never ask. He put the thought out of his mind.

They returned to Moscow that night by airplane. The flights from Kiev to Moscow were all full for days in advance, but real money in the right hands got them on a flight that night. Chapman and Fall rode in the galley with the stewardesses, and Joanna and Jennifer rode up front with the flight crew. An empty jump seat was given to Joanna, while Jennifer sat in the navigator's seat and the navigator stood.

During the flight, Chapman asked Fall how he had found them. "I took a chance," Fall said. "But once I realized you were probably gone, it was either take a chance on catching you and failing, or let you go and fail for sure. So I thought about how I'd try to get out if I were you.

"You couldn't just fly out to the West. Probably you wouldn't try to fly at all—you have to give a name to get airline tickets, even internally, and you'd have to show a passport to fly. For any real international flight you'd have to go through full passport control with the border guards. Maybe the police would have given your name to the border guards and maybe they wouldn't, but it would be a risk. So you'd want to get out without going through passport control. If you took a chance that the police weren't checking passenger names on internal flights, you could fly to Alma-Ata or Minsk or Kiev, because there's still no passport control on flights that used to be domestic in the days of the Union. They're still treated as domestic flights. But for the same reason, they're erratic. You might wait for days to get out, and you couldn't do that."

"I could have driven." Chapman didn't like hearing his reasoning unraveled by someone else, not even his lawyer.

"You might be able to drive out, but foreign-registry cars are still rare on the roads, and the police still take note of them. You couldn't stop at any hotels, and it would be several days before you'd know if you had made it. Not much fun with a wife and child in the car.

"That really left you only one way out—by railroad. No one asks for your name if you don't buy your tickets in advance, and there's no passport control on the trains either. Your only real choices were Kiev or Minsk. That got me down to a fifty-fifty chance. I decided it on politics: Kiev is more independent of Moscow than Minsk is. If the Russian police asked for you back, the Belorussians might send you back, but the Ukrainians probably wouldn't. So I went to Kiev."

"What if we'd gone to Minsk?" Brad asked, unamused.

"I sent Misha to Minsk, just in case—although I knew he'd have more trouble convincing you to come back than I would. Now the biggest risk is that he'll get stuck there and won't be back by the time Judge Pskova convenes court tomorrow morning. But I think he'll make it. He took plenty of dollars."

"I'll bet you think you're smart, don't you, Alex?"
"That's part of the service."

Although both Ukraine and Russia were sovereign nations,
flights from Kiev to Moscow still arrived at a domestic-flights
airport, not at Sheremetyevo Airport where the international
flights arrived from outside the old Union; there still was no
passport check on passengers arriving in Russia at the "domestic" airport. No record showed that Bradley Chapman and his
wife and daughter had ever left Russia; no record showed that
they had ever returned.

The city slept, and there was no pursuit.

# 50

IT WAS PART OF THE JOB OF THE DEPUTY PROSECUTOR FOR INVESTIGA-
tions of the office of the Moscow City Prosecutor to be available
at all hours, every day, for police business. Crime didn't wait for
the Deputy for Investigations to get his beauty sleep. He was
always available to put his signature on warrants for search or
arrest, or to advise an investigator on whether such things were
needed, and he was proud of it. But that didn't mean he had to
like it.

He didn't like it, and investigators knew that.

So he thought it bold of Chief Investigator Major Volkov to
appear at his apartment late on a Sunday evening, even with a
half hour's notice by telephone. On Sunday night, what couldn't
wait until Monday morning?

The Deputy for Investigations had always thought of Volkov
as a steady man, up to now, a man not given to panic. Young
investigators sometimes imagined an investigation would go
away if they left it alone overnight. But crimes didn't go away,

and neither did proofs of them. Volkov was an old hand. He went all the way back to Krylov's day. He should know crimes didn't go away.

The Deputy for Investigations opened the file that Volkov had brought with him. "There's a lot here," he said, "for a case that you just opened yesterday. Yesterday—on a Saturday! Does your wife throw you out of the house on weekends, Volkov?"

Volkov didn't answer. He saw that none was expected.

"What is it you want? After-the-fact authorization for a search conducted on an emergency basis?" The Deputy for Investigations scribbled his signature on that paper. "Damn, you've been busy. Authorization to detain and interrogate one Minin, Anton Antonovich. Son of a bitch, you don't go after little fish, do you, Volkov. Do you know who this Minin is?" He didn't wait for an answer. "Authorization to detain and interrogate one Marchenko, Grigory Artyo . . . mo . . . General Officer of the Ministry of . . . Holy shit, Volkov! What have you got here?"

"The supporting documents are attached."

"I *see* they're attached. I can read, damn it! But an MBR general? Are you trying to start a war?"

"Close to one, maybe."

"What the hell does that mean?" But Volkov saw that an answer wasn't expected. The Deputy for Investigations read the request again. Then he read the record of Brick's interrogation, attached. Then he looked at Volkov again. "You know who Marchenko is?"

"Yes."

"Son of a bitch." It was hard to tell if the Deputy Prosecutor was referring to Marchenko or just to the situation. "I can't sign this," he said at last. "It'll have to wait until morning. I'll give it to the Prosecutor himself. We'll see if his is as big as he boasts."

"If it has to go to the City Prosecutor himself, maybe at least you should call him tonight to let him decide for himself whether to wait until morning?"

The Deputy for Investigations knew that Volkov had him there. He might not want to call the Prosecutor late on a Sunday night; but calling was better than deciding not to call the Prosecutor late on a Sunday night, when he had been directly asked to, and later having the Prosecutor decide that he should have called. Every bureaucrat's first rule was to avoid making decisions; but if the only choice was to make one of two decisions, every bureaucrat's rule was to make the small one and force someone else to make the big one.

He went to the telephone. He dialed, waited a long time, looking increasingly like changing his mind, then he stiffened. "Pavel Ivanovich, sorry to disturb you. I've got an investigator here. Volkov. He's requesting authority to interrogate a suspect, says it's urgent. . . . Yes, sir, I know it's late. But he says a witness's life may be in danger. . . . Who does he want to interrogate? Well . . . a general of the Ministry of Security. . . . What? Why, yes . . . it *is* Marchenko. . . . Yes, all right, sir. We'll come right over."

The Deputy for Investigations turned with the telephone dangling in his hand. "Apparently, there's more going on than I know about, Volkov. You can brief me on the way to the Prosecutor's apartment."

"If City Prosecutor Linnik knows about it already, there's more going on than I know about too," Volkov said.

When they reached Linnik's apartment, Yuri Kol'tsov was there, too, crossing and uncrossing his skinny legs on the Prosecutor's couch. Kol'tsov was the other Deputy Prosecutor, in charge of trials rather than investigations. Seeing Kol'tsov there, the Deputy for Investigations was even less happy than he had thought he was going to be.

Linnik's wife served them coffee, smiled, and vanished into the bedroom.

"So," Linnik said to Volkov. "What's this you've handed us, Major?"

"Something we'll wish we hadn't touched," the Deputy for Investigations said. "There's enough shit on this to stick to everybody."

"We don't have to touch it," Kol'tsov said. "Marchenko has already offered to take it out of our hands."

"He's done *what?*" It was an impolite interjection by Volkov, the junior officer present. He didn't care.

Linnik said, "General Marchenko has asked us to petition the court to send the case back for investigation, and to send it to the Ministry of Security."

"On what basis?" Volkov demanded. This was more than impolite, but Linnik seemed not to notice.

"That's a state secret. An Absolutely Secret secret. But we can hardly question a request of our sister service, can we? At least General Marchenko certainly hopes we can't."

"It's transparent," Volkov said. "He's trying to bury the case. And he's in it up to his neck."

"Which puts him in an an awkward position," Linnik said. "Burying himself." No one laughed except Linnik. "Well, what shall I do about it? We don't know where Marchenko is now, but we know where he's going to be in the morning. He's going to be in court. As much work as he's done to get us to bring him there, he's not going to back out now. So why not let the court decide?"

"There's a good reason to let the court decide," Kol'tsov agreed. "You could even argue that we can't do anything else. It depends on what we want to interrogate Marchenko about. You could argue that it's about a new case—murder, attempted murder, and so forth—and if that's so, then the City Prosecutor could order him interrogated. But you could also argue that it's related to the case already before Judge Pskova—which I think it is; in that case, it's out of the Prosecutor's hands. Only the court has the power to order anything to be done. The court would have to send the case back for additional investigation before we could detain or arrest suspects."

"Spoken like a true lawyer," Linnik said.

One thing that made Kol'tsov nervous about his superior officer was that he never knew whether the Prosecutor was being ironic.

"So," Linnik said, "I think it's decided. "Our suspect Marchenko is going to appear in court tomorrow on his own request to have the case sent back for further investigation. As I understand from Major Volkov, the defendant's lawyers are going to present a new witness to try to persuade the court to do the same thing. And the prosecution wants to interrogate Marchenko. Well, let's let the court decide. That's what courts are for."

"You can't just wash your hands of this," Volkov objected. "You know who this Marchenko is, don't you?"

"Aside from being a general of the Ministry of Security, you mean? Yes, Major, I know who he is. We all know who he is. I attended the Militia Academy, too, somewhat before your time. I'll drink a toast to General Krylov when Marchenko is sentenced. And I won't ask any questions about why you didn't get a warrant to search this apartment that's mentioned in your papers. But until then, the court is the place for this to be decided." Linnik added, in a tone far gentler than insubordination normally received, "I think it will be better this way, Major. No one can claim that the militia or the *Prokuratura* acted out of revenge. And as for the court . . . Pskova's a law-and-order judge. Even if she's afraid of the MBR, she'll be on the side of the Prosecutor." He turned to Kol'stov. "It should make for an interesting morning, Yura. I wish I could be there with you."

# 51

MARCHENKO FELT THE WAY HE ALWAYS FELT ON THE MORNING OF battle.

As he dressed, he went over in his mind what he had done and what he would do. He was not satisfied, but he had played his hand as well as he could up to now. If it was not a strong hand, he could not help that.

He looked at himself in uniform in the mirror. His hair had gone gray, but it was still a soldier that looked back at him. His belt was ten centimeters larger than the first one he had worn as a soldier: the ravages of desk work. He decided he should add his award ribbons. He wouldn't have worn them to the office, but his mission for today was to convince a judge, and if awards helped, better to wear them. He took off his jacket, hunted in his top drawer behind his pistol for the rows of ribbons, and began to fasten them to the jacket.

He wondered, now, if he was doing the right thing, going to court. It was a risk. He did not like this Deputy Prosecutor, who was a weak man. It was bad to put your fate in the hands of weak men. But sometimes you had no choice.

But the letter asking for the case to be turned over to the Ministry: that was good. Only a bold man would have written it. Maybe it was even a good thing that the Deputy Prosecutor had questioned the missing number from the chief of the department. A short, confidential talk with the Officer of the Day had opened the office of the chief of the department for a few moments. Why would the Officer of the Day deny a favor to a friendly general, when the general was in position to return the favor many times over? A few minutes: that was all it took to locate the register of letters. The Deputy Prosecutor would get his numbered letter. Only a bold man would have done that.

Still it was risky. But what wasn't? Life itself was risky. And after all the work he had done, there was no going back now. It was like the Kabul airport. Going forward was dangerous, but when you were ready, it was worse to go back. Forward was the chance of glory. Behind was nothing but defeat.

And anyway, he had no choice. He had, in a sense, made this decision long ago when he took the oath of service to the Committee and to the Motherland. What he did now, he had to do, for the good of the country.

And yet . . . that woman.

He put his jacket back on and looked again at the soldier in the mirror. A soldier who had done what had to be done for his country.

He wished it could have been otherwise with the woman.

But that was weakness. With her alive, the case would never be in safe hands.

It had to be done. Whatever he wanted for himself, it had to be done for the good of the country.

He started to close the drawer, and as he did so, he saw the pistol again, lying there.

And if everyone failed him? What then?

Who would there be to do what had to be done?

Why did it have to be her?

He opened the drawer again and took out the pistol in its holster and unbuckled his belt and threaded the holster onto it and rebuckled the belt. Then he snapped the magazine out of the butt of the pistol and looked to see that the full load of cartridges was in it and snapped it back into the pistol.

# 52

ON MONDAY MORNING SLAVIN MET CHAPMAN AT THE COURT. JOANNA was with her husband. When she looked around, Slavin supposed she was wondering where Fall was, but she didn't ask.

Slavin waited in the courtroom for the Prosecutor to arrive. He intended to have a word with Kol'tsov about the witness he intended to present. But Kol'stov, when he came in, was not alone. An officer was with him.

"Who's that?" Chapman asked.

Slavin didn't answer.

Slavin had never seen Marchenko in person, but he knew him at once. Marchenko looked the right man to be a Hero of the Soviet Union. He was a tall man, in his fifties now but still athletic and handsome in uniform, with a star on each shoulder and award ribbons on his chest, and even a pistol on his belt. Slavin was surprised at the pistol, for he had been a soldier, and he knew that a soldier not on field duty should not be armed.

Marchenko sat down in the first row of seats behind the Prosecutor.

Slavin said nothing to Kol'tsov.

It was five minutes later when Fall reached the court building with Inna. They had taken a roundabout route to the north of Moscow and arrived from the direction opposite to his office.

They parked in front of the court and left the car there, although that was illegal. Fall was willing to let the car be impounded, just so he got Inna inside the courtroom.

Inna walked gingerly in Slavin's galoshes. She was wearing blue jeans, an old duffle coat, and a broad-brimmed hat with her hair put up under it. She didn't look quite like a man, but she didn't look like a woman deputy of the Supreme Soviet, either.

The courtroom was on the third floor. Fall and Inna walked quickly up the stairs. A women's lavatory was on the second floor. Inna stopped there to change into a dress, to be the woman they had not wanted her to be on the street. Fall went on ahead, taking the last flight of stairs two at a time. Between the end of the stairs and the courtroom door was a row of chairs for witnesses to wait outside the courtroom. A bored-looking court guard was sitting in the one next to the door.

Fall opened the courtroom door to show Slavin that he was there, then waited for Inna in the hall. He had timed his arrival for exactly ten-thirty, the hour the trial convened. Judge Pskova was a demon of promptness.

Fall would rather have been inside the courtroom; but Slavin had convinced him that they could not afford the risk of offending Judge Pskova with such a breach of decorum—allowing a witness to be present for any part of the proceedings—for it had still seemed to Slavin that everything hinged on Pskova's agreeing to hear a surprise witness.

Fall nodded to the guard outside the door as he passed back in front of him and sat down one chair away.

Slavin started to go out into the hall to talk with Fall, to discuss what it meant that Marchenko was there; but Pskova and her two People's Assessors came through the doorway at the front of the courtroom and settled down at the judges' desk.

Judge Pskova said, "I understand there may be a petition this morning. Comrade lawyers?"

Slavin rose and was surprised to see Kol'tsov rise at the same time. "Comrade President," Slavin said, "I petition the court to hear an additional witness who is not identified in the case, and further to hear this witness immediately, out of the usual order. I have the witness waiting in the corridor outside the courtroom."

Judge Pskova said, "Comrade Prosecutor? I see you're on your feet already. Does that mean you have an objection?"

Kol'tsov said, "I don't have an objection, Comrade President; but I do have a question—whether the purpose of presenting this witness is to ask the court to send this case back for further investigation. Because I also petition the court to send this case back for further investigation on the basis of newly discovered evidence."

"Yes, somehow I thought you might. Do you want to present any witnesses also, Comrade Prosecutor?"

"Not at this time, Comrade President. My petition is made on the basis of evidence that cannot be revealed in court because of its secret nature. General Marchenko of the Ministry of Security, whom I believe you have met, is here to support his Ministry's request."

Marchenko shifted in his seat. Perhaps he was ready to rise and speak, but Judge Pskova said nothing to him.

"Comrade Advocate," the Judge said to Slavin, "do you object to the Prosecutor's petition?"

"I object if it means that my witness would not be heard in court." Slavin straightened to his short full height. "The witness is Inna Romanovna Korneva, a People's Deputy and a member of the Supreme Soviet of the Russian Federation."

As he said this, he looked directly at Marchenko.

Marchenko bit at his lower lip for an instant, but if he was startled to hear that Inna was alive and present, he gave no other sign of it.

Slavin said, "What People's Deputy Korneva has to say will change considerably the court's view of this case given by the evidence previously available. We ask you to excuse us for not identifying her earlier, but she came into possession of the evidence to which she will testify only within the last three days. But the primary reason for hearing her now is that we fear that any delay may lead to attempts on her life. There has been at least one such attempt within the last forty-eight hours. At this moment she is sitting in an unguarded corridor outside this courtroom. We ask you to permit her to testify immediately to

323

preserve her evidence. We also ask for additional security for this courtroom while she is testifying."

"To preserve her evidence? What about preserving her life, Comrade Advocate? You don't think the life of a deputy of the Supreme Soviet is worth this court's consideration?"

"I don't mean to suggest that, of course."

"I didn't think you did. Well, Defendant: do you have any objection to this witness? I guess not, since your lawyer wants her."

"I have no objection," Chapman said.

"Comrade Prosecutor?"

Kol'tsov looked at Marchenko with the look of a man helpless to avoid his fate—except for a small smile on his lips. "No objection."

"People's Assessors?" Pskova looked to her left and right as she asked this, but she knew the lay judges weren't going to object to anything she wanted. "No? Then bring Witness Korneva in."

Inna was not sitting in the corridor outside the courtroom. She was just coming up the stairs when the Court Secretary stepped out the door and called her name. She still walked slowly and carefully, but she had taken off the hat, and her hair flowed loose about her head. "Here," she called, starting to hurry as best she could.

The guard beside the door stood up. He was a lean man with sunken cheeks and a hawk nose, and it seemed to Fall that his uniform fit him ill.

Inna turned from the top step onto the landing leading to the courtroom.

The thin guard methodically slammed the courtroom door into the Court Secretary, drew the pistol from the holster at his belt, and took careful aim at Inna, frozen four steps away beside the corner post of the stair railing. He held the pistol in both hands. He took one more step toward her as Fall leaped to his feet.

Fall never heard the gun go off, nor did he feel the bullet tear through his flesh. He had a vague impression—or was it only a memory of a story someone told him?—of a breaking railing and a wall spinning past and the hard edges of the stairs below. And clearer—so very clear—his hands on someone's throat, though whose he couldn't say, smashing a head against the hard edges of the stairs again and again and again and again, and the blood pouring down the hard edge of a stair.

Whose blood?

# 53

THE SOUND OF TWO SHOTS BROKE THROUGH THE OPEN DOOR OF THE courtroom and echoed and echoed and echoed from the wide stairway.

Half the people in the room leaped to their feet. Then they froze there, not knowing what to do. Slavin leaped up, too, and dashed for the doorway. To reach it he had to cross in front of Marchenko. He was startled to see Marchenko rise up with a look of horror on his face and then sink back and cover his face with his hands.

The stairway, when Slavin reached the rail, was for an instant almost empty. It was like a stage set: a broad yellow wooden stair, lit from above by a skylight, and halfway down, three figures—two men lying like broken dolls across the stairs in a pool of blood, like broken mechanical dolls winding down with jerky movements, and standing over them a woman. A pistol lay two steps down. One of the mechanical dolls was a court guard in uniform, and the other was Alex Fall with his hands on the guard's throat, unable to rise but repetitively raising the guard's head and bashing it to a pulp on the stairs. And then suddenly the set was clogged with guards coming up the stairs. One of them raised his pistol and brought it down on Fall's head. The woman screamed and fell over Fall to protect him.

Slavin ran down the stairs to intervene. He slipped halfway down, fell and slid down several steps, got to his feet again, and arrived as the guards were trying to drag Inna away from Fall and Fall away from the man he was choking. "Stop!" he shouted. "I'm a lawyer!" He wondered for an instant why he had said that. To make himself the better target for a beating? "I'm an officer of the court! You've got the wrong man! That's not a guard! That's not a guard! That's an assassin!" He kept shouting it until his sheer assertion of authority backed the police away from Fall. "Don't touch the pistol!" he warned a guard who was stopping to pick it up. "It's evidence."

The guards separated Fall from the assassin. Inna knelt on one stair with Fall's head and shoulders in her lap. She would not let anyone touch him. He was unconscious.

Joanna came running down the stairs. "Oh, Alex!" She knelt beside Inna, then hugged her and cried.

Inna looked around for the first time, recognized Joanna, put one of her hands on Joanna's arm. The guards cleared the stairs of everyone else; the two women knelt together until an ambulance arrived.

They relinquished Fall to the stretcher bearers. He had never opened his eyes. Inna followed the stretcher down the stairs and to the door.

Slavin was there. "You can't go, Inna Romanovna," he said. "The physicians won't let you be with him. And you still have a duty here."

"I want to go with him."

"You'll do him more good here."

They turned back and went up the stairs together.

Looking up, Slavin saw Joanna standing alone in the center of the wide stairway, looking down at them; above her, behind the rail outside the courtroom, Brad was looking down at her.

Slavin knew, when he returned eventually to the courtroom, that Marchenko might easily have escaped in the commotion, and he half-expected not to find him there; but the General was still sitting in the same place. His face was calm, but he looked as if he might have been weeping once, though perhaps a long time ago.

The machinery of justice settled slowly back into place: the attorneys, the judges, the guards, and the Court Secretary.

"Everyone quiet down!" Pskova commanded. "We have work to do." All the discussions ended. Pskova said, "Court Secretary, call the witness People's Deputy Korneva."

Limping badly, Inna came through the door with two guards, one leading and one following. Her face was tearstained. Her dress was brown with drying blood.

Slavin had a sudden premonition that Marchenko would draw his service pistol and kill her in the courtroom, although he knew it was absurd. Still, he looked suddenly at Marchenko but found the General had covered his eyes with one hand; the other clutched his chest.

Pskova said, "It is my duty to warn you, Deputy, that it is a criminal violation for a witness to lie. Do you understand that?"

"Yes, I do." Her voice was hoarse with spent tears.

"I'm sure you do. Please sign the Secretary's record, my dear. Do you want to sit down?"

"Yes, please."

"Please do."

A guard moved a chair up to her, and Inna sat down and folded her hands in her lap. She found herself looking at her hands, which were touching Fall's blood on her dress. She tried to move them, but there was nowhere clean. She put them back.

"Are you all right, my dear?"

"Yes. It's not my . . ." She seemed to choke a little. "It's not my blood."

"Can you tell us the story of what happened to you?"

"Yes."

"Please."

Inna began, and as she spoke, her voice grew stronger. The hoarseness left it, and she was no longer aware of her hands.

"I am a People's Deputy of the Russian Federation, and a member of the Supreme Soviet. My subcommittee has been holding hearings on proposed legislation to combat corrupt activities, which have a negative impact on the economy of our country."

It was like a little speech. Beginning was the hard part. Once you began, it was easy.

"Another member of our subcommittee is Antipov. Vasily Ivanovich. He has always been very opposed to foreign investment as a prime source of corruption. Many people are. After our hearings concluded on Friday, he invited me to meet some friends of his who shared the same concern, he said.

"I went with him to a compound, an old Party facility, I guess, with several dachas and a hotel, and there, in one of the dachas, I met several of Antipov's friends. One of them is here this morning."

"Here? In court?"

"Yes. General Marchenko."

Inna looked at him.

He had not been looking at her when she spoke. He had sat with his head still bent and his eyes still covered by his left hand. But when she stopped speaking and looked at him, he sat up. He put down his hand and looked at her, looked into her eyes. He saw that they were red with old tears. Not tears for herself; for someone else.

Maybe, in a better world, they could have been tears for him.

He felt the weight of the pistol on his hip. It oppressed him.

"What happened at the dacha?" Judge Pskova prompted gently. She wanted to ask who else had been there, how long they had met—the thousand questions from which a lawyer builds testimony. But they would wait. The lawyers would ask them, if she didn't. They would wait.

"We talked. We talked about our country, and how it should be, and who should be allowed to help us build it. We talked about soldiers, and their duty to do what is right. We talked about who owns the JorSov joint venture, and who should own it, and who will own it in the future. We talked about whether Vladilen Viktorovich Turbin had been murdered, and why."

"Were you told he was murdered?"

"I was told he was murdered, and why, but not by whom."

"Why was he murdered?"

"Because he wanted to keep the ownership of the Russian half of JorSov for himself."

"You said you talked about who should own it? What was said about that?"

"The people in the dacha, Antipov's friends—they intended to own it."

"So that makes the question of 'who' pretty easy, doesn't it?"

"At least it gave me an opinion."

"What happened next?"

"They asked me to join them. They offered me a share of the ownership of JorSov. When I refused, General Marchenko asked me to work with them anyway. I said I would consider it and said I was going home. As Antipov was by then too drunk to drive, they insisted I be driven home."

"Who insisted?"

"General Marchenko and . . . Minin. Anton, I don't recall his patronymic. His driver and guard took me in his limousine. I believed they had instructions to kill me. I jumped from their car just in front of a train at a crossing, but one of them followed me with a gun. I fled into a cemetery, and when he still followed me, I hit him with something—a grave marker, I think—and took his gun."

Judge Pskova was heard to murmur under her breath—but heard only by the People's Assessors seated next to her—"*Molodyets!*" It was a Russian word of approval, based on the word for a young hero.

Kol'tsov, seated in front of General Marchenko, thought he heard the General mutter the same word, but he doubted it could be so.

"I walked through the forest until I came to a railway, and I walked to a station and broke in and found a telephone. I called Alex Fall, who came for me . . ." Here the witness broke briefly into tears. "And now I'm here."

"Are there any questions from the participants in the trial?" Judge Pskova asked. "Comrade Prosecutor?" Her own voice had grown suddenly rough. She did not trust it for any more questions now.

Inna did not know how long she spent as a witness. It might have been minutes or hours. Kol'tsov asked her questions, then Misha, and then Judge Pskova again, and even one of the People's Assessors, the woman. Then the judge released her.

"Please, may I leave?" Inna asked. "I'll come back if you want. But I don't know where they've taken Alex."

"May you leave? I have no objection. Do the participants in the trial object if Witness Korneva is excused?"

Kol'tsov rose, seeming reluctant to be the one to do it. "I understand the witness's urgent desire to leave, but there may be some additional questions she could give evidence on. I'm sorry, but I ask that she remain in the court."

Pskova looked hard at the Prosecutor. "If you're sure . . ." He said nothing. She turned back to Inna. "Well, I'll have to keep you here, my dear. Please take a seat." She said to Kol'tsov, "I hope we can make this short."

"I hope we can."

"All right, then, Comrade Prosecutor. You petitioned to have this case sent back for further investigation at the request of the Ministry of Security, based on a letter signed by General Marchenko. Are you ready to proceed?"

"I'm ready, Comrade President. In view of the testimony the court has just heard, I ask that the court call General Marchenko as an additional witness. It will be no inconvenience to the court, since, as you know, the witness is already present."

"So I noted," Pskova said. "If he was going to be a witness, he shouldn't have been in the courtroom. Well, but we have to live our lives from where we are." She turned to Slavin. "Comrade Advocate, any objection?"

Slavin had none.

Kol'stov said, "In this regard, Comrade President, I have some additional documents and physical evidence that I would ask the court to consider in connection with this petition."

"Comrade Advocate?" Pskova asked.

Again, Slavin had no objection.

Kol'tsov carried a box to the judges' bench.

Pskova said, "General, please come forward. And remember, it's a criminal offense to lie." After Marchenko had signed the Secretary's record, she said, "You've had the advantage of hearing the testimony of People's Deputy Korneva, General. What's your story?"

The General stood straight and tall. "I'm afraid People's Deputy Korneva misunderstood what was being said to her. From a friendly conversation about the needs of our country, she imagined a plot including theft and multiple murders! I'm only a soldier, not a lawyer used to orating in courts of law, so I hope you'll forgive me if I tell my story in a straightforward way."

"We'll all forgive you, General. The more straightforward the better. But tell me," Pskova asked, departing from her usual method of interrogation, "if Deputy Korneva imagined all those things she told us of, how did she imagine *this?*" From the box Kol'tsov had given her she took a service pistol, holding it awkwardly by the very end of the butt, and waved it in the direction of General Marchenko. "This, I take it," she said to the Prosecutor, "is the weapon that Deputy Korneva testified she took from the man who pursued her into the graveyard?"

"It is," Kol'tsov said.

"Witness Korneva," the Judge said, "did you hear that? Is it true that this is the pistol?" She put it back into the box and held the box out to the Court Secretary, who carried it back to Inna.

"There are hundreds of thousands of those in the world," Marchenko said. "It's a standard service pistol. With the current breakdown of law and order, they are unfortunately available almost anywhere. The People's Deputy could have got one from a hundred sources in Moscow."

"You're suggesting she lied about how she got this?"

"I'm suggesting that the fact that she had it doesn't mean she got it in any particular way."

"What about it, Deputy Korneva?" the Judge asked. "Is it the one you took from that man?"

"I'm sure it is," Inna said from where she sat.

"How do you know?"

"It has these pictures engraved on it. The crest of the USSR on one side. I don't know what's on the other side. Some kind of shape."

Slavin saw that Marchenko had suddenly gone tense.

The Judge said, "Let me see it again, may I?"

She turned the pistol in her hands. It was clear she was no marksman. "Interesting engraving. Yes, there's the USSR crest on the left side. And what *is* this on the right?" She offered the pistol to the two People's Assessors. The woman, Bitova, glanced at it and passed it back, but the man, Tushin, studied it with interest. "It's Afghanistan," he said.

"What's that?"

"The engraving," Tushin said. "It's the map of Afghanistan."

Pskova took the pistol back and studied it. "Hmf. You could be right."

"*That's* not standard issue," Tushin said. "Neither is the USSR crest. Or they weren't when I was in the Army."

Kol'tsov said, "The court will find that in the witness statements in the file I've just given you, there is an explanation of the engraving."

"Do you want to point out what it is," Pskova asked, "or shall we wait for it? I assume you're going to present witnesses—unless they're not alive or available."

"I can present the witnesses," Kol'tsov said. "It may take a little time to get them here."

"Comrade President, perhaps I could save the time if I may ask one question," Slavin said.

"It's irregular, Comrade Advocate, but you have permission."

Slavin was surprised. Irregularities never happened in Pskova's court. Inna's testimony must really have affected her. "About the pistol. General Marchenko is carrying his service pistol."

"I have authority to carry it," Marchenko said to the judge. "My work is connected with dangerous cases."

"I wasn't questioning the General's right to carry it," Slavin said. "I wonder if we could compare it to this pistol that's in evidence—the one that Deputy Korneva could have picked up anywhere."

Marchenko was facing the judges, facing away from Slavin. Slavin saw the back of his neck redden, and he knew that his guess was right.

"Comrade Prosecutor?" Pskova said. "Do you object to asking your witness if we may examine his pistol?"

"No objection, Comrade President."

"May we see your pistol, General?"

Marchenko stood for a moment, stiff and tall. Then, with great care, he unsnapped the flap of his holster and drew his pistol. He held it a moment in position to fire, then took it in his other hand, reversed it, and handed it butt-first to the judge.

"Is it loaded?" Pskova asked.

"Certainly it's loaded," Marchenko answered. "What good is an unloaded pistol?"

Judge Pskova laid it carefully on the desk and looked at it. She turned it over, looked again. Then she looked at Marchenko. "It has the same engravings."

Marchenko said nothing.

"Where did you pick yours up, General?" she asked.

The General knew that, when the time came to surrender, there was no point in being a fool. A man could fight to the death on the battlefield, but not in a courtroom. There, he could only look like a fool. And he had given up his weapon: it was too late for the bullet for himself. And the bullet for her? Could there ever have been one?

"I didn't 'pick it up.' " He looked at Inna as he spoke. He looked into her eyes until she looked away. "It's from Afghanistan. I gave my whole platoon pistols like it—or the survivors. After we took the Kabul airfield."

"The court will keep this for now," Pskova said. "It will be attached to the case." She put it in the box with the other.

It wasn't the pistol alone that did it. Volkov's file by itself would have been enough in the end. But it was the pistol that Slavin was proud of. The pistol brought the questions to a point so much faster.

Judge Pskova asked, "About this other pistol, General. The pistol that the prosecutor has asked be attached to the case, that Deputy Korneva described taking from a man who followed her into a graveyard at night. Do you know the man who carried that pistol? I remind you that it is a criminal offense to lie."

"I know him."

"We'll return to that. Now, do you know the man who attempted to kill Deputy Korneva outside this courtroom?"

"I do not."

333

"Do you know anything about the way in which he came to be here this morning?"

"I do not. The Internal Army are a different organization from mine."

"Do you maintain that he was really a court guard?"

"I don't know. Someone said he appeared to be."

"You didn't go into the stairway to look, I observed. Why not?"

"I assumed that the matter was in professional hands."

There were more questions, many more. Pskova had a question for every sentence in the reports Kol'tsov had given her. Then she invited the People's Assessors to ask questions. They declined. Pskova said, "Is there anything more?"

"On the basis of the testimony we've heard," Kol'tsov said, "I petition the court to send this case back for further investigation, to find additional witnesses, and to add charges."

"Comrade Advocate?" She looked at Slavin.

"The defendant supports the Prosecutor's petition," Slavin said.

"Then the court will recess to discuss the decision on the petitions to return this case for further investigation. But first, Witness Korneva, I think you can leave now. Any objection, Comrade Prosecutor?"

Kol'tsov had none.

"I wish I had guards to send with you," Judge Pskova said. "But all I have is guards for prisoners."

"I don't need a guard," Inna protested.

"I'm afraid that maybe you do. Well, I'll ask the captain of the court guards to call for a militia guard for you. And to give me a report on where you are every hour, to be sure you're safe. Comrade Prosecutor, maybe you could help him with that."

"I'll call my office," Kol'tsov said.

Pskova rose and the two People's Assessors followed her into the judges' chamber behind the front wall of the courtroom.

Marchenko sat alone. He did not look at anyone, but he felt that the eyes of all of them were on him, and that their eyes were on his empty holster.

A soldier who lost his weapon was no soldier at all.

Slavin joined Chapman and they both walked to the back of the room where Joanna was sitting. "What's going to happen now?" she whispered. She would have whispered anyway in this room, but with Marchenko sitting in the front row she felt even more wary, though he'd given no sign he could understand English.

"I don't know," Slavin said. "The court will decide. I think they have to send the case back, since the Prosecutor asked as well as us. I don't think they can send it to the Ministry of Security, with this evidence. But of course many people are still frightened of the MBR."

"I don't think Judge Pskova is one of them," Joanna said. She added, "Is there some way we can find what's happening to Alex?"

Slavin realized that he had forgotten about Alex. His mind had been only on one thing. When a witness was testifying, he saw nothing, heard nothing else. Yet, that was what a lawyer's mind should be on in court. Was that shameful? "We can try to call," he said. "Do you know where they took him?"

"Inna didn't know. She was going to look for him."

Before Slavin could decide what to do, the judges returned. Slavin was surprised they were back so soon. It was either a good sign or a bad one. He rushed to the defendant's counsel table.

At the same time, there was the sound of feet in the hall outside the courtroom door. The door pushed open a crack. Joanna caught the glance of an eye from under a military hat. She wanted to ask Slavin what was happening, but there was no chance.

The door slid closed.

Judge Pskova asked, "Court Secretary, is everyone back in the courtroom?" The Secretary affirmed that the necessary parties were present. "The decision is being pronounced," Pskova said. Everyone rose. Pskova took several handwritten pages from a red leather folder and began to read.

"The court finds that, on the basis of the petitions of the Prosecutor and the defendant and of the information attached to the petitions and presented in court, this case should be sent back for further investigation, for identification and interrogation of additional witnesses.

"The court finds that there is insufficient support for the request presented by the Ministry of Security to have this case sent to that Ministry, without additional facts showing the basis for the request. The Prosecutor is directed to ask for additional information from the Ministry of Security.

"The court finds that certain persons, among them Marchenko, Grigory Artyomovich, in order to conceal their participation in other crimes that are still the subject of investigation in this case, conspired in the attempted murder of Korneva, Inna Romanovna, People's Deputy and member of the Supreme Soviet of the Russian Federation.

"The court has decided to initiate a criminal investigation against Marchenko, Grigory Artyomovich, as a defendant in this case, on the basis of Articles Seventeen, Fifteen, and One-oh-two of the Criminal Code of the Russian Federation, persuading another person to attempt murder, with aggravating circumstances.

"The court has decided that the measure of prevention appropriate in this case, taking into account the gravity of the crime of which Marchenko is accused, is that he be taken under arrest. This decision can be appealed by the Prosecutor or by General Marchenko."

The doors of the courtroom swung suddenly open, and an officer and four additional guards rushed into the room. They surrounded Marchenko, then turned to face the judges.

"Guards, you may remove the prisoner."

For the first time that day, Slavin smiled.

Judge Pskova rose, followed by the People's Assessors, and left the courtroom. The guards hurried Marchenko out the main door into the corridor and down, around the bloodstain spread across the stairs.

As the crowd drained from the courtroom, Slavin edged his little party—his client, his client's wife, and himself—toward the prosecutor, Yuri Kol'stov. "It's been an interesting case, Yuri Alexandrovich. With a most unusual outcome."

Kol'tsov looked at Slavin thoughtfully, and at Chapman. "The case has certainly taken an unusual turn, Advocate. It's obvious that there was more to it than met the Investigator's eye at the time he reached his first conclusions. Your client may have been to some extent a victim himself. Presumably, further investigation will determine that."

Chapman started to agree, but Kol'tsov went on, ignoring him: "Still, it's my duty to say that in my opinion the evidence still strongly suggests that bribery and theft of state property have occurred. The Russian side contributed a vast amount of property to the joint venture. It's an unbelievably low value that the JorSov accounts assign to that property.

"We may be seeing you again."

Chapman said nothing until they had left the building. Then it was as if a sudden lowering of air pressure allowed him to boil over. "I can't believe it!" Chapman raged. "Do I have to go through this all over again? Why did I come back here? Alex promised me that it was all going to be over!"

"He didn't promise you," Joanna said.

"He said with Inna as a witness, I'd win the case!"

"Well, you haven't lost it yet," Slavin said. "Very few things are easily finished in Russia. We begin; we lose our innocence; we endure. In a few days I'll talk with the Chief Investigator, and then we'll decide how much to worry. Today I'm saving my worrying for Alex."

They learned that night from Inna that Fall had been flown to a hospital in Germany. He was in critical condition, with a shoulder smashed by a bullet and with head injuries from the fall onto the stairs and the blow of a policeman's pistol butt.

Brad and Joanna sat outside after Slavin left, silent under the Moscow twilight. "You want to go be with him, don't you?" Brad said.

"Someone should be with him. I hate the thought of him alone. You still can't cross the city limits, and it will take days for Misha or Inna to get German visas. He saved your life, Bradley."

"He saved *her* life."

"Yours too. If they'd killed Inna . . ."

"There was other evidence. Slavin would still get me off, Inna or no Inna."

"You didn't sound so confident this afternoon."

He sipped at his iced tea, thinking how Slavin only drank tea hot. Had to preserve his throat for the benefit of his clients, he said. Odd duck. But a real lawyer. "You're right," he said. "You'd better go."

"I'll come back when Inna gets there."

"You're becoming great friends with Inna."

"I want to be."

Once the case was sent back, Slavin should not have been able to learn how the further investigation was going, but some rules are observed through the fingers, as the Russian saying goes. With Marchenko's arrest, Slavin had more friends than ever in the militia. So he already had some feeling for the status of the case when he went to see Volkov a few days later in Volkov's office.

The Investigator opened the conversation. He had none of the informality he had displayed after Slavin came to his apartment about Inna. "I've received your petition to dismiss the case against Chapman, and I've forwarded it to the investigating officer. The case has grown too big for me. It's gone up the line. To the top."

Slavin waited.

"Even if I had the case, it's still my opinion that your client is guilty of the crimes I charged him with. The fact that other, worse crimes were committed by others is no defense."

Still Slavin waited, although in other cases at this point he would have begun to sweat for his client.

"It's a mockery to have his kind on the streets, preying on the weakness of our nation."

"You know that my view of the facts is different," Slavin said. "And I had hoped that the testimony that was given in court might have convinced the Prosecutor's office to take a broader view of the case."

"I was talking of my own view, not necessarily that of the Prosecutor's office. And not necessarily my own view of all aspects of the case." Volkov sat upright in his chair, a man doing a duty he did not like, but it was his to do. "I understand that in light of new information—information that did not exist at the time this case was initially forwarded to the court—the conclusion of the Prosecutor's office will be that the case against your client should be dismissed. The wheel of justice has rolled past him."

"Thank you, Maxim."

They both stood, awkwardly. Then suddenly Volkov offered Slavin his hand. "Thank you, Misha." He clasped Slavin fiercely, in the hug that is no offense to a Russian man.

When Slavin left the office, he was applauded down the halls by a crowd that rushed to the doors. Parnov and Shumsky were among them.

Brad celebrated the good news that night with Slavin alone on the back deck. Joanna was still gone. They drank a bottle of champagne that Slavin had brought, and then a bottle of vodka and some cognac. "I can't take it with me," Brad said. "We'll clean out the liquor cabinet, Misha. We'll get so tight in the pale moonlight, and dance by the light of the moon, the moon . . . and dance by the light of the moon." Misha laughed as Chapman threw bottles one by one over the fence into Ed Miller's back yard.

After that, while Joanna was still gone, Brad started packing the household. When she returned after a week, the house was full of boxes—an end of something.

Fall had rarely been conscious, she said, but he was out of danger. "I don't know if he even knew I was there."

That evening, Joanna found Brad starting a fire in the fireplace. It was a chilly evening, as Moscow evenings could be even in August. "That's a good idea, Bradley," she said. "It makes me think of home."

"I thought it would get us off to a good start. And I needed to clear out some old papers. Old papers, old thoughts." He stuffed an envelope into the bottom of the papers under the kindling and lit it and watched the flames consume it and send the smoke up the chimney and out into the cold Moscow air.

# 54

Fall and Inna returned from Germany the day before the Chapmans were due to leave Moscow.

Inna drove him to Brad and Joanna's going-away party. He was still too weak to protest much at her driving, which was as new and delicate as the pin in his shoulder. "You've learned a lot while I was unconscious," was all he said.

"The wife of an American has to know how to drive," she said. "And I'm no worse than Misha."

"No, you're not. Are you marrying an American?"

"I hope so. Have you closed your offer?"

"You know I haven't. Don't you still have your sheep to care for?"

"You know I have. But I've decided nationalism isn't a good basis for choosing a husband." She added, "It's not a good basis for choosing a deputy, either. If they don't like me married to an American, they can vote for someone else."

"What if I go back to America?"

"What if what if? Do you want me to marry you or don't you?"

"I want you to marry me, Innochka."

That was the point where the car went off the road.

Ed and Betsy Miller threw the party. Brad and Joanna were the guests of honor, but Fall and Inna—to their embarrassment— were the stars, even though they arrived late. "We had car trouble," Fall said.

"Tough driving with a bum shoulder," Ed Miller sympathized.

"Yeah. Yeah, it is."

\*      \*      \*

340

Brad was holding forth in praise of his defense team. "Fall was good," he said, agreeing in part with Betsy Miller, "but it was Slavin who was brilliant. Slavin would even get Marchenko off."

Slavin, who had brought a new female acquaintance to the party (the Court Secretary at the Chapman trial, quite pretty with different glasses), smiled modestly. "Well, sometimes it's best not to predict too much success," he said. "But I think a good lawyer could do something for General Marchenko, if he asked."

"Misha!" Betsy Miller cried. "No one could save that good-for-nothing! Could they? Certainly no one *should!*"

"Well, the case presents certain features," Slavin said. "In spite of all the circumstances, I believe there's no evidence that he personally threatened anyone, nor even that he directly ordered anyone to do so. He always acted on the diagonal. One could infer that he intended the results, but good cross-examination of witnesses often exposes inconsistencies. It would be hard to prove conclusively even that he intended to obtain a share of JorSov for himself. It's incontrovertible that he forged certain official documents, of course, but that's a little thing. And done in a good cause, too—the defense of the Motherland. At least as he saw it. It's a defense with sound historical antecedents. No, I think there's certainly scope for lawyering in his defense. As for 'should'—what kind of legal system is it that lets only popular defendants have lawyers?"

Betsy Miller was scandalized. "Would you really defend him, Misha?"

"Probably I would have a conflict of interest, since I would have to try to show that actions of certain JorSov officials were dangerous to the Motherland, if not actually illegal." Slavin loved playing to an audience, especially where there was a woman to be impressed.

"God, I hope he hasn't asked you!" Betsy Miller exclaimed. "Has he?"

Slavin smiled—a beatific smile that glowed in his eyes.
"Has he?"

Late in the evening Fall went outside for fresh air. The chill made his shoulder hurt, but he ignored it. He wandered next door and sat down on a chair on Brad Chapman's deck and looked at the birch grove. He supposed it was for the last time. Or maybe not. The new American co–General Director of JorSov would be moving in here when Brad and Joanna left. JorSov was still his client. Misha said Volkov was going to bring charges concerning Turbin's death and Shubina's, but that wouldn't stop Russian nationalists from trying to get foreigners out. Nothing ended.

He heard steps in the grass. He looked around, more cautious than he used to be. It was Joanna. She sat down in the chair beside his.

"I never got a chance to thank you," she said.

"I guess I left kind of suddenly. I heard you were there—in Germany. But I never saw you. I woke up too late."

"Wasn't it always that way?"

"I guess it was. I'm sorry it was."

"Yeah. Me too." She smiled. "You were so helpless. I could have ravished you. Maybe I did. How will you ever know?"

"I'll see it in my dreams."

"I hope it's good." They said nothing for a little while. Then she said, "Congratulations on your engagement."

"Thanks."

"She got a hell of a guy."

"I keep telling her that."

"But you got a hell of a woman too. You never thanked me for putting you together."

"Betsy Miller is taking credit for that."

"But we know better."

"Yeah." Without looking at her he reached out toward her and found her hand reaching toward him. They sat side by side holding hands in the dark.

"Take care of Jen in Minneapolis," he said.

"I will. Will you write to her?"

"Sure."

"I'll take care of Brad, too."

"I know you will."

Nothing ended. Nothing but innocence.